Drive-In Creature Feature

Edited by
Eugene Johnson and Charles Day

D1413753

Dedicated to:

My partner in life Angela and my four wonderful children for standing by my side. My family. My grandparents, who raised me by nurturing my creativity. To God. My great friends J.P. Linkous, Rebecca Johnson, Luke Styer, Lia Staley, and Jim Staley, for always standing by me. To all the authors and artists Jim and Neal for their belief in this great project and their support.

Special thanks to my friends and mentors Scott, Paul, Taylor, Joe, Ty, Lisa, Jonathan, Elizabeth, Cortney, and Jason, for all the help and guidance working on this project and more.

The Indiegogo campaign supporters. To my publisher, friend, mentor, co-editor, Charlie Day for believing in me, this anthology, and through the bad and good never giving up on me or Drive-in Creature Feature!

-Eugene Johnson, June 7, 2016

Acknowledgements

Huge thank you to everyone who's purchased a copy, pledged to our Indiegogo campaign, promoted us on their social media venues, or pre-ordered from our website. It means a great deal to all of us who worked behind the scenes to bring this book together. I also need to thank so many for your patience, as this was a very long endeavor, with a few bumps and obstacles in the way, that Eugene and I managed to clear. This allowed us to finally get DRIVE-IN CREATURE FEATURES off the development table and ready to be read by all those who've been waiting . . . like forever.

Finally, I need to thank our authors. Without them there would be no book. Your patience and understanding has never gone unnoticed. We appreciate you hanging in there with us until the end. Now the fun begins. You all rock.

Of course the whole team at Evil Jester Press & Comics. Joseph, John, Bryan, Erik, Bri, and our newest member, Sarah, who came in and helped us get our product out to so many more people. Jim and Scott, and Even William Neal McPheteers, who despite all the work he was doing, took the time out to create an awesome cover for us. Thanks to each and every one of you.

However, I owe so much to the master behind this whole project, Eugene, Skip, Johnson, who brought this all to life. A man so committed to DRIVE-IN CREATURE FEATURES. I just know he had many sleepless nights, because I was there with him on the phone or texting each other about how to make this the best book it could be. Hey. My friend. We did It. I'm so proud to hold this book.

So again, thank you to all the readers.

Grab your popcorn, hotdogs and soda! Let's get back in our cars, turn the volume up on our speakers hanging off our windows, and let's enjoy the good ole times.

Charles Day, M.P.A., B.A.,

CEO/Publisher

Evil Jester Press & Evil Jester Comics

Table of Contents

INTRODUCTION BY
F. PAUL WILSON

Jim Kavanaugh

F. Paul Wilson

F. Paul Wilson was born toward the end of the Jurassic Period and raised in New Jersey where he misspent his youth playing with matches, poring over Uncle Scrooge and E.C. comics, reading Lovecraft, Matheson, Bradbury, and Heinlein, listening to Chuck Berry and Alan Freed, and watching Soupy Sales and horror movies. He sold his first story in the Cretaceous Period and has been writing ever since. (Even that dinosaur-killer asteroid couldn't stop him.)

He's written in just about every genre - science fiction, fantasy, horror, young adult, a children's Christmas book (with a monster, of course), medical thrillers, political thrillers, even a religious thriller (long before that DaVinci thing). So far He's got about 55 books and 100 or so short stories under his name in 24 languages.

INTRODUCTION

F. Paul Wilson

Park-In Theaters…that's what they were called at first. The first official, free-standing, permanently located Park-In opened in 1933 in – where else? – My home state of New Jersey. They multiplied slowly through the thirties, limped through the gas rationing of WWII, but surged to new popularity with the post-war motorization of America, especially during the 1950s.

They became known as Drive-Ins and were great for families. A mother and father could take the whole gang to a Disney movie or a western or even a Doris Day rom-com without hiring a babysitter. If the kids (usually admitted free under a certain age) got bored, they could fall asleep on the back seat. For teenagers, it allowed them some privacy, and the phrase "passion pit" entered the American lexicon.

No wonder the drive-in numbers grew to 4-to-5,000 screens at their peak in 1960. They were cool.

What else helped drive their growth during the 50s? Monster movies, of course. Movies with *big* monsters – what the Japanese call *daikaiju eiga. I count 40 or so big monster epics released during that decade. What kicked off this blitz of daikaiju eiga (besides nuclear testing paranoia)? If you say The Beast from 20,000 Fathoms*, you're almost right. For the true answer you've got to consider what film helped get *Beast* green-lighted. I'll give you a hint: It had been a monster hit two decades earlier.

That's right. *King Kong.*

After its initial release in 1933, RKO rereleased *Kong* every 4-6 years or so. But when, in 1952, they presented it for the fifth time (a censored version with no chomping on natives or cops or undressing Fay Wray), they added advertising on that new-fangled thing called TV. It grossed $4M. This was unheard of. A twenty-year-old film grossed almost as much on rerelease as it had on all its previous releases combined? Crazy!

That very same year Warner Bros started production on a giant monster film called in *The Monster from Beneath the Sea*. The script included scenes of a huge dinosaur rampaging through Manhattan, just like *Kong*. Was the greenlighting a coincidence? I don't think so. The film was released the following year as *The Beast from 20,000 Fathoms*, the same title as the Ray Bradbury story that inspired it. Following the example of *Kong*'s rerelease the year before, they saturated the few existing TV channels at the time with the *Beast* trailer.

That was when Li'l F learned that he was a *daikaiju* fan.

I was only seven, yet to this day I clearly remember the moment I first saw that trailer (in black and white, of course). It opens with an A-bomb explosion, then a series of avalanches, followed by a glimpse through an Arctic snowstorm of a huge dinosaur. But this trailer doesn't play coy. It shows you the creature demolishing a lighthouse (the centerpiece of Bradbury's story) and then rising from the East River to wreak havoc on the streets of Manhattan – crushing cars, knocking down walls, panic everywhere. Big white letters fill the screen:

THE BEAST!

THE BEAST!

THE BEAST FROM 20,000 FATHOMS!

I lived in Hackensack, NJ, a few miles across the Hudson River from Manhattan. We received a total of six TV feeds at the time (cable TV was at least a quarter century away): CBS, NBC, ABC, WNEW, WOR, and WPIX. After seeing that trailer – we called them "previews" back then – I began frantically switching channels (manually, of course) to see if I could find another station playing the *Beast* trailer. Eventually I found one. And another. I watched with my face pretty much pressed against the screen. (Think the face-hugger and John Hurt's space helmet.)

Lil F was in love.

I had to see this movie. *Had* to. And I had no doubt that I would. Just a few months previous I'd gone to the Oritani Theater with a friend to see the new Martin and Lewis film, *The Caddy*, so no problem going to see *Beast*. Right?

Wrong. I'd gone to see *The Caddy* in the cool weather. This was summer, and summer was polio season. Polio is a virus that can cause a condition called poliomyelitis or "infantile paralysis." Most polio-infected people don't even know they have it; some get flulike symptoms and get over it. But an unfortunate 1% experience varying degrees of paralysis, the most serious involving the phrenic nerve. Without the phrenic nerve, you can't move your diaphragm, and if you can't move your diaphragm, you can't breathe. These poor kids wound up in big cylindrical chambers called iron lungs. (Think of spending all day, every day, lying in something like an MRI scanner.)

Polio stopped being a problem with the arrival of the Salk vaccine in 1955, but before that, movie theaters were considered dangerous. When you packed kids together in an enclosed space, you put them all at risk for polio. Later generations have no idea (polio has been controlled for over half a century) and many members of my generation – the first wave of boomers – have forgotten the plague mindset involving movie theaters in the early 50s.

So, no way was I going to see *Beast*. I was crushed. (Don't forget, this was before VCRs and DVDs and DVRs. The only way you got to see a film after its theatrical release was hit or miss on a Saturday afternoon double feature at the local theater. Maybe.)

But I was rescued by…the Drive-In.

After weeks of constant pestering, I convinced my father that I couldn't catch polio in the family car, so he relented and took my brother and me to the local drive-in to see *The Beast from 20,000 Fathoms*.

After impatiently suffering through animated dancing hot dogs and juggling bags of popcorn, we finally got to the feature. A glorious night, an epiphany in black and white. I confess to puddling up a little when they killed the beast. Even at that age I realized it was only being true to its nature.

Spurred by the success of *Beast* (I'm guessing here), the Japanese shot *Gojira* and released it the following year. (It would take two years before an Americanized version of *Godzilla* reached US shores.)

In 1954 my dad took me to *Them*. After that, with the polio scare over, I returned to the indoor screens for the likes of *It Came from Beneath the Sea, Tarantula, The Black Scorpion, The Deadly Mantis,* the laughable *The Giant Claw,* the very cool *Twenty Million Miles to Earth, The Blob,* and so on.

But when I got my driver's license at seventeen, it was back to the drive-ins, sometimes with my girlfriend, sometimes with a bunch of guys and a couple of six packs for a gorefest. I remember the members of my garage band piling into a car to go see *A Hard Day's Night*.

But technology, domestic / international politics, and simple economics were conspiring to sound the death knell of the drive-in. The oil crisis of the 70s made everyone stingy with their mileage; they'd watch TV rather than waste gas going to a drive-in. And for anyone owning one of those relatively new VCRs, the decision to stay home was a no-brainer. To make matters worse, the oil crisis also spurred a national shift to daylight savings time, forcing drive-ins to start their shows an hour later, cutting off much of their traffic for family films. Add to that the inexorable rise in the value of their land with the attendant higher property taxes and the writing was on the wall.

Result: From a peak of nearly 5,000 screens in the early 60s, the number had fallen to less than 350 by 2014. All the beloved drive-ins of my youth are now either strip malls, flea markets, or garden apartments. Despite recurrent talk of a resurgence, I'm not holding my breath. The digital projectors necessary to show new releases these days cost a bundle and aren't feasible for a single-screen theater.

5

But do not let your hearts be troubled. Eugene Johnson has called on some of the best writers in the world to hold up mirrors to those films we loved. Some of the writers here are simply talented fans of drive-ins and creature features, and some have actually written those features.

I thought I had only memories of those days. Now I have these stories as well.

And so do you.

F. Paul Wilson
The Jersey Shore

The Curse of the Amazing Colossal Thing From Outer Space

EXTRATERRESTRIAL KILLING MACHINE

Drive-In Creature feature Anthology *presents a* **S.G. Browne** *story* **The Curse of the Amazing Colossal Thing From Outer Space** *edited by* **Eugene Johnson** *and* **Charles Day** *produced by* **Evil Jester Press** A T Alien Terror Creature Violence *Copyright 2016*

S.G. Browne

S.G. Browne is the author of five novels, including *Less Than Hero*, *Big Egos*, *Lucky Bastard*, *Fated*, and *Breathers*, as well as the eBook short story collection *Shooting Monkeys in a Barrel* and the heartwarming holiday novella *I Saw Zombies Eating Santa Claus*. You can learn more about his books at www.sgbrowne.com. You can also follow him on Twitter at @s_g_browne or on Facebook at Facebook.com/SGBrowneAuthor.

THE CURSE OF THE AMAZING COLOSSAL THING FROM OUTER SPACE

S.G. Browne

Reeb takes a deep drag on the half-smoked joint, the cherry glowing bright orange in the waning twilight like our own little personal sun, then passes the joint to me and exhales. For a moment the cloud of smoke lingers above us, as if Reeb's soul has escaped the confines of his body for a breath of fresh air. I wouldn't blame it. If I were Reeb's soul, I'd sure as hell want to step out every now and then, maybe take a bubble bath. Then the smoke drifts away, leaving Reeb a husk of human detritus without a soul.

Or maybe that's just the pot talking.

"You ever think about the end of the world?" Reeb asks, his eyes fixed on the western sky as he passes the joint.

Reeb and I are sitting on a couple of sun-bleached lawn chairs in the bed of my Dodge truck, sharing a joint and a twelve-pack of Olympia and watching the stars come out. We do this every now and then,: park off-road a couple miles north of Route 95 outside of Tonopah, hoping to catch sight of a UFO or a flying saucer while avoiding the crowds that flock to the Extraterrestrial Highway around Rachel and Area 51. We've never seen anything other than a few shooting stars and a couple of jack rabbits humping, but we don't really care. The pot and the beer are the main attractions.

"Think about it how?" I say, and take a hit.

Reeb finishes off his beer. "Like what you would do if it happened."

I empty my lungs in little puffs of smoke that drift up toward the indigo sky littered with the discarded light from a million dead stars. Or maybe it's a billion. It's hard to keep count. I pass the joint back to Reeb. "I hadn't really given it much thought. Why?"

9

"Just something that seemed worth thinking about," Reeb says, one hand digging around in the ice chest, his gaze still fixed on the same point in the sky about three beer cans above the glowing horizon.

Reeb doesn't usually think anything's worth thinking about unless it's beer, pot, or pussy, so I follow his gaze until I see a star so bright it has to be a planet. Except the longer I look, the brighter it grows.

"Is that a satellite?" I say.

Reeb shakes his head. "Don't think so."

We sit in silence and watch it grow bigger, now nearly twice as bright as any of the other stars in the sky, and it's definitely descending.

"It looks like it's coming right for us," I say.

"Yep," Reeb says, matter-of-fact, like it's nothing more than a tumbleweed.

I don't know if it's the pot, the beer, or Reeb's contagious nonchalance, but I don't feel any sense of urgency to get out of the way.

"Hey Mur?"

"Yeah," I say as the celestial object races toward us, dark and red, like a blood moon plummeting toward the earth.

I expect Reeb to give some kind of sentimental affirmation of our friendship. Or maybe a confession, like he killed someone or he was gay. Then he says, "We're almost out of beer."

Five seconds later the meteor roars past about twenty stories up and directly overhead—the heat blasting us like someone opened the door to a cosmic furnace. We stand up in unison and turn to watch the red ball of fire slam into the earth about a mile away, burrowing through the desert for about another quarter mile before finally coming to a stop.

We both turn to look at each other, neither one of us able to find the words to describe what we just witnessed.

"That was fucking awesome!" Reeb says.

I stand corrected. *Fucking awesome* pretty much captures the moment, so I just nod my silent agreement.

"Let's go check it out!" Reeb says, like a kid on Christmas morning.

Reeb climbs behind the wheel of my truck, so I give him my keys and we drive east to the impact point, the Dodge's brights lighting up the way. When we get there we find the earth scorched by a black scar a good ten feet wide and four feet deep that runs just over a quarter mile through the dirt and sagebrush, while several cactus lay broken and scattered to the sides like the bodies of dead soldiers.

Along the edges of the scar some kind of reflective formations have sprouted up. Once we get out of the truck we realize they're crystallized glass sculptures, each of which stands about three feet high on a single two-inch thick column and topped by what looks like half a dozen or so withered fronds. In the wash of the truck's headlights, they look like miniature, frozen, un-watered palm trees lining the dead road to an

10

apocalyptic oasis.

Or maybe I'm just really stoned.

"It's meteor art," Reeb says, running an appreciative hand along one of the formations like he's caressing a woman's thigh.

"*Meteorite* art," I say. "A meteor is what it's called before it hits the earth."

"Meteor art sounds better," Reeb says. "Hey, do you think that's copyrighted?"

Reeb and I walk along the edge of the scar until we reach the meteorite's final resting spot, which is a couple of feet below us beneath a cactus tree with a dozen spires that serve as the crater's headstone.

"That what a meteorite's supposed to look like?" Reeb asks.

I shake my head. "I don't think so."

Instead of an irregular shaped piece of space debris, the meteorite is smooth and white and appears perfectly round like a giant, luminous cue ball. Almost as if the moon had been sanded and buffed and polished to a high shine before being loaded into a cannon and fired at the earth. Except the moon is sitting three-quarters full just above the mountains in the east.

"What do you think it is?" Reeb takes out the joint and sparks it back up.

I shrug. "Your guess is as good as mine."

We stare down at the round, white, glowing orb half-buried in the scorched desert, passing the joint back and forth. Sobering up was probably the smarter course of action, but when you encounter a giant cue ball from outer space, getting stoned seems like the thing to do.

As I take a drag on the joint, something cracks and hisses and I jump away from the edge of the scar, half-expecting the cue ball to split open and some alien creature to come clambering out. Then I realize it's just Reeb opening the last can of Oly.

"Hey, how hot do you think that thing is?" Reeb asks.

While it's not smoking or giving off any steam, it did create a quarter-mile long skid mark of charred desert.

"Probably pretty hot," I say.

Reeb takes a drink of his beer, then gets this raised-eyebrow, crooked-grin expression he always gets whenever he comes up with an idea.

"What?" I say.

Still wearing his crooked grin, Reeb walks around the edge of the crater until he reaches the cactus tree.

"What are you doing?" I ask.

"I want to see how hot it is." He leans forward with one outstretched hand and tips the can of Oly until some beer trickles out and drops into the crater, landing on the scorched earth a foot from the meteorite.

"Shit, hold on," Reeb says, like I'm waiting on him for something.

11

He tests one of the spires of cactus for support, muttering "ouch" three times in succession before he finally takes off his sweatshirt and wraps it around his hand; then he leans out again, pouring the beer into the crater.

As soon as the beer hits the cue ball, the liquid crystallizes and turns to glass, shooting up toward the beer can. Just before the crystalized beer reaches his hand, Reeb lets go of the can and the column of glass flares out at the top like a frozen Fourth of July fireworks display.

"Holy shit!" Reeb says.

While the single column of frozen beer is less than half the width of the other glass sculptures, the top reminds me of the dead palm trees that line the quarter mile of scorched desert. Except rather than withered palm fronds, these look more like tentacles.

Off to the south, more than half a dozen sets of headlights appear in the growing darkness, headed our way. Maybe lookie-loos. Maybe military. Maybe men in black. Whoever they are, they're closing fast.

"Reeb, we've got company."

"Just a second," he says and unzips his pants.

"What the fuck are you doing?"

"Taking a piss," he says with a drunken grin.

I glance down at the white glowing orb and the frozen beer sculpture with the tentacles, then I glance back along the blackened desert at all of the other sculptures lining the scar.

"Hey Reeb, I don't think that's a good idea."

"Why not?"

Reeb doesn't give me a chance to elaborate before he releases his bladder.

The urine hits the giant cue ball and immediately crystallizes at the point of impact, turning to glass as it races back along the stream of urine toward Reeb. I know without him saying so that he thinks he can shut off the stream before the frozen urine reaches him, but good timing has never been Reeb's strong suit.

Reeb's playful expression turns to wide-eyed shock as the crystallized urine shoots into his urethra. He opens his mouth to scream but before any sound comes out, he turns to glass and freezes, his hands still holding his cock like a pornographic Greek statue. Pan caught in a moment of orgiastic self-gratification. Dionysus giving a golden shower.

"Holy shit," I say, taking a tentative step toward him. "Reeb? Hey Reeb?"

He doesn't respond and I don't know what to do, but when your best friend turns into a statue after crystallized urine shoots into his pecker through his pee hole, you have to at least make an effort.

I take a couple more steps forward, not all that sure I want to get any closer, just in case what happened to Reeb is contagious. The thought of jumping into my truck and getting the hell out of there waves its hands

12

in the air, trying to get my attention, but I can't just abandon Reeb. We've known each other since we were kids. He's my best friend. Plus he has the keys to the Dodge in his front pocket.

"Reeb, you in there?"

The approaching headlights are less than half a mile away. From the silhouettes of the vehicles racing along behind the headlights I'm pretty sure they're not lookie-loos. Even if I could make a break for it I wouldn't get far before they caught up to me, so I take one last hit on the joint and toss it into the crater before popping a breath mint.

A few moments later a dozen military vehicles arrive in a cloud of dust and humorless efficiency. Barricades are set up and a perimeter established with guards carrying intimidating guns. Floodlights are turned on to light up the impact point, while half a dozen figures in white decontamination suits and blue particle masks and black rubber elbow gloves climb down into the scar and start collecting samples.

Three uniformed figures approach me, two of them armed and flanking the third, who doesn't look happy to see me. I get the feeling he never looks happy to see anyone.

"What happened here?" he says, confrontational and accusatory, like all of this is somehow my fault.

I used to get the same kind of attitude from my mom.

It seems pretty obvious what happened here, but it's probably not a good idea to point that out to Colonel Dickhead, so I keep it simple.

"We were just drinking some beer and checking out the meteorite," I say, motioning toward Reeb's frozen figure while trying to sound sober. "Then my friend pissed on it and turned into a glass sculpture."

"How long ago was this?" Colonel Dickhead asks.

"A few minutes ago," I say.

He turns to one of the men in decontamination suits who is standing at the top of the crater near Reeb. "Disconnect him."

"Are you sure, Colonel?" the man says from behind his blue heavy duty particle mask.

"Don't question me," the colonel says. "Just do it."

"Yes sir." The man in the decontamination suit walks up to Reeb, then takes out a small hammer and what looks like a two-foot long chisel, which he places on the frozen stream of urine a couple of inches from the end of Reeb's pecker. He gives the chisel a single *whack* and the stream of urine shatters and falls into the crater, taking an inch of Reeb's manhood along with it.

"Man, that's not cool," I say.

Colonel Dickhead gives me a cold, appraising glance, then turns to his minions. "Get him out of here."

"Hey," I shout as the two armed guards escort me away from the crater. "Aren't you going to do anything to help him?"

Colonel Dickhead doesn't respond but just turns his back on me.

I glance at Reeb, his mouth open in an un-birthed scream and his hands holding what's left of his pecker. For a second I think I see his face twitch, like a wink or a muscle spasm, but then it's gone. Or maybe it was just my imagination.

When we reach the military truck, one of my two escorts pulls out a pair of plastic restraints and zips my wrists together in front of me while the other guard opens the passenger door. Before they can pack me into the passenger seat, there's a loud *crack* from the crater and someone shouts, "Something's happening!"

Colonel Dickhead starts barking out orders as armed guards run toward the crater while the guys in contamination suits run in the opposite direction. My armed escorts and I are nearly a hundred feet behind the crater so I don't see anything at first and I think that this time maybe the crack I heard *was* the giant cue ball splitting open. Then I see movement along the top of the cactus, like a snake curling around one of the spires. When a spotlight turns on the cactus I realize it's not a snake but a tentacle.

"Stay inside!" says one of my escorts before he shoves me into the truck and closes the door, then runs off toward the crater with his buddy, their guns drawn.

When authority figures tell me to do something I usually do the opposite. A lesson I learned from my father. But when the authority figures have large semi-automatic guns, I'm likely to make an exception. Except I can't just leave Reeb out there. I don't know what's going on or what I can do to help him, but I have to try.

I grab the handle with my cuffed hands and open the door. Lots of people are shouting now, a mixture of authoritative commands and barely controlled panic. More floodlights turn toward Reeb and the cactus, lighting them up like a movie premiere as I step out of the truck and look around for a sharp edge to cut away my wrist restraints.

There's another *crack* and a second tentacle appears, waving in the air beside the cactus. Whatever is coming out of the cue ball must be huge because those tentacles are at least twenty feet long and look like they can do some serious damage. And Reeb is at ground zero.

I'm trying to figure out if I can make it across a hundred feet of desert to Reeb before the tentacles crush him or knock off more of his body parts when I realize the tentacles aren't coming out of the giant cue ball. They're coming out of Reeb, one on either side of him.

I freeze next to the truck and stare at my best friend, struggling to believe what I'm seeing. It doesn't seem possible. Just half an hour ago the two of us were sitting in the back of my Dodge, watching the sunset and getting stoned. Now I'm under military arrest and Reeb is a glass statue with tentacles sprouting from his arms.

Colonel Dickhead shouts out commands and draws his revolver, which he aims at Reeb, while a dozen soldiers take up positions in a

14

perimeter around my best friend, a few of them wearing what appear to be canisters on their backs.

I can't see Reeb's face and for that I'm thankful, because the next moment the back of his head splits open with another loud *crack* and a third tentacle slips out, wraps around the base of the cactus tree, rips it out of the ground, and swings it at Colonel Dickhead like a cleanup hitter unloading on a 3-and-0 fastball down the middle of the plate.

Colonel Dickhead flies more than fifty feet in the air before crashing into one of the floodlights, knocking it and the Colonel out of commission, while the other tentacles dispatch half a dozen nearby soldiers with a couple of *flicks* and *snaps*.

All of this takes place in a matter of seconds.

Gunfire erupts as three more tentacles sprout out of what remains of Reeb and joins the others, silencing the guns and extinguishing another floodlight. The tentacle with the cactus swings again, this time connecting with a trio of soldiers wearing canisters. One of the soldiers depresses his trigger before impact and flies through the air like a human comet, a trail of fire tracing his path before he lands at the edge of the barricade and goes up in a fiery *whump*.

Another soldier stands in a jeep behind a mounted machine gun and starts firing. One of the tentacles whips out and grabs hold of the jeep and flings it into the air in a single motion. The jeep flies into the night sky, the soldier screaming as he tumbles out of the vehicle and plummets to his death, landing head first twenty feet away from me with an audible *snap*. When I look up, the jeep is coming right at me.

I run and dive to the ground an instant before the jeep slams into the truck, metal and glass crunching and exploding behind me. When I get to my feet, there's only one remaining floodlight and it's hard for me to see what's happening, just the occasional highlighted tentacle swinging through the air and the silhouettes of the other tentacles wreaking havoc.

A round of gunfire erupts, then another, but it's less like a counter attack and more like the death throes of the last un-popped kernels of Jiffy Pop popcorn. Another flamethrower shoots out a jet of flame and gets snuffed out, along with the remaining floodlight.

Somewhere in the darkness, someone is screaming for Jesus.

When the attack finally comes to and end less than a minute after it began, the only light remaining other than the three-quarter moon is the high beams of my Dodge lighting up the crater where half a dozen tentacles the size of trees wave back and forth where Reeb used to be.

An alarm goes off in my head, flashing red, telling me to run away but instead I just stand there, waiting to see what happens next. I've never been good at probability and statistics, but I figure when you're staring at a giant tentacled creature from another planet that just wiped out at least three dozen armed military troops in less than a minute, drawing attention to yourself isn't the best way to improve your chances of survival.

15

The tentacles continue to wave back and forth in the air until one of them stops and points west. Two of the others follow suit, almost like they're communicating with one another. A fourth tentacle disappears from view and returns a moment later with the giant cue ball held protectively in its grasp.

When the creature starts moving I expect it to glide along the desert like some kind of terrestrial squid or octopus. Instead, it walks away on some form of appendages. Not exactly legs but more like a pair of enormous, flexible tubes. From where I'm standing, the creature appears to be at least three stories tall.

It's hard to believe something that big came out of Reeb.

Once the creature is far enough away, I walk over to the edge of the crater and, in the wash of the headlights from my truck, I look for any remaining signs of Reeb, hoping that he's somehow still alive; hoping that I'll find him in a pool of extraterrestrial ectoplasm or cosmic afterbirth. But all I find is a bunch of shattered glass, one crystallized foot, and the frozen, disembodied inch of Reeb's dong.

"I told you it wasn't a good idea," I say.

I walk back to my truck and use the edge of the front bumper to cut away my wrist restraints, then I reach into the ice chest for a beer until I remember that Reeb drank the last one. He also had the rest of the pot in his back pocket. Hopefully one of the military trucks still has the keys in the ignition or else I'm going to have a long, sober walk back home.

Nearly a mile away and following the same line as the extraterrestrial skid mark, the silhouette of the creature moves along the desert, several of its tentacles waving in the air as it heads west toward the Monte Cristo Mountains, like it's retracing the path the giant cue ball took when it entered our atmosphere and is following some kind of invisible, cosmic trail of bread crumbs. Either that or it's going to meet a spaceship that will take it back home.

"Water," a voice says from behind me.

I turn and see one of the guys in the white decontamination suits standing on the other side of the crater, his suit torn and his particle mask gone, though he's still wearing one of the black elbow gloves.

"Sorry," I say. "I don't have any water. And Reeb drank the last beer."

"That's where it's headed," he says. "It's looking for water. For the orb."

"For the orb?" I say. "You mean the giant cue ball?"

He nods. "That's how it reproduces."

"No shit," I say.

I look back at the creature and decide if that's the case, it might be a good idea for me to go as far and as fast as possible in the opposite direction. After all, if the orb can create just one of those things from a single stream of Reeb's urine, imagine how many it can create with a swimming pool, or a lake, or an ocean.

"Hey," I say to the guy in the decontamination suit. "This isn't the end of the world, is it?"

He looks at me, then turns to follow the path of the creature. "It might be."

"That's a bummer."

I guess I should have listened to Reeb and given more·thought to what I would do if the world ended. But it's not like you ever expect your best friend to piss on a meteorite and cause Armageddon.

The sound of a steady *thwup thwup thwup* turns my attention to the sky, where several helicopters approach, searchlights playing across broken vehicles and dead bodies and the empty crater. The guy in the decontamination suit waves his hands over his head and gestures west. The helicopters hesitate a moment, then turn and follow the creature toward the Monte Cristo Mountains, toward Mono Lake and California and the San Francisco Bay Area.

Toward the Pacific Ocean.

ANT FARM

They will Exterminate the Human Race!

Drive-In Creature Feature Anthology *Presents a* **Lisa Morton** *story* **Ant Farm** *edited by* **Eugene Johnson** *and* **Charles Day** *Produced by* **Evil Jester Press**

IT | Insect Terror
Bloody Violence

Copyright 2016

19

Lisa Morton

Lisa Morton is a six-time winner of the Bram Stoker Award®, a screenwriter, a novelist, and a Halloween expert whose work was described by the American Library Association's *Readers' Advisory Guide to Horror* as "consistently dark, unsettling, and frightening". Her most recent releases are the non-fiction books *Ghosts: A Cultural History* and *Adventures in the Scream Trade.* She lives in the San Fernando Valley, and can be found online at www.lisamorton.com.

Website: http://www.lisamorton.com
Facebook: https://www.facebook.com/lisa.morton.165
Twitter: https://twitter.com/cinriter

ANT FARM

Lisa Morton

I was working on Hollywood Boulevard when the giant ants came for me. Although, truthfully, they weren't really "giant". I mean, they were big, sure, but more like…large ants. Whatever you'd call an ant the size of Lassie.

It was 1975, and I'd come west from Indiana because there was a revolution happening in Hollywood. I'd been living in my small Indiana town, writing plays that everyone thought were too good for the local theater company. I'd agreed. I belonged in Hollywood, with the new wave of filmmakers who were shaking things up, making movies like *The Godfather* and *The French Connection* and *Taxi Driver*, movies that were realistic and tough and stripped of phony glamour. It didn't matter that I was female and had a degree in English from a state university and knew absolutely no one in California.

I'd arrived with a suitcase and a portable typewriter, and I got lucky almost right off the bat: After only two nights in a sleazy hotel on Sunset Boulevard where the pool area always smelled like pot, I found a roommate: Charlene Moss was a tall, pretty brunette who wanted to be an actress. Unfortunately, Charlene's enthusiasm outstripped her talent, but because she was willing to work hard – and take her clothes off – she'd found work in a few B movies. She was from Iowa, and we got along great.

I landed a job working at a bookstore on Hollywood Boulevard called Pickwick's. It was a big three-story ode to literature, and despite the occasional drunk or pervert who wandered in off the street it wasn't a bad day job for a wannabe writer.

It was a quiet Thursday afternoon and I was running the register when a guy came into the store who almost made me laugh. He was maybe 40, with a pinstriped suit, plaid tie, and hair positively sopping with BrylCreem. Everything about him, from his oversized sunglasses to his too-loud voice, screamed HUSTLER.

He glanced around the store, then came up to the counter and flashed me a grin that he probably thought was irresistible. "Hi, sweetheart. I'm hoping you can help me find somebody who works here – Barbara Maxwell?"

My first thought was, *I'm gonna kill whoever tried to set me up with this jerk.* My second thought was to tell him Barbara Maxwell had suffered a terrible fall from a ladder in the Poetry section and passed away.

But I was also curious – who *was* this guy? – so instead I said, "That's me."

He thrust out a hand and shook mine vigorously. "Barb, I guessed that might be you! Charlene said you were smart, and you look smart."

It suddenly all made sense: Charlene had just been cast in a small part in an ultra-cheap horror movie called *Dr. Blackyll and Mr. White.* She'd be playing a hooker who gets murdered in the first reel, after Mr. White tears her blouse off (of course). Charlene had tossed me the script, and I'd laughed out loud: It was 46 pages of the worst dialogue imaginable, punctuated by scene descriptions that said things like *Mr. Blackyll kills her hard.* "Who makes this stuff?" I asked.

"Ever hear of Roger Corman?"

I was impressed; I'd done enough homework on Hollywood to know Corman was the King of the B's. "Sure. He made all those movies with Vincent Price, right?"

"I don't know – I guess. Anyway, this guy's about four rungs below that. He makes Corman look like MGM. His name's Marv Simonson. Get this: About ten years ago Marv inherits these rental properties when his dad kicks the bucket. One day Marv has to oust a tenant who's a year behind on his rent, and when he goes into the apartment he finds all these cans of unused movie film. So Marv, being the entrepreneur that he is, decides to make a movie with it. He hooks up with some kid fresh out of college who works for free, and in a week they shoot this soft-core detective movie called *Big Dick Cracks the Case.* It makes Marv a little money and he's hooked." Charlene had gone on to describe Marv's legendarily awful taste in clothes ("think bad acid trip meets Sears catalog").

I knew that's who I had to be looking at. "You must be Marv Simonson."

"Ah! Charlene talked about me, huh?"

"Don't worry, it was all good." Well, except for the part about how in her audition he'd told her to stop reading the lines and take off her blouse.

"And she said the same about you." Charlene had told me that she'd mentioned me to Marv, but I hadn't thought anything about it. "In fact, she said you're a helluva writer – excuse my French."

"Oh…" I was about to say more, but I broke off to ring up a guy buying a copy of *Helter Skelter.* Marv waited impatiently and then said,

"Look, can you take a break? This'll be worth it, I promise."

"Let me check."

I found my manager, Dave, and asked for fifteen minutes. Marv and I went up to the second floor to talk. "Let me tell you something," Marv started, "I didn't get where I am by not trusting my gut, and my gut tells me you're a talented writer – the kind of writer I like to work with. You want to get into the pictures, right?"

"Sure." It was true. I'd written two screenplays, I'd made the rounds of production companies and agents, but so far I hadn't gotten anywhere.

"Let me cut to the chase, Barb: I need a screenplay, and I need it *quick*. You think you can write quick?"

"How quick?"

"I need it a week from Monday."

Today was Thursday.

I gaped in disbelief. "Ten days? A whole screenplay?"

"Yeah. I mean, if you don't think you can do it –"

"I can do it." Those four words escaped my mouth without my volition, damning me. I'm not stupid – I knew something was rotten with this whole deal – but I was a desperate Hollywood hopeful like about a hundred-thousand other newbies in this town. "What's it about?"

"Let me show ya something..." Marv was carrying a battered leather case. He lifted it up, unzipped the top, and pulled out some photos. "It's a horror picture, and there's your star."

He handed me the stills: The first one showed a fat guy dressed as a security guard, standing in front of a row of cages that held ants that size of my dog back home, Rudyard. The second one showed another security guard, a thin young guy with a squirrelly mustache, holding one of the ants at the end of a stick with a wire noose around it. I had to admit they looked pretty good, despite the laughable idea of German shepherd-sized ants.

"Is that cool or what?"

"It is cool. Are they puppets?"

Marv's grin slid sideways just far enough to tell me something wasn't right with his story. "I work with this guy who's a genius at special effects. He just made these giant ants for a museum exhibit, but the show closed and he got the ants back. So, we're gonna make..." Marv grinned at me and raised his hands, moving them as if spelling out the words across a grand marquis, "...*Ant Farm*."

"*Ant Farm*." I wasn't entirely successful in hiding a derisive snort.

Marv didn't seem to notice. "But it doesn't stop there – we've got a star, too: Mara Duran."

I searched my memory, but couldn't come up with a match. "Mara Duran...?"

23

"Star of *Queen of Wolf Island*!"

That rang a slight bell – it brought up memories of squatting before our old black-and-white television on a summer afternoon, being mesmerized by the sight of an attractive woman growing facial hair under a full moon. "Wasn't that made back in the '50s?"

Marv waved a hand in irritation. "Yeah, sure – that's why I can get Mara so cheap nowadays. She's a little past her prime, but the fans love her. I've got her under contract for a gangster picture, but I figure I can cut her loose from that for a day and get two movies out of one contract. So you write me a script in a week for those ants and Mara Duran, and I'll pay you five-hundred for it. Whattaya say?"

What I should've said was, "How many people have already turned this down?" Or, "Five-hundred? No thanks."

Instead, my brilliant response was, "Uh…okay."

"Great!" Marv reached into his leather case again and came back up with a sheaf of carbon copies and a pen. "I got two copies of my standard contract right here. You just scribble your Jane Hancock on page ten of both and we're good to go."

I took the contract and glanced through it, seeing phrases I didn't understand like "throughout the universe in perpetuity" and "first right of refusal."

Marv thrust the pen at me impatiently. "Ahhh…you sign on the last page…"

I started to question, but instead I signed.

Marv gave me one copy of the contract, a business card, and the following words of wisdom: "Just remember: No kids, no animals, no special effects except the ants, no fancy props or sets, no crowd scenes, and no more than six speaking roles."

"What's left?" I asked, genuinely perplexed.

Marv tapped his forehead and smiled. "Imagination, sweetheart. That's why I'm paying you the big bucks."

***

FADE IN:

INT. LABORATORY – NIGHT

Handsome young scientist THOMAS ("TOM") CRANE is pacing back and forth before a large sealed metal door; a window inset in the door glows with the brilliance of atomic energy. Tom stops to check a meter by the side of the door, then adjust a dial beside the meter.

TOM

We're almost there, Maggie…

Tom's lab assistant is MAGGIE MacRAE, a lovely brunette whose white lab coat doesn't hide her curvy figure. She checks a clipboard against a gauge and looks up at Tom in excitement.

24

> MAGGIE
> *The U-235 count is in the*
> *right range now.*
> TOM
> *Think of it, Maggie:*
> *If this works, we can solve all*
> *the world's food problems.*
> *No one will ever go hungry*
> *again, thanks to our enhanced*
> *food production.*
> MAGGIE
> *I just want to see a*
> *blueberry the size of a*
> *basketball.*
> *Tom LAUGHS with her.*

***

By Friday night I had the first fifteen pages of *Ant Farm* done. I gave them to Charlene to read; I had, after all, written the female lead for her.

"A scientist," she said, smiling, nodding. "That'd be a nice step up from hooker."

"Do you like it so far?"

"Yeah, but...I can tell you what Marv will say: You've got fifteen pages here and nobody dies yet."

I restrained an urge to gape and said, instead, "But there's an ant attack by page seven. The first attack is on Maggie – your character – and since you're the lead, I can't kill you this early on."

Charlene tossed the pages back to me. "Then you better rewrite it and add a janitor or somebody for the ant to kill."

"Okay. Thanks for the tip."

I started typing again.

***

INT. LABORATORY
One of the ant's front legs smacks Tom hard. He flies back against the steel lab door and is knocked out. Maggie cowers back against a desk as the ant advances on her. She remembers the phone on the desk and grabs the receiver.

> MAGGIE
> *(into phone)*
> *This is Tom Crane's lab, we've*
> *got a situation here and*

25

need help - !

The ant charges Maggie. She SCREAMS, drops the phone, and raises her hands to shield herself as the ant approaches. The ant gets closer...closer...Maggie tries to back away, but stumbles and goes down...the ant gets closer – and the door to the lab bursts open. A SECURITY GUARD rushes in, gun drawn, ready to shout something – but he sees the ant and breaks off in astonishment. The ant turns to him, forgetting Maggie. The guard FIRES twice, but the ant doesn't slow down. It attacks the guard, who SCREAMS as the ant's mandibles rip a chunk from his upper arm.

***

It was Saturday night when Charlene read my first batch of rewritten pages. "Better," she said. "Marv will probably like that." But she was frowning.

"'Probably'? Why not 'definitely'?"

"Well...the ant should probably rip my clothes off before the guard comes in."

"You're kidding. You *want* that?"

Charlene shrugged. "No, but Marv will."

***

By Wednesday I had half the script – 40 pages of ant-smashing brilliance.

Charlene read it that night. She finished and said, "Overall, it works." Not "it's great" or "I love it," but "it works." Well, I probably had no right to expect anything more.

"So where doesn't it work?"

Charlene considered. "I don't get the point of the scene with the old lady in her apartment."

"Oh, that's the part for Mara Duran."

"Mara Duran? Marv's putting her in this?"

"Yeah. Is it okay?"

"In that case – it's Shakespeare, honey."

***

INT. MRS. KOBRITZ'S LIVING ROOM – NIGHT
Elderly MRS. KOBRITZ sits on her living room couch, reading a romance novel; SOFT MUSIC plays from a small stereo unit. The music stops abruptly, and Mrs. Kobritz stops knitting long enough to look up, irritated.
MRS. KOBRITZ
Oh, honestly, Sylvester,

26

I wish you'd leave that
record player alone.
The lights FLICKER. Now Mrs. Kobritz is a little unnerved.
MRS. KOBRITZ
Sylvester...?
There's a noise from outside, like a flower pot CRASHING. Mrs. Kobritz
sets her knitting aside now and rises.
MRS. KOBRITZ
(to herself)
I swear, that cat will be
the death of me.
A new sound comes: Something SCRATCHING at a window.
MRS. KOBRITZ
Hang on, I'm coming...
Mrs. Kobritz hobbles slowly across her living room to the window that
looks into the back yard. She looks out, calling:
MRS. KOBRITZ
Sylvester?
She sees something that makes her frown and squint and press closer to
the glass.
MRS. KOBRITZ
What in the -?
Suddenly her eyes go wide, and she stumbles back as the head of one of
the giant ants appears at the window. The elderly woman SCREAMS and
raises her hands protectively. The window is SMASHED inward by an
oversized ant leg that reaches for human prey. Mrs. Kobritz rushes to the
front door, trying to escape. She flings it open – and another ant is there!
She SCREAMS again, and the ant is on her. Blood splatters the camera as
we HEAR Mrs. Kobritz being TORN APART just out of frame.

***

On Thursday I dropped off the first half at Marv's office. On Friday I got a call from somebody named Frances Walker. He said he was the director of *Ant Farm* and he wanted to go over some notes with me.

We met at Marv's office. I'd expected another young kid fresh out of school, but instead I was met by a man who looked close to sixty and smelled like a distillery. Charlene had already given me the dirt on him: He'd been a successful cameraman until he'd developed a serious drinking problem, at which point his last name and choice of booze had formed an unholy alliance that led to his nickname "Johnnie". He'd been on the skids until Marv Simonson had given him a second chance...since Johnnie provided the camera equipment for the movies free of charge, and even shot them while directing. Johnnie and Marv had made ten movies together, one of which – a sex romp called *Who's Minding the Store?* –

had even been a modest hit on the Midwest drive-in circuit.

Johnnie had his own office in Marv's suite, and as he sat down behind his desk he fanned my pages out in front of him. I took the seat opposite and waited, trying not to wince at the alcohol fumes wafting off him.

"I like it," he said as he scanned the pages. "Dialogue's not too thick, moves fast…we've got a couple of problem areas, though, like here on 18…" He pulled the indicated page out of the stack and scanned it. "There's a flamethrower."

I stared in confusion until Johnnie explained: "I know Marv – he's not gonna shell out for a flamethrower in one scene. Make it a shotgun."

"Okay."

"Oh, and one other thing: The female lead, Maggie – my girlfriend's gonna have a hard time with some of that scientific jargon, so tone that down a little."

"Your…girlfriend?"

"Yeah – didn't Marv tell you? She's playing the lead. She was a non-negotiable part of my deal."

"Oh."

Johnnie fixed me with a hard stare. "Is there a problem?"

"No. I just…I was writing the lead for my friend Charlene Moss."

Johnnie leaned back, waving a hand. "Oh, Charlene's great. We want her in this, but just not in the lead. You can write her somethin' else nice."

"Right."

I took the pages back and left, happy to be free of the miasma of alcohol surrounding Johnnie.

***

EXT. MRS. KOBRITZ'S HOUSE – NIGHT
An attractive brunette news reporter, CAROL LANFORD, stands before Mrs. Kobritz's small suburban house, speaking into a microphone. Behind her, we see a cop examining a shattered window.
                    CAROL
            This is Carol Lanford coming
            to you live from Orange Avenue
            in the East Valley, where police
            are investigating reports that
            some sort of "giant bug" attacked
            the home of an elderly woman. The
            woman, Elena Kobritz, was found
            dead on the scene, and witnesses are reporting –
            (she glances down at a notepad

just out of frame)
- "some sort of bug, like an ant
but the size of a large dog."
Investigators say –
She breaks off as she hears a strange CLACKING NOISE behind her.
CAROL
Hold on, we're hearing something strange…Greg, are you picking that
up? Folks there's some sort
of sound out here, like –
She breaks off as a giant ant appears in the frame, its mandible halves
CLACKING together hungrily. Carol SCREAMS and staggers back. The
ant rips off Carol's blouse before it turns to the camera, and we hear the
CAMERAMAN SCREAM. The frame goes down as the camera is dropped,
and a giant ant leg steps into the picture. Then the shot GOES TO BLACK
as the leg apparently grinds down on the camera.

***

"Do you like it?"

Charlene finished reading and looked up, grinning. "I love it."
She impulsively threw her arms around me. "Thank you *so* much."

"You're welcome."

She released me to glance at the pages again. "You go up to page
65 here. Are you going to be finished in time?"

I nodded. "I know the ending. Two cops with no lines, Tom, and
Maggie battle one giant ant with shotguns. Johnnie was pretty clear on
that."

Charlene sighed. "Hey, it is what it is. Welcome to Hollywood."

***

I dropped off the finished script on Sunday evening at 7 p.m.
Marv was bent over a desk with Johnnie, moving little slips of paper
around. They both looked up expectantly as I entered.

"You got it?" Marv asked.

I tossed all 82 pages of *Ant Farm* on the desk in front of them.
"There it is."

Marv immediately flipped to the back. "A little long, but we can
trim."

Johnnie nodded.

My stomach did a flipflop.

"Oh, hey, Barb, you're gonna love this handsome young kid we
got for Tom."

"I'd like to see him."

Marv flipped through a stack of head-shots on his desk, but pulled

29

out a Polaroid and tossed it to me. It was a portrait of a thin guy with a bushy mustache, trying (badly) to smile. It took me a few seconds to remember where I'd seen him before. "Wasn't this guy in one of the ant photos you showed me?"

"Yeah – hey, kid, you got a great memory! Trust me, this guy – Enrique – can act."

I looked at the picture again. Enrique was in his security guard uniform, just like he'd been in the photo with the ant. "Is he a security guard?"

"He's just played a lot of 'em. Trust me, you'll like him when you see the finished picture."

"'The finished picture'? Won't I be on the set?" I'd already asked for next week off from the store. Dave had thrown a little fit, but finally gave in.

"Oh, sorry, sweetheart, but we've got a pretty strict rule about not allowing writers on the set."

"Why?"

Johnnie turned his red-rimmed eyes on me and actually sneered. "Trust me, kid – it's for the best."

***

So I went to work that week after all.

Charlene was scheduled to film her big scene on Thursday night. They were shooting on a real street in Santa Clarita, up in the hills just north of the San Fernando Valley. "You know, if you want to watch some of the shooting, tonight would be your best chance, since it's on location."

"Really? But Johnnie and Marv don't want me on the set..."

"Trust me, there are always onlookers around locations. They won't even notice you."

Her call time was late – 10 p.m. – and since I'd be done with work by then I decided to chance it. I mean, I *was* curious...or, should we say, dying to see my brilliant words come to life.

That night Charlene dressed in her best business outfit (supplying her own costume), and then we piled into her car and headed north up into the hills, where lots of new housing developments were under construction. Charlene kept checking the map they'd given her – this whole area was so new that street signs weren't even all in place yet.

"Why would they be shooting out here?"

Charlene snorted before answering, "Because nobody lives here yet and they can get in and out without a permit."

Finally we spotted some bright movie lights and a bunch of people milling around. "You know," Charlene said, as she parked at the edge of the circle of cars and trucks, "this looks pretty isolated, so maybe you should stay in the car until I scope it out."

30

"Right."

Charlene climbed out and I scooted down low enough so that I could still see out. As she walked forward, a guy with a baseball cap and a notebook glommed onto her and hustled her over to a small table with mirror and chair where a make-up lady started working on her.

I couldn't stand it. I had to know. I stepped stealthily out of the car and ran to where I could stand unseen behind a big truck. It was dark, and I could peek around the edge of the truck without being seen.

As I watched, Marv appeared, walking up to Charlene. He threw some pages down in front of her and then whispered to her. She noticeably sagged, dropped her head, reluctantly nodded. Marv patted her shoulder and moved off.

After a few seconds, Charlene rose from the make-up table and started walking back to the car. I hissed at her in the semi-darkness and asked her what had just happened.

"Surprise, surprise: new pages."

"What? New pages? From who?"

"Probably Marv." She tore off her nice jacket, handed it to me, and then unbuttoned the top three buttons on her blouse. "I'm a hooker again, coming to visit a client."

"But that's not -"

Before I could finish, a voice called, "Charlene, we need you on set NOW!"

Charlene answered, "Coming!" She threw me a last look before walking back to the set.

As I watched, secretly fuming, Johnnie discussed the scene with her. I couldn't hear exactly what they said, but he was obviously telling her to walk toward one of the (empty) houses, then stop on a mark, react to a sound, see something. She nodded.

Johnnie moved the camera into position; an assistant checked the lens. There was no rehearsal, of course.

But there was something else: a sudden anxiety in the crew. Everything went quiet for a second. All heads turned toward a truck parked a few vehicles away from me. I heard some sort of commotion, a man shouting obscenities.

Then, from the back of that truck, came a fat guy in a security guard uniform leading an ant at the end of a pole. An ant the size of a large dog.

An ant that was obviously *real*.

The fat man had been in the photo I'd seen. The ant in that photo had been real, too. I tried to remember details of that photo – the row of cages. Like something in a laboratory.

I realized then just how much I'd been scammed by Marv: he'd somehow gotten his hands on real giant ants, probably from some experiment. He'd paid these security guards to steal them. And he'd paid me to write a movie for them.

I nearly ran forward then and told Charlene to get back in the car…but instead I watched, stunned.

Charlene's eyes went wide as she took a step back, wobbling on her heels. "Marv…what the *hell* is that?"

"It's okay, sweetheart, Bert's got it totally under control."

Bert – the fat guy – didn't look like he had anything under control; he was staggering and struggling as the ant pulled against the noose. A second man came out of that same truck, leading another ant. The ants were both an angry shade of red with black abdomens; their pool-cue-length antennae twitched, mandibles clacked together. Their eyes darted here and there, and part of me supplied, *seeking victims*.

The second man was dressed in a white lab coat, but I still recognized Enrique, the other man from the photos, the man who was playing my scientist hero. He wasn't bad-looking, but he seemed preoccupied, eyeing Charlene –

"Enrique -!" That was Bert. He was yelling because Enrique had nearly lost his grip on the bar he used to guide the ant.

Enrique, grinning arrogantly, turned to answer – and then he *did* lose his grip. The ant moved with surprising speed, dragging the heavy bar attached to the wire collar around its throat.

Bert shouted incoherently and tried to grab the bar as the ant shot past him, but the ant abruptly stopped, turned, and sank its mandibles into his reaching hand. He shrieked and let go of the ant he was still trying to control.

Now they were both loose.

Everything happened at once. Crew people screamed and ran. Bert rolled on the ground, clutching the bloody bite holes in his right hand. The ants charged.

For a second I thought they were going for Charlene, who kicked off the heels and bolted toward me in a way no tripping-over-her-own-stupid-feet horror movie heroine ever had.

But she wasn't their target. Later, I'd wonder if ants are somehow attracted by the smell of alcohol, because they went straight for Johnnie Walker. His mouth opened in silent, abruptly sober shock as they sank their jaws into his legs. He went down, and the ants' glistening black abdomens curled under, driving fist-sized stingers into him over and over.

Enrique pushed his lab coat aside, and I saw that he still had his security guard uniform on beneath it. He pulled a pistol and aimed it in the direction of Johnnie and the two ants, but Marv leapt forward, frantically gesticulating. "No, don't!"

I expected him to say something like, "Don't shoot – you'll hit Johnnie!" Instead, he said, "We still need the ants!"

As Enrique debated, not re-holstering the pistol, the young boom operator ran up, paused just long enough to gauge the situation, and then reached down and snatched both the ants' poles. He struggled for a second, but then managed to pull them away from Johnnie.

It was too late; Johnnie was foaming and shaking, bleeding from a dozen wounds. We all watched in silent horror until the seizures faded and ceased. Johnnie was dead.

Marv walked over to the b-roll cameraman, and I heard him say, half under his breath, "You got all that, right?"

**

By three that morning, the envelopes of cash had arrived from Marv, one each for Charlene and me, along with a reminder that our contracts contained confidentiality clauses.

The production assistant who dropped the money off told us that the ants had come from a local university investigating ways to control the dangerous spread of fire ants. Enrique had approached Marv with the deal: he'd get two of the ants out of the lab if Marv gave him the acting career he'd always wanted.

The paper the next morning had an article about how director Frances "Johnnie" Walker had suffered an allergic reaction to an insect bite on the set of his newest movie, and had been pronounced dead a short time later.

Of course Charlene and I debated going to the police, but the more we went over the story, the crazier we sounded. Then Marv offered Charlene the lead in his next movie – "And you don't even have to play a hooker" – and me a three-picture deal. Charlene took her offer; I turned mine down. But most importantly, we stayed quiet, like the rest of the crew.

**

Two months later, Marv invited us to the premiere of *Ant Farm*. It would be taking place at a drive-in in Ontario.

"A drive-in?" So much for fantasies of a red-carpet premiere, klieg lights limning the Hollywood skyline.

"It's the only theater where it's opening in Southern California. Marv's going to promote it, though, and he wants us to be there to sign autographs."

"I don't think I can do it, Charlene. Nobody will care about the writer, anyway…especially since I probably didn't end up writing *any* of it."

Charlene's perfect brow furrowed, and she took my hands in her hers. "Barb…would you please go, for me? I've never done a premiere before, and my agent says it'll be great for my career, but…well, I need moral support."

I had to admit, a tiny part of me was curious, despite the nightmares I still had about seeing Johnnie Walker murdered by a giant ant. "Okay. But only for you."

＊

Just past sundown, we found ourselves in a line of cars threading into Ontario's Luxe Drive-In. We pulled into a spot, got out, and spotted a crowd around the snack bar. "That got to be it," I said.

We walked to the crowd while trailers for movies with titles like *Supervixens* and *The Giant Spider Invasion* played on the screen behind us. As we worked our way through the gawkers, the previews and ads for the snack bar ended, and *Ant Farm* began. I had to turn back for a few seconds and watch, feeling a little surge of pride.

The actors' credits came just after the title. There was Charlene's name, on a card with three others. After the actors came the cinematographer (Frances Walker), the production designer (Frances Walker), and finally the writer…

Frances Walker.

And below that, "Barbra Maxwel." Yes, they misspelled my name.

"Barb, baby!" I turned just as Marv clamped a hand onto my arm and dragged me forward. "This is the writer of the picture, folks!"

A lukewarm round of applause went up from the crowd. I was standing next Marv, while Charlene stood on the other side. Next to her was Maggie MacRae, with a smile that looked more like a grimace. Enrique stood beside her, wearing his white lab coat.

And next to Enrique was Bert, with his right hand still bandaged, while his left held onto a pole with a giant ant on the other end.

I gaped, too stunned for a few seconds to do anything else. I swear that ant turned and looked at me, its eyes cold with need.

Marv must have seen my reaction, because he leaned over and said, "Be cool, baby – it's just here for a few pictures, that's all."

I blinked, blinded, as flash bulbs went off.

"*Smile*," Marv hissed at me.

I didn't smile. I stared at the ant.

A kid, no more than eight or nine, pushed through the crowd, fascinated by the ant. He started to reach out.

Bert struggled, one-handed, with the pole. Even Enrique frowned.

I'd had enough. I stepped out of the line, ignoring Marv shouting behind me, gave the ant a wide berth, came up behind Bert and yanked out his holstered pistol.

Some of the onlookers gasped.

I lowered the gun and blew the ant's head off.

The kid cried as ant goo spattered him. He dodged back into the crowd. Bert stared in shock at the headless ant body on the other end of his pole. All eyes turned to me for a moment –

And then Marv stepped forward, grinning, raised his hands, and yelled, "It's all part of the show, folks!"

They bought it. To the sound of clapping, I handed Bert his gun and walked away.

The next day I gave notice at the store and to Charlene, and a week later I was back home in Indiana, where my parents and Rudyard the collie were happy to see me.

***

That was forty years ago. I never wrote another screenplay. I went back to college, got a master's degree, and discovered I liked teaching. I still write plays sometimes, and I'm happy if maybe twenty people ever see them.

Last week *Ant Farm* was on some cable station. I was horrified when I came into the living room and saw my husband Bill watching it. He was smiling, almost transfixed. "You know, honey, this isn't as bad as you make it sound. God, I remember seeing this when I was a kid and loving it."

I stood there in my living room, forty years removed from the worst experience of my life, staring in disbelief at my beloved husband, and I realized: it didn't matter how bad *Ant Farm* was, or that a man had died making it, to middle-aged audiences who would catch it on some cable channel and stop to watch. They'd be taken back to a moment in their lives when they'd experienced careless freedom and fearful wonder, when a movie had given them the gift of a lifetime memory. It wouldn't matter whether the movie had been good or bad, because they'd only remember *this*.

"No," I said, taking my husband's hand, "I guess it's not that bad."

35

SUCKERS!

TERROR TO THE LAST DROP...

Drive-In Creature Feature Anthology *presents a*
Ronald Kelly *Story* **Suckers!** *edited by* **Charles Day**
and **Eugene Johnson** *produced by* **Evil Jester Press**

BT — Blood Curdling Terror / Creature Violence

37

Ronald Kelly

Ronald Kelly has been writing his unique brand of Southern-fried horror for nearly thirty years. His work includes such novels as *Undertaker's Moon, Blood Kin, Burnt Magnolia, Fear,* and *Hell Hollow*, as well short story collections like *Cumberland Furnace, Midnight Grinding, The Sick Stuff,* and *After the Burn.* He lives in a backwoods hollow in Brush Creek, Tennessee with his wife and three young'uns.

SUCKERS!

Ronald Kelly

Bertrand Pinet opened the letter from the New Orleans Coroner's Office, knowing very well that he would not like what he read.

He unfolded the sheet of paper, bypassed the medical jargon that seemed to be verbal overkill to his Acadian mind, and found the morsel of information that he was looking for. *The subject's cerebrum and cerebellum seems to have been forcefully removed, leaving the majority of the medulla oblongata intact. Liquefied remnants of the brain were evident in minute quantities within the cranial cavity. The source of the tissue's extraction was a 5.3 centimeter circular opening in the rear of the skull, located between the lambdoid suture and the posterior fontanelle.*

"Sweet Virgin Mary!" the sheriff of St. Adeline Parrish said softly in a thick Cajun accent. "We got some bad shit goin' on."

Almost immediately, his dispatcher and secretary poked her head through the door of his office. "You say something, Sheriff?"

"No, ma'am, Miss Evangeline," he said, quickly slipping the letter beneath a stack of paperwork. "Nothin' to worry your pretty head over."

Evangeline Dupree – seventy-two years of age, rail thin, with hair as black as a cottonmouth's back – eyed Bertrand suspiciously. "Do that letter pertain to those bodies found in the bayou?"

"Maybe… but that be official police business, Miss Evangeline. Being as you're not a police lady, but in the administrative branch, you needn't concern yourself about it."

"Don't you be giving me that, Sheriff," she said haughtily. "I'm a tax-paying citizen here of St. Adeline, so's it *is* my business!" She frowned, her eyes bugging behind her horn-rimmed spectacles. "Folks being found dead, heads and bodies caved in, *empty*, some sucked dry of every last drop of blood… it's hellacious! You ask me, that doctor out yonder near Roubechoix Point is the one up to no good. Out there by his lonesome, doing God knows what!"

"Now you go leaving Otis Louviere alone," Bert told her. "He's a fine doctor and I got no reason of suspecting him of anything. Besides, he's a scientist doing wondrous things. Remember how he treated Aileen Chauvin's smallest girl? The one with the gimpy leg three inches too short? Louviere, he gave her shots and that leg grew right on out, pretty as you please. Miraculous!"

"Satan's balm is more like it! Louviere out there, thirty-eight years old, no wife, no young'uns, living in the boonies with his laboratory of potions. He's not to be trusted, that man."

"You are of a sour disposition this morning, Miss Evangeline," said Bertrand wearily. "Leave the poor man be."

The old woman began to return to her desk. "Get the lead out of your toot-toot, Bertrand, and earn your dollar. Find out what – or *who* – is responsible for what is going on!"

That's what I be trying to do, he thought, disgruntled. *Meddling, old bitch-lady.*

Bertrand Pinet looked at the coroner's letter peeking out from beneath the papers and considered taking the crime photos from his bottom drawer; photos of sunken bodies, drained of fluids and organs snapped by a digital camera he had purchased at the Wal-Mart in Baton Rouge. He thought better of it, though. If Evangeline caught sight of those pictures, she would be out in the middle of the street like a brass band, telling everyone within earshot.

With a groan of effort, he left his chair and walked outside. As he was climbing into his jeep, a voice crackled over the radio. It was his deputy, Armand Fruge.

"I'm out here south o' town, Sheriff... at Clovis Thibodaux's pier. We got us another one and fresh!"

Bertrand shook his head and turned his key in the starter. "Hold on... I'm a-coming."

***

Sheriff Pinet was headed down the boardwalk of the pier, when he saw his deputy and Clovis Thibodeaux standing at the end, looking down into the water.

Clovis was old – hell, he was old when Bertrand was born thirty-six years ago – and made his livelihood trapping and fishing, or so he claimed. The elderly man was thin as an eel and mean as a gar, and if he bathed, no one had ever laid witness to it. He wore the only set of clothes anyone had ever seen him in; an oily baseball cap, flannel shirt, faded overalls, and knee-length waders. His constant companion, a one-eyed bluetick hound named Pierre, lay next to him with his head on his paws and his tail drumming the boards.

"Where is he?" Bertrand asked his deputy.

"In the water, among the pilings," Armand told him. "But it be a

40

she, not a he."

Bertrand walked up to the edge of the pier and looked down. A skinny woman with stringy brown hair with cherry red highlights floated in the murky water. Her tattooed arms were pale blue and slightly bloated, and she was dressed in an orange tank top and cut-off denim shorts. One foot still wore a green rubber flip-flop, while the other was bare and pruny.

"Let's get her out," the sheriff instructed. The three of them got down on hands and knees, and lifted the corpse from the water. Despite the fact that it was water-logged, the body seemed surprisingly light.

Gently, they turned her over and laid her out on the boards of the pier.

"Well, I'll be damned," said Bertrand. "Rosella Rivette." He grimaced. His wife, Zenobia, would be mighty upset. Rosella had been her best friend in high school. They'd gotten their first tattoos together at Gustave's House of Ink.

"Didn't she serve eighteen months for meth possession?" asked Deputy Fruge.

"Twelve," the sheriff clarified. "Another six for prostitution."

"The gal had a rough life, she did," Clovis told them. "Her papa, he lavished more affection on her than was proper."

Bertrand looked at him. "Jacked the springs with her, did you?"

The old man shrugged his narrow shoulders. "A couple of times or three, I suppose."

They stared at the woman's face. It was sunken in, the same way Wayne Mazerolle's head had after the brains had been sucked out of the back of his skull, according to the autopsy report. "Well, she ain't gonna get no dates now, for damn sure," said Armand.

The sheriff knelt and laid a hand on her stomach. The flesh was flaccid, the abdomen hollow underneath. The pressure of his hand caused the corpse to release a loud, wet fart that was both comical and nauseating at the same time. Nasty black water shot from the frayed legs of her shorts, pooling on the boards.

"Get back, gents," warned Clovis. "Watch your shoes!"

Bertrand studied the body for a long moment, then took a Case pocket knife and folded out the sharpest blade. He pushed back her head with the toe of his boot and jabbed the steel into her carotid artery.

"Shit!" declared Thibodaux. "What you gone and done?"

"Just testing a theory." And the lawman's hunch proved right. No blood was in the artery at all. Rosella Rivette had been bled completely dry.

"What would do that to someone?" the deputy wondered.

Clovis's ancient eyes peered off across the swamp. "I'm thinking I be knowing."

"What then?"

41

"Been seeing some frightful things out yonder," he told the two. "Peculiar things whilst I've been out fishing."

"You mean poaching," Bertrand clarified.

"Naw, naw… fishing."

"More like poaching," the sheriff said once again. "Gator… maybe out of season?"

"Catfish," the old man insisted. "A snapping turtle or two." He glared at Bertrand. "You want to contradict or listen to what I be saying to you?"

The sheriff backed off a bit. "Go on."

A spooked look shown in the elderly man's eyes. "As I be saying, seen some mighty queer things out there. Ticks as big as softballs and skeeters the size of Ol' Pierre there, with wings five feet across. Flying across the evening sky in formation, like a flock of gooses, they were."

"You certain you weren't drinking that old kick-ass shine you like to brew?" asked Bert. "Maybe you seen them giant swamp spiders, too. La Sanguinaire?"

"I ain't lying, Sheriff! I seen them things with my own twin eyes!" Clovis looked as if he'd had his feelings hurt. "You don't be thinking much of me, do you, Pinet?"

"Can't say as I do. But go on."

Clovis cleared his throat and continued. "Found some critters on the banks of the bayou and on the sand bars… rabbits, coons, a white-tail deer… hollowed out like an empty sack. Touched 'em with a stick and their bones just gave way, collapsed. One critter… a good-sized possum… had something living inside it. Thrashed around, twisting and turning, like a snake, but it weren't none. Didn't prod it to see, neither. Afraid I was, that it would slither out and grab hold of me!"

"Still sounds like a gallon drunk of skull-bust, in my opinion," Bertrand said skeptically. "Any idea where these things came from?"

"Not sure about the ticks or the thing in the possum, but the skeeters, they be flying from the direction of Roubechoix Point."

Armand's eyes widened. "That there crazy doctor! Louviere!"

The sheriff looked irritated at his deputy. "Not you, too."

"It be true!" said Clovis. "I swear to it on my Mee-ma's grave, bless her soul. It was Otis Louviere's house that they flown from."

"Everybody gotta have them a scapegoat," said Bertrand, shaking his head. He looked down at the whore's body. "I'm going to the jeep to call Mr. Dubois to bring his hearse. I suppose we be sending poor Rosetta to the morgue in N'Orleans, as well."

"If'n they have enough tables and drawers left by now," said Clovis, eyeing the sunken woman with distaste.

***

42

That night, Bertrand and his wife sat at the kitchen table, sharing a bottle of Pernod Ricard, most of which his woman had downed. Zenobia had wept tears over Rosetta, for they had been inseparable up until graduation, when they had parted for their separate paths in life.

"She was a good 'un, Rose was," Zee sobbed, taking another swallow from a jelly jar glass with Scooby Doo on the front. "She was wild and couldn't keep her legs together ten minutes, but she had herself a good heart, she did."

Bertrand took the bottle and capped it. "That enough for you tonight," he told her. "You know liquor gives you the runs. Best leave it alone."

"Look in on the babies, will you, Bertrand?" she asked, leaving the kitchen and dropping dizzily onto the cushions of the living room couch. "I think I'm in no condition to play mommy. My head is swimming like a seasick fish."

Bertrand nodded and left her there. He walked down the narrow hallway to the children's room at the far end of the house. The bedroom light was off, but a small nightlight glowed from an outlet near the closet. He could barely see his daughter, Ophelia, in her toddler bed and his infant son, Philippe, in his crib. Bertrand crossed the floor in his sock feet, kissed them both on the forehead, then crouched down and scratched their mutt-dog, Gambit, behind its floppy ears. Satisfied, he left the room and started back to the living room, certain that Zee would likely be stretched out on the couch and sound asleep.

He was nearly there, when he heard a dry rasping sound behind him. He turned just in time to see something long and pale slither into the children's bedroom.

His heart hammered in his chest. *What the hell was that?* he thought. He stood there, frozen in his tracks, listening for the sound of Gambit growling or barking. The dog did neither. *That be odd. Ol' Gambit wouldn't let a house fly get ten feet from the young'uns without pitching a fit.*

Bertrand walked to the hall closet, opened it silently, and took his service revolver from the gun belt hanging on a peg inside. He checked the loads. Five in the chambers, one empty beneath the hammer. Slowly, he walked down the hallway and peeked through the open door.

All seemed as it had before, but he knew that was a lie. Something had entered the

room. *A snake?* The thought coated his heart with ice. He cocked the gun, turning the cylinder, and bringing a round into line. Cautiously, he stepped inside, holding the .38 pistol ahead of him.

It was a moment before he realized that all was *not* as he had left it. The floor of the bedroom between the bed and crib was empty. Gambit was nowhere to be seen.

Step by step, he traveled the length of the room, looking from left to right. The palm of his hand grew slick with sweat, making the walnut grips of the Smith & Wesson difficult to hold. *Come on, Gambit, boy. This is not like you. Did you find that ol' viper and make a midnight snack of him?*

He was nearly to the bedroom window, when he heard the sound of something gasping for breath… or, rather, *strangling* for breath. It came from the far side of his daughter's bed, near the closet. Carefully, he stepped around the whitewashed footboard, until he could see what was happening in the glow of the nightlight.

Gambit lay on the floor entwined by a constricting length of twisted white muscle. It wasn't a snake, though; not a swamp snake nor a boa or python. This thing was nearly six feet long and strangely flat… not round and thick like a serpent. He watched in terror as the thing slowly and methodically forced its way through Gambit's open mouth and down his throat into the depths of his bowels. The dog was dying; he could see the glassy look in the canine's dark brown eyes.

What is it? he wondered. *Oh dear God, it looks like… like a…*

Bertrand knew that firing his gun was out of the question. He laid the revolver on a toy box nearby and quietly raised the bedroom window. Gathering his nerve, he bent and grabbed the convoluted mixture of dog and writhing monster, intending on carrying it to the open window and tossing it out.

That was when dear, sweet Ophelia woke up and sat straight up in bed. She scrubbed the sleep from her eyes. "Daddy?" asked the girl. Then, seeing what was in his hands, she began to scream.

A moment later, Zee had snapped on the bedroom light. Stunned, she stood in the doorway, her face pale and her eyes as wide as saucers. "Bertrand! What is that thing?"

The sheriff said nothing at first. Then he stared at the ugly thing in his hands, squirming and thrashing as it made its way, inch by torturous inch, down the little dog's throat. "Lord help us all, Zee… I do believe it is… a *tapeworm!*"

Then he stepped to the window and flung it far off into the darkness of the Louisiana night.

Soon, Zee had grabbed their daughter, while Bert held his crying son close to his chest. Together, they stood at the window. The light cast its glow upon the dewy grass of the yard outside. They caught a glimpse of pale motion as the long, flat creature slithered toward the thicket that bordered the edge of the Pinet property, dragging the motionless carcass of the dog behind it.

Holding the squalling Philippe in the crook of one arm, he reached down with the other and took the gun off the top of the toy box. "Grab the diaper bag," he told Zee. "I'm taking you to your mama's."

"Where you be going then?" she asked, wild with fear.

"To find out what's happening here in St. Adeline Parrish," he told her. "And I do believe I know where to go about finding the answer."

***

It was nearly midnight when Bertrand Pinet parked his jeep by the highway. Taking a twelve-gauge shotgun from the back seat, he slowly made his way across the marshy earth that bordered the dark waterway of Roubechoix Point.

Before leaving the house, he had called Armand and told him to round up Clovis Thibodaux, his john boat, and every gun they could gather, and meet him at the dock behind the old Louviere house. After finding four organ-ravaged and exsanguinated bodies during the past two weeks – as well as the monstrous tapeworm that had killed poor Gambit – the Cajun lawman knew that they had no time to waste. The threat had to be identified and eliminated, more by force than by due process of law.

The old, two-story plantation house had once been the heart of a sugar plantation owned by the Louviere family back in the mid-1800s; a majestic palace built of money and power, immaculately white and surrounded by tall cypress trees laced with long beards of Spanish moss. But now, nearly a hundred and seventy years later, it was simply a deteriorating remnant of the Old South and its forgotten days of glory and prosperity.

Bertrand cautiously traveled down a worn path through a dense thicket of high thistle and blackberry bramble. Up ahead, the old house – scrubbed bare of its white paint by decades of harsh weather and humidity – loomed before him. All the windows were dark, like the empty sockets of a skull, except for a single one on the ground floor, which glowed brightly, casting a long slice of yellow light across the trail of moss and black earth.

He was halfway to the old mansion, when he heard the singing of crickets cease. Bertrand stood, frozen, in the silence for a long moment, then heard a peculiar noise echo from the direction of the bayou. He peered into the darkness, but could see nothing over the tall brush. Then the noise – a shrill, high-pitched *buzzing* – seemed to lift skyward and head straight toward him.

The sheriff looked toward the pale orb of a full moon. His heart leapt in his chest when he saw several dark forms silhouetted in its glow. He considered turning and running back to the jeep, but it was too late. The squadron of airborne monstrosities was suddenly descending upon him.

They were mosquitoes… giant ones. He remembered Clovis telling him of skeeters as big as Ol' Pierre the coonhound with wings five feet across. These were much larger, about the size of a year-old calf with a wing-span of six and a half feet or more. Even in the gloom, he could see that the body and legs of the pest alternated in bold stripes of black

45

and white, identifying it as a tiger mosquito, a species common in the area's bayous and deltas. Bertrand recalled jokes that had been going around for years; how the mosquito was the state bird of Louisiana. Looking at the things that swooped toward him, that wisecrack seemed more accurate and less humorous than it had before.

He lifted his pump shotgun and fired, peppering one with double-ought buckshot. The skeeter crumpled in mid-air and dropped to the marshy earth. He dispatched a couple more, then heard buzzing coming up fast from behind. He whirled to fire, but a giant skeeter dropped low and knocked him bodily off his feet. The twelve-gauge went spinning off into the thicket. Bertrand found himself lying on his back in the damp earth, staring up at six of the winged creatures hovering directly overhead.

He shucked his .38 revolver from its holster, just as one of the things dropped and lit on his right leg. One of its suckers – long and firm and as thick as a garden hose, punched through the denim of his jeans and burrowed into the meat of his thigh, searching for an artery to drain. He screamed at the pain and fired twice at the thing; missing once, before striking it in its limber body. The skeeter shrieked with an ear-piercing insectile cry and flew off, dragging its sucker out of Bertrand's leg. He felt warm blood soak his pants leg from the ugly hole in his thigh.

The scent of blood seemed to drive the hovering group of mosquitoes wild. They dipped and dived, their dark eyes gleaming hungrily at him. There were five of them and only three rounds left in his gun. He fired at one, but his target bobbed and weaved, dodging the shot. Bertrand was certain they would drop, en masse, and completely drain him of his blood, when a loud report cracked through the night... a rifle shot. One of the winged monsters veered sharply and slammed into the trunk of a cypress tree, dead before it hit. A volley of gunshots rang out and the others fell about him in loud thuds, bony legs kicking and wings fluttering until they grew still in death.

"You okay, Sheriff?" asked Armand Fruge, running from the direction of the dock. Clovis followed closely behind, holding a Winchester rifle in his wrinkled hands. "Damn! You been shot?"

"Naw, one of them giant skeeters lit on me and sunk its sucker into the meat of my leg," Bertrand told him. "Hurts like hell, but it ain't bleeding near as bad as it was before." With some effort, he got up and limped toward the big house. "I'm going to find out what's going on. Ain't natural, what I've been seeing tonight."

Clovis kicked at one of the fallen skeeters. It was as limp and light as an empty trash bag. "Hooo boy! Don't that be the honest truth."

***

Soon, they were on the front porch and banging on the big double doors of ornately-carved oak. No one answered at first, then they heard the sound of a deadbolt disengaging and one of the doors swung open. A pudgy, middle-aged man wearing thick-lensed glasses and a lab coat stood there. He held a 9mm pistol in one hand and his face was blanched and pale with fear.

"Quickly!" he hissed, his magnified eyes looking warily into the dark sky overhead. "Come inside!"

Once they were in the spacious foyer of the plantation house, Otis Louviere locked and bolted the door securely. He looked at the gun in his hand and self-consciously crammed it into a pocket of his lab coat. "So, what brings you here at this time of night, gentlemen?"

"What in blue blazes have you been doing up here, Louviere?" demanded the sheriff.

"Making himself some big-ass monsters!" accused Clovis, eyeing the doctor with contempt.

Louviere raised his hands in defense. "Not intentionally. Things... well, they've sort of gotten a little out of hand."

"A *little*?" declared Armand. "Four innocent folk dead, they innards sucked out, and the sheriff here with a hole in his leg big enough to drive a Buick through!"

"Come into my laboratory," he told them. "I will fix up Bertrand's leg and tell you what's happening."

***

Soon, the doctor was administering first aid and telling his story. "For several years I have been experimenting with growth hormones, hoping to develop a strain strong and stable enough to cure such physical anomalies as dwarfism and birth defects. I have had some success with several children here in the Parrish, but the strain was too weak to effectively treat adults. So I launched a new series of tests and increased the strength to a much greater potency. Initially, I used small animals as my test subjects: squirrels, rabbits, possums. But the strain seemed to be more than they could handle and they died within hours. So I lessened the potency and tried other subjects. Parasitic insects and worms seemed to absorb and sustain the hormone best. There were plenty of species to be found here in the swamp. But halfway through my tests, something went wrong. Their metabolisms and their rate of absorbing and processing the hormone caused them to grow to gigantic proportions. The bigger they became, the more aggressive they grew. I tried to contain them, but I returned to the lab one morning to find that they had escaped... into the swamp."

"What all did you experiment on?" Clovis asked him.

"Common varieties of parasitic organisms indigenous to our area," Louviere told him. "Mosquitoes, ticks..."

"Tapeworms," added Bertrand.

47

The doctor's eyes enlarged behind the lenses of his glasses. "So, you found it?"

The sheriff nodded. "It found me... or, rather, my dog. Killed him. Crushed him like a boa constrictor and forced its way down its throat."

"Alas, poor Pierre, he is dead, too," said Clovis. He glared hatefully at the doctor. "Earlier tonight, something, it latched onto his side and sucked his guts clean out. Nothing left but an empty sack of bones and hide."

Armand removed his hat solemnly. "Poor Gambit and Pierre! Gone to that great coon hunt in the sky."

The old man wiped his eyes with a filthy bandana. "A beautiful sentiment! Thank you, Deputy."

When the doctor had finished working on Bertrand's leg, the lawman limped to one of the laboratory windows and looked out. "So, what can we do to fix this problem, Doctor?"

Louviere's face grew as pale as lard. "Our only course of action would be to venture into the swamp and destroy the test subjects. I would prefer to capture them alive for further study, but they have grown much too aggressive and too dangerous."

"And, after they are destroyed, you will discontinue your experiments," emphasized the sheriff.

"Yes," said the scientist. "What about the people who were killed?"

"I reckon you'll be brought up on manslaughter charges... for bringing about their deaths. I'm sorry but I don't see any way to avoid that."

Otis Louviere nodded. "I suppose that is a fair price to pay for my stupidity."

Bertrand looked at the men around him; saw the grim expressions in their eyes. "Okay, then it's settled. Let's get it done."

***

They left by the mansion's rear door and headed through the darkness in the direction of the bayou. Clovis Thibodaux's john boat was tied there, waiting for their dreaded excursion into the dark depths of the swamp.

The four climbed into the boat, silently watching for menacing movement in the night. Clovis disengaged the rope that was tethered to the dock and, starting the engine, sent them slowly down the channel, toward the heart of the bayou. The old man clicked on a spotlight. It cast a swath of pale illumination upon the dark waters and the gnarled cypress trees that stood to either side, their limbs bowing low and dangling thick with Spanish moss.

48

For a while, all they saw were gators lying on the mossy banks and a few snakes resting on rocks and low-hanging branches, maybe a gar or a barnacle-crusted snapper. Then, the further into the swamp they traveled, those familiar life forms dwindled, almost as though becoming extinct. Even the night birds and insects were silent, if they were even there at all.

The boat was moving beneath a particularly dense canopy of moss-laden branches, when something began falling out of the trees.

At first, Bertrand thought they were brown pie plates, although the idea seemed downright ludicrous. Then one of the flat objects fell across his back and scuttled sluggishly up the nape of his neck, heading for the rear of his skull. He knew then exactly what it was. "Ticks!" he yelled. Reaching around, he grabbed the parasite and flung it away. It landed in the dark water of the channel with a loud splash.

Clovis and Louviere fought with the things as they caught hold and hung onto their clothing. Then, behind him, Armand Fruge began to scream.

The old man directed the light toward the rear of the john boat. The deputy was covered with them. The giant ticks had bitten deep and dug in; sucking hungrily at his head, chest, back, and belly. There was even one hanging from the junction of his groin. As he dropped to the floor of the boat, Bertrand and Louviere rushed to his side.

"Get us the hell outta here!" the sheriff ordered. Clovis did as he was told and soon they were away from the tick-infested branches, into open water.

Armand was flailing and hollering in agony. "It hurts, oh dear Jesus!" he hollered. "The pressure! I can't stand it!"

"What can we do?" asked the sheriff.

Louviere regarded the poacher. "Do you have a knife? Two if you have them?"

Clovis drew a long-bladed knife with a wicked point from a sheath on his hip and handed it to the doctor. He found a curved skinner in a compartment near the boat's dash and gave it to the sheriff.

"The heads are anchored deep," said Louviere. "We'll have to carve them out. But we'll need to do it quickly." He pointed to several of the monstrous ticks. Their flat bodies were beginning to swell, filling with fluid and tissue.

They went to work on Armand's head first. It took some doing, but they finally disengaged the tick's mandibles from the back of the deputy's skull. It left an ugly hole about the size of a quarter in the skin and bone. Bertrand removed his shirt and tied it around Armand's head, then went to work on another parasite. The man wailed and screamed as the knives whittled and carved, digging deep craters around the tick's stubborn heads. Finally, all were off. They heaved the ugly creatures over the sides of the boat, where they bobbed on the water like partially-

49

inflated balloons. Louviere went to work, binding the deputy's wounds. They bled profusely and organs and tissue were even protruding from a few of the gaping bites.

"Turn this thing around, Clovis!" Bertrand ordered. "We gotta get Armand to the hospital!"

The metallic cocking of a hammer caused the two to turn around. Otis Louviere stood behind them, holding the 9mm steadily in his hand. "No," he said calmly. "We will be proceeding." He nodded to several wire cages Clovis had sitting in the bed of the boat. "And we will be bringing back as many specimens as possible." A small grin crossed his chubby jowls. "Or, rather, *I* will. You two gentlemen will receive a bullet for your troubles and will feed the gators, while I return to St. Adeline and continue my work."

"Treacherous son-of-a-bitch!" cussed Clovis. He looked at the Winchester leaning nearby, but knew he would barely get three steps within reach before Louviere gunned him down.

"Proceed," the doctor insisted, his voice as cold as the blued steel in his fist.

Onward into the far reaches of the swamp they traveled. Each man was on the alert for fleeting motion or unusual sounds that would herald the presence of more parasites. But, for a half hour, there was nothing. The swamp seemed empty of wildlife.

***

Around three o'clock in the morning, Clovis slowed the boat to a halt and let the engine idle.

"Why did you stop?" asked Louviere.

"Something's in the water," the old man told him. He turned the spotlight on the churning currents ahead of the bow. Several long, glistening objects broke the surface, before sinking into the dark depths again.

"Gators?" asked Bertrand.

"No. They look too soft and slimy. And too big."

The doctor motioned threateningly with his gun. "Remember, whatever we find goes back with me."

"These won't be fitting into no damned cage," Clovis said. He turned and looked at the man. Suddenly his ancient eyes widened in horror. "Sacre bleu!"

Puzzled, the doctor looked over his shoulder and his heart froze.

Something was rising up out of the dark waters behind the boat. It was black and glistening and impossibly large; tubular, like a worm, but much thicker. If it had eyes, Louviere could not see them. All he could see was its open maw ringed with hooked, shark-like teeth.

"It's..." Bertrand was at a loss for words at first, then found them

50

as the thing lurched and swayed. "It's a *leech*!"

The creature emitted a guttural gurgling sound as it found its victim and lowered, much quicker than anyone expected for such a cumbersome organism. Louviere cried out, fired twice with his pistol, and then was swallowed – from the chest up – by the fanged mouth of the monstrous leech. Its teeth anchored deeply and its dark body began to pulsate as it sucked hungrily at its prey. Bertrand and Clovis could hear the doctor's muffled screams. His shrieks echoed within the gullet of the beast as his arms and legs jerked spasmodically.

It's sucking him clean out! thought the sheriff with horror. *Like I'd suck the innards from a boiled crawdad!*

Then, abruptly, the leech rose another seven feet into the muggy night air. The doctor's feet kicked wildly, dislodging a shoe, then the awful screaming stopped and he grew limp. With a loud splash and a gurgle, the monster descended back into the depths of the bayou, taking Otis Louviere's remains with it.

The sheriff and the poacher stood there for a long moment, watching and listening. The swamp was still around them and so was the water. Nary a ripple broke its mirror-like surface. Nothing else appeared… hungry, searching for sustenance.

At the back of the boat, Armand moaned, oblivious to what had just taken place.

"Let's get on back to town, Clovis," Bertrand suggested.

"Yes, sir," he agreed with a nod. "I be more'n ready to be rid of this dark place and the horrors that dwell here."

Clovis deftly turned the boat and started back up the channel. Above the bearded limbs of the cypress the night sky was like black velvet, studded with a million rhinestone stars.

Bertrand crouched next to his deputy. "We gonna get you some good help, Armand," he told him. "It's over."

"I think not, constable," said Clovis from the bow. "Look!"

Bertrand stood up. The old man was directing the beam of his spot along the banks of the bayou. Partially submerged in the still water and clinging to the exposed roots of the cypress trees were dark, waxy cylinders of some sort; narrow and pointed at the ends.

"What the hell is all that, Clovis?" he asked.

"Be looking like skeeter eggs to me," the poacher told him. The man's wrinkled face was pale and full of fright. "They be thousands of them!"

The sheriff thought for a minute. "Can we burn them?"

"I got me a two-gallon can of gasoline here, but that ain't gonna do much. We'll have to come back and get 'er done… and pray that they don't hatch before we do."

Bertrand Pinet shuddered. The thought of a massive, buzzing swarm of giant mosquitoes descending upon his hometown of St. Adeline

51

Parrish was terrifying to even imagine. "Let's go then."

Clovis nodded grimly and, pushing the john boat's engine to the limit, they silently headed back up the dark channel of the bayou for home.

The Yattering and Jack

Jim Kavanaugh

Impossible to hide when the Demon has come to collect!

Drive-In Creature Feature Anthology *Presents a*
Clive Barker *story* **The Yattering and Jack** *edited*
by **Eugene Johnson** *and* **Charles Day** *Produced by*
Evil Jester Press | DH | Demonic Horror / Satanic Images | *Copyright 2016*

Clive Barker

Clive Barker was born in Liverpool in 1952. He is the worldwide bestselling author of the *Books of Blood*, and numerous novels including *Imajica, The Great and Secret Show, Sacrament* and *Galilee*. In addition to his work as a novelist and short story writer he also illustrates, writes, directs and produces for the stage and screen. His films include *Hellraiser, Hellbound, Nightbreed* and *Candyman*. Clive lives in Beverly Hills, California.

THE YATTERING AND JACK

Clive Barker

Why the powers (long may they hold court; long may they shit light on the heads of the damned) had sent it out from Hell to stalk Jack Polo, the Yattering couldn't discover. Whenever he passed a tentative inquiry along the system to his master, just asking the simple question, "What am I doing here?" it was answered with a swift rebuke for its curiosity. None of its business, came the reply, its business was to do. Or die trying. And after six months of pursuing Polo, the Yattering was beginning to see extinction as an easy option. This endless game of hide and seek was to nobody's benefit, and the Yattering's immense frustration. It feared ulcers, it feared psychosomatic leprosy (condition lower demons like itself were susceptible to), worst of all it feared losing its temper completely and killing the man outright in an uncontrollable fit of pique.

"What was Jack Polo anyway?"

A gherkin importer; by the balls of Leviticus, he was simply a gherkin importer. His life was worn out, his family was dull, his politics were simpleminded and his theology nonexistent. The man was a no-account, one of nature's blankest little numbers—why bother with the likes of him? This wasn't a Faust: a pact-maker, a soul-seller. This one wouldn't look twice at the chance of divine inspiration: he'd sniff, shrug and get on with his gherkin importing.

Yet the Yattering was bound to that house, long night and longer day, until he had the man a lunatic, or as good as. It was going to be a lengthy job, if not interminable. Yes, there were times when even psychosomatic leprosy would be bearable if it meant being invalided off this impossible mission.

For his part, Jack J. Polo continued to be the most unknowing of men. He had always been that way; indeed his history was littered with the victims of his naiveté. When his late, lamented wife had cheated on him (he'd been in the house on at least two of the occasions, watching the

55

television) he was the last one to find out. And the clues they'd left behind them! A blind, deaf and dumb man would have become suspicious. Not Jack. He pottered about his dull business and never noticed the tang of the adulterer's cologne, nor the abnormal regularity with which his wife changed the bed-linen.

He was no less uninterested in events when his younger daughter Amanda confessed her lesbianism to him. His response was a sigh and a puzzled look.

"Well, as long as you don't get pregnant, darling," he replied, and sauntered off into the garden, blithe as ever.

What chance did a fury have with a man like that?

To a creature trained to put its meddling fingers into the wounds of the human psyche, Polo offered a surface so glacial, so utterly without distinguishing marks, as to deny malice any hold whatsoever.

Events seemed to make no dent in his perfect indifference. His life's disasters seemed not to scar his mind at all. When, eventually, he was confronted with the truth about his wife's infidelity (he found them screwing in the bath) he couldn't bring himself to be hurt or humiliated.

"These things happen," he said to himself, backing out of the bathroom to let them finish what they'd started.

"Que sera, sera."

Que sera, sera. The man muttered that damn phrase with monotonous regularity. He seemed to live by that philosophy of fatalism, letting attacks on his manhood, ambition and dignity slide off his ego like rain-water from his bald head.

The Yattering had heard Polo's wife confess all to her husband (it was hanging upside down from the light-fitting, invisible as ever) and the scene had made it wince. There was the distraught sinner, begging to be accused, bawled at, struck even, and instead of giving her the satisfaction of his hatred, Polo had just shrugged and let her say her piece without a word of interruption, until she had no more to unbosom. She'd left, at length, more out of frustration and sorrow than guilt; the Yattering had heard her tell the bath-room mirror how insulted she was at her husband's lack of righteous anger. A little while after she'd flung herself off the balcony of the Roxy Cinema.

Her suicide was in some ways convenient for the fury. With the wife gone, and the daughters away from home, it could plan for more elaborate tricks to unnerve its victim, without ever having to concern itself with revealing its presence to creatures the powers had not marked for attack.

But the absence of the wife left the house empty during the days, and that soon became a burden of boredom the Yattering found scarcely supportable. The hours from nine to five, alone in the house, often seemed endless. It would mope and wander, planning bizarre and impractical revenges upon the Polo-man, pacing the rooms, heartsick, companioned only by the clicks and whirrs of the house as the radiators cooled, or the refrigerator switched itself on and off. The situation rapidly became so desperate that the arrival of the midday post became the high-point of the day, and an unshakable melancholy would settle on the Yattering if the postman had nothing to deliver and passed by to the next house.

When Jack returned the games would begin in earnest. The usual warm-up routine: it would meet Jack at the door and prevent his key from turning in the lock. The contest would go on for a minute or two until Jack accidentally found the measure of the Yattering's resistance, and won the day. Once inside, it would start all the lamp-shades swinging. The man would usually ignore this performance, however violent the motion. Perhaps he might shrug and murmur: "Subsidence," under his breath, then, inevitably, *"Que sera, sera."*

In the bathroom, the Yattering would have squeezed toothpaste around the toilet seat and have plugged up the shower head with soggy toilet paper. It would even share the shower with Jack, hanging unseen from the rail that held up the shower curtain and murmuring obscene suggestions in his ear. That was always successful, the demons were taught at the Academy. The obscenities in the ear routine never failed to distress clients, making them think they were conceiving of these pernicious acts themselves, and driving them to self-disgust, then to self-rejection and finally to madness. Of course, in a few cases the victims would be so inflamed by these whispered suggestions they'd go out on the streets and act upon them. Under such circumstances the victim would often be arrested and incarcerated. Prison would lead to further crimes, and a slow dwindling of moral reserves—and the victory was won by that route. One way or another insanity would win out.

Except that for some reason this rule did not apply to Polo; he was imperturbable: a tower of propriety.

Indeed, the way things were going the Yattering would be the one to break. It was tired; so very tired. Endless days of tormenting the cat, reading the funnies in yesterday's newspaper, watching the game shows: they drained the fury. Lately, it had developed a passion for the woman who lived across the street from Polo. She was a young widow; and seemed to spend most of her life parading around the house stark naked. It was almost unbearable sometimes, in the middle of a day when the postman failed to call, watching the woman and knowing it could never cross the thresh-old of Polo's house.

This was the Law. The Yattering was a minor demon, and his soul-catching was strictly confined to the perimeters of his victim's house. To step outside was to relinquish all powers over the victim: to put itself at the mercy of humanity.

All June, all July and most of August it sweated in its prison, and all through those bright, hot month's Jack Polo maintained complete indifference to the Yattering's attacks.

It was deeply embarrassing, and it was gradually destroying the demon's self-confidence, seeing this bland victim survive every trial and trick attempted upon him.

The Yattering wept. The Yattering screamed.

In a fit of uncontrollable anguish, it boiled the water in the aquarium, poaching the guppies.

Polo heard nothing. Saw nothing.

***

At last, in late September, the Yattering broke one of the first rules of its condition, and appealed directly to its masters.

Autumn is Hell's season; and the demons of the higher dominations were feeling benign. They condescended to speak to their creature.

"What do you want?" asked Beelzebub, his voice blackening the air in the lounge.

"This man..." the Yattering began nervously. "Yes?"

"This Polo..." "Yes?"

"I am without issue upon him. I can't get panic upon him, I can't breed fear or even mild concern upon him. I am sterile, Lord of the Flies, and I wish to be put out of my misery."

For a moment Beelzebub's face formed in the mirror over the mantelpiece.

"You want *what*?"

Beelzebub was part elephant, part wasp. The Yattering was terrified.

"I—want to die." "You cannot die."

"From this world. Just die from this world. Fade away. Be replaced."

"You will not die."

"But I can't break him!" the Yattering shrieked, tearful. "You must."

"Why?"

"Because we tell you to." Beelzebub always used the Royal "we," though unqualified to do so.

"Let me at least know why I'm in this house," the Yattering appealed. "What is he? Nothing! He's nothing!"

Beelzebub found this rich. He laughed, buzzed, trumpeted. "Jack Johnson Polo is the child of a worshiper at the Church of Lost Salvation. He belongs to us."

"But why should you want him? He's so dull."

"We want him because his soul was promised to us, and his mother did not deliver it. Or herself, come to that. She cheated us. She died in the arms of a priest, and was safely escorted to—"

58

The word that followed was anathema. The Lord of the Flies could barely bring himself to pronounce it.

"—Heaven," said Beelzebub, with infinite loss in his voice. "Heaven," said the Yattering, not knowing quite what was meant by the word.

"Polo is to be hounded in the name of the Old One, and punished for his mother's crimes. No torment is too profound for a family that has cheated us."

"I'm tired," the Yattering pleaded, daring to approach the mirror. "Please. I beg you."

"Claim this man," said Beelzebub, "or you will suffer in his place." The figure in the mirror waved its black and yellow trunk and faded.

"Where is your pride?" said the master's voice as it shriveled into distance. "Pride, Yattering, pride."

Then he was gone.

In its frustration the Yattering picked up the cat and threw it into the fire, where it was rapidly cremated. If only the law allowed such easy cruelty to be visited upon human flesh, it thought. If only. If only. Then it'd make Polo suffer such torments. But no. The Yattering knew the laws as well as the back of its hand; they had been flayed on to its exposed cortex as a fledgling demon by its teachers. And Law One stated: "Thou shalt not lay palm upon thy victims."

It had never been told why this law pertained, but it did. "Thou shalt not..."

So the whole painful process continued. Day in, day out, and still the man showed no sign of yielding. Over the next few weeks the Yattering killed two more cats that Polo brought home to replace his treasured Freddy (now ash).

The first of these poor victims was drowned in the toilet bowl one idle Friday afternoon. It was a petty satisfaction to see the look of distaste register on Polo's face as he unzipped his fly and glanced down. But any pleasure the Yattering took in Jack's discomfiture was canceled out by the blithely efficient way in which the man dealt with the dead cat, hoisting the bundle of soaking fur out of the pan, wrapping it in a towel and burying it in the back garden with scarcely a murmur.

The third cat that Polo brought home was wise to the invisible presence of the demon from the start. There was indeed an entertaining week in mid-November when life for the Yattering became almost interesting while it played cat and mouse with Freddy III. Freddy played the mouse. Cats not being especially bright animals the game was scarcely a great intellectual challenge, but it made a change from the endless days of waiting, haunting and failing. At least the creature accepted the Yattering's presence. Eventually, how-ever, in a filthy mood (caused by the remarriage of the Yattering's naked widow) the demon lost its temper with the cat. It was sharpening its nails on the nylon carpet, clawing and scratching at the pile for hours on end. The noise put the demon's metaphysical teeth on edge. It looked at the cat once, briefly, and it flew apart as though it had swallowed a live grenade.

The effect was spectacular. The results were gross. Cat-brain, cat-fur, cat-gut everywhere.

Polo got home that evening exhausted, and stood in the doorway of the dining-room, his face sickened, surveying the carnage that had been Freddy III.

"Damn dogs," he said. "Damn, damn dogs."

There was anger in his voice. Yes, exulted the Yattering, anger. The man was upset: there was clear evidence of emotion on his face.

Elated, the demon raced through the house, determined to capitalize on its victory. It opened and slammed every door. It smashed vases. It set the lampshades swinging.

Polo just cleaned up the cat.

The Yattering threw itself downstairs, tore up a pillow. Impersonated a thing with a limp and an appetite for human flesh in the attic, and giggling.

Polo just buried Freddy III, beside the grave of Freddy II, and the ashes of Freddy I.

Then he retired to bed, without his pillow.

The demon was utterly stumped. If the man could not raise more than a flicker of concern when his cat was exploded in the dining-room, what chance had it got of ever breaking the bastard?

There was one last opportunity left.

It was approaching Christ's Mass, and Jack's children would be coming home to the bosom of the family. Perhaps they could convince him that all was not well with the world; perhaps they could get their fingernails under his flawless indifference, and begin to break him down. Hoping against hope, the Yattering sat out the weeks to late December, planning its attacks with all the imaginative malice it could muster.

Meanwhile, Jack's life sauntered on. He seemed to live apart from his experience, living his life as an author might write a preposterous story, never involving himself in the narrative too deeply. In several significant ways, however, he showed his enthusiasm for the coming holiday. He cleaned his daughters' rooms immaculately. He made their beds up with sweet-smelling linen. He cleaned every speck of cat's blood out of the carpet. He even set up a Christmas tree in the lounge, hung with iridescent balls, tinsel and presents.

Once in a while, as he went about the preparations, Jack thought of the game he was playing, and quietly calculated the odds against him. In the days to come he would have to measure not only his own suffering, but that of his daughters, against the possible victory. And always, when he made these calculations, the chance of victory seemed to outweigh the

60

risks.

So he continued to write his life, and waited.

Snow came, soft pats of it against the windows, against the door. Children arrived to sing carols, and he was generous to them. It was possible, for a brief time, to believe in peace on earth.

Late in the evening of the twenty-third of December the daughters arrived, in a flurry of cases and kisses. The youngest, Amanda, arrived home first. From its vantage point on the landing the Yattering viewed the young woman balefully. She didn't look like ideal material in which to induce a breakdown. In fact, she looked dangerous. Gina followed an hour or two later; a smoothly polished woman of the world at twenty-four, she looked every bit as intimidating as her sister. They came into the house with their bustle and their laughter; they rearranged the furniture; they threw out the junk food in the freezer, they told each other (and their father) how much they had missed each other's company. Within the space of a few hours the drab house was repainted with light, and fun and love.

It made the Yattering sick.

Whimpering, it hid its head in the bedroom to block out the din of affection, but the shock-waves enveloped it. All it could do was sit, and listen, and refine its revenge.

Jack was pleased to have his beauties home. Amanda so full of opinions, and so strong, like her mother. Gina more like *his* mother: poised, perceptive. He was so happy in their presence he could have wept; and here was he, the proud father, putting them both at such risk. But what was the alternative? If he had canceled the Christmas celebrations, it would have looked highly suspicious. It might even have spoiled his whole strategy, wakening the enemy to the trick that was being played.

No; he must sit tight. Play dumb, the way the enemy had come to expect him to be.

The time would come for action.

At 3:15 on Christmas morning the Yattering opened hostilities by throwing Amanda out of bed. A paltry performance at best, but it had the intended effect. Sleepily rubbing her bruised head, she climbed back into bed, only to have the bed buck and shake and fling her off again like an unbroken colt.

The noise woke the rest of the house. Gina was first in her sister's room.

"What's going on?"

"There's somebody under the bed." "What?"

Gina picked up a paperweight from the dresser and demanded the assailant come out. The Yattering, invisible, sat on the window seat and made obscene gestures at the women, tying knots in its genitalia.

Gina peered under the bed. The Yattering was clinging to the light fixture now, persuading it to swing backward and forward, making

61

the room reel.

"There's nothing there—" "There is."

Amanda knew. Oh yes, she knew.

"There's something here, Gina," she said. "Something in the room with us, I'm sure of it."

"No." Gina was absolute. "It's empty."

Amanda was searching behind the wardrobe when Polo came in. "What's all the din?"

"There's something in the house, Daddy. I was thrown out of bed." Jack looked at the crumpled sheets, the dislodged mattress, then at Amanda.

This was the first test: he must lie as casually as possible. "Looks like you've been having nightmares, beauty," he said, affecting an innocent smile.

"There was something under the bed," Amanda insisted. "There's nobody here now."

"But I felt it."

"Well, I'll check the rest of the house," he offered, without enthusiasm for the task. "You two stay here, just in case."

As Polo left the room, the Yattering rocked the light a little more. "Subsidence," said Gina.

It was cold downstairs, and Polo could have done without padding around barefoot on the kitchen tiles, but he was quietly satisfied that the battle had been joined in such a petty manner. He'd half-feared that the enemy would turn savage with such tender victims at hand. But no: he'd judged the mind of the creature quite accurately. It was one of the lower orders. Powerful, but slow. Capable of being inveigled beyond the limits of its control. Carefully does it, he told himself, carefully does it.

He traipsed through the entire house, dutifully opening cupboards and peering behind the furniture, then returned to his daughters, who were sitting at the top of the stairs. Amanda looked small and pale, not the twenty-two-year-old woman she was, but a child again.

"Nothing doing," he told her with a smile. "It's Christmas morning and all through the house—"

Gina finished the rhyme.

"Nothing is stirring; not even a mouse." "Not even a mouse, beauty."

At that moment the Yattering took its cue to fling a vase off the lounge mantelpiece.

Even Jack jumped.

"Shit," he said. He needed some sleep, but quite clearly the Yattering had no intention of letting them alone just yet.

"Que sera, sera," he murmured, scooping up the pieces of the Chinese vase, and putting them in a piece of newspaper. "The house is sinking a little on the left side, you know," he said more loudly. "It has

been for years."

"Subsidence," said Amanda with quiet certainty, "would not throw me out of my bed."

Gina said nothing. The options were limited. The alternatives unattractive.

"Well maybe it was Santa Claus," said Polo, attempting levity. He parceled up the pieces of the vase and wandered through into the kitchen, certain that he was being shadowed every step of the way. "What else can it be?" He threw the question over his shoulder as he stuffed the newspaper into the wastebin. "The only other explanation—" here he became almost elated by his skimming so close to the truth, "the only other possible explanation is too preposterous for words."

It was an exquisite irony, denying the existence of the invisible world in the full knowledge that even now it breathed vengefully down his neck.

"You mean poltergeist?" said Gina.

"I mean anything that goes bang in the night. But, we're grown-up people aren't we? We don't believe in Bogeymen."

"No," said Gina flatly, "I don't, but I don't believe the house is subsiding either."

"Well, it'll have to do for now," said Jack with nonchalant finality. "Christmas starts here. We don't want to spoil it talking about gremlins, now do we?"

They laughed together.

Gremlins. That surely bit deep. To call the Hell-spawn a gremlin. The Yattering, weak with frustration, acid tears boiling on its intangible cheeks, ground its teeth and kept its peace.

There would be time yet to beat that atheistic smile off Jack Polo's smooth, fat face. Time aplenty. No half-measures from now on. No subtlety. It would be an all-out attack.

Let there be blood. Let there be agony. They'd all break.

***

Amanda was in the kitchen, preparing Christmas dinner, when the Yattering mounted its next attack. Through the house drifted the sound of King's College Choir, "O Little Town of Bethlehem, how still we see thee lie…"

The presents had been opened, the G and T's were being downed, the house was one warm embrace from roof to cellar.

In the kitchen a sudden chill permeated the heat and the steam, making Amanda shiver; she crossed to the window, which was ajar to clear the air, and closed it. Maybe she was catching something.

The Yattering watched her back as she busied herself about the kitchen, enjoying the domesticity for a day. Amanda felt the stare quite clearly. She turned round. Nobody, nothing. She continued to wash the Brussels sprouts, cutting into one with a worm curled in the middle. She drowned it.

The Choir sang on.

In the lounge, Jack was laughing with Gina about something. Then, a noise. A rattling at first, followed by a beating of some-body's fists against a door. Amanda dropped the knife into the bowl of sprouts and turned from the sink, following the sound. It was getting louder all the time. Like something locked in one of the cupboards, desperate to escape. A cat caught in the box, or a—Bird.

It was coming from the oven.

Amanda's stomach turned, as she began to imagine the worst. Had she locked something in the oven when she'd put in the turkey? She called for her father, as she snatched up the oven cloth and stepped toward the cooker, which was rocking with the panic of its prisoner. She had visions of a basted cat leaping out at her, its fur burned off, its flesh half-cooked.

Jack was at the kitchen door.

"There's something in the oven," she said to him, as though he needed telling. The cooker was in a frenzy; its thrashing contents had all but beaten off the door.

He took the oven cloth from her. This is a new one, he thought. You're better than I judged you to be. This is clever. This is original.

Gina was in the kitchen now. "What's cooking?" she quipped.

But the joke was lost as the cooker began to dance, and the pans of boiling water were twitched off the burners on to the floor.

Scalding water seared Jack's leg. He yelled, stumbling back into Gina, before diving at the cooker with a yell that wouldn't have shamed a samurai.

The oven handle was slippery with heat and grease, but he seized it and flung the door down.

A wave of steam and blistering heat rolled out of the oven, smelling of succulent turkey-fat. But the bird inside had apparently no intentions of being eaten. It was flinging itself from side to side on the roasting tray, tossing gouts of gravy in all directions. Its crisp brown wings pitifully flailed and flapped, its legs beat a tattoo on the roof of the oven.

Then it seemed to sense the open door. Its wings stretched them-selves out to either side of its stuffed bulk and it half-hopped, half-fell on to the oven door, in a mockery of its living self. Headless, oozing stuffing and onions, it flopped around as though nobody had told the damn thing it was dead, while the fat still bubbled on its bacon-strewn back.

Amanda screamed.

Jack dived for the door as the bird lurched into the air, blind but vengeful. What it intended to do once it reached its three cowering victims was never discovered. Gina dragged Amanda into the hall-way with her father in hot pursuit, and the door was slammed closed as the blind bird flung itself against the paneling, beating on it with all its strength. Gravy seeped through the gap at the bottom of the door, dark and fatty.

The door had no lock, but Jack reasoned that the bird was not capable of turning the handle. As he backed away, breathless, he cursed his confidence. The opposition had more up its sleeve than he'd guessed.

Amanda was leaning against the wall sobbing, her face stained with splotches of turkey grease. All she seemed able to do was deny what she'd seen, shaking her head and repeating the word "no" like a talisman against the ridiculous horror that was still throwing itself against the door. Jack escorted her through to the lounge. The radio was still crooning carols which blotted out the din of the bird, but their promises of goodwill seemed small comfort.

Gina poured a hefty brandy for her sister and sat beside her on the sofa, plying her with spirits and reassurance in about equal mea-sure. They made little impression on Amanda.

"What *was* that?" Gina asked her father, in a tone that demanded an answer.

"I don't know what it was," Jack replied.

"Mass hysteria?" Gina's displeasure was plain. Her father had a secret: he knew what was going on in the house, but he was refusing to cough up for some reason.

"What do I call: the police or an exorcist?" "Neither."

"For God's sake—"

"There's *nothing* going on, Gina. Really."

Her father turned from the window and looked at her. His eyes spoke what his mouth refused to say, that this was war.

Jack was afraid.

The house was suddenly a prison. The game was suddenly lethal. The enemy, instead of playing foolish games, meant harm, real harm to them all.

In the kitchen the turkey had at last conceded defeat. The carols on the radio had withered into a sermon on God's benedictions.

What had been sweet was sour and dangerous. He looked across the room at Amanda and Gina. Both, for their own reasons, were trembling. Polo wanted to tell them, wanted to explain what was going on. But the thing must be there, he knew, gloating.

He was wrong. The Yattering had retired to the attic, well-satisfied with its endeavors. The bird, it felt, had been a stroke of genius. Now it could rest a while: recuperate. Let the enemy's nerves tat-ter themselves in anticipation. Then, in its own good time, it would deliver the coup de grâce.

Idly, it wondered if any of the inspectors had seen his work with the turkey. Maybe they would be impressed enough by the Yattering's

65

originality to improve its job prospects. Surely it hadn't gone through all those years of training simply to chase half-wit-ted imbeciles like Polo. There must be something more challenging available than that. It felt victory in its invisible bones: and it was a good feeling.

The pursuit of Polo would surely gain momentum now. His daughters would convince him (if he wasn't now quite convinced) that there was something terrible afoot. He would crack. He would crumble. Maybe he'd go classically mad: tear out his hair, rip off his clothes; smear himself with his own excrement.

Oh yes, victory was close. And wouldn't its masters be loving then? Wouldn't it be showered with praise, and power?

One more manifestation was all that was required. One final, inspired intervention and Polo would be so much blubbering flesh.

Tired, but confident, the Yattering descended into the lounge.

***

Amanda was lying full-length on the sofa, asleep. She was obviously dreaming about the turkey. Her eyes rolled beneath her gossamer lids, her lower lip trembled. Gina sat beside the radio, which was silenced now. She had a book open on her lap, but she wasn't reading it.

The gherkin importer wasn't in the room. Wasn't that his footstep on the stair? Yes, he was going upstairs to relieve his brandy-full bladder. Ideal timing.

The Yattering crossed the room. In her sleep Amanda dreamed something dark flitting across her vision, something malign, some-thing that tasted bitter in her mouth.

Gina looked up from her book.

The silver balls on the tree were rocking, gently. Not just the balls. The tinsel and the branches too.

In fact, the tree. The whole tree was rocking as though someone had just seized hold of it.

Gina had a very bad feeling about this. She stood up. The book slid to the floor.

The tree began to spin.

Christ," she said. "Jesus Christ." Amanda slept on.

The tree picked up momentum.

Gina walked as steadily as she could across to the sofa and tried to shake her sister awake. Amanda, locked in her dreams, resisted for a moment.

"Father," said Gina. Her voice was strong, and carried through into the hall. It also woke Amanda.

Downstairs, Polo heard a noise like a whining dog. No, like two whining dogs. As he ran down the stairs, the duet became a trio. He burst

66

into the lounge half expecting all the hosts of Hell to be in there, dog-headed, dancing on his beauties.

But no. It was the Christmas tree that was whining, whining like a pack of dogs, as it spun and spun.

The lights had long since been pulled from their sockets. The air stank of singed plastic and pine-sap. The tree itself was spinning like a top, flinging decorations and presents off its tortured branches with the largesse of a mad king.

Jack tore his eyes from the spectacle of the tree and found Gina and Amanda crouching, terrified, behind the sofa.

"Get out of here," he yelled.

Even as he spoke, the television sat up impertinently on one leg and began to spin like the tree, gathering momentum quickly. The clock on the mantelpiece joined the pirouetting. The pokers beside the fire. The cushions. The ornaments. Each object added its own singular note to the orchestration of whines which were building up, second by second, to a deafening pitch. The air began to brim with the smell of burning wood, as friction heated the spinning tops to flash-point. Smoke swirled across the room.

Gina had Amanda by the arm, and was dragging her toward the door, shielding her face against the hail of pine needles that the still-accelerating tree was throwing off.

Now the lights were spinning.

The books, having flung themselves off the shelves, had joined the tarantella.

Jack could see the enemy, in his mind's eye, racing between the objects like a juggler spinning plates on sticks, trying to keep them all moving at once. It must be exhausting work, he thought. The demon was probably close to collapse. It couldn't be thinking straight. Overexcited. Impulsive. Vulnerable. This must be the moment, if ever there was a moment, to join battle at last. To face the thing, defy it, and trap it.

For its part, the Yattering was enjoying this orgy of destruction. It flung every movable object into the fray, setting everything spinning.

It watched with satisfaction as the daughter twitched and scurried; it laughed to see the old man stare, pop-eyed, at this preposterous ballet.

Surely he was nearly mad, wasn't he?

The beauties had reached the door, their hair and skin full of needles. Polo didn't see them leave. He ran across the room, dodging a rain of ornaments to do so, and picked up a brass toasting fork which the enemy had overlooked. Bric-a-brac filled the air around his head, dancing around with sickening speed. His flesh was bruised and punctured. But the exhilaration of joining battle had overtaken him, and he set about beating the books, and the clocks, and the china to smithereens. Like a man in a cloud of locusts he ran around the room, bringing down his favorite books in a welter of fluttering pages, smashing whirling Dresden, shattering the lamps. A litter of broken possessions swamped the floor, some of it still twitching as the life went out of the fragments. But for every object brought low, there were a dozen still spinning, still whining.

He could hear Gina at the door, yelling to him to get out, to leave it alone.

But it was so enjoyable, playing against the enemy more directly than he'd ever allowed himself before. He didn't want to give up. He wanted the demon to show itself, to be known, to be recognized.

He wanted confrontation with the Old One's emissary once and for all.

Without warning the tree gave way to the dictates of centrifugal force, and exploded. The noise was like a howl of death. Branches, twigs, needles, balls, lights, wire, ribbons, flew across the room. Jack, his back to the explosion, felt a gust of energy hit him hard, and he was flung to the ground. The back of his neck and his scalp were shot full of pine-needles. A branch, naked of greenery, shot past his head and impaled the sofa. Fragments of tree pattered to the carpet around him.

Now other objects around the room, spun beyond the tolerance of their structures, were exploding like the tree. The television blew up, sending a lethal wave of glass across the room, much of which buried itself in the opposite wall. Fragments of the television's innards, so hot they singed the skin, fell on Jack, as he elbowed himself toward the door like a soldier under bombardment.

The room was so thick with a barrage of shards it was like a fog. The cushions had lent their down to the scene, snowing on the car-pet. Porcelain pieces: a beautifully glazed arm, a courtesan's head, bounced on the floor in front of his nose.

Gina was crouching at the door, urging him to hurry, her eyes narrowed against the hail. As Jack reached the door, and felt her arms around him, he swore he could hear laughter from the lounge. Tangible, audible laughter, rich and satisfied.

Amanda was standing in the hall, her hair full of pine-needles, staring down at him. He pulled his legs through the doorway and Gina slammed the door shut on the demolition.

"What is it?" she demanded. "Poltergeist? Ghost? Mother's ghost?" The thought of his dead wife being responsible for such wholesale destruction struck Jack as funny.

Amanda was half smiling. Good, he thought, she's coming out of it. Then he met the vacant look in her eyes and the truth dawned. She'd broken, her sanity had taken refuge where this fantastique couldn't get at it.

"What's in there?" Gina was asking, her grip on his arm so strong it stopped the blood.

"I don't know," he lied. "Amanda?"

Amanda's smile didn't decay. She just stared on at him, through him.

"You do know." "No."

"You're lying." "I think…"

He picked himself off the floor, brushing the pieces of porcelain, the feathers, the glass, off his shirt and trousers.

"I think… I shall go for a walk."

Behind him, in the lounge, the last vestiges of whining had stopped. The air in the hallway was electric with unseen presences. It was very close to him, invisible as ever, but so close. This was the most dangerous time. He mustn't lose his nerve now. He must stand up as though nothing had happened; he must leave Amanda be, leave explanations and recriminations until it was all over and done with.

"Walk?" Gina said, disbelievingly. "Yes…walk…I need some fresh air." "You can't leave us here."

"I'll find somebody to help us clear up." "But Mandy."

"She'll get over it. Leave her be."

That was hard. That was almost unforgivable. But it was said now. He walked unsteadily toward the front door, feeling nauseated after so much spinning. At his back Gina was raging. "You just can't leave! Are you out of your mind?"

"I need the air," he said, as casually as his thumping heart and his parched throat would permit. "So I'll just go out for a moment."

No, the Yattering said. No, no, no.

It was behind him, Polo could feel it. So angry now, so ready to twist off his head. Except that it wasn't allowed, *ever*, to touch him. But he could feel its resentment like a physical presence.

He took another step toward the front door.

It was with him still, dogging his every step. His shadow, his fetch; unshakable. Gina shrieked at him, "You sonofabitch, look at Mandy! She's lost her mind!"

No, he mustn't look at Mandy. If he looked at Mandy he might weep, he might break down as the thing wanted him to, then every-thing would be lost.

"She'll be all right," he said, barely above a whisper.

He reached for the front door handle. The demon bolted the door, quickly, loudly. No temper left for pretense, now.

Jack, keeping his movements as even as possible, unbolted the door, top and bottom. It bolted again.

It was thrilling, this game; it was also terrifying. If he pushed too far surely the demon's frustration would override its lessons?

Gently, smoothly, he unbolted the door again. Just as gently, just as smoothly, the Yattering bolted it.

Jack wondered how long he could keep this up for. Somehow he had to get outside: he had to coax it over the threshold. One step was all that the law required, according to his researches. One simple step.

Unbolted. Bolted. Unbolted. Bolted.

Gina was standing two or three yards behind her father. She didn't understand what she was seeing, but it was obvious her father was doing battle with someone, or something.

"Daddy—" she began.

"Shut up," he said benignly, grinning as he unbolted the door for the seventh time. There was a shiver of lunacy in the grin, it was too wide and too easy.

Inexplicably, she returned the smile. It was grim, but genuine. Whatever was at issue here, she loved him.

Polo made a break for the back door. The demon was three paces ahead of him, scooting through the house like a sprinter, and bolting the door before Jack could even reach the handle. The key was turned in the lock by invisible hands, then crushed to dust in the air.

Jack feigned a move toward the window beside the back door but the blinds were pulled down and the shutters slammed. The Yattering, too concerned with the window to watch Jack closely, missed his doubling back through the house.

When it saw the trick that was being played it let out a little screech, and gave chase, almost sliding into Jack on the smoothly polished floor. It avoided the collision only by the most balletic of maneuvers. That would be fatal indeed: to touch the man in the heat of the moment.

Polo was again at the front door and Gina, wise to her father's strategy, had unbolted it while the Yattering and Jack fought at the back door. Jack had prayed she'd take the opportunity to open it. She had. It stood slightly ajar: the icy air of the crisp afternoon curled its way into the hallway.

Jack covered the last yards to the door in a flash, feeling without hearing the howl of complaint the Yattering loosed as it saw its victim escaping into the outside world.

It was not an ambitious creature. All it wanted at that moment, beyond any other dream, was to take this human's skull between its palms and make a nonsense of it. Crush it to smithereens, and pour the hot thought out on to the snow. To be done with Jack J. Polo, forever and forever.

Was that so much to ask?

Polo had stepped into the squeaky-fresh snow, his slippers and trouser-bottoms buried in chill. By the time the fury reached the step Jack was already three or four yards away, marching up the path toward the gate. Escaping. Escaping.

The Yattering howled again, forgetting its years of training. Every lesson it had learned, every rule of battle engraved on its skull was submerged by the simple desire to have Polo's life.

It stepped over the threshold and gave chase. It was an unpardonable transgression. Somewhere in Hell, the powers (long may

70

they hold court; long may they shit light on the heads of the damned) felt the sin, and knew the war for Jack Polo's soul was lost.

Jack felt it too. He heard the sound of boiling water, as the demon's footsteps melted to steam the snow on the path. It was coming after him! The thing had broken the first rule of its existence. It was forfeit. He felt the victory in his spine, and his stomach.

The demon overtook him at the gate. Its breath could clearly be seen in the air, though the body it emanated from had not yet become visible.

Jack tried to open the gate, but the Yattering slammed it shut.

"Que sera, sera," said Jack.

The Yattering could bear it no longer. He took Jack's head in his hands, intending to crush the fragile bone to dust.

The touch was its second sin; and it agonized the Yattering beyond endurance. It bayed like a banshee and reeled away from the contact, sliding in the snow and falling on its back.

It knew its mistake. The lessons it had beaten into it came hurtling back. It knew the punishment too, for leaving the house, for touching the man. It was bound to a new lord, enslaved to this idiot-creature standing over it.

Polo had won.

He was laughing, watching the way the outline of the demon formed in the snow on the path. Like a photograph developing on a sheet of paper, the image of the fury came clear. The law was taking its toll. The Yattering could never hide from its master again. There it was, plain to Polo's eyes, in all its charmless glory. Maroon flesh and bright lidless eye, arms flailing, tail thrashing the snow to slush.

"You bastard," it said. Its accent had an Australian lilt.

"You will not speak unless spoken to," said Polo, with quiet, but absolute, authority. "Understood?"

The lidless eye clouded with humility. "Yes," the Yattering said.

"Yes, Mister Polo."

"Yes, Mister Polo."

Its tail slipped between its legs like that of a whipped dog. "You may stand."

"Thank you, Mr. Polo."

It stood. Not a pleasant sight, but one Jack rejoiced in nevertheless. "They'll have you yet," said the Yattering.

"Who will?"

"You know," it said, hesitantly. "Name them."

"Beelzebub," it answered, proud to name its old master. "The powers. Hell itself."

"I don't think so," Polo mused. "Not with you bound to me as proof of my skills. Aren't I the better of them?"

The eye looked sullen.

71

"Aren't I?"

"Yes," it conceded bitterly. "Yes. You are the better of them." It had begun to shiver.

"Are you cold?" asked Polo.

It nodded, affecting the look of a lost child.

"Then you need some exercise," he said, "You'd better go back into the house and start tidying up."

The fury looked bewildered, even disappointed, by this instruction. "Nothing more?" it asked incredulously. "No miracles? No Helen of Troy? No flying?"

The thought of flying on a snow-spattered afternoon like this left Polo cold. He was essentially a man of simple tastes: all he asked for in life was the love of his children, a pleasant home, and a good trading price for gherkins.

"No flying," he said.

As the Yattering slouched down the path toward the door it seemed to alight upon a new piece of mischief. It turned back to Polo, obsequious, but unmistakably smug.

"Could I just say something?" it said. "Speak."

"It's only fair that I inform you that it's considered ungodly to have any contact with the likes of me. Heretical even."

"Is that so?"

"Oh yes," said the Yattering, warming to its prophecy. "People have been burned for less."

"Not in this day and age," Polo replied.

"But the Seraphim will see," it said. "And that means you'll never go to that place."

"What place?"

The Yattering fumbled for the special word it had heard Beelzebub use.

"Heaven," it said, triumphant. An ugly grin had come on to its face; this was the cleverest maneuver it had ever attempted; it was juggling theology here.

Jack nodded slowly, nibbling at his bottom lip.

The creature was probably telling the truth: association with it or its like would not be looked upon benignly by the Host of Saints and Angels. He probably *was* forbidden access to the plains of paradise.

"Well," he said, "you know what I have to say about that, don't you?"

The Yattering stared at him frowning. No, it didn't know. Then the grin of satisfaction it had been wearing died, as it saw just what Polo was driving at.

"What do I say?" Polo asked it.

Defeated, the Yattering murmured the phrase.

"Que sera, sera."

72

Polo smiled. "There's a chance for you yet," he said, and led the way over the threshold, closing the door with something very like serenity on his face.

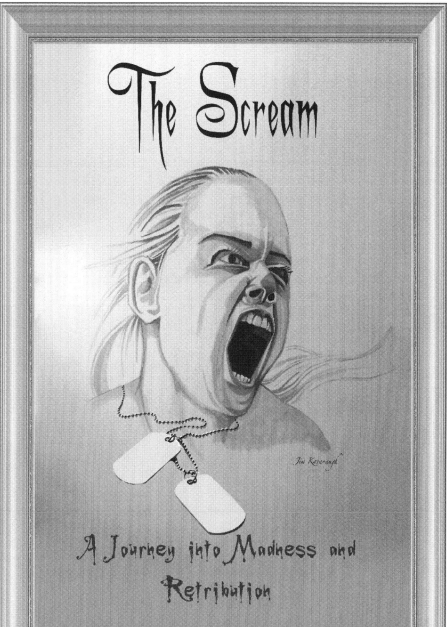

The Scream

A Journey into Madness and Retribution

Drive-In Creature Feature Anthology *Presents* a **Jonathan Maberry** *story* **The Scream** *edited by* **Eugene Johnson** *and* **Charles Day** *Produced by* **Evil Jester Press** ST Sheer Terror / Ghostly Images *Copyright 2016*

Jonathan Maberry

Jonathan Maberry is a New York Times bestselling author, 5-time Bram Stoker Award®-winner and comic book writer. He writes in multiple genres including suspense, thriller, horror, science fiction, fantasy, action, and steampunk, for adults and teens. His works include *Kill Switch, Rot & Ruin, The Orphan Army, Patient Zero, V-Wars, Captain America*, and many others. And he is the editor of several high-profile anthologies including *The X-Files, Nights Of The Living Dead*, and *Scary Out There*. Several of his works are in development for movies and TV. He is a popular workshop leader, keynote speaker and writing teacher. He lives in Del Mar, California. Find him online at: www.jonathanmaberry.com

THE SCREAM

Jonathan Maberry

In the spring of the year before, Jenny Mitchel went to war.

Bobby stayed home. This time Bobby stayed home.

He went with her all the way to the gates of the base when she had to report. He held her as tightly as he could, and she bent down to kiss his face. Then she smiled that smile of hers, hefted her duffle bag, blew him a final kiss, and went to join the others. Men and women. All so young. All going to war.

He told her that she didn't have to go. They could get married now. They could have a kid. Or, if the doctors couldn't help them manage it, they could adopt. It wasn't her war to fight. She couldn't change what had happened to him. She did not need to go and try to find justice over there, because this was war and there was no justice. No matter how hard she fought, no matter where in Iraq or Afghanistan or Syria she went, there was no chance she would ever find the person who built the IED. Wars were like that. It was as indifferent and unfair as the fact that the other three men with Bobby died and he did not. Only part of him died. The rest had come home to her. So why did she think that she had to go over and try and make it right?

What was 'right' anyway?

Jenny walked away, her back straight and strong, moving well on good legs, the heavy duffle carried with ease. Bobby sat in his chair, feeling as cold as the chrome wheels, and watched her go. He kept his smile on his face for as long as he could. Until it broke off and the pieces fell and he had to turn away in case she looked back.

Jenny went off to war and Bobby went back to their house. He wheeled himself up the ramp and into the living room. It had always been a small house, he thought.

Until now.

Now the goddamn thing was vast. Filled with noise and shadows and a complete and total emptiness of her. They had put up pictures of the two of them smiling. From before. One beautiful picture of her in a bikini

77

top, straw-colored hair blowing in the Ocean City sea breeze. A photo that had been taken on the happiest day they'd had since he got out of the V.A. hospital. She looked radiant. Like a sea goddess, with her pale Irish skin that showed blue veins on the swell of her breasts. That dusting of freckles, the red of her smiling mouth, the white of her teeth, the bottomless green of her eyes. Bobby had taken the photo from the point of the beach that was as far as she could push his chair. He made a joke and Jenny had thrown back her head and laughed as if the whole world was theirs. A laugh that was as free as a child's but every single bit a woman's. *His* woman's laugh. Captured by his phone's camera, saved, printed, blown up, framed, mounted on the wall. Looking at him in the emptiness of the living room.

With every single day since she went away the laugh looked less happy to him. He sat and stared at it. Hour after fucking hour.

They say unexpected laughter can sound like screams if you don't know what it is.

Smiles were like that, too. That was something Bobby came to understand as he looked at her open mouth. She looked like she was screaming.

Jenny screamed in his dreams, too.

As did he.

-2-

Jenny was gone for five months.

Bobby got emails from her for most of that time. Emails, some actual letters delivered by the postman, and once a package filled with sand and a heart shaped rock she'd found.

Then there was nothing for a week.

Then a man from the army came by the house. A very young officer in a very crisp uniform. A lieutenant, but Bobby could not remember his last name. Or his face. The officer perched stiffly on the edge of the couch, holding a cup of coffee he did not drink, and told him what he was allowed to say. He was sorry he said. So sorry.

"How did she die?" asked Bobby.

"She died bravely," said the officer. "Serving her country."

"No...*how* did she die? Was she shot? Was it a bomb?"

The lieutenant smiled the kind of smile that looks like a wince. "I don't know the full details..."

"What *do* you know?"

The lieutenant set his coffee cup on the table and stood up very slowly. He was very tall and there was a window behind the couch with a sunny sky that turned him to a dusky silhouette. Bobby thought he looked like the angel of death.

"What matters, sir, is that Jennifer Mitchel was a good solider who laid down her life in the service of liberty. We should celebrate her sacrifice and honor her commitment to this great nation."

There was more. There's always more, but Bobby stopped listening. The picture on the wall kept screaming at him. The lieutenant couldn't hear it, but Bobby could. Jenny screamed and screamed and screamed and Bobby closed his eyes and clamped his hands over his ears.

When he opened his eyes the living room was as silent as it was empty.

Bobby would have taken the picture down and smashed it, but he couldn't quite reach it.

He tried, though.

He tried so hard.

-3-

Bobby dreamed of her that night.

Of course he did.

In his dreams he still had two working legs instead of useless meat and bone that was decaying to nerveless junk inside his burned skin. In his dreams Bobby could walk and he could run, and he ran and ran, drawn by the sound of her screams.

He was back in Afghanistan, in one of the mountain passes that are baked by the sun all day and turn to winter at night. Amid a nightmare landscape of deadfalls, box canyons, endless cave systems, valleys where no one goes unless they are dealing death or running from it, cliffs over which bodies are dropped and never found. Places where wind shears and gusts throw helicopters against unforgiving walls, where tanks won't go and Humvees go to die. Blighted lands filled with carrion birds, scorpions, sand snakes, and biting spiders that no one has yet named. A place that seems like it could only exist in bad dreams but which is more than real. As the Russians found out. As the U.S. military found out. A place that is heartbreakingly beautiful from any distance but merely heartbreaking up close.

Alexander the Great conquered it once. Then the Muslims. Almost no one since. It breaks those who try as surely as it breaks those who fight to defend it. No one wins there because it isn't worth winning. That was a truth Bobby knew once he'd gone there for the first time as a young soldiers. It was a truth everyone on any side of the fight knows with absolute certainty. And, for some reason no one that Bobby ever met or read about, its lack of importance was why people fought so hard for and against it. It was a philosophic point, a patch of ground sown with shell casings, irrigated with blood and yielding a hardy crop of pain.

That's how Bobby saw it.

It was part of the poetry he wrote when he was alone. It was in the lyrics of the songs he composed on his guitar during the long nights over there. And it was the secret whispered by the music of his dreams. It called to him.

She's here, it sang.
Come and find her.
She's here.

In his dreams Bobby could walk and he could run, and he never tired, even as he ran naked through the mountain snows or climbed the jagged peaks. In his dream he was not a broken, helpless man. In his dreams Bobby was something else. Stronger than a man. Less vulnerable. Angrier, hungrier, faster, relentless.

The thing he became in his dreams would never stop looking for Jenny.

How could it? Why would it?

So, in his dreams he ran and ran and ran. Calling her name. Screaming it as loud as her picture had screamed at him. The echoes of that scream punched into the sides of the mountains and flew back at him, cutting like knives. It startled dark night birds from their hidden holes and they flung themselves into the air, all in a blind panic that made them collide and shriek and fall and swoop back up from the stony ground to go soaring over the crags and tors.

"Jenny!" he cried, but his voice sounded like those shrieking birds.

In the dream he saw a glow in the distance. A fire. A camp built into the shelter of a ledge of rock, hidden from the sky. There were camels and goats. There was a single spavined dog that was too old to be any use as a sentry. There were guards, but their rifles were slung, their knives sheathed, their eyes drawn to the cooking fire, their minds numb with the knowledge that they were in a place no one could reach. Not without making noise. Not without alerting them.

Except that Bobby ran without noise because this was a dream. No, because it was a nightmare and he was the thing in the dark. Even he didn't know what he was. Not an animal. Certainly not a man. Not anymore. Not even now that he had his legs back. He was something else. Less tangible, less real. A ghost, perhaps, or one of the *djinn* that haunt the legends of Iraq and Iran. Something like that. Maybe whatever he was had no name. No real name.

He ran and leapt and clawed and climbed and scurried and tore at the rocks with fingernails that were hard as iron.

Looking for her.

Looking for Jenny.

It did not matter that Jenny was dead. It didn't matter that her body was being shipped home to New Jersey. It didn't matter that the envelope of flesh that looked like the woman he loved was no longer here in these mountains. *She* was here. She died here, and she would always be here.

That was the secret known to the Bobby-thing that ran through the Afghan night. It's what made him run so fast and hard. It's what made him so hungry. It's what made him howl into the night.

These were the men who had taken Jenny from her. He knew that without know how he knew. Just as he knew what things had been done to her. To her flesh. These same hills had echoed with her screams, and somewhere here in this hell of ice and rock those screams were still trapped. That was how this worked. The screams of the dying are supposed to fly up into the sky, to disperse, to fade away and take the soul of the dying with them.

Except when they could not.

He knew –absolutely knew—that it was like that. He knew that there were houses whose walls could trap a scream as easily as these unforgiving mountains. A scream trapped likewise trapped the screamer.

Bobby knew that. When his Bradley had rolled over the IED and half of him died, he screamed. As he lay there painted in the blood of his platoon, feeling his flesh melt, believing that death was about to lift him out of that wreckage and take him home, Bobby had screamed. And part of him *had* died there, so he believed that his screams haunted these same hills.

Part of him and all of Jenny.

These men had torn the screams from his Jenny and even though she died out here, her screams had never faded away. They had wandered, lost and desperate, into the open mouths of caves and become trapped. Forever trapped.

Hell was not an abstraction. It was a place. It was many places, and this was one of them. These mountains.

Jenny's soul had been torn from her and become lost here.

Bobby screamed out her name and it roused everyone in the camp. The old dog began barking hysterically, but its eyes were as bad as its ears and it faced the wrong direction. The camels screeched and honked in panic, kicking at each other and at the men, and jerking their heads against the ropes that held them to a stump of a withered tree. Men kicked their way out of bedrolls and grabbed for their guns, standing back-to-back and pointing their barrels at the goat path while the goats themselves bleated and shrank back against the wall of the cave.

Bobby's scream had reached them long before he did. They were awake, alert, prepared.

But they were not prepared for him.

No.

The dream turned red and wet, and new screams tore the night.

-4-

Bobby woke in utter darkness, drowning in it, and he swam upward toward the light. He burst from the dream with a cry, his body

81

bathed in sweat, stinking of the terror of that dream. His sheets were knotted around his waist and legs.

It took him a long, long time to understand that.

The sheets were knotted around his legs.

His legs, his legs, his useless dead legs.

How could the sheets be knotted around them? How could he have kicked and thrashed with ruined flesh and inert bone?

How?

How?

How?

He lay there, propped up on elbows, staring down the length of the bed at what he saw by moonlight.

In his mind he heard the echo of his scream and the paler echo of the screams of the men in that camp. Ghost screams, though.

Because he was here and they were thousands of miles away and he was a cripple. And his woman was dead and lost.

But...

The sheets were twisted around his legs.

"Jenny...," he whispered to the night.

And the night, perverse and filled with possibilities, whispered back in her voice.

"*Bobby...*"

-5-

There were dreams every night.

Only at night, though, because they were not daydreams. They were not nightmares either, but they belonged to the night. Bobby knew that and understood it.

It took him a month to go mad.

As mad as he needed to be.

It took six months to plan everything and then nearly a year to pay for it. He sold Jenny's car. He sold the house. He sold everything that was worth selling. This was going to be expensive and he was not a rich man. The house was good, though. He got almost a quarter of a million for it. More than he thought. More than he'd need.

There were fees and equipment to buy. People to hire here, people to hire there. Hands to be greased, here and there. More there, though, because that's how it worked.

He got asked the same questions a lot. By friends, by relatives – his and hers; by people in the government, including someone Bobby was certain worked for Homeland security. Eventually by the press.

"Why go back?"

At first he couldn't give a good answer, but because he was grieving and because he was disabled people cut him slack. Over time, though, they asked again and again, wanting a better answer. And Bobby realized that sketchy answers created obstacles. Good answers elicited support and opened doors.

"It's all about forgiveness," he told a public relations office from the army. "I can't move forward with my life if I hold onto hate. I already lost too much to that. Now I have to accept what's happened and let it go."

It was a good answer. He'd rehearsed a dozen versions of it before he tried it out. It made the man from the army go all glassy-eyed. When he used it on an old friend from his former unit, his friend tweeted it out.

And then it was all over the internet. Twitter, Facebook, Tumblr, even tagged to a picture of him and Jenny that wound up on Pinterest. He was *that* guy. The man who had lost everything and wanted to go to the place where it had been taken from him and find peace and closure.

The first book offer came in seven months into his campaign. The movie deal was closed less than a week later.

That almost made Bobby smile. A movie. The producer who optioned it and the screenwriter who became attached to the project both thought they were going to make an inspirational tearjerker of a tragic love story. It would win awards, they said. It would win an Oscar. They were sure of it even though no one had yet written a word of the book or the script. The story was that good, they told him.

Yeah. The story was good.

But Bobby knew the producer and the writers were wrong about one big thing. This wasn't going to be a tender love story, even though love was the core of it all. It wasn't going to be a tear-jerker even though Bobby wept every day, and would probably weep all the way to the last. And it wasn't a heart-stirring story of forgiveness and closure.

Well, closure maybe.

Bobby knew that it wasn't that kind of story, and a movie would probably never be made. Not once the trip was finished. By then the producer and writers would know that it was a totally different kind of story. And, who knows, thought Bobby, maybe they would make that other kind of film.

A horror film.

Because that's what Bobby wanted it to be.

-6-

They threw a party for him.

That was funny. Bobby had to wheel himself into a toilet stall at the VFW hall so he could laugh without anyone hearing him.

A party? Really? A fucking party?

The mayor of Ocean City shook his head. The producer was there, along with a director and the actor who was going to play him in the

83

movie. Ethan Hawke. Which was weird because except for them both being skinny white guys Hawke didn't look anything like Bobby. The press was there. Officers from his old unit were there.

Lots of speeches, lots of photos.

Bobby could not remember a single word of any of them. He couldn't remember what he'd said. It was a blur, and while he sat on the plane the following day, he let it all slide off of him the way mud will sluice off when you stood in the rain. It felt like that.

He dozed on the plane and dreamed of running in the hills.

Running.

Hunting.

He woke angry, as he was often angry. Scared, as he was often scared. Filled with doubt, as he was always filled with doubt. The dreams were always the same. The hunt, the chase, the red carnage, the taste of blood, the satisfying sound of bones breaking between his teeth, the texture of skin as it tore beneath his nails. All of that was good. That part of it was delicious and satisfying in ways that no longer made him feel strange or guilty or ashamed.

What made him angry about this dream –and all of the others— was that it ended too soon. It ended with death but not with discovery. It ended with him finding the camp with the men, the right men; but it ended before he found *her.*

She was there, though. So close. So maddeningly close. He could hear her screams on the wind. So close to the place where Bobby did his killing. So close to where Jenny died. That was her place, where she would be from now until forever. Bobby knew and understood that. He even thought that she heard him as he hunted and killed. Heard and came looking for him.

But the dreams always ended too soon.

Bobby pawed at the tears in his eyes and looked out at the night. The plane had so far yet to fly.

So did he.

-7-

After the movie deal was finalized Hollywood location teams handled a lot of the more complicated logistics of the trip. They had the money, the experience, and the drive. They made sure he could get as close to the spot where Jenny died as they could manage. They hired private contractors –mercenaries— to provide security. It was all very exciting for everyone. Even Bobby thought it was kind of cool, though privately he was simply grateful that so many obstacles had been handled so easily.

It was like fate, or at least that's how he took it.

So much of the process was taken out of his hands that for a while

84

Bobby felt like he was floating on an outgoing tide. He was sure that during some of that process he wasn't quite there. He drifted in an out of himself. In and out of dreams. The heat and the cold of Afghanistan drew him away from his broken body in different ways. The heat pushed him into vivid memories of pain, of laying broken and charred inside the Bradley, of the hot taste of blood –not his own—in his mouth, the feel of it on his skin.

The cold took him somewhere else.

The cold sent him running deep, deep into himself. Into the nightmare landscape high up on the slopes of the mountains that now rose around him. To narrow passes and steep defiles and into the hungry mouths of caves. Chasing memories. Chasing dreams. Chasing a desperate hope of finding Jenny. Chasing her, while the demons of doubt and dread pursued him like dogs.

And then the day came when he was there.

Actually there.

"You sure this is what you want?" asked the producer. They were on a flat shelf of rock beside a path that whipsawed up through the hills.

"Yes," said Bobby. "This is great. Thanks."

The producer looked dubious, but he nodded. "You okay if we record this? We can let the cameras run. They're digital. We can leave you alone."

It was something they'd discussed. Background, they called it. So the Ethan Hawke could study the footage and reproduce the scene when they shot the movie. If there was anything worth using.

"That's fine," said Bobby. "But I want to be alone for a while? Let the cameras run, but nobody else up here until I call? Okay?"

The producer nodded and after a reluctant pause, turned and trudged down the hill to their camp, leaving Bobby alone. Night was falling over the mountains and already the day's heat was being leeched away. Cold stabbed him like a knife.

That was okay.

It was more than okay.

The colder it got, the sharper the stab, the easier this was going to be.

Somewhere in these mountains not too many miles from where he sat, the Taliban killers were making their camp. Tying up their camels and goats. Feeding the spavined dog, building a fire against the cold. Maybe they were aware of the Hollywood Americans down here. Probably. He hoped so. It seemed more apt.

The cold tore through his sweater and coat and found his scarred flesh. It really did feel like a knife. The pain was real and it he was too thin, too frail, too sick to have any resistance. This kind of cold could kill him, and he knew it.

So he took off his coat and threw it over the edge of the cliff. The sweater followed, and the shirt. He couldn't manage the pants, but that wouldn't matter. It was a few degrees above freezing and in half an hour it would be well below. His skin burned with the same intensity as it had when he'd been in the destroyed Bradley.

That was good, too.

He shivered, his teeth chattering, his breath shuddering with each labored exhale. The cold was so intense up here in the brutal wind. He could feel shriek wanting to claw its way out but he clenched against it, forcing it back, keeping it inside. It wasn't time for that yet.

He wheeled his chair over to the very edge of the drop-off. The cameras, triggered by motion sensors, turned to follow like a host of silent witnesses.

The sun fell off the side of the world and huge shadows collapsed around him, bringing an even deeper cold. Inversion coaxed the winds into a howling storm of icy blades that slashed at him.

He risked a single word. Her name.

"Jenny…"

It came out hoarse and wrong and fractured. So he said it again. Louder. Needing the wind to take it from him and carry it to her. He opened his mouth and shouted.

"*Jenny!*"

Only it wasn't what came out.

Not her name. Not a word. The wind drew back and stabbed him with all of its force at the moment he tilted his head back to yell.

What came out was a scream.

A long, long scream. So long. So loud. So much bigger than he was. It was massive. A scream of pain, a scream of love. A scream of need.

As the scream slammed into the walls and flew back at him, Bobby felt sagging forward, nodding out of the chair, felt himself falling toward the infinite blackness over the edge. He fell.

And fell.

But the scream still rose above him.

He never felt his body land. He wasn't in it when it struck the rocks.

The scream rose and flew out into the darkness and it carried him with it. What there was of him. What was left of him. What mattered of him.

On dark wings of cold night air he flew through the mountain passes, climbing higher, calling out in a voice of darkness. In a scream.

There was a light below. A campfire in the mouth of a cave hidden in the craggy hills. Bobby saw it and swept downward. Then suddenly he was running. He had no idea where this new body had come from or what it was composed of. What did that matter? The answers might have mattered before his old body fell; it did not matter at all to this

86

body. He had muscles to run, claws to climb, teeth to bite. If there was a name for what he was, it belonged to someone else's vocabulary. Maybe the Taliban soldiers would know. Maybe they would name the thing that came hunting them in the night.

Maybe.

But Bobby did not care.

He ran up the slope toward their camp and as he drew close he screamed once more. The scream of what he was. The scream of something that lived now in these mountains. The scream of a thing that belonged in this nightmare landscape.

And far above him, coming from deeper in the hills, reaching him first as a whisper that escaped from a cave or some other hidden, lonely place, came a sound.

Another scream.

Higher, sharper.

Familiar. So familiar.

Answering his cry.

It sounded again. Closer now.

Hungry.

Coming to join him.

Coming to share the hunt.

Growth Spurt

Terror That Will Grow On You!

Drive-In Creature Feature Anthology *presents a*
Joe McKinney *story* **Growth Spurt** *edited by*
Eugene Johnson *and* **Charles Day** *produced by*
Evil Jester Press | ET | Environmental Terror / Disturbing Images | *Copyright 2016*

Joe McKinney

Joe McKinney has his feet in several different worlds. In his day job, he has worked as a patrol officer for the San Antonio Police Department, a DWI Enforcement officer, a disaster mitigation specialist, a homicide detective, the director of the City of San Antonio's 911 Call Center, and a patrol supervisor. He played college baseball for Trinity University, where he graduated with a Bachelor's Degree in American History, and went on to earn a Master's Degree in English Literature from the University of Texas at San Antonio. He was the manager of a Barnes & Noble for a while, where he indulged a lifelong obsession with books. He published his first novel, *Dead City*, in 2006, a book that has since been recognized as a seminal work in the zombie genre. Since then, he has gone on to win two Bram Stoker Awards® and expanded his oeuvre to cover everything from true crime and writings on police procedure to science fiction to cooking to Texas history. The author of more than twenty books, he is a frequent guest at horror and mystery conventions. Joe and his wife Tina have two lovely daughters and make their home in a little town just outside of San Antonio, where he pursues his passion for cooking and makes what some consider to be the finest batch of chili in Texas. You can keep up with all of Joe's latest releases by friending him on Facebook and following him on Twitter at @JoeMcKinney.

GROWTH SPURT

Joe McKinney

The homeless were restless. It wasn't even fully dark yet, and already they were gathering under the Fine Silver Pkwy Bridge, bustling with a sort of mute agitation. Doc had come down early; hoping to get a dry spot for the night, but now it didn't look like that was going to happen. Too many people were moving into the area.

A big South Texas rainmaker was gathering overhead. Lightning ripped across the belly of the sky and thunder followed, rattling his teeth. He knew he'd get drenched if he didn't find shelter soon, but all the activity made him nervous. Crowds usually meant trouble, and Doc had survived on the streets for a long time because he knew how to avoid trouble.

He stopped a man named Bobby Earl and asked him what was going on. "It's Jackson," Bobby Earl said. "Something's wrong with him. He's got something on his skin."

"Which Jackson? The black guy?"

"No, Big Jackson, with the beard. Always wears the Oakland A's cap."

"Yeah, yeah, I know him," Doc said. "You say he's got a rash?"

Bobby Earl shrugged. "Don't look like no rash I ever seen. It's all green."

"Green?"

"Yeah. It's nasty looking. Go and check it out if you want."

Doc went under the bridge and saw a bunch of guys running around collecting sugar packets. The junkies believed the sugar helped with the shakes, but Doc knew that wasn't the problem. Jackson was a drinker. He never touched heroin, and if he had the DTs, sugar wouldn't do a thing to help him.

Somebody yelled out Doc's name. The others called him Doc because he could bandage a dog bite or even set a broken bone when he had to, but it was just a nickname. The only thing he knew about medicine was what he'd learned in the U.S. Army's Field Medic School thirty years earlier, and he'd forgotten most of that.

A woman named Carla took him to Jackson, and one glance was all it took for Doc to know Bobby Earl was right. That was no rash.

Jackson was stretched out on a bedroll. The others had tried to make him comfortable, but he still looked bad. His skin had grown over with something that looked like moss. It was thick and spongy to the touch and vibrantly green; moist like the bark on a rotten log.

Doc turned Jackson's chin one way and then the other, lifting it so he could see his throat. The moss was white and delicate around the throat, almost like cobwebs. He pulled at it gently with his finger and realized that it was much stronger than cobwebs.

The same cobweb-like stuff was growing in the pits of his arms and in the spaces between his fingers.

"Jackson, can you hear me? It's me, Doc."

Jackson's eyes were crusted over with a slick green film that looked like transparent algae. Doc could see Jackson's eyes moving lazily beneath the film, but he couldn't tell if Jackson could see him or not.

Either way, it didn't look like Jackson was feeling any pain.

In fact, the noises he made sounded like those of a man dreaming he was rolling in a pile of money.

Thunder boomed over them, and a moment later the rain came hard and heavy, the sound of falling water drowning out even the slapping of the car tires on the bridge above them.

Doc studied Jackson and his disease in the lightning flashes, his mind going through the possible causes. "Does anybody know if he's been drinking from that canal by the railroad yard again?"

No one knew for sure.

"He smells good," said one of the onlookers, trying to be helpful.

Another man slapped him on the shoulder and told him to shut up, but Doc had noticed the smell too. When he leaned in close to look at the mossy stuff on Jackson's chest, he could smell the sweet, ozone odor of clean air.

It was almost intoxicating.

Doc pulled back the blanket the others had put over Jackson's legs, and everybody gasped. He'd been wearing jeans and heavy boots, but there was little left of the denim and leather.

The moss had eaten most of it away.

And it was different than the moss on his chest. It was thick and ropy; more like ivy, with broad flat leaves the size of a man's palm.

Hundreds of little yellow nodules that looked like dried figs were nestled at the base of the leaves. Doc rolled one of the nodules between his fingers, but it didn't feel like anything vegetable. More like hot, wet human skin.

He tugged gently on one of the vines and felt its hold on Jackson's skin. It gave a little, but only just a little.

"Help me get this off him," Doc said to the others, and a dozen pair of hands reached in and pulled at the vines.

Somebody managed to get a vine loose and yanked it hard, causing Jackson to erupt in a horrible, gut-wrenching scream. He bolted upright and thrashed at the hands on his body, slapping them away with surprising strength and speed.

The others scattered. They hid behind pillars and grocery carts and anything else they could put between themselves and the screaming man-bush of moss and vines that Jackson had become.

Only Doc held his ground. He tried to calm Jackson, but couldn't reach him. The man was too far-gone.

Jackson spun around, still screaming, the moss and vines curling around him and dragging over the ground like the train of a bride's wedding gown.

Doc tried to steer him back down to the bedroll, but Jackson pushed him away.

He ran into the rain and headed for the canal.

Doc ran after him. A few of the others left their hiding spots and followed at a cautious distance. As lighting flashed above them and the rain came down in shimmering silver sheets, Jackson ran across the access road and jumped down the embankment to the canal.

He hit the water at full speed and disappeared beneath its black surface. Doc stopped at the bank, staring at the spreading ripples.

The crowd crept closer for a better look.

"Why did he do that?" somebody asked.

Nobody answered.

They stood on the bank for several minutes, the rain coming down all around them. When Jackson didn't come back up, they drifted back to the bridge in small sad groups of twos and threes.

Doc was the last to leave.

***

The rains stopped just before morning, though dawn never really broke. The sky remained a thick gray sagging belly of threatening storm clouds with no trace of sun.

Around ten o'clock Doc went down to the canal.

Overnight the banks had become a dense jungle of moss and vines, fifteen feet high in some places.

It was vibrantly green and pearled with water drops, except for the little yellow nodules that looked like dried figs. They were denser and firmer than they had felt the night before. And they weren't growing singly, as they had on Jackson's body. Now they were clustered in groups of three on long green woody boles that reminded Doc of bamboo, except that in quite a few places the boles curled over and seemed to reach

93

toward the road, like an old woman's gnarled fingers.

Every time he squeezed one of the nodules, it released more of that intoxicating odor of clean air and ozone, and he had to shake himself loose from its spell.

The poppies will get them, he thought, and smiled.

And just as quickly set his mouth in a frown against the memories that flooded into his mind. He remembered being ten years old and on his belly in his parent's living room, watching *The Wizard of Oz* on an ancient Delmonico set his dad loved so much. Those were the good years, the sepia years, before his mom died of the cigarettes she couldn't quit and his dad was still taking his medication regularly. But when she died – and he was still thankful it had been quick, barely three months from diagnosis to the funeral home – and his father stopped caring about the meds and the mood swings got more and more violent…well, the Army started to look pretty damn good, even if it did mean heading off to Vietnam.

He closed his eyes and measured out his breaths and pushed all that from his head. Nothing good ever came of lingering on the past. Not to Doc's way of looking at things.

He opened his eyes and took a long moment to study the banks of the canal.

There was no sign of Jackson.

Doc hoped he had simply slipped into the night and found someplace to sleep it off, but as he looked around at the vegetation choking the banks, he couldn't get past the feeling that something bad had happened.

He walked back up the embankment, rubbing his hands. They'd been itching fiercely since he woke up.

He rubbed them against the thighs of his jeans and looked at his palms. They were bright red and raw; yellow blisters had formed a sort of bracelet around his wrists.

He pulled his sleeves over the blisters and followed the access road to his regular intersection along the interstate. The freeway had an upper and a lower level there so that if it started to rain again he could stand out of the wet and still be in the intersection.

He took a worn piece of cardboard out of his pack and unfolded it so passing motorists could see where he'd written, "I'M A VET HOMELESS ANYTHING WILL HELP," in great big black letters.

Almost as soon as he opened his sign, a white-haired woman in a big shiny Buick put a five-dollar bill in his hand and gave his fingers an encouraging squeeze.

"Bless you, ma'am," he said, and she smiled.

A woman named Elizabeth worked the opposite corner. Her gig was a baby doll she'd found in a dumpster. She wrapped the doll in a soiled blanket and sat at the light pretending to sooth it, a worn, beleaguered look on her face. She usually brought in three hundred bucks

94

or more a day doing that. Doc never made that much. On a good day, he could make forty with the God loves you bit. But he was having a much better day than usual. By noon, he'd made fifty bucks. Traffic was heavy and the lights were long, giving him plenty of time to walk up and down the rows.

It seemed like everybody was in a giving mood.

Later that afternoon a cop rolled up on Elizabeth's corner.

He must have been having a bad day, Doc figured, because he jumped out his car yelling, grabbed the doll from Elizabeth, and slapped its head against the curb until it broke apart in his hands.

There was chaos after that.

Cars swerved around the angry cop. One driver lost control, glanced off another car stopped at the light, and careened into the oncoming lanes, causing a six-car pile-up that completely shut down the intersection.

Soon traffic was backed up for a mile in every direction. People were honking, and a few even got out of their cars to yell at the cop. Most people were so pissed they made a point to stop and give Doc whatever change they had, just to spite the cop.

If it hadn't been for his itching, burning skin, which had been getting steadily worse all day, Doc might have felt vindicated for all those years of acting servile and beaten to every bully with a badge that chased him off a good corner.

But the show ended eventually, and the intersection went back to normal. Doc patted his pockets, which were swollen with bills and coins and a pack of smokes some truck driver had given him, and he figured he'd done well enough for one day.

He asked Elizabeth if she wanted to join him for a beer and a hot dog, and together they walked up to the gas station at the next intersection.

"I heard about Jackson," she said to Doc as they sat under the awning of the gas station. "Carla told me."

"Yeah," he said, rubbing the back of his neck. Now that he was out of the intersection, his skin felt like it was on fire.

It started raining again.

"Any idea what it was?" she asked.

"No," he said. "I've never seen anything like it."

She nodded, drank some of her beer. "Do you think he was in pain?"

"Maybe," Doc said. "I don't know. It'd be a small mercy if he wasn't."

Elizabeth snorted at that. She was a junkie, twenty years on the horse. She fed her habit by turning tricks when the baby doll bit didn't pay, so she knew all about mercy. Knew about it the way a slave knows about freedom, as some impossibly cruel dream they beat you for having.

They stayed under the awning for a long time while Elizabeth drank the rest of her beer and Doc tried to soothe his burning skin. Finally, feeling light-headed from the pain, he told Elizabeth he was going back to the bridge.

She smiled at him, and before he could ask her why, she stood up on her toes and kissed his cheek.

He looked at her with a curious smile. "What was that for?"

"Thanks," she said. Her smile was full of crooked and yellow teeth, but it was kind, and genuine. "You're a good man, Doc. Thanks for trying to help. Most people don't."

He nodded and stepped into the rain. To his surprise, he found the pain went away as soon as his skin got wet. It still itched, and it was raw to the touch, but it *did* feel better.

He walked back to the bridge, fully aware that something was wrong with him. His hands were bloated and unnaturally red, and the yellowish blisters he'd covered earlier with his sleeves had spread up his arms and were beginning to bubble across his neck.

He thought about going to the free hospital and having it checked out, but he was so very tired, and the thought of walking another three miles into downtown was just too much to ask of his worn out legs.

Instead, he went to the bridge, found a dry spot, and drifted off to sleep.

***

That night Doc had a strange and wonderful dream. He stood in a field beneath a blue and yellow-banded sky and watched as the wind sent waves through tall green grass.

That wasn't grass.

More like bendy green reeds topped with yellow balls.

Like something out of *The Wizard of Oz*.

He felt warm, and complete, yet when he looked down, the body he had known for so long was gone. A thick, green woody bole, like bamboo, had replaced his legs and torso, and where there had once been arms and fingers, there were now round, moist leaves dancing in the breeze, soaking up the sun.

Everything was as it should be, and as he glanced along the field and the waves of grass that wasn't really grass, he knew the peace of a baby in his mother's arms.

This was home. He knew that on some deep, atavistic level.

And then something changed. He felt himself rising into the air, his essence reduced to an iridescent membrane, like a soap bubble.

The waves of grass sank farther and farther away from him, until soon they were out of sight, part of the indistinct coloring of a planet shrinking into space.

He felt the searing cold and darkness of the long void, and the eons of sleep that followed.

He remembered waking beneath blue skies, with dry crumbling ground beneath him. It was a hard, cold land, but there was water and iron, enough in the soil for him to feed on.

This ground *could* be a home, though he knew he would always miss the blue and yellow skies of the birthing place.

Doc was slow to wake the next morning, and the dream still tasted sweet on his lips. It was difficult to open his eyes, and he couldn't feel his legs. But strangely, he felt very calm, very rested.

He lingered over the dream, and over his past. Doc had been alone, living on the road, for nearly forty years, since coming home from the war, and never in all that time had he felt such warmth, such joy. In his dream, he was clean, and the air in his lungs smelled sweet, like ozone.

Only when he tried to sit up and rub his eyes did he realize something was holding him to the ground. Slowly, with great difficulty, he pulled himself up and looked over his own body.

He'd become a carpet of vines.

There were dozens of piles of vines just like him under the bridge; dozens and dozens of dreamers.

His first impulse was to grab at the ropes and pull, but as he held them in his hands and caressed the hundreds of fig-like nodules, his belly began to warm as from a shot of whiskey. Warmth pulsed through his entire body, calming him, satisfying him.

He was thirsty, and he thought of the quiet black water of the nearby canal.

Doc got to his feet and shuffled into the sunlight. The familiar noises of cars rushing overhead were gone and all that remained was the soothing whistle of the wind through the grass.

Though he wanted the canal, his mind wasn't able to totally let go. He needed to see for himself. He walked up to the edge of the freeway and looked south toward downtown. From where he stood, Doc could see far into the distance.

Huge tracts of the city were green. The green covered the roads and the houses and long, ropy lengths of it hung from the roofs of the skyscrapers.

He felt short of breath and clumsy, but at the same time he was immensely happy, for he knew the green was spreading.

Doc walked down the embankment, trailing his vines behind him.

Soon, he sensed, the nodules would spread their soap bubble seeds across the waiting earth.

He looked forward to that.

As he stepped into the still, black water of the canal he couldn't help but think of the day before and smile.

It had been a wonderful day.

So many lovely people had lent him a helping hand.

William F. Nolan

William F. Nolan writes mostly in the science fiction, fantasy, and horror genres. Though best known for coauthoring the acclaimed dystopian science fiction novel *Logan's Run* with George Clayton Johnson, Nolan is the author of more than 2000 pieces (fiction, nonfiction, articles, and books), and has edited twenty-six anthologies in his fifty-plus year career.

Of his numerous awards, there are a few of which he is most proud: being voted a Living Legend in Dark Fantasy by the International Horror Guild in 2002; twice winning the Edgar Allan Poe Award from the Mystery Writers of America; being awarded the honorary title of Author Emeritus by the Science Fiction and Fantasy Writers of America, Inc. in 2006; receiving the Lifetime Achievement Award from the Horror Writers Association in 2010; and as recipient of the 2013 World Fantasy Convention Award along with Brian W. Aldiss. In 2015, Nolan was named a World Horror Society Grand Master.

A vegetarian, Nolan resides in Vancouver, WA.

JAZZ KILL

William F. Nolan

E-mail from the New Orleans Mayor's office:

"In the aftermath of the catastrophic failure of levees during Hurricane Katrina, we urgently need your expertise in designing a workable new system. Please call the office directly..."

Over the phone, Mayor Benoit offered Doug Belford a substantial sum to relocate to Louisiana for this "vital" assignment. Doug didn't hesitate; as an experienced consultant to the U.S. Army Corps of Engineers, this job represented a golden opportunity. He agreed to fly out the following weekend.

Doug's wife, Julia, was equally enthusiastic. Her eyes were glowing as she paced the living room of their modest Santa Monica home. "I can't wait to go. Wow! New Orleans, here we come!"

"You're not going," Doug declared. "I can wrap this job up in a few months. Meanwhile, somebody has to run the house, take care of Zipper and K.C."

"Cats are very adaptable," she said. "They'll fit right in to a New Orleans apartment."

He shook his head. "We can't put this place up for sale," he replied. "Hell, we just spent a fortune in renovation. We'd take a big hit selling it now."

"Who said anything about *selling* it? We'll find some renters while we're gone."

Doug lowered his gaze, sighing. "Yeah... I guess we could do that, but—"

"No 'buts' about it: I *am* going!" Her tone was determined. "You have your hobby—all that weird occult stuff—and I have mine. *Jazz*, baby, jazz. Don't think you can jaunt off to Louis Armstrong country and not take little ole me along. Not damn likely."

So it was settled: They would both fly to New Orleans.

***

101

To Julia, the flight seemed endless. She could barely contain her excitement. "They play jazz in all the clubs along Bourbon Street," she said. "Ten... twelve bands... all playing at once. My God, Dougie, that's heaven!"

"For a nutcase like you, sure," he said, grinning at her. "I happen to prefer Mozart."

She stuck out her tongue at him. "Ole stick-in-the-mud Belford."

"At least it's classic mud!"

They laughed together.

What Doug Belford did not know, was that the dark flood from Hurricane Katrina had borne, in its murky aftermath, something terrible from the deep, uncharted sea. The storm had unleashed something very savage into the historic city of New Orleans, something that would create fear and havoc and death.

Something monstrous.

***

The Mayor's office was expansive, colorfully decorated in an Asian motif. His desk was mounded with official papers. He was a handsome black man with a firm handshake. Dark-eyed and bulky, he was proud of his toughness, explaining to Doug how he worked out for an hour each day in a gym in the State Building. "Got to keep in shape," he affirmed in a rich, full-toned voice. "As the Bard said, 'Man is of mortal flesh'—or was that Mark Twain?" He chuckled, waving Doug to a deep red leather chair.

"Were you in working for the government during Katrina?"

"No. But I remember it vividly," the Mayor replied. "Dreadful. Eighty per cent of the city flooded. Thousands dead."

"I heard the figure was around fifteen hundred."

"Granted, the actual number is in dispute... regardless, we can't let this sort of thing happen again." He leaned forward, dark hands tented. "That's why you're here, Doug... Uh, you don't mind if I call you Doug?"

"Not at all, Mr. Mayor. We'll be working together for quite a while."

"You're a godsend, Doug." He pressed a button on his desk. "Ms. LeBlanc... please send Gordon in."

A tall, trim-bodied man in his mid-thirties, wearing a NOPD uniform, entered the room. He was ruddy-faced with steady gray eyes.

"This is our new Chief of Police, Gordon Linge," said the Mayor. "Gordy, this is Doug Belford; he's here to help redesign our levees."

Linge and Belford shook hands. "Big job," the chief declared. "Sure you can handle it? Crescent City's depending on you."

"I can handle it," Doug assured him. "You'll need to construct

102

better seawalls, based in concrete, high enough to check major hurricane flood waters. Also need more reclamation of the bayou from overdevelopment. We'll have to work closely with the Army Corps of Engineers to rebuild the Mississippi Delta back to the way it was before the oil companies. Take some time, but it can be done. Worked for Galveston, after all."

"Sounds good," said Linge, checking his watch. "Have to run. Got a real crisis on my hands."

"I just flew in this morning," said Doug. "What's the problem?"

Linge took a newspaper from the Mayor's desk and handed it to Belford. "Read this, today's paper. They're calling these poor folks victims of the 'Saint City Killer.' Disgusting."

Bold news headlines told the story, describing the eighth in a series of random, bizarre homicides generating fear and panic among the citizens of The Big Easy. The murders, all gruesome, all terrifying, lacked a known motive. The story claimed that "the police are baffled."

"Baffled, yeah," nodded Linge. "They got that right. I'll say one thing—this wacko doesn't discriminate. Kills men, women, children, old folks, black or white. Then *gnaws* on the bodies, stealing parts off of them—eyes, tongues, fingers and toes. Leaves little bones and weird voodoo fetish items drenched in sea water and kelp around the victims, too. This is one sick individual."

Doug bit his lower lip, thinking. "This has all the earmarks of something else... something supernatural almost," he said.

Linge frowned, eyes tight on Belford. "What do you mean?"

"Hobby of mine," nodded Doug. "You may be dealing with someone far more dangerous. Maybe not even entirely human—"

The chief laughed, shaking his head. "Takes all kinds, eh?" Linge shrugged. He checked his watch again. "I'm overdue for a meet with the press. They want answers I don't have." Ignoring Belford, he nodded curtly to the Mayor and left the room.

***

"So how did your visit with Mayor Benoit turn out?" asked Julia later that afternoon.

"He's okay," said Doug. "But I sure didn't score with the police chief."

Julia nodded. "I've been reading the paper all about this murder spree. Knowing you, ten-to-one you told the chief it was some kind of hocus pocus. Something supernatural, am I right?"

"You guessed it," Doug admitted. After a pause he added: "He didn't seem too pleased."

She nodded, taking a sip of water. "I'm *not* surprised."

"So I'm fruitcake, is that it?"

103

"When it comes to the spook stuff? *Yeah*—you're pretty far around the bend."

He regarded her, a little hurt. "But... what if I'm *right*? What if there is an evil creature—"

Julia sat up abruptly, a loud yawn interrupting their discussion. "Look, Dougie, I'm tired; I, need to hit the sack, huh? I've got a shot at singing with 'The Group' at the Junkanew Club here in town this Friday. They put out prime sound. Their trumpet player is sen*sational*. If they like what I do I'm... well... I'm really up for this gig."

"Congrats darling! I've always said you have a wonderful voice." He poured some red wine for them both, and they tapped glasses. "Here's to success at long last! You're hipped on jazz and I'm hipped on weirdness. That's us." He grinned at her.

"Yeah," she nodded. "That's us... the odd couple!" And she grinned back.

***

Julia did well on her Junkanew tryout, and was signed with 'The Group' as lead singer that weekend. Doug was busy at his office in the State Building, pouring over plans, sketching ideas for the redesigned levees, but after reading a lurid news account of the latest murder, he took time out to appear at police headquarters for a talk with Chief Gordon Linge.

"All the bodies," said Belford, "have something in common: a unique mark *bitten* into each victim, as though they had been in the water, like a shark had been at them—"

Linge glowered at him. "That info should *never* have been leaked," he said. "It's strictly police business. Damn press sticks their nose into everything."

"I've been doing some research—"

Linge held his hand up, a strained smile touching his lips. "Do me a favor, huh? Stick to drawing little pictures of the levees and how to fix them. Leave the gumshoe stuff to the experts."

Doug ignored the hostility.

"So you're an expert on homicide now? I thought you were some type of *engineer*..."

Doug forced a smile, straightening. "Obviously can't rely on the NOPD, can I?"

Chief Linge sat back in his chair, crossing his arms. "Get the fuck out of here, Belford. And *don't* be stupid, or I'll bust your ass."

Doug left the room, closing the door behind him.

Linge stared after him. "*Dick*."

***

104

The Junkanew was thronged with its usual Saturday night crowd: teens in graphical tee-shirts, a trio of white-haired old ladies in wheelchairs, drunk girls in Daisy Dukes, wide-eyed tourists mesmerized by the raucous tide of jazz surging from a raised bandstand in the center of the room. Julia was onstage, in a sequined silver gown, belting out her own rendition of "When the Saints Come Marching In." As the song ended, the applause was thunderous.

Doug was at a front table facing the stage. He was proud of his wife, proud of her obvious talent, but he had other things on his mind. Now, he raised a hand, gesturing to Julia. She nodded, saying something to the band—and the music changed—from period jazz to a haunting, exotic drum-led beat that vibrated through the crowd, lulling, intense, and hypnotic.

This was special music that Doug had asked Julia to have 'The Group' play. At first she objected, looking over the pages of sheet music he handed her with a skeptical eye." It's a *jazz* club, Doug. Why would we play weird stuff like this?"

"You'll just have to trust me on this, Julia. I know that what I'm asking is off the wall, but please... just trust me, okay?"

Reluctantly, she agreed.

***

Now, as the atonal music flowed through the room, Doug sat tensely, on edge, right hand gripping a Saturday Night Special under the table. He had discovered, in his online research that this particular music had been shown to exert a hypnotic effect; drifting out the open door on foggy Carondelet Street. Would it lure the killer into the club?

Doug realized it was a long shot. What if the person—or *thing*—stalking these dark streets, failed to hear the music that he had so carefully chosen? *What then?*

"We'll be back in a few minutes!" Julia told the audience as the band left the stage.

As the group took a dinner break, he waited for his wife to come to the table. Doug looked at his watch: 12:32 am.

Then he heard a terrified cry from backstage.

Julia? Doug leapt from the table, knocking his drink over. He pushed through the crowd. *"Julia?"* He brought the gun up.

At that moment, a fiendish horror materialized, shielding itself behind his wife as it tried to leave the club through a side door. One of its suckered tentacles, sword-sharp, was tight against her neck as the thing's multiple eyes burned with unholy fire, mouth agape with needled teeth.

"My God, don't shoot, Doug!" she pleaded, voice strained with fear. "It'll kill me if you shoot!"

Doug knew what he had to do. *It'll kill her anyway unless I kill it first.* But what if he missed?

Thrusting Julia's limp body forward, razored tentacle at her throat, its slimy, seaweed-draped figure glistened in the half-light of the stage area, bloated body pulsing with alien life.

Aim for the head... Only chance. The entire club was in panic.

Doug squeezed the trigger. The gun roared. Again... and again... and again. Six times.

The enraged creature released its death hold on Julia and staggered forward, howling madly, clawing at its bullet-shattered skull. It slammed into Doug, smashing aside a table, throwing them both to the floor. A second razored tentacle sliced viciously into Doug's leg as he attempted to twist free. Despite its terrible wounds, the creature's strength was incredible.

I'm going to die, Doug told himself, blood soaking his leg. *I'm going to fucking die!*

The creature lashed out blindly, mewling and screaming in its death agony; at last the sea-beast heaved, blood bubbling from its fanged mouth. The unblinking eyes glazed. Finally, after a tortured breath, it ceased all movement. Doug watched to be sure it was dead, repulsed by its barnacle crusted, part-fish, part-humanoid body. Some of the muddy fins and scales on the creature had bits of netting and twigs clinging to them... and even what appeared to be small voodoo fetish items—bits of bone, little dolls, animal parts—entwined in the fleshy strings of matted algae covering its foul-smelling body. *What the hell* was *this thing... where did it* come *from?*

Stunned, Doug held his wife close, murmuring: "It's over. It's over now."

***

A couple months later, after the investigation had closed regarding the Junkanew Club shooting, Doug and Julia were cleared to return home to L.A.

The protective levees had been designed and were ready to be built, the Saint City Killer had been stopped; they were headed home.

Home to Santa Monica...

Home to their cats...

Home to their normal life...

Doug Belford's job was done.

106

Terror From The Briny Depths

Jim Kavanaugh

Sea Creature From the Darkest Regions Of The Abyss !

Drive-In Creature Feature Anthology *presents a* **Elizabeth Massie** *story* **Terror From The Briny Depths** *edited by* **Eugene Johnson** *and* **Charles Day** *produced by* **Evil Jester Press** *copyright 2016*

OH | **Oceanic Horror**
Sea Creature Terror

Elizabeth Massie

Elizabeth Massie is an award-winning author of novels, short fiction, media-tie ins, poetry, and nonfiction. Her more recent works include the novels *Hell Gate*, *Desper Hollow*, the novelization of *Versailles* (based on the French mini-series of the same name), and *Night Benedictions*, a collection of gentle thoughts, poems, and meditations on the goodness of the night.

Elizabeth has won the Bram Stoker Award® twice –for her novel *Sineater* and her novella *"Stephen"* –and the Scribe Award for her novelization of the third season of Showtime's original television show, *The Tudors*. A long-time fan of classic horror and science fiction movies, one of her favorite activities is watching *Svengoolie* on Saturday nights as he presents the old cinematic gems with flair and good humor. She lives in the Shenandoah Valley of Virginia with her husband, illustrator Cortney Skinner.

TERROR FROM THE BRINY DEPTHS

Elizabeth Massie

Anna clutched the ship's railing and looked out at the foam-capped waves. The briny spray was refreshing, spattering her cheeks and arms with misty droplets. It was so good to be free of solid ground and sailing – well, by way of a motorized dolphin-watching ship – a half-mile off shore on the great Atlantic Ocean. There was something primal about the sea, something mysterious and moving and brilliantly powerful.

"Hey." Greg moved up to the railing beside Anna. He put his arm around her shoulder and drew her close. "Nice, huh?"

"It really is," said Anna. She brushed back a strand of red hair. "This is the first time I've been out on the ocean, and I love it. Strange, isn't it? I'm a mountain girl. I was raised by my dad in the Blue Ridge. Yet, still, the ocean seems to be so familiar. As if it knows me. As if I have a connection to it."

"Ah, baby," said Greg, running his thumb along the back of Anna's neck. "You're such a dreamer. Head in the clouds, mind on such silly things. Don't worry, once we're married you'll have enough to keep busy. Cooking. Cleaning. Planning parties. Raising our children. No time for crazy thoughts."

Anna grimaced. It was all she could do to keep from shrugging Greg's arm off her shoulder. Yes, she'd agreed to marry him. Yes, they had already set the date, a short two months away. Greg had even bought a brand-new 1958 Lincoln Premiere convertible to take on their honeymoon to Niagara Falls. The fact that he was recently graduated from law school and was now a freshman partner in the Virginia law firm of Fleming, Yaber, and Armstrong was certainly attractive. He would be able to provide all the creature comforts a newlywed couple could want.

Anna's own youth had been one of meager means, spent with her father in a three-room mountain house, tending chickens, milking cows, and swimming in algae-covered ponds. Financial stability was a big plus when it came to marrying Greg, whom she'd met while waitressing at the Conner Gap Diner in western Virginia. But recently, Anna had begun seeing and hearing parts of her fiancé's personality that set her teeth on edge.

"You'll never want for anything," Anna's father, once a poor traveling salesman and now a poor mountain farmer, had said of the relationship. "I'll be able to sleep soundly, knowing my daughter is well cared for."

And so Anna had done her best to endure Greg's irritating quirks.

"Dr. Pepper?" asked Greg, giving Anna's shoulder a squeeze.

"That would be nice. Thank you."

Greg sauntered off across the deck to the boat's enclosed cabin, where a white-capped ship's mate sold pretzels and soft drinks to the dolphin-watch customers.

"It'll be all right," Anna whispered to herself as she watched Greg disappear into the cabin. "I'll get used to it. He's not a bad guy. There is a lot a good in him, I know."

"Look!" shouted a little boy from the ship's bow. "Mommy, I see dolphins!"

"Yes, there they are!" his mother said.

The tourists hurried to the front of the boat, where they *oohed* and *ahhed* over the flashes of silver fins and tails.

Anna stayed put, enjoying her temporary solitude. She put her arms on the railing, her chin on her arms, and gazed down at the foamy water.

And there, staring up at her from inches below the water's surface was a huge, black, glistening eye.

The eye blinked.

Anna screeched and stumbled backward.

"Anna!" Greg was there, holding two bottles of Dr. Pepper, kneeling beside her. "What happened? Are you hurt?"

"I…" she began. "I saw an eye! A huge eye! Big, dark, almost as wide as this boat!"

Greg helped Anna to her feet. "An eye? Honey, you must have just seen some floating garbage."

"No, it was an eye. It was gigantic! It was *horrible*!"

Greg led her back to the railing. "Look," he said.

"I'm afraid to."

"I said *look*!" Greg's voice had lost its patience. Anna forced herself to look over the railing.

The water rose and fell, foam and brine and white caps. There was no giant eye below the surface.

"I saw it," Anna insisted. "I really did, Greg!"
"You saw a reflection of something, or maybe even a large jellyfish."

"No, it was…"

"It was not an eye."

But it was an eye! Anna thought but did not say any more. Greg wouldn't believe her and the discussion would only turn into a debate. He loved to be right.

"Now, let's go see the dolphins," said Greg. He took Anna's hand and led her up to the bow, elbowed his way through the crowd, and made room for the two of them at the railing. "There they are! Jumping, performing! Almost as if they know we're watching them. Do you see them?"

Anna nodded.

Greg pulled Anna close. "What a nice trip. I just wish this was our honeymoon, if you know what I mean."

Anna knew. She gave Greg a wearied smile. And as she looked back out at the dolphins, and then out across the vast expanse of sea, she thought she heard something whisper her name. It made the flesh on her arms prickle.

Anna....Anna.....Anna....!

But again, she said nothing. I would only lead to yet another debate.

***

The creature swam the sea, deep, where sunlight's tendrils were little more than faint ribbons, her long, massive, scale-covered body undulating and coiling as she moved, feeding angrily on anything that got in her way. She breathed as a land creature, rising up twice an hour to lift her giant head above the ocean's surface and draw in air before diving down again, exhaling blasts of gas and fire that boiled and scalded the waters around her. Her cavernous mouth, filled with spear-sharp teeth, could devour a whale in four bites. Two bat-like wings the size of a schooner's sails protruded from her flesh behind her mouth and served as fins.

Frustration and confusion drove her onward through the deep waters, from the tropical oceans to the frigid seas of the poles, back and forth, knowing she was cursed but not remembering why. On occasion she would rise up to the shallows and ram into a boat, overturning it and sending the occupants to their deaths. But primarily she was driven to swim, to move place to place, searching desperately, furiously, for something she could not find and could not recall.

But then, in the moderate, blue-green waters off the coast of Virginia, she felt it.

A bright, almost painful surge.

There was something here she knew. Something vague but powerfully familiar.

A name formed in her mind, and she rose up toward the daylight,

111

her giant black eyes staring, looking, seeking.

And with all her might she thought the name that had come to her.

Anna! Anna!
Anna!

***

They were vacationing at the Cavalier Hotel in Virginia Beach, an elegant, seven-story, seaside establishment built in 1927 on a hillside overlooking the shoreline and a private outdoor dance pavilion on the sand. The hotel was five-star, serviced by stoic, white-jacketed and white-gloved waiters and bellboys, smiling concierges, and dutiful housekeepers in starched uniforms. Greg would accept nothing but the best.

As was proper, Anna and Greg had their own rooms. However, Greg had insisted that the rooms be adjoining. While he expected his bride to wear white during the wedding ceremony, he certainly didn't expect her to be a virgin. Anna found his lovemaking to be tedious and orchestrated, nothing like the passionate, clumsy coupling she'd experienced with her teenaged boyfriend, Buck, back in the mountains. But she would get used to it, she knew. She was resilient. She was a survivor.

They dressed for dinner; Greg in a tailored suit and Anna in a green silk gown Greg had bought for her. He ushered her around the dining room, making sure all the customers saw the red-haired beauty on his arm. A string quartet in the corner played tame versions of current favorites – "Rockin' Robin," "Lollipop," and "To Know Him is to Love Him."

Their table was next to a large window overlooking the hotel's wide, sloping lawn, the sandy private beach and pavilion, and the Atlantic beyond it. They dined on shrimp, filet mignon, and champagne. Anna didn't care for the shrimp and so dabbed hers with coatings of sauce to mask the taste. The steak was perfect, however. The champagne, bubbly and delicious.

The world began to darken outside. The lawn, beach, and ocean took on the same pewter hue. As Greg finished his last sip of champagne, he reached for Anna's hand.

"How about a stroll before retiring?"

Anna nodded. "That would be nice," she said. That seemed to be a pat answer these days. As long as he wasn't asking something beyond her ability to tolerate, she would agree. She would deem it "nice." That kept Greg happy and Anna out of a debate.

The night air was salty and damp. Dark clouds drifted overhead, obscuring the stars and moon. Greg said little, guiding Anna along the boxwood-edged pathways, past the koi pond, down to the patio and its white benches. They sat side by side, Greg looking at Anna, Anna looking

112

down across the darkened lawn to the black sea. Faint strips of white became visible as the waves rose, folded over, and crashed onto the beach.

As Greg put his arm around Anna and leaned in to kiss her, the voice from the sea rose up on the salty air, an urgent whisper louder than before.

Anna! Anna!

Anna gasped and jumped to her feet. "Listen, Greg!"

"Anna, cut it out!" Greg glared at her from the bench.

"Didn't you hear it? It called my name! Something from the ocean called to me!"

"What the devil are you talking about?"

"Something...something out there knows me!"

Greg stood, grabbed Anna by the arm, and slapped her. Anna gasped.

"Some women claim they have a headache to stop their men from being affectionate," said Greg, "but not you, you and your blasted imagination!"

"No, that's not what's going on here. Honestly, I heard it call me. I heard it on the boat today, too, after I saw the eye in the water. I heard it, but didn't want to say anything to you."

"Why not?"

Anger roiled in Anna's chest, bubbling up, stronger than her fear. "Because...because of this very thing! Because you treat me like a child. You don't want to hear anything that is counter to what you think or want. If you loved me, you would hear what I have to say without needing to shut me up. If you loved me, you would care!"

"Oh!" said Greg. Even in the darkness she could sense the red of rage flowering on his cheeks. "So now I don't care? Give me examples of how I don't care. I don't care because I paid for that green dress? I don't care because I planned this vacation? I don't care because I gave you a diamond ring and asked you to be my wife?"

"Do you hear yourself? It's always about you! I didn't want this green dress, I wanted the red. But you said red didn't look good with my hair. I preferred a smaller ring but no, you got the one you liked best. But that's not what I'm talking about. I'm talking about what I think, what I feel! You always dismiss me, Greg!"

"So you want to break off our engagement?"

"I didn't say that."

"It sounds like it!"

"Greg!"

Bristling, Greg marched off up the pathway, heading for the hotel. Anna dropped down onto the bench, her head in her hands. What a mistake to accept his proposal! But, what a mistake to let him go. Her father would benefit as much as she would. And she loved her father more than anyone on Earth.

113

Maybe Greg was right. Maybe she was too fanciful, too imaginative. Maybe she was…

"Maybe I'm just insane."

The darkened clouds began to rain. Anna let the rain drench her, let them mingle with her tears, until she could take the chill no more. She went inside to warm up. And back up to the fourth floor to make amends with her betrothed.

***

She seethed in white-hot frustration, writhing angrily beneath the waves like a giant earthworm on a sun-scorched sidewalk. Her wings thrashed madly. She bellowed out great bursts of fire, feeling as if she would explode. Ocean creatures for miles fled for their lives.

Anna!!

She had seen Anna, there on the deck of a boat. Up through the rippling waters she had seen Anna's face, and a memory had slammed back into her brain.

Anna, it is you!

Anna, you were stolen away from me!

Anna, my daughter!

***

Anna and Greg made love. It was as it always had been. Anna tolerant; Greg arrogant and boring. When it was done, he held her and told her how it would be even better once they were married. After a good twenty minutes, she excused herself to shower and return to her room. She wanted to lock the adjoining door, but knew that would only create a new slew of debates.

Clean and exhausted, she fell asleep.

And she dreamed.

She dreamed of an island. Palmetto trees shading the sandy soil, crabs skittering amid the sea oats. Tar shacks. Clothes drying on lines and little roadside stands from which handmade baskets and quilts were sold. Small gardens enclosed with wire fences. Dark-skinned people singing and speaking in a language she couldn't understand. Kind people, smiling people.

But there was another shack. It was set apart from the others on a spit of land that had no trees, no sea oats, only rocky soil. It smelled bad, and even with no trees, it seemed to be in constant shadow.

Anna, now a very small child, stood outside the shed on the rocky spit, staring across the inlet to the other huts and the cheerful men, women, and children coming and going. She waved at them but they didn't see her. Or they didn't want to. She tried to call out "Hello!" but there was no sound to her voice.

"Anna!"

The command came from inside the shed.

Anna did not want to go, but her feet forced her to do so. Inside, on a stool, sat a thin woman with dull red hair and fingernails as long as claws. She was stitching a small cloth doll, and chanting and spitting on the fabric as she did. The cloth doll cried pitifully with each stitch.

Oh, my God! This woman is a witch, Anna thought.

"Bring me that jar!" the woman demanded. She pointed to a wooden shelf on which various glass containers sat, filled with oily liquids. "Quickly!"

Anna went to the shelf, but each jar she touched exploded beneath her fingers. When Anna looked at her hands, she saw that they were bleeding profusely, the fingers severed at the joints and lying on the dirt floor.

"Clumsy!" shouted the witch. "How dare you break my jars!"

"No, please…" began Anna.

"Humbalan! Humbalan!" wailed the witch.

With that utterance, Anna felt her body lock up, tightly, as if she were suddenly made of wood. Not a muscle moved. Even her lungs stopped working, and she stood there for many long, terrifying, painful seconds.

Then the witch snapped her fingers. Anna could breathe again. As she bent over and sobbed, the witch laughed. A bellowing, screeching laughter that seemed to singe the very air.

***

Anna awoke to the sound of a screeching alarm and shouts from the hallway.

"What's happening?"

"Is it a fire?"

"No, no! Not a fire!"

"What is it?"

"Did you see it? Oh, my God!"

"We have to evacuate! Get away from here! Hurry! Hurry!"

The door to Anna's room blew open and Greg was there, his hair wild with sleep, his eyes huge with terror.

"Something's coming!" he screamed. "I heard them yelling from out on the lawn! Something's coming up from the sea!"

Anna stumbled for Greg, and they raced into the hallway, joining the river of hotel guests, some of whom were banging on the elevator buttons in an attempt to hurry them up, some of whom were pushing past each other and down the stairs, yet others of whom were heading for the plate glass window on the east end to see what had caused the sirens, the

115

terror. Greg forced his way through the crowd, dragging Anna with him, up to the window.

Where they stood.

And stared.

The scream that formed in Anna's chest was stopped cold it its tracks.

In the ocean waves down below the lawn and beach, illuminated by a full moon that had broken through the clouds, there had risen the most enormous, horrific thing Anna had ever seen. A sea serpent two hundred feet tall at the least, as wide as a freight train, with giant, leathery wings battling the air. The mouth of the hideous monster opened to bellow, revealing vicious teeth. A column of flame shot from the mouth, out and down, igniting a nearby pier and the restaurant atop it. Then, the creature, propelled by its dreadful wings, lurched up and out of the ocean, its tail dragging the sand and crushing the dance pavilion like a bug.

It leapt again, heading up the hill toward the hotel.

"What is that?" screamed Anna.

No one answered. No one knew. Some remained at the window and screamed as others turned and fled for the stairs and elevators.

The hotel alarm continued to blare, a mechanical wail that offered nothing to those who heard it but a sense of panic. No direction. No advice.

We are doomed!

***

She remembered it all now.

Curses on them all, I remember!

She was a leviathan, the most horrifying of all sea creatures, created by one great collective *wudu* curse of the Gullah people on South Carolina's small, wind-swept Cootuh Island. Damned to swim the ocean in a state of constant confusion, anger, and misery.

She had once been a woman named Chloe, and a witch of great power. She lived in a shack on a rocky spit of land with her young daughter, Anna, whom she had been training to follow in her footsteps. Chloe had thrived on her magic, charming young men to her bed when she wanted them, bringing disease and crop failure to those whom she disliked, and causing "accidents" – broken bones, crushed spines, amputated fingers or limbs – to others on a whim.

But then the Gullah of many nearby villages had joined forces to curse and stop her. They had been jealous of Chloe's powers, of course, terrified of her spells, and unwilling to tolerate her any longer. Unable to destroy her, their combined spell had morphed her into the giant monster of the Atlantic, had scrambled her memories, and set her out to swim and suffer for eternity.

116

The leviathan did not know what had happened to Anna, but someone, somewhere had taken her and raised her. And now, Anna, full grown, was here.

She had seen Anna on a boat.

She sensed Anna in the hotel on the hill.

I will have my daughter back!

With a thrust of her powerful tail and flapping of her wings, the leviathan leapt farther up the slope toward the hotel, her body coming down atop vacationers who had made the deadly mistake of racing out onto the front lawn. She heaved a great bolt of fire at the hotel, at the roof went up in an instant. Screams could be heard from the building, and the sounds pleased her more than anything had pleased her in years.

Another flapping of wings, another leaping of her tremendous body, and she landed within yards of the hotel with an earthshaking thud. Now, with her huge black eyes, she could see inside the windows, see the terror in the faces of those who were frozen in place, staring out at the creature.

Where is Anna!?

Her gaping maw released another burst of fire that drove against the windows of the top two floors, blowing them inward, setting people aflame, hurling them backward in a writhing, wailing jumble.

Where is my daughter?!

And then she saw her. Anna, standing at the window on the fourth floor amid another clot of terrified humans, staring up in disbelief and horror.

***

She remembered it all now.

Living in the shack on the rocky spit with her mother Chloe, an angry, powerful witch. Anna trembling in her tiny shoes as her mother concocted potions, bearing brutal beatings for not learning spells and incantations quickly enough, doing her best not to cry, because crying only made things worse.

She remembered one bug-infested, humid morning. The Gullah people gathering where the rocky spit left the island, their voices rising in a deafening chant. Chloe racing from the shack, shrieking at the chant, morphing and growing into a hideous, gigantic, snake-like creature that they then drove into the ocean waters and away. A kind traveling salesman agreeing to take her far away from Cootuh Island and raise her as his own.

Yes, she knew now.

The creature out the window, raised up like a monstrous, winged cobra, was her mother. Chloe, the leviathan, had come to claim Anna. To keep her prisoner? To kill her? Anna couldn't know. But even as her heart thundered and her breaths came in jagged, painful gasps, she knew she

117

had to do something to stop her. If she didn't, Chloe would continue to kill and maim innocent people. Much as she had when in human form.

The remaining people beside her at the window dispersed and ran, back to the stairs, the elevators, weeping, screaming. Anna turned to reach for Greg, but he was gone. Off with the others, escaping without her, his selfishness no more clear than in that moment.

So be it.

Anna looked back at the window. The gigantic black eye lowered level to the window. Anna raised her trembling hand.

"Mother," she whispered.

The leviathan's mouth twisted in what could have been a smile, though Anna knew better. Anna jumped back as one wing slammed into the window glass, shattering it into flying shards. The wing then reached in, wrapped tightly round Anna's body, and drew her out into the night air.

With three powerful leaps, the leviathan returned to the ocean, Anna in her cold, clammy grasp. She could feel its sense of victory as the monster breached and then dove into the water. Anna caught a breath before they went under, though the impact nearly knocked it out and away.

Chloe meant to drown her. Meant to kill Anna. Meant to punish her for existing and living upon the Earth even as Chloe was damned to live in the sea. Meant to punish her daughter for being what she could no longer be.

But I am a witch's daughter! I am not powerless!

I remember!

Oh, yes, I remember!

And so, as the leviathan swam deeper, Anna opened her mouth and in a muffled yet audible voice cried, *"Humbalan! Humbalan!"*

The leviathan's powerful tail ceased its moving. Anna scrabbled from the grasp of the leathery wing and kicked her way to the surface as the mighty creature sank like a stone. No longer able to swim. No longer able to come up for air.

And as she swam to shore, toward the light of the burning hotel and the flashing lights of the city fire engines, Anna thought back on what she'd remembered.

Her powers. She would be fine. Her father would be fine.

She was resilient, a survivor.

If Greg ever bothered her again, he would be sorry.

Anna smiled.

THE FOREST THAT HOWLS

GRISLY HORROR!

Jim Kavanagh

Drive-In Creature Feature Anthology *Presents a* **Michael Paul Gonzalez** *story* **The Forest That Howls** *edited by* **Eugene Johnson** *and* **Charles Day** *Produced by* **Evil Jester Press** *Copyright 2016*

BT | Bigfoot Terror
Frightening images

Michael Paul Gonzalez

Michael Paul Gonzalez is the author of the novels *Angel Falls* and *Miss Massacre's Guide To Murder and Vengeance*. A member of the Horror Writers Association, his recent short stories have appeared in *Gothic Fantasy: Chilling Horror Stories*, *18 Wheels of Horror*, *the Booked. Podcast Anthology*, *HeavyMetal.com*, *the Appalachian Undead Anthology* and the forthcoming anthology *Lost Signals*. He resides in Los Angeles, a place full of wonders and monsters far stranger than any that live in the imagination. You can visit him online at MichaelPaulGonzalez.com

THE FOREST THAT HOWLS

Michael Paul Gonzalez

Sheriff John Manley hated dragging people in to the drunk tank. They always smelled bad. Even if they managed to keep their internal affairs in order and avoid filling the back of the car with vomit or urine, they'd still leave a lingering fug of old booze and sweat that never aired out of the upholstery. He begged the state every year to retrofit the car with a plastic backseat, but it wasn't in the budget. The only thing worse than taking in one alkie was having to haul in two of them.

He stops his cruiser next to the blinking lights of a pickup truck. It's half in a ditch, the pulsing hazards illuminating two men sprawled on the ground. They scramble to their feet when they see him and hustle to the car, pounding on the hood and begging to be let in. It was still early enough in the afternoon that just asking the next question put Manley in a foul mood.

"You two been drinking?"

They rush to the driver's window so quickly that Manley's hand instinctively shoots down to the butt of his sidearm. They jockey for position outside of his window, pushing and shoving each other, a stream of nonsensical babble rattling back and forth.

The only key phrases that he can pick out are *they're still out there* and variations on *tore Steiney apart*.

Manley reaches up and hits the siren for a couple of short blats, shoving his door open so fast that both men scramble backwards and fall on their butts.

"Quiet," Manley growls. They remind him of bobblehead dolls, wide-eyed, heads whipping around trying to view every side of the forest at once. Can't be booze, had to be meth or something worse.

He points at the man to his right. "You. Talk. What happened?"

"We was gonna find a Squatch," he says, his eyes nearly bugging out of his head. His fingers fumble with the stained, curling hem of his BUSH QUAYLE '92 T-shirt.

"Mister. Sheriff. Sir. Officer. Please," the other man says.

121

"Tch," Manley clicks his teeth and snaps his finger at the second man, silencing him. He quickly points the finger back at the first man, who recoils as if the digit is loaded. "Are you two out here alone?"

The man nods so hard that Manley expects to hear a noise like a nickel rattling in an empty paint can.

"...'cept fer Todd," the second man says.

"We gotta--" the first one yelps. Manley snaps his fingers again and the man's lips purse shut.

"Who's Todd?" Manley asks.

"Our friend," the first man says. "Todd Steinhour. Drinking buddy. Steiney."

"What's his name?" Manley asks, indicating the other man on the ground.

When the second man starts to answer, Manley glares him into silence.

"Huck," the first man says. "I mean, Sawyer."

"His name is Sawyer?" Manley asks. "And you call him Huck?"

"Like the book, you know. It's like... you know, a joke. There's the book Huck Finn, and his last name is... I mean... guess you had ta be there," the man says.

The beginnings of a long-afternoon headache tingle at the base of Manley's skull. He holds his palm up for a long second, then points at the second man, Huck. "What's his name?"

"Why'incha just ask 'im?"

"Because I'm asking you."

Far away, the sound of a large branch snapping echoes through the trees, reverberating like a pistol shot.

"Aw shit, they're coming," Huck says. "You gotta take us in! You gotta move!"

"What," Manley asks again, "is his name?" pointing at the first man.

"Hank," Huck barks.

"Last name?"

"Hicks. Both of us," Huck says.

"You don't say?" Manley shakes his head.

"Naw, it's our last name. We're brothers," Huck says.

"That's your names?" Manley mutters. "Huck and Hank Hicks? Jesus Christ, I should have just gone into plumbing. Now. How did your truck come to rest here in the ditch?"

"Look, Officer, I don't mean ta be disrespectin' yer authority, but there's somethin' out there that wants us dead. You gotta help us, right? Says so there on your car!" Hank points at the back of the cruiser.

A cold wind whips between them, scattered drops fall from the dark clouds.

"I'm gonna put you in the back. We're gonna keep talking. I'm gonna crack the window open, and if either of you two Hicks tries to climb out, I will put a bullet in your ass, are we clear on that much?"

The Hicks boys nod and scramble to their feet. When Manley reacts, hand near his hip, they slow down. Huck raises his hands above his head. Hank offers his hands for cuffing. When they catch each other's eyes, they switch positions.

Manley swings the back door open. "Just get the fuck in there, okay?"

He slams the door behind them without bothering to let them get comfortable, then walks over to the pickup truck to assess the damage.

He leans his head into the cloud of stale beer smell, peeking in the open driver's side window. The whole cab is at a steep angle, all of the empties piled in the passenger footwell. The glove compartment hangs open, stuffed full of unpaid tickets and various papers, all weighed down by a box of rifle ammo.

The bed is covered in a battered camper shell. All of the windows are busted out, possibly from the force of the crash. The sides are heavily scratched and dented, not unusual for a truck that wanders these parts of the woods. Most of the residents had a daily driver for work and a beater that they'd take out into the woods for fishing and camping. There was an odd regularity to the damage, not the kind of thing you'd see from tree branches scraping. Looked more like someone had taken several baseball bats to the truck.

Manley moved around to the back of the truck and popped the camper shell top, a mere formality since all of the glass was missing. He tried to drop the tailgate, but it wouldn't move.

"There's a trick to it!" Hank yells from the car.

"And that blood ain't ours! I mean, we didn't do it!" Huck shouts. This was followed by a yelp as Hank presumably jabbed him in the ribs.

Manley frowns at them, hand near his holster. He leans his head in. The bed is mostly empty, but then he sees it, a puddle of blood at the back of the bed. Following the trail up, a dark streak that travels up the inside of the tailgate to a smear of blood on the top of the gate, still shiny and wet. It looks like someone was beheaded over the edge of the tailgate.

"What in the honest hell," Manley mutters, hustling back to the cruiser. He grumbles, "Shut the fuck up, both of you," as he slides into the car.

He exhales, thinking for a minute. Take them in now, stay here and set up a crime scene? Backup isn't an option as the only other two deputies on duty might as well be on Mars. It would take them hours to get here.

Manley picks up his radio and calls for dispatch, receiving nothing but static in return. He makes a mental note to write down the first mile marker he sees and starts the car up.

123

"Oh thank Jesus!" Hank shouts. "Thank you Lord, he's movin'. Take us in! Take. Us. IN! Get us the Hell out of—OW!"

Manley slams on the brakes, sending both men rocketing into the steel mesh partition that separates the front from the back. "Let's get a couple of things straight here. I don't know what either of you two have done, but if you've broken the law I'll see that you pay for it. If someone else is trying to hurt you, I will do my best to keep you safe. I'm gonna ask you questions, but you don't have to answer them until you have a lawyer present. There's your rights. With that out of the way, let's get to the truth and make life easy on everyone."

"Thank you sir," Huck says.

"Is that deer blood in the bed of your truck?"

Hank looks at Huck and shakes his head.

"It's…not. It's not…human. We think."

"Okay. How did the blood get in the truck?" Manley leaves the question of what the blood came from for the moment. They're probably trying to cover up poaching. He's always careful not to ask leading questions that can be used against him later to scuttle a case. Not *Why did you kill him* or *who killed him*, just give them enough slack to hang themselves.

"Sir, you will not believe us if we tell you the truth. I'm only tellin' ya that much so's you don't slam on the brakes again and crush us."

"What's the truth?"

"Steiney got… kilt by… a… sir, aw hell, I dunno how t'start…"

"It was a Sasquatch, sir," Huck says. "An army of them. They took him away screamin' and they was comin' fer us next. You see what they did to the truck! We was outta control and—OW!"

This time the car fishtails from the force of Manley's braking. He pulls over and throws the car in park, turning around in his seat.

"Okay. I don't know what you're on right now, but my advice to you is that if you can't offer me any useful information right now, your best course of action is silence, you got me? I don't know what you poached. Plenty of different things out of season right now, and I'm sure you're not trying to--"

"We's sober as ghosts!" Hank says.

"What's that s'posed ta mean? Sober as—ghosts ain't real, dummy! Sir," Huck says, "We ain't been drinking. I mean, not fer the past few hours. Not since we got ta the… look, if you'll kindly drive down the road, I swear I'll give ya the short version of what happened. I mean, Steiney could still be alive out there, and we gotta find 'im!"

Manley took off his sunglasses and hat and set them gently in the seat next to him. He put the car in drive and slowly pulled back out onto the mountain road.

"Talk," he says.

124

"We moved out here from Kentucky, see, work on the gas pipeline up near Sumner. We was out trying to kill a weekend, get away from the wives and kids fer as long as we could, put some miles between us and our everyday troubles. Prollem with drivin' away from your troubles is they's always more troubles waitin' somewhere else," Huck says. "We wanted to make a movie out here in the woods, see? We was at the bar talking about how we could maybe get a Sasquatch on video and sell it to the news, or one o' them groups s'always out here pokin' around the woods. I mean, we know fakin' the video isn't the right thing ta do, and we're, y'know, invokin' the Fifth Amendment in case what we says here is--"

"I don't give a shit if you were out here to make pornos," Manley says. "Just get to what happened."

"Not! We wasn't! No. No! No. Look, we was plannin' this whole thing fer days. Weeks. And one night this fella at the bar hears us talkin', and says he could take us all out to where there's some Sasquatch action. Like real Sasquatch. Steiney got real excited at that. Me and Hank figgered we'd find a good spot to make the film, but if this dude was the real deal, maybe we could bag a real Squatch and be done with it. Millionaires! So this guy at the bar, Buck was his name, I think, or maybe Bug, he had a thick accent I couldn't quite place, well that man was the spittin' image of what we figured a fer-real bigfoot hunter would look like. He tells us no guns, right? I mean, we never go out in the woods without 'em, but he's real insistent on this. Cameras only. So, fine. We'll keep 'em out of sight, right? No harm, no foul."

"I'm pretty sure it was Buck," Hank says, "Not Bug. Guy just had a weird accent. You ever hear of a guy named Bug? We asked him couple times to repeat it, but it sounded different every time, like even he wasn't sure of his name. Big fella, he was. Six and a half foot if he was an inch. Arms like tree trunks. Head like a pile o' rocks. You ever see them drawn's o' cavemen, with the big foreheads and the big faces? I mean, he was kind of like that. Folks see me and Huck and Steiney, and they'd call us mountain men, but this guy was the real deal. You could tell he walked the walk. Big bushy beard. Clothes look like he lived in 'em full time, too."

"So here was the plan. Saw this thing on TV, the Patterson-Gimble thing, the movie? The shaky recordin' o' that big furry lump goin' out there?"

"Gimlin."

"Huh?"

"Patterson-Gimlin are the guys that made the movie," Manley says, silently cursing himself for entertaining this line of conversation.

"Steiney said we was gonna get somethin' on tape no matter what," Huck says. "He had a fur suit under the shell in his pickup. Said if we couldn't find one, we could fake it and nobody would know. Buck

125

thought that was the funniest thing. Steiney was gonna show him the suit, but he said no. And I wish he had looked, 'cuz we was hidin' our rifles under that suit. Y'don't go out in the forest without guns, that's just crazy. If he'd'a seen it, he'd a said no and left us at the bar and that woulda been that. "

"But he didn't, and we's only thinkin' about the money. So there we was with our million dollar idea," Huck says, "Takin' a ride out in a convoy of pickups. Steiney hopped in with Buck and they took the lead. We just followed 'em out here. I mean, Buck gives us all maps at the beginning, but after a couple o' beers it just got easier to follow the truck 'stead of tryin' ta pay attention to the map. Can't read that typeographical maps anyways."

"Topological. No! Topographical," Hank says.

"I get it," Manley says.

"We had good maps," Hank says.

"Yep. We drove out there, got off the main roads onto the side roads, got off the side roads and onto fire roads, got off the fire roads and onto unmarked trails… we was driving through gullies, busting through brush, and I had no idea how we was ever gonna find our way back home. I honked fer everyone to stop and I told Buck he better know what he was doin', and he jes' look at me like I was a child, you know? That kind of stern look where your old man doesn't have to say a word and you just gotta trust he has the whole thing under control."

"So we drove until dusk and set up camp," Huck continues. "Spent the night around a fire and Buck started tellin' us stories about what to expect. He said the squatches are nomadic. They don't set up in one spot fer too long, but they was also territorial. Like they'd be in one spot fer the fall and another fer summer and so on. And he says there's tribes of 'em, like there's not really such a thing as Sasquatch, or that there *is*, but that's just the name of one tribe. The bravest one, or the dumbest I guess, that always finds itself out near human contact."

"He said people din't really have a word fer the tribe we was trackin'," Hank says. "So we spent the first night tellin' stories and buildin' the fire and we all hit the tents early so's we could get up at the crack o' dawn. And all night I couldn't sleep cause I kept hearin' this noise."

"Steiney said he heard it too! You ever hear a dog do that high pitched whine, kinda sounds like a faucet that's been turned on jes' enough to let air come out the pipe but barely any water? Just a breathy *heeeeeeeee* kinda noise? Spooky as hell," Huck's eyes go big, as if this conveys the weight of the fear he felt.

"Well, I was afraid, I'll admit it," Hank says. "Didn't want to poke my head out, but I did eventually, because the thing was, the noise didn't move. It was comin' from the same spot, at the same volume, from only a few feet away. And I zipped my tent down just enough to peek out,

126

and what did I see but Buck sittin' upright there by the fire. Couldn't tell if he was sleepin' or not, but that noise was comin' from him! I could see his back movin' in time with the sound. And I thought maybe that was his snorin', right? But then he'd stop sometimes, and wait, and then his head would nod a little and he'd start in with that noise again in a different pattern. He was talkin' in some kind of Sasquatch Morse code."

"Fascinating," Manley says.

The car approaches an intersection. Manley slows down and drums his fingers on the wheel. A piercing scream breaks the silence.

"Coyote," Manley says, noting the fear on the men's faces.

"That wasn't no—drive! You gotta drive!"

The scream returns again, rhythmic and undulating, this time echoed and answered by a different scream from the other direction. Right or left, Manley would be driving toward one of the two sounds.

"They're trackin' us," Hank whispers.

"Right to remain silent," Manley grumbles at him.

Manley pulls a forestry service map from the door pocket and consults it for the fastest way back into town. It was getting near dusk and these roads always got tricky once the sun went down.

"Listen to me," Manley says. "I'm not trying to coerce you in any way, shape or—you guys understand what *coerce* means?"

"I guess so," Hank says.

"I'm not claiming you're guilty, but you said you came up here with a man named Buck and a friend. That friend is missing now, and you have blood on your truck. I'm going to have to come back here with a team of deputies and possibly state troopers so we can sweep the forest up there looking for him. That's a lot of time and a lot of money, and our taxpayers can frankly afford neither. So if you know where your friend is-- and again, I'm not asking you to tell me what happened to him, just where he might be--it will make all of our lives much, much easier."

"It wasn't Steiney's blood!" Hank cries. "We shot one o' them. Lord help us, we jes' thought… I mean we thought it was like a huntin' trip. Figgered this Buck guy would want to be cut in on any trophy money. Buck set us up in a clearing with a camera, said he was gonna go check the creek and see if anythin' was happenin' that way. He was gone for over an hour. I mean, he told us no guns, but goddamn if we was gonna sit in the middle o' nothin' without bein' able ta defend ourselves, and—and one o' *them* came out. Tall as me! A girl, I think, 'cuz I could see titties. I know that sounds stupid, but I saw 'em, I don't mean it in a nasty way, I just… I saw 'em and thought Buck was tryin' ta fool us with one of *his* friends in a suit. Thought maybe he paid off Cecilia Dockins from the bar, she's always doin' pranks like that. But then the thing stood up, and there ain't no suit that good. There ain't no mask that realistic, with teeth and… and it roared, and I don't know. I just…suddenly I had the rifle leveled and felt it pop against my shoulder, and this thing's face…her face just

127

fell, you know? All scared and confused, and I don't… I never killed nobody before! I hunt, but I ain't never shot a person, and I thought I did. Thought I kilt Cecilia. Her face, you could see the hurt, like she just din't understand what was happenin'."

Tears form in Hank's eyes. "We jes' stood there fer a minute with the body. Din't know whether ta scratch our watches or wind our butts, ya know? But when we realized what we had…we was happy. Thought our ship had come in. We made sure ta get plenty of pictures. Propped her up, held her arms way out so's you could see the arm span, the foot size, the weird skull shape. We could sell the photos first and then sell the body to science. Thought we was rich, man. Then Buck came runnin' back 'cuz of the noise, and he saw what happened, he… he just freaked out and grabbed Steiney by the back of the neck and smashed his vidya camera, and then… they came. They all came out of the forest and surrounded us and—we just started runnin'. Had ta listen to Steiney screamin' fer us ta come back, and then just plain screamin', and then nothin'."

A pickup truck approaches from behind, coming to a stop behind the cruiser. Hank hears the growl of the engine first and turns to look. He starts slapping Huck's shoulder.

"Huck! Huck! It's him! It's…it's…it's…"

"Sherriff, Officer, sir, that is the truck that's…Bug. Buck. The guy! It's the guy!"

Manley exhales. He rolls his window down and barks the siren twice, motioning for the truck to drive up next to him. It's a monstrous old pickup, beat to hell, the paintjob more rust than pigment.

The window rolls down and a large man leans over to the passenger side. Hank and Huck each press against the side window, trying to peer up to see if they can get a look at the driver.

"Help you, Officer?" a low voice says. It sounds like gravel sliding down a deep muddy river.

Hank and Huck turn pale and instantly press themselves against the opposite side of the car.

"It's him," they whisper.

"We seem to have had an incident out here, and I'm hoping you wouldn't mind answering a few questions for me," Manley says.

There's a silence so long that Manley thinks the guy has passed out. A loud *thunk* as the truck drops into gear and slowly rolls forward. It turns right at the intersection and stops a few yards down the road, safely out of the way of any potential traffic, not that there ever was any up here this time of day. Manley tucks in behind the truck, leaving his flashers on. He tries to radio in to dispatch, but there's no answer other than static squawk. He shakes his head, then pops the door open.

"You ain't callin 'fer backup? Mister, that guy is responsible fer--"

128

"Right to remain silent. And keep your voices down. You want him to run away? Right now he might be the only thing standing between you two and a very lengthy trial."

Manley slams the door and walks toward the truck. "Go ahead and shut her down for me, sir. Thanks."

He stops at the corner of the truck and peeks into the bed. It's streaked with what looks like dried blood. There's torn clothing, old rags, a large shovel. None of it unusual for this neck of the woods.

"You mind stepping out while we talk?" Manley says, stopping a few feet behind the driver's door.

"No problem," the voice rumbles.

The door pops open with a shriek of rusty metal. The largest man that the Sherriff has ever seen clambers down. Easily close to seven feet tall, he was as muscular as the two men had described him.

"You been camping?" Manley asks.

"That what those two say?" the man asks, jutting his chin at Manley's car.

"If you could just answer my questions, I'd be obliged," Manley says.

"Not camping. Hunting. They wanted to see Sasquatch, so we went," the man says.

"Your name Buck?"

"Some people call me that," Buck says.

"Okay, Buck. And what did you--"

A piercing shriek sounds from over the ridge. It echoes across the sky before it's picked up down the road. When that callback dies off, another shriek comes from the other direction down the road.

"I don't patrol this side of the mountain too often. You seem like you know this area," Manley says. "Lotta coyotes out here?"

Buck nods, his face impassive. "Good eatin'."

"Lotta stuff for them to hunt this time of year?"

"Good eatin' for us," Buck says. "Serves us well when there aren't any people around."

"And what does that--"

And now the shriek is loud, so loud that Manley feels like he's inside of it, like the scream is a force of nature that freezes every muscle in his body and turns his blood to ice. It's all around him, echoing, rising and falling, swirling among a cacophony of breaking tree branches and the sound of deep bass drums, rhythmic, running like heavy feet.

His hand instinctively drops to his revolver, but before he can unsnap it, something hits him from behind like a truck. It takes him a few tumbles before he realizes he's rolling across the road and down into a ditch. He splays his legs to stop his momentum, coming to rest just a few inches from a skinny tree just off the other side of the road. His vision is

129

blurry, tinged with white. Each time he blinks he sees shapes moving in the forest, large and looming, circling him, waiting.

From across the road, there's a sound like gunshots, but regular and fierce, like someone's banging away a solo on Satan's drum kit. He reaches for his revolver, but the holster is empty. He scrambles to his feet and runs back to the road. What he sees stops him short. He mistakes it at first for a small group of bears attacking the cruiser, but bears couldn't grow that big. Bears couldn't wield sharpened tree branches and makeshift clubs.

There's a noise behind him like tires squealing on asphalt, but it's bouncing, the scream a very large creature might make if it was running. His head explodes in pain and the world turns purple and white, and then silent.

***

When Manley opens his eyes again, the world has gone upside down. His wrists and ankles burn, his nose and ears feel stuffed with mud. His head throbs in time with a furious and insistent thudding that bumps beneath him. The trees are moving, swaying in the wind. Running. Dancing. His brain slowly comes back online, piecing things together as quickly as it can.

Not trees dancing. Legs. Great, furry, muscular legs. The drums are footsteps. He's tied to a large branch that's being carried along by the big man, Buck, and someone behind him. To either side, great creatures stomp and clear the brush. The sky still has enough sun left that it backlights the creatures. He can't tell what they are, but they can't be human. His brain checks out again and the world goes dark.

***

He wakes, this time seated on the ground, his arms bound in front of him. His feet are tied to a stake in the ground. Buck crouches in front of him, his filthy plaid flannel shirt illuminated by flames from a nearby bonfire.

Someone will see the smoke, Manley thinks. *Help will come.*

He remembers that *he* is the help that would notice these things.

"Awake?" Buck asks.

Manley nods, trying to keep his eyes on the big man and ignore the seated forms of the hairy giants around the fire. There are at least a dozen of them.

"We have a problem," Buck says, his mouth pursing in a grim smile. "The men you were with have committed a crime. They must pay. I must pay for my part in it. But you may be able to help me. Ours are the only lives at stake here, you and me, everything else is decided."

Manley stares at him, unsure of how to proceed. Normally, he'd lean on the badge, tell anyone holding him captive that they were about to have the full weight of the law come down on them. He had a feeling the

130

only law out here was what the creatures around the fire deemed appropriate.

"You need to let me go," Manley says.

"Let you go?" Buck asks. "Not, let us go?"

"Where are the Hicks?"

Buck chuckles. "Hicks. Yes. Yes they are. They're across the fire. They will be dealt with. I'm sorry you have to see this, but I'm also glad you turned up today."

"Kinda like a bad penny that way," Manley says. "Look, I'm unarmed, near as I can tell. There's more of you than me. You look like you could toss me back to Snoqualmie on your own. Just saying, there's really no need to keep me tied up."

Buck thinks on this a minute, then turns to the fire. "*HAKKAH! Hargh, Chaq-chot.*"

The creatures around the fire shrug their shoulders. Buck stands up straight, so tall that Manley can barely see his face behind his massive barrel chest.

"You will not run," Buck says. "If you escaped, what would you do? Tell everyone you see about what happened here. Who would believe you?"

"I'm not even sure if I can walk right now. Your boys there did a number on me."

"Boys? No. Those are our youngest men and women. They are sometimes unaware of their own strength."

Buck reaches down and plucks the stake from the ground, untying Manley's legs.

"Your hands stay tied for now. Stand." He pokes one finger under Manley's armpit and hoists him up.

"Jesus," Manley mutters. He hadn't been lifted that way since he was a toddler.

As soon as he's on his feet, he's greeted with drunken shouting from across the fire.

"Sherriff! Officer! Sir! You gotta help us. You gotta--"

The air splinters under the force of the sustained roar of all of the creatures around the fire. Manley concentrates on stopping his knees from knocking together. The Hicks brothers fall silent.

"You will not speak," Buck tells them.

Their shirts have been stripped off and tied around their wrists. They're bound to a tree by a thin rope around their necks and foreheads, holding their heads perfectly still.

"These men came out here to kill," Buck says.

"Why don't you let me take them in and see that justice is done?"

"Not your justice. Ours."

"Pardon my ignorance, but are you part of a federally-recognized tribe? What jurisdiction do you have--"

131

"This is our land. It has always been and will always be. Men keep taking more and more of it. Where are our children supposed to--"

"I'm sorry, again," Manley says. "You keep saying 'our' like... I mean... look, don't hurt me for this, but you don't exactly look like those others by the fire. Whatever they are."

"Some of us assimilate," Buck says. "We must learn about your society and watch it carefully so that we may continue to survive."

Manley stares at Buck, then looks over at the fire, where some of the other creatures have stood to face him. His eyes dance back and forth between the hairy behemoths and the giant mountain man.

"I shave," Buck says. "It's tedious."

Manley nods as if he understands.

"Years ago, one of our tribe was captured on film, and since that day, more and more people come every year trying to duplicate the footage. Humans are aggressive and not to be trusted. It wasn't long before they stopped coming with cameras and started bringing guns. We had to do something. So we watch, and learn."

"I'm not sure that gives you the right to..." Manley drifts off, unsure how to finish.

"Exactly," Buck answers. "The right to kill. Who has such a right? And why? Would you not kill to protect your family? Did you not swear an oath to protect and serve those in your community?"

"Yes," Manley says. "So you can understand the predicament you're putting me in here."

"We pick a spot in the forest to live. Somewhere remote. Untouched. We live here until man stumbles through. We watch them kill the deer. We watch them pollute the air, cut down our trees, sully our rivers. We abide that. When too many come, we find a Sasquatch hunter with a camera. We bring them out here to let them 'capture' one of us on camera. That gets other humans excited. They all come to that spot in the forest while we're busy moving on, somewhere deeper, ignored and unseen. I find the people to bring. That is my job. It is my job to make sure that they don't bring weapons. I thought these men were unarmed. I bit my tongue while we traveled, even as they wouldn't stop talking about how glorious it would be to kill one of us."

"It wasn't supposed to be like that!" Hank shouts, then winces as one of the creatures threatens him. "We was jus' comin' ta make movies! Steiney was the one brought the guns and wouldn't --"

Hank falls silent as a massive wooden club pulps his head against the tree behind him. One of the creatures holds the bloody weapon, then draws it back again and smashes what's left of Hank's head until his body drops, dangling from the rope around his neck. Huck starts screaming beside him.

The creature turns to Manley and drops the bloody club, screaming, tears in its eyes, a look that Manley understands perfectly.

"They shot her daughter," Buck says. "They took turns posing with the body. They smiled. They smiled!" Buck roars at Huck. "My fault that her daughter has been desecrated."

"But I didn't... I didn't shoot! It was Steiney! Please! Please Officer, tell them they can't do this! You gotta protect me, ya gotta help, officer--"

Huck is silenced as a sharpened spear slams through his neck and into the tree. His feet dance in the twigs and dirt so fast it sounds like the static of a TV tuned to a dead channel. The creature turns the spear, wrenching it back and forth until Huck's head pops free from his neck and topples to the ground.

Buck hangs his head. "It is my fault that she died. I never should have brought the men into the woods."

The tribe turns to face Manley and Buck, closing ranks and blocking the light from the fire. Manley looks at Buck. "Please don't kill me."

"That is up to you," Buck says. "In our tribe, there are three like me who may contact humans. One who teaches, an old one. One who roams. And a young one who learns. It is the greatest honor and the greatest responsibility the tribe can bestow upon us. Our job is to keep humans away, to learn where they're going so we can avoid them, to find the most determined among them and discredit them. I didn't know he had a weapon. I didn't know."

A smaller Sasquatch approaches Buck wielding a club. It points the club at the ground and growls until Buck slowly lowers himself into a sitting position.

"The choice is yours," Buck says to Manley. "I am to face death for my part in her loss. That I found you was a small miracle. I can still be punished. You may yet live on."

"I didn't know I was on trial," Manley says.

"I have made a request of the tribe. They will let you live if you take me back to your town, arrest me for the murders of these three campers. I will spend the rest of my life in prison as atonement for what happened to our lost one. You will say nothing else of what you saw here. You will be a hero."

"And if I say no?"

Buck looks at the tribe surrounding them, lets the silence of the forest and their resolute stillness speak for them. "Don't say no."

"You're going to kill me unless I become an accessory to murder."

"You already are, every day, just by living out here. Actions you don't think twice about echo through these woods for decades. Every year, we have less and less land, less food, more pollution."

"I can't--"

133

"Find a way to *can*," Buck says. "For both of us. This is as close to justice as we can hope for."

Manley spits on the ground, his mind racing for an escape. "Where's my car?"

"It's been moved off of the road. I can lead you back to it easily. The tribe planned to destroy it. I told them to leave it alone and dismantle the Hicks' truck instead. You will take me to town, and I will confess."

Manley ignores the sick feeling in his gut, tries to keep his back as straight as possible. He nods, and the tribe circles them again. One of the Sasquatch moves to Hank's corpse and tears the shirt from his body. He scuttles behind Manley and binds it around his eyes. Manley squeezes his eyes shut, tells himself that the cold wetness is just mud or water from the forest floor.

The leaves and branches rustle around him. The ground pulses with the thud of the tribe's steps. He winces at their growled conversations, feels like he's surrounded by angry bears. After an interminable silence, there comes a distant scream, a unified howl that will echo in Manley's mind every time he sees a full moon over the forest. From beside him, three, short, sharp barks.

"They will watch you. For the rest of your life. Speak of anything else you've ever lived, but never speak of this until the day you die."

The blindfold is yanked away. He's alone in the clearing with Buck, the headless corpses of the hunters arranged around the base of a large tree. The campfire has been extinguished. Buck holds a large burlap sack, wet and bulging.

"Evidence," Buck says, then lays a massive hand on Manley's shoulder and spins him roughly. "Walk."

***

A year and a half later, Manley rolls down the highway in his civilian vehicle, an old SUV that's seen better days. It would only need to make one more trip.

He was a bonafide celebrity. Book deals. Movie deals. All of it. The man who captured the King County Chopper. The trial was quick and efficient, the evidence indisputable, and yesterday Buck had officially been sentenced to three consecutive life terms in prison for the murders of the Hicks brothers and their friend. Justice was served.

Manley felt like hell. In court, after the verdicts, he had to bite the inside of his cheek when the Hicks family came over to thank him. When they walked away, he hustled to the bathroom and lost his lunch. He was a damned liar. A hero cop and a disgrace to his badge. He'd still cash the checks.

He'd tried to go fishing a few times to clear his head, shortly after bringing Buck in to town. It was too loud in the forest now, even when nothing made a sound. Everything was too close and too vast and formless.

134

He arrived the next day in the desert outside of Palm Springs, where he settled in to a small trailer on a vast patch of treeless land. During the day, the bottle helped keep the echoes of the two men's screams out of his head. At night, when the coyotes were hunting, he'd stay awake, red-eyed and drenched in cold sweat, clutching his gun to his chest.

He aimed at every shadow that moved, and when the howls came, he joined them, raving into the cloudless sky, the closest thing to a confession he'd ever offer the world.

-THE-
NUCKELAVEE
A HELLBOY STORY

WHO WILL SURVIVE THE MARAUDING HORSEMAN FROM THE SEA?

Jim Kavanagh

Drive-In Creature Feature Anthology *Presents a*
Christopher Golden & Mike Mignola *story*
The Nuckelavee *edited by* **Eugene Johnson** *and*
Charles Day *Produced by* **Evil Jester Press**
Copyright 2016 MH | Medievil Horror equestrian terror

137

Christopher Golden

Christopher Golden is the *New York Times* bestselling, Bram Stoker Award®-winning author of such novels as *Of Saints and Shadows, Tin Men, Strangewood* and *Snowblind,* and the editor of such anthologies as *Seize the Night, The New Dead*, and the upcoming *Dark Cities.* With *Hellboy* creator Mike Mignola, he is the co-creator of two cult favorite comics series, *Baltimore* and *Joe Golem: Occult Detective.* Golden was born and raised in Massachusetts, where he still lives with his family. His original novels have been published in more than fourteen languages in countries around the world.

Please visit him at www.christophergolden.com

Mike Mignola

Mike Mignola is best known as the award-winning creator/writer/artist of *Hellboy,* now celebrating its 22nd Anniversary! He was visual consultant to director Guillermo del Toro on both *Hellboy and Hellboy 2:The Golden Army* films. He also co-authored (with Christopher Golden) two novels *Baltimore, or, The Steadfast Tin Soldier and the Vampire* and *Joe Golem and the Drowning City.* Mignola lives in southern California with his wife and cat.

THE NUCKELAVEE

A Hellboy story by
Christopher Golden & Mike Mignola

The old man had a shuddery way about him, a fidgety, near-to-tears aspect to every glance and gesture that said he'd jump at every shadow, if only he had the strength. If only he weren't so damned old. But his eyes weren't old. His eyes were wild with terror.

It was a cold, clear evening in the north of Scotland, and the sky was striped with colors, from a bruised blue on one horizon to the pink of sorrow or humiliation on the other. The rolling hills that surrounded the crumbling stone estate had no name save for that of the family which had resided there for more than five hundred years: MacCrimmon.

"That's it, then. Just as I said. It's dry as kindling, now, and ne'er will run again," said the old man, whose name was Andrew MacCrimmon.

He was the last of them.

MacCrimmon's wild eyes darted about like those of a skittish horse, as though he waited for some shade to steal upon him. Night had not quite fallen, and already, it seemed the man might die of fright, heart stilled in his chest so as not to be heard by whatever he feared might be hunting him.

Whatever it was, it had to be horrible, for the old man stood on the slope of the hill beside a creature whose countenance would give a hardened killer a week of restless nights and ugly dreams. Hellboy carried himself like a man, but his hooves and tail, his sawed-off horn-stumps, and his sheer size spoke another truth.

There were those who thought him a devil. But Andrew MacCrimmon would have sought help of the devil himself if he thought it would have done him any good.

"You'll stay, then, won't you?" the old man asked. "You must."

Hellboy grunted. He stared at the dry river bed, gazing along its path in both directions. It didn't make any sense at all to him, but he hadn't been there more than fifteen minutes. Just a short way up the bank of the dry river was a small stone building. When the water had still run through there, it would have stood have in, half out of the river.

"What's that?" Hellboy started off toward the stone structure.

"Ye don't understand," the old man whimpered. "Ye've got to help me. I was given to understand that ye do that sort of thing."

As he approached the small building, Hellboy narrowed his eyes. The thing was ancient. Older, even, than the MacCrimmon place, which stood on the hill behind them. It wouldn't have been called a castle; too small for that. But it was too big to be just a house, and too dilapidated to be called a mansion.

But this other thing . . .

"What is this?" he asked again.

"It's as old as the family," the old man told him. "Been there from the start. My grandfather told me he thought it was the reason the MacCrimmons settled here."

Hellboy studied the structure, the ancient stone was plain, but overgrown with ivy save for where the water would have washed across it before the river had gone dry. Centuries of water erosion had smoothed the stone, but Hellboy could still make out the faintest impression of carving. Once upon a time, there had been something drawn or written on that stone surface, but it was gone now.

Curiously, he clumped down into the dry river bed and around the other side of the edifice. His hooves sank in the still damp soil. There was something else on the river side of the building. Set into the stone, there was what appeared to be a door.

"How do you get in there?" he asked.

The old man whimpered.

There were no handles of any kind, nor any edges upon which he might get a significant grip. Still, Hellboy tried to open the door, to no avail.

"Please, sir, ye must listen to me," MacCrimmon begged.

Hellboy paused to regard him. The man's long hair and thick, bristly beard were white, and his face was deeply lined. He might have been a hermit, a squatter on this land, rather than its lord. Of course, "lord" was a dubious title when it referred to the crumbling family home, and a clan which no longer existed.

"Go on."

"The river was here before us, but the legend around the doom of Clan MacCrimmon was born right here on this hill. When the river goes dry, the legend says, it'll mean the end of Clan MacCrimmon. I've no children, ye see. I'm the last of the clan. Now that the river is dry, death will be coming for me.

"I knew it right off," the old man said, becoming more and more agitated. "Took three days for the river to run dry. Three days, you understand?"

Hellboy grunted. "Not really."

140

It was then that he noticed that the river wasn't completely dry. A tiny trickle of water ran past the door, past the building. It wasn't more than three inches wide, and barely deep enough to dampen the earth, but it was there. Hellboy reached down to put his finger into the water, and MacCrimmon cried out as if in pain.

"No, you mustn't! It's the doom of the MacCrimmons, don't you see? When the water stops running, the doom of my clan will be released."

"That's . . . interesting." With a shrug, Hellboy stepped up onto the slope again. "So what do you expect me to do?" he asked, massively confused by the old man's babbling. "Some legend says you're gonna die, I don't know how I'm supposed to deal with that."

The old man clutched at Hellboy's arm with both hands, eyes flicking back and forth in that disturbing, desperate twitch.

"You'll stay for dinner," he said, but it wasn't really question. "You'll stay, and you'll see."

It was a very long drive back to anywhere Hellboy might stay that he wouldn't be shot at by local farmers or constabulary, so when Andrew MacCrimmon urged him on, he trekked up the hill to the crumbling manse alongside the old man. It was a gloomy place, a testament to entropy, with barely a whisper of the grandeur it must once have had.

***

Once they had entered, Hellboy saw that he had not been entirely correct about its origins based on his initial observations. While the manse itself was no more than three hundred years old, it was built around an older structure, a cruder, more fundamental tower or battlement, that must once have served as home and fortress for whomever had built it.

MacCrimmon Keep, someone at the BPRD had called it. Hellboy hadn't understood before, but now he saw it. This was the keep, and the rest of the place had been built up around it.

When they had settled inside, the old man brought out cold pork roast and slightly stale bread. There was haggis as well, but it looked like it might have gone over somewhat. Not that Hellboy was the world's greatest expert on haggis, but there was a greenish tint to it that made him even less likely to eat it than if he'd been trapped for a week on Everest with nothing to gnaw on but coffee grounds and it was a choice between haggis or his fellow climbers -- which was pretty much the only way he would've eaten haggis even if it were fresh.

"Sorry I don't have more to offer," MacCrimmon muttered, a mouthful of questionable haggis visible between what was left of his teeth as he spoke. "The cook and t'other servants left three days ago, when the river started to slow. They <u>know</u>, y'see. They know."

When the meal was done, MacCrimmon seemed twitchier than

141

ever. The manse was filled with sounds, as every old building is -- a sign of age like the rings in a tree stump. The old man must have been familiar with most of those sounds, but now they frightened him, each and every one. He seemed to draw into himself, collapsing down upon his own body, becoming smaller. Decaying already, perhaps, at the thought of death's imminent arrival. Or imagined arrival.

"Cigar?" he asked suddenly, as if it were an accusation.

Hellboy flinched, startled. "Sure."

MacCrimmon led him to the library, which was larger than the enormous dining room they'd just left. Two walls were lined floor to ceiling with old, desiccated books, but Hellboy's eyes were drawn immediately to the other walls. To the paintings there, above and around the fireplace -- where the old man now built a roaring blaze -- and around the windows on the outer wall. Clan MacCrimmon came to life on those walls, in the deep hues and swirls of each portrait, but none of them was more vibrantly powerful than the one at the center of the outer wall. It hung between two enormous, drafty, rattling windows, and seemed, almost, a window itself. A window onto another time, and another shade of humanity. For the figure in the portrait was a warrior, that much was clear.

"Clan MacCrimmon?" Hellboy asked, glancing at the other portraits on the wall.

The old man seemed reluctant even to look at the portraits, but he nodded his assent as he handed Hellboy a cigar. With wooden matches, they lit the sweet-smelling things and began to smoke. After a short while in which nothing was spoken between them, the old man looked up at the portrait of the warrior that hung between the windows.

"That'd be William MacCrimmon. A warrior, he was, and fierce enough to survive that calling. Old William lost his closest friend in battle in 1453, and promised to care for the other warrior's daughter, Margaret."

Hellboy took a long puff on the cigar, then let the smoke out in a huff as he studied the old man. MacCrimmon was warming to the story of his ancestor, clinging to it as though it were a life preserver. It might only have been a way to pass the time, but Hellboy wondered if, in some way, it was the old man's way to keep his fears at bay, just for a while.

"Though already quite old for his time, William fell in love with Margaret, and married her. It was a sensible thing, perhaps the best way to care for the girl. Trouble was, Margaret was a Christian. William had to make some changes. He wasn't from the mainland, ye see. But from the Isle of Malleen. Margaret wouldn't hear of living on the island, for there were stories, even then, of the things which thrived on Malleen."

Hellboy raised an eyebrow and scratched the stubble on his chin. "Things?"

For the first time since he began the story, MacCrimmon looked at him. The old man grinned madly.

142

"Why, the fuathan, o' course. Ye've never heard of them?"

Hellboy didn't respond. Considering the job, he didn't study nearly as much as he should. The old man didn't seem to notice, his attention drawn back to the portrait of his warrior ancestor.

"Old William had known the people, the fuathan, since he was a bairn, ye ken. Shaggy little beasts that might be men if not for the way nature twisted their bodies. The legends say they hated men, but not so, not so. They were the servants and allies of the islanders, and held malice only for those from the mainland.

"Still, when William married Margaret, and chose to remain here in the North Country, rather than return to the island, the fuathan had no choice. They came along. It were they who built the original keep, and that pile out in the river bed. It were they who made the river run, so the legend goes, for the fuathan were ever in control of the water.

"What it was built to house, the legends dinna say, but the story has it that they raised it in a day, and the keep itself in a week, all the while, making certain Margaret MacCrimmon would never see them. There's a circle of stones in the wood over the hill that were used for worship. The fuathan lived there, in the wood around the circle, and the clan grew with both the new religion and the old faith."

Hellboy shivered. He'd heard similar stories dozens of times, about the encroachment of Christianity into pagan territories, one family at a time. But in this case, with the results crumbling and gloomy around him, it seemed far more tangible. Honestly, it gave him the creeps. The clash of old and new faiths could not have been a healthy one. He had to wonder what it had done to the offspring of that union, down across the centuries.

The old man seemed to have run out of steam, though he still stared at the portrait of the warrior. And there was something odd about that portrait, something that held the eye. Hellboy tore his gaze away, took a puff of his cigar, and turned his attention on the old man again.

"So you live here alone, now? I mean, except for the servants who ran off?"

"Last of the clan," MacCrimmon agreed, apparently forgetting that he'd told Hellboy that already. "Alone here since my brother died."

With the fat cigar clenched in his teeth, the old man moved to the stone fireplace, the blazing light flickering over his features. There were faded photographs in silver frames on the mantel, and MacCrimmon pulled one of them down and handed it to Hellboy. In the corner, a dusty grandfather clock ticked the seconds by, its pendulum glinting with the light of the fire as it swung back and forth.

In the photograph, two young men flanked a beautiful girl, whose raven hair and fine china features reminded Hellboy of a woman he had once known. He pushed the thought away. The two men were obviously MacCrimmon and his brother. Though Andrew had grown old now,

143

though his face was wrinkled and bearded, the eyes staring out of that photograph were the same.

Wild, even then. Hellboy had to wonder if the man had ever been sane.

He handed the photograph back to the old man. "Who's the girl?"

MacCrimmon set his cigar on the stone mantel, and stared at the photo, a dreamy look relaxing his features for the first time since Hellboy had arrived.

"That'd be Sarah Kirkwall. She was here all that long summer. This photo was taken the day before me brother Robert announced that they were to be engaged." The old man frowned, and rubbed distractedly at his forehead. When he spoke again, his voice was lost and far away. "They lived here, with me, until Robert . . . died. I told Sarah she could stay, that I'd care for her, just as Old William MacCrimmon had taken care of Margaret five hundred years ago. That she could . . . marry me."

The anguish in the old man's voice was horrible to hear, and Hellboy felt the sadness in that old stone dwelling creeping into his bones.

"So you married?"

The old man shook his head, still staring at the photo. "It were Robert she loved. When he died, she . . . went away. I never did marry. Sarah was the girl for me. There never were anyone else."

MacCrimmon looked even older now, shrunken, staring down at the photograph as though trapped, now, in that other time, back when. Hellboy thought again of the portrait of the warrior on the wall, how it looked almost like a window on another time, and seemed to draw you in. The photograph in the silver frame had the same effect on the old man.

Hellboy scratch the back of his neck, where what hair he had was tied back in a knot. "How did Robert die?" he asked.

The frame tumbled from the old man's hands and shattered on the stone in front of the fireplace. Hellboy prepared to catch MacCrimmon, thinking he must be about to collapse, but the old man just stared at his hands, the spot where the frame had been. Slowly, he reached out and took his cigar from the mantel, and pulled a long puff on it.

"Ten years ago, this very night," MacCrimmon said.

He seemed almost calm, and then a shudder ran through him and he turned and looked at the grandfather clock. When he spoke again, his voice cracked with a panic he could no longer hide.

"Ten years ago tonight," he repeated. "He died at three minutes past nine."

Hellboy glanced at the clock. It was only a few minutes before nine then, half a dozen minutes to go before the dreadful anniversary.

With that edge of panic still in his voice, the old man continued. "He was three days sick, dying, before he went at last. Just as the river was three days, drying up. Now it's almost time. The last trickle will run through the dry bed out there, and he'll come for me."

144

Minutes ticked by and Hellboy just watched the old man in silence. The cigar burned in MacCrimmon's hand, but he made no effort to smoke it. Then, suddenly, the old man glanced at the burning weed in his hand, and he narrowed his gaze, as if seeing it for the first time. With a tremor of disgust, he threw the cigar into the fire, which now had begun to burn low. The flames flared up inexplicably, tendrils of fire lashing out at the stone masonry, then dying down again.

The grandfather clock chimed nine.

Andrew MacCrimmon dropped to his knees before Hellboy, tears beginning to slip down his craggy features.

"Save me!" he pleaded.

Hellboy only looked at him dubiously.

The clock continued to chime.

As if he'd been startled by some sudden noise, the old man turned his head and glanced about, eyes more wild than ever, hands on his head as though he might hide himself away.

"Did ye not hear that? It's the doom of the MacCrimmons!"

"It's just the clock," Hellboy told him.

The old man rushed to one of the wind-rattled windows and threw it open. He leaned out, but Hellboy knew that from that angle, there was no way MacCrimmon could see what he was looking for. The river bed, of course, and that little stone building the man had insisted was built by horrid little fairy creatures.

"Not the clock! Don't you see? It's him. It's *it*. The stream's gone dry, and it's coming out; battering down that door. It's coming up the lawn now, coming for me!"

The old man turned from the window and fell again at Hellboy's feet. He clutched the bottom of Hellboy's duster and buried his face in it, whimpering, muttering.

Hellboy frowned. "Did you bury your brother in that little building out there?"

"You saw that place," the old man stammered. "There's no way to open it from the outside, but . . . from the inside . . . no. Robert's cremated and his ashes are in a niche at St. Brendan's, where they ought to be. But . . ."

MacCrimmon gripped his jacket even more tightly, his voice barely a whisper. "There, you *must* hear it. It's coming for me. His ghost has set it free. There! It's broken down the door. Can't you hear it on the stairs?"

Hellboy heard nothing. He looked down at the old man and felt a little sorry for him, though he had a strong suspicion what had driven him so completely mad.

"You killed him."

The old man wailed. "Robert has loosed the doom of the MacCrimmons on me for murderin' him. I fed him poison and sat by those three days while it killed him. I did it for her, I did it for the girl, and it wasn't ever me that she wanted . . ."

His voice trailed off after that. He fell quiet, listening. Then the old man jerked, suddenly, as if he'd been pinched.

"It's there now!" he screamed, voice raspy and hoarse. "In the hall, just outside the door. Please, help me. Take me with you. Kill me! Anything. Just don't let that thing take me!"

Despite the old man's mad cries, however, the room was silent save for his blubbering and the ticking of the clock. On the face of that antique timekeeper, the long hand had moved inexorably along so that it was now four or five minutes after nine o'clock. The anniversary of Robert MacCrimmon's death had come and gone.

"Don't have a heart attack or anything," Hellboy said. "Look, I'll show you."

He reached for the door knob, shaking his head ruefully. But just as his fingers touched it, the door came crashing down at him, tearing off its hinges and slamming Hellboy to the floor.

"Jeez!" he shouted in surprise.

As he tried to get out from under the heavy door, a sudden and tremendous weight was put on it from above, pinning him there. Hellboy grunted in pain, struggled to move, and could not. There was a horrid stench, like nothing he had ever smelled before, death and rot and fecal matter, blood and sweat and urine, matted horse hair and putrefying fish, and something else, something worse than all of those disgusting odors combined.

Then, without warning, the weight was removed. Something stepped off the door and into the room. Hellboy summoned his strength and his anger, and tossed the shattered door off him. He glanced around, and then he saw it, one of the most horrifying monstrosities he had ever laid eyes on. It was like a huge, equine creature that might have been a horse if it had any skin. Instead, there was only naked purple muscle and white tendons and swollen black veins. Growing out of its back was a human torso, also stripped of skin, with a head that swung about wildly as if there were no bones in its neck. Its huge mouths, both human and horse, gaped open and that stink poured out, almost visible, like breath in winter.

Its long arms snaked out and grabbed hold of old man MacCrimmon, and hauled him up onto the back of its horse segment. Hellboy started to roar, started to lunge for it, but a hoof lashed out and cracked against his skull, and he went down hard on the floor of the library, not far from the blazing fire.

By the time he shook off the blow, the creature was gone, the old man's screams echoing through the house and down the hillside. Hellboy rose, ready to give chase, but the fire flared again, and he turned to see that it was blue now. Tendrils of blue flame shot out of the blaze and

146

seemed to touch each of the portraits in turn, ending with that of William MacCrimmon, founder of the clan.

Blue fire seemed to seep into the portrait, becoming paint, becoming one with the history in that window on that past. It truly was a window now, and through it, Hellboy could see the old warrior moving, turning to glare into the library with a stern countenance, cold and cruel in judgement. Tendrils of blue flame jumped from portrait to portrait, and the painted images of the warrior's descendants were somehow erased from their own frames, to appear behind the original, the founder. That portrait seemed to grow, with all of them standing therein, arms crossed before them, glaring down like inquisitors.

Then the portrait burst into flame, and Hellboy heard an enormous crack. The keep, the part of the MacCrimmon homestead that had been built so long ago by the fuathan, began to fall, to collapse down into the remainder of the house. The shelves and books in the library were set aflame, but the flame was nearly snuffed out as the walls collapsed, tumbling toward Hellboy.

He ran for one of the huge windows, not daring to look at the burning, living painting, at the ghosts of the clan MacCrimmon, for fear he might be sucked into that collective past. Hellboy crashed out through the window and fell twenty feet to the hillside below. The walls were crumbling in on themselves, but several stones came falling after him, and he rushed to avoid being crushed or buried.

He could hear Andrew MacCrimmon screaming, down the hill, where the river bed was now completely dry. Hooves pounding the grass, Hellboy gave chase. Where the river had run, he saw hoof prints from the beast in the soft, damp earth. As he passed the structure that stood on the river's edge, he saw that the stone door he had found impossible to open now hung wide. Seconds after he crossed the dry river bed, he heard a kind of explosion, and turned to see that even that stone structure had been part of the chain reaction. It was nothing but rubble now.

The doom of the MacCrimmons had come, all right.

There came another scream. Hellboy glanced up the opposite hill and saw the beast disappearing over its crest, looking like nothing more than a large horse bearing two riders. But the way its raw, skinless form glistened wetly in the moonlight . . . it was no horse.

***

When he reached the top of the hill, however, neither beast nor man were anywhere in sight. Hellboy crouched in the spot he had last seen them, and found a trail. It was relatively easy to track; the beast was so heavy that its hooves left prints in the hardest, dryest ground.

Hellboy followed.

Hours passed, and he made his way across farms and estates,

through groves and over hills, and finally he came to a town on the north coast, the tang of the ocean in the air, the sound of the tides carrying through the streets. It was after midnight, and most of the residents had long since retired for the evening. In the midst of the town, on a paved road, he lost the trail. Hopelessly, he looked around for someone who might have seen something. After a minute or two, he spotted a portly man slumped in a heavy, old chair on the porch of what appeared to be some kind of mercantile.

"Hey, wake up," Hellboy said, nudging the portly man with the weight of his stone hand.

The man snorted, blinked his eyes open, and let out a yell of surprise and fear. The odor of whiskey came off him in waves.

"Quiet," Hellboy snapped. "I'm just passing through."

"Thank the Lord for that," the man said in a frightened whisper.

"You see anything strange go through here?"

The man stared at him as if he were insane.

"Anything *worse*?" Hellboy elaborated.

"Depends on your definition of strange, I suppose," the man said. "Two men came through, not long ago. Two men riding the same horse. Only one of them wasn't riding. He *was* the horse. That's pretty strange."

"You see where it went?" Hellboy demanded.

"Down to the rocks," the man replied. "Down to the sea. And that old one screaming all the way. Weren't a surprise, though. I'd scream too, that horse, and the whole thing smelling like a fisherman's toilet."

His voice trailed off and he moaned a bit, and fell back to sleep, or into unconsciousness. The whiskey had claimed him again.

Hellboy scratched his chin and looked along the paved road to the rocks and the ocean beyond. He could hear the waves crashing, and he started to walk toward them. At the end of the road, he stopped where the rocks began. There was a cough off to his left, and he turned to see an old woman standing on the front stoop of her home in a robe that was insufficient for the chill ocean breeze.

"It was a Nuckelavee," she told him.

Hellboy looked at her oddly, but she didn't even turn her face to him. She just stared out at the ocean.

"When I was but a wee girl in the Hebrides, my father told me a story. He were coming home late one night, and a Nuckelavee come up out of the ocean and chased him. He only escaped by jumping over a little stream of fresh water. The monster roared and spit and with one long arm snatched off me father's hat, but he got away clean save for a pair of claw marks to show off to prove the truth of it."

Now she looked straight at Hellboy for the first time.

"He was luckier than that old man tonight. That's certain."

Hellboy nodded and looked out across the waves again. He could see a dark hump in the distance, out on the ocean.

148

"What's that?"

The old woman hesitated. At length, she spoke, her voice low and haunted. "'Tis the Isle of Malleen. But don't ye think about goin' out there. It's not a place fit for man, nor e'en a thing such as yourself. There's only evil out there, dark and cruel. If that's where the Nuckelavee was headed, no wonder the old man were screaming so."

Hellboy consider her words, staring at the island in the distance.

"I guess maybe he deserved it," he said after a bit. "I'm starting to wonder if maybe all it did was take that old man home. And I think there'll be hell to pay when he gets there."

The wind shifted, then, and for a moment, it seemed as though he could hear a distant scream, high and shrill and inhuman. But then the waves crashed down again on the rocks, and it was gone.

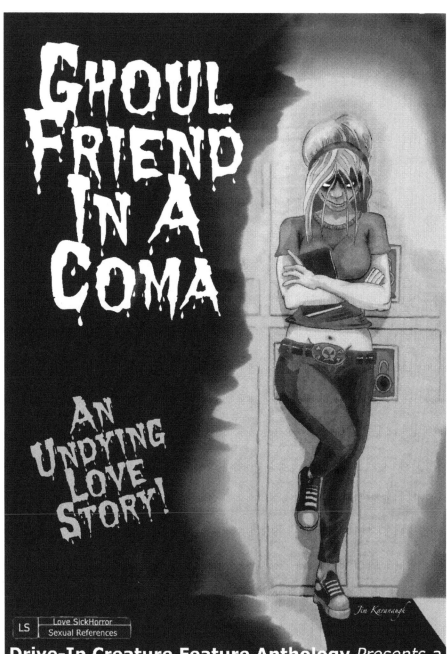

Jim Kavanaugh

Drive-In Creature Feature Anthology *Presents a*
John Everson *story* **Ghoul Friend In A Coma**
edited by **Eugene Johnson** *and* **Charles Day**
Produced by **Evil Jester Press** *Copyright 2016*

John Everson

John Everson is a staunch advocate for the culinary joys of the jalapeno and an unabashed fan of 1970s European horror cinema. He is also the Bram Stoker Award®-winning author of *Covenant* and seven other novels, including the creature feature spiderfest *Violet Eyes*, the erotic horror Bram Stoker Award® finalist *NightWhere*, and his latest, the seductive backwoods tale of *The Family Tree*. Other novels include *Sacrifice, The Pumpkin Man, Siren* and *The 13th*. Over the past 20 years, his short stories have appeared in more than 75 magazines and anthologies. His fourth fiction collection, *Sacrificing Virgins*, was released from Samhain Publishing at the end of 2015. For more information on his obsession with chili peppers, as well as his fiction, art and music, visit www.johneverson.com.

GHOUL FRIEND IN A COMA

John Everson

You know, whether they're dead, alive, or somewhere in between... all girls are the same. They want your undivided attention. "Love, love me do." There was never a better four-word phrase written to describe girls.

Maybe that's why I started to notice Regina. She seemed so quiet and shy. So totally NOT like the other girls. She was pretty, I guess, in a quiet way, too. But she didn't really let you notice. She always wore loose jeans and t-shirts, usually with some kind of longer shirt buttoned over them, sleeves half-rolled up. Except when it got really hot. She didn't do much with her hair, but it was snow-blond and looked full and glossy despite her lack of effort; she wore it curled loosely over her shoulder. Mostly, she let strands of it hang down half over her face, which hid her eyes much of the time. The guys in class didn't pay her any attention; they were all focused on the spandex and lip-gloss girls.

Maybe that's why I noticed her. The cheerleader mallrats just annoyed me. I couldn't stand to listen to them. And certainly none of them ever talked to me.

Don't get me wrong though, that's not to say I didn't have a girlfriend. Amy planted herself next to me at the lunch table every day, and I had learned a long time ago not to try to walk home from school without her. I can't say that I ever actually asked her out. And most of the time she was around, I'd frankly have preferred to be by myself. But... she was useful when it came to working on term papers. And my mom loved her. That alone made it worth keeping her around. Mom left me alone when Amy was over.

So, anyway... you can imagine that I had to be careful of my eyes for Regina. I'd never even really talked to her. I figured she was pretty smart though, because she took more sick days than anyone I knew – and she still managed to pass her tests, at least in the classes I had with her – English Lit and Calculus.

Today was one of those days that I noticed her seat was empty.

153

Normally I wouldn't have worried, but then right after 7th period, the principal came on the overhead with an announcement.

"This is a reminder that the Renfield Meadows curfew remains in effect. Please make sure if you are walking or bicycling to go straight home today. Be safe, not sorry. Thank you."

The bell rang then, and everyone jumped up to head for the door.

Shit. The last time they made one of those announcements, there'd been a freshman missing. That was almost a month ago, and they still hadn't found the body.

"Who do you think it is this time?" Amy said, latching onto my arm in the hallway. I resisted the urge to yank my arm away when she wrapped her fingers around it. Every day I reminded myself that she gave me a cover. As long as she was my "girlfriend," I didn't have to deal with a bunch of other shit. I wore Amy like a security blanket. That sounds lousy, I know but hey... she was happy... I was, mostly, happy. It worked, okay?

"Another dorky freshman who wandered into the forest preserve, you think?"

I shrugged. "Maybe."

She laughed, and leaned her head on my shoulder as we walked. I blew a ringlet of her black kinky hair out of my mouth.

"Will you walk me home and keep me safe?" she asked.

I shrugged again. "Maybe."

I was a real catch of a boyfriend, I know. But she never seemed to notice.

"C'mon," she said, yanking me forward. "I want to stop at Burger Palace on the way. I'm starved."

Nobody was ever going to look at Amy and worry about her being starved, but I knew better than to argue. At least when she had food in her mouth, she shut up for a minute. OK, maybe only 30 seconds, but I took what I could get.

***

The next morning, I saw Regina walking down the hall and it's weird to say, but when I saw her, I instantly felt better. I still hadn't heard who the latest kid was that was missing, so I guess part of me had wondered if it was her. But no, there she was, head down with an armload of books. Just as I noticed her, and felt better knowing she was okay, I saw one of the spandex girls pull a typical mallrat move. Sandra Tolley held one arm out, right in front of Regina. A second later, that arm connected with Regina's stack of textbooks, and that carefully stacked pile was suddenly up in the air. You could barely hear it above the noise of a hallway full of kids, but I heard the books hit the tile with a sharp *slap, slap...slap*. A couple pieces of loose-leaf flew into the air and disappeared in the rush of milling teens. I saw Sandra stifle a laugh just before she gave the most unauthentic apology ever. "Oh, I'm *sooo* sorry," she said to Regina. "You really should watch where you're walking though."

With that, she disappeared into the crowd to join her friends as Regina scrambled to reclaim her stuff.

I bent down to pick up her history book, and grabbed a couple assignment pages that already had shoe marks on them. "Here you go," I said, as we both stood.

She looked at me through a loose lock of hair the color of fresh cream. "Thanks," she whispered. "You didn't have to."

I shrugged. "But I wanted to."

Her lips seemed to smile, just a little, and I realized for the first time that her eyes were blue; pale, piercing, ice blue.

"Well, thanks then." She said. I could barely hear her voice above the din around us. And then came a voice that I could hear above every other.

"There you are!" Amy said. She slapped a mitt full of fingers around my biceps and pulled me to the side a step. "I waited for you at your locker, but you never turned up."

I shrugged. "I got here a little early and was heading to class when I..."

"When you decided to chat with Weird Girl? What did she want?"

I looked away from her and saw that Regina had already vanished.

"Nothing," I said. "Someone pushed her and I helped her pick up her stuff."

Amy smiled and ran her hand across the back of my head. Kind of like she was petting a dog. "Well, aren't you just a Knight in Shining Armor. Maybe tonight you can carry my books for me, huh?"

The warning bell saved me, and after a perfunctory kiss we separated and went opposite directions to class.

***

It was only a week later that we got another one of those "watch your back" announcements over the loudspeaker. Joe Watson groaned behind me and said out loud what we were all thinking. "Holy shit, another one?"

"Joseph!" Mrs. Powers yelled, but it didn't matter. The final bell went off and we bolted like a stampede for the door. Curfew or not, killer or not, we all just wanted to be out of that school.

"You think it's someone from Heller High?" Phil asked, falling into step next to me.

I shrugged. "Doesn't really matter. It wasn't us, and they still

155

haven't caught the guy."

"How do you know it's a guy?" Amy asked. I could hear the breath catch in her throat; she'd obviously run to catch up, not wanting to miss a minute of *my* conversation with *my* friend. "You know there are female serial killers too."

"She's right," Phil said. "Girls can be nastier than guys."

"Gotta agree with you there," I said.

"What do you mean by that?" Amy said, and punched me in the shoulder.

"Hey," Phil said, changing the subject. "Do you guys want to get together tomorrow night? Watson got a 12-pack off his older brother, and we were going to drink 'em out by County Line."

"What about the curfew?" I asked.

"We'll stay hidden. You know that ditch we used last month? It's perfect. It's unincorporated, so the cops don't patrol it, and it's deep enough that you can't really see it from the road."

"And the killer?"

"That bitch is not going to fuck with a group of us."

I took a glance at Amy. She was no longer happy with the female killer idea, I could tell.

"I'll have to see if I can sneak out."

"You could come study at my house," Amy said.

"That's a good excuse," I agreed.

"No... I meant, you really could come over."

"What time, Phil?" I asked, ignoring her point.

"Probably get there around 9, after it's dark."

"Perfect," I said. "See you then."

Phil nodded and took off towards his block. Amy was irritated that I was choosing beer in the ditch over an evening at her house. It was refreshing. She didn't say anything for about three blocks. And then finally...

"So what time are you picking me up?"

***

While it was possible to hide out in the ditch and not be seen, Phil and Joe and Larry were not exactly trying too hard. Amy and I rode our 10-speeds out to the spot, because it was only a couple miles. We'd just passed the Rollin Pesticide plant at the end of the industrial park when I spotted them up ahead. Their flashlights bobbed back and forth from the side of the road and occasionally caught on the undersides of the trees nearby.

Two minutes later, we dropped the bikes at the bottom of the grassy gulch. Joe held out a bottle to each of us. "Happy hoppy Saturday!"

I held it up. The bottle was brown, and the label was dominated

156

by a frog with an enormous belly. HopOrtunity, the label said.

"Is it any good?" I asked.

Joe shrugged. "Who cares? It's beer and it's free."

There was some wisdom in that. Something along the lines of "Don't look a gift horse…"

I took a swig, and the bitter metallic taste slapped me across the face. When I breathed out, I could taste it in my nose.

I raised an eyebrow and took a breath before looking around. The road behind us was empty, but I could see the parking lot lights from the industrial park just a quarter mile down the road. "Where did you park?" I asked. I knew that someone had driven; there were no bikes in the ditch but ours.

Phil pointed to the trees. "Right back there."

There was a small gravel drive just a few yards away that cut across the ditch and wound back into the scrub trees beyond.

Next to me, Amy started to cough. I turned to look, and her mouth was crinkled up in a horrible grimace. She held the bottle out in front of her like it was poison.

Phil laughed, and took the bottle from her hand. "Not Hoppy with it?"

"That tastes like kitchen counter cleanser!" she said.

"No worries," Joe said. He rooted around in a duffel bag for a minute, and came up with a clear bottle with a plain label. All I could read on it was the word "Vodka."

"Always have a fallback position," he explained.

Amy smiled. "You're the best," she said. I could see her sneaking a glance at me to see if I was noticing how happy Joe had made her. I suppose she wanted me to feel guilty. I just took another swig of my beer. I reached out a hand to Phil and took back her abandoned bottle. "I can take care of that for her," I said.

Amy shook her head, visibly annoyed that I wasn't reacting. "You wouldn't have a Coke by any chance, would you?" she asked.

"I'm a boy scout," Joe said.

"You're the best!" Amy purred, and kissed him on the cheek. She glanced back with a "look at me" grin, and I raised my bottle to toast her.

I could tell that wasn't the reaction she was going for. But jealousy? She wasn't going to get that from me.

"Don't chug all of that," a voice came from the ground beyond Phil and Joe. Lydia propped herself up on one elbow, taking a break from roto-routing Larry's tonsils. "I want some when I'm done here."

With that she buried Larry's face in her hair again, and Phil snorted. "By the time she's 'done there' we're going to be on the way home."

He turned on a boom box and pretty soon the ditch was rocking with both laughter and guitars. It was a good Friday night in the Middle of

157

Nowhere U.S.A.

About an hour later, as Amy lay with her head in my lap and Phil was going on about the godlikeness of his newest favorite guitarist (he had a new guitar hero every month), Joe suddenly stopped in mid-sentence and barked, "kill the radio."

Phil slapped his hand on the volume, and everyone was quiet. I understood why a second later, as the sound of crunching gravel came from nearby.

I was staring in just the right spot to see the car, as it turned off the two-lane and crept towards the trees. And I could see the driver clearly as the car crossed over the ditch. There was no mistaking that pale face and even lighter hair. It was Regina.

She was driving an old beat-up Toyota. I'd seen her in it at school, so it only took a glance and I was sure it was her. She didn't seem to see us in the ditch below as she crossed over and then began to speed down the lane to disappear into the trees.

"What's back there?" Joe asked, just before he turned the radio back on.

"Might be an old farmhouse or something," Phil said. "There aren't any subdivisions this far out."

"Huh," Joe said. "Never had anyone go down that road while we were here before."

Amy piped up. "Well, that's it, party's over. Guess you'll have to find a new ditch to drink in!"

Joe shook his head. "Seven bottles left. We've got a while to go. You'd better just talk to your vodka."

Amy smirked and put the bottle to her lips. She'd already downed the Coke and hadn't asked for another. After a minute, she squeezed my hand. "Take a walk with me?"

I knew better than to refuse. "OK, but let's not go too far," I said. I looked at Phil and said "Be back in a bit."

We stood up and Joe tossed a bottle cap at my head. "Where you guys goin'," he drawled. "Don'tcha wanna get nasty down here in the ditch like Lydia and Larry? They'll make room!"

"We'll be back," I said, and crawled up the steep incline towards the trees. We followed the gravel road back a few yards until the mix of oak and pine branches obliterated the stars overhead. And then suddenly Amy was pushing me against the trunk of a huge rough-barked oak, and sticking her boozy tongue down my throat. Her lips felt warm and moist and swollen, and I have to admit, I enjoyed having her chest pressing against mine. I could feel the hard cup of her bra through my t-shirt.

Her hands were around my neck and then grabbing at the zipper of my jeans. "Mmmm, I have missed you all week," she whispered as she slipped one hand inside my briefs to grab the tip of my quickly expanding manhood. Okay, maybe teen-hood. But... right then, I felt man-ish. That's

158

for sure. And all of my bitching about Amy's annoying controlling ways disappeared when she got my belt undone, and I pulled her shirt over her head.

She could be a bossy bitch, but she knew what to do when she was naked, or half-naked, anyway.

And after drinking a quarter of a bottle of vodka, she was even more energetic than usual. I did my best to reciprocate, because I definitely appreciated what she was doing.

A while later, she rolled over on the forest floor and swore. "Ow, there's a pine needle up my ass!"

That, I assumed, signaled the end of our little field trip, and I grabbed for my shirt and pants and stood up. Her bra was in my jeans, and I fished it out and tossed it to her. I had to stop and watch as she slipped one arm through, and shrugged her breasts into the white lace. You could say a lot about Amy, and a lot of it not very complimentary, but you could not deny that she was stacked.

"Quit gawkin' and get dressed," she said. "I want more vodka. If you're a good boy, maybe I'll let you peek again later."

I doubted that. She was about 15 minutes from being thoroughly trashed. I hoped she was going to be able to ride her bike home.

"Thanks for bringing me," she said. "I'm having a good time."

"Me too," I said, as she took my arm. Just at that moment, something like a scream sounded from deep in the forest.

"What the fuck?" Amy said.

We stepped onto the gravel of the winding road and peered down its length into the depth of the forest. I could just make out the faint light of a house back there.

Something shrieked again, but fainter this time.

"Owl?" I said.

"That was not a fuckin' owl," Amy answered. The more she drank, the more she swore, I had noticed.

We stood there for several minutes, breathing quietly. Listening.

But the sound didn't come again.

"Come on," Amy said finally. "We should get back with the others."

A few minutes later we were back in the midst of laughter and a pounding bass beat. "I hope *you* were a boy scout," Phil laughed. I took a beer from him and only answered with a smirk. An hour or so later, we all staggered out of the ditch, and headed home under the light of a million stars. It was way past curfew.

***

On Monday, I noticed Regina's seat was empty in English class. Normally, I wouldn't have thought too much about it; she was gone at least a day every week it seemed like. But… it occurred to me – much belatedly – that she had driven down that gravel road on Saturday night… the same road where we'd heard something a little later that sounded like a scream. What if she had gotten home and the Renfield County Killer had been waiting for her?

The thought bugged me throughout the day; I had Calculus class too, where I was also confronted by her empty chair.

After school, I decided to go for a bike ride. Mom was still at work and Amy had softball practice, so I was on my own.

I headed out onto the two-lane towards the industrial park, and pulled off the road at the ditch where we'd been drinking Saturday night. The telltale frog labels stared at me from the deepest edge of the drop off. I laid the bike over them, and crawled up and out of the ditch to walk down the gravel towards where Amy and I had made out. Towards the house I assumed was hidden back there.

And my assumption was correct.

The road wound around and suddenly I was standing in a small clearing, with a two-story cedar-framed cottage tucked at the edge. A stand of oaks and maples climbed into the sky behind the green-mossed shingles of the place; I could see the gutters were overflowing in pine needles, leaves and acorns.

I stood there looking at the place, assessing the sagging screens and the weathered wooden porch that stood four steps up from the gravel drive. And suddenly I didn't know what the hell I was doing here. I was just assuming this was her house. If Regina answered the door, what was I going to say? "Hi, I thought you might have been killed two days ago so I finally decided to ride out and see." Or what if her mom came to the door and asked if I was a friend of her daughter. "Um, well, not really…"

I almost turned around right then. But I'm stubborn. Hell, I've stuck with Amy this long, haven't I? I don't let go of things when I should.

So after fidgeting in place for a while, I walked up the warped wooden steps and stood in front of the old wooden door. I almost knocked. And then something made me walk to the family room window instead. I wanted to see what I was getting in to. I leaned past the drapes on the side windows until I could see in through the glass to the room beyond.

It took a minute for the scene to register.

I saw a brown couch, sitting right beneath the window, and a beige carpet that extended across the room to end where another room, and a stretch of tile began. The family room led straight into the kitchen. It looked like a big kitchen, with dark wood cabinets that stretched to the ceiling, and an old white refrigerator on the left side of the room next to a stove.

All of those things registered before my mind allowed me to see

160

the elephant in the room.

Well... not an elephant exactly.

A dead body.

Two, actually.

From the color of the hair, I was reasonably sure that one of them was Regina.

Oh mother fuckin' shit.

It was her that had screamed on Saturday. I'd been just a few yards away and I'd done nothing. And now...

I started to back away from the window, ready to run to my bike, truth be told. And then the faintest voice whispered in the back of my head, *"what if she's still alive and just unconscious and you leave her yet again... maybe then she'll be dead by the time someone comes back here."*

I didn't want to know. But I *had* to know.

I put my hand on the front door knob, assuming that my white knight's efforts would easily be rebuffed and I'd have no choice but to leave.

But... the knob turned.

I could hear my heart pounding in my head as I stepped onto the carpet.

What if the killer was still here?

Two days later?

I tiptoed across the carpet and then knelt on the edge of the tile just a couple feet away from that otherworldly blonde hair. Both bodies were naked, and a pool of dried blood extended across the tile all around them, but most of it seemed to stem from the neck of the body next to Regina. It was another girl; from what I could tell, she looked about our age. Her brown hair was twisted and matted in blood, but her face was down towards the floor and away from my view. Regina's face lay in the same direction, as if she was staring at the girl's back. If they'd been in a bed, they might have been cuddling. Their hips were cupped together. The creamy curve of Regina's butt gave me a hard-on in spite of the hideous situation. The girl was... had been... beautiful.

I extended my hand slowly. It shook as I held it over Regina's head. Gently, cautiously, I laid it down on that white-blond hair and stroked it, gently.

Poor girl. She'd barely ever talked to anyone, and someone did this to her and her friend. I was actually kind of surprised to see her with someone... I didn't think she'd had a friend in the world.

Her hair was soft under my hand, and I ran my fingers down it all the way to her shoulder.

My breath caught, as my fingers touched the soft curve of her arm. *Too little, too late, chicken-shit,* I thought. *If you ever had a chance it's gone now.*

Regina suddenly moaned and rolled onto her back.

161

My eyes must have bugged out of my head as I saw hers open. Her face was splattered with dried spots of blood, and where her cheek had touched the floor, it looked like a solid bruise of dusky red.

"Hi there," she said softly, blinking a couple times, and then adjusting her jaw back and forth. I could see her chin shift. "What are you doing here?"

"You're alive!" I said.

"Yeah, I guess so," she said, and sighed as she pushed herself up to a sitting position. Her breasts were small, but perfectly smooth. They were also streaked in dried gore.

"What day is it?" she asked.

"Monday," I said.

"Damn," she said. "I missed school again, huh."

"Um, yeah. What did he do to you?" I said. My voice was a church whisper.

"Who?" she asked.

"The guy who did this," I said. "It was the Renfield County Killer, wasn't it? How did you escape?"

"I didn't escape," she said. "Nothing to escape from."

"I don't understand," I said. "Then what happened?"

Regina put her hand on my shoulder. "You know how you guys were partying in the ditch on Saturday?"

"You saw us?" I said.

"You weren't trying too hard not to be seen."

I shrugged.

"Well, I was having my own party up here."

She held one arm across her chest, covering herself, but raised the other to touch my cheek.

"You were worried about me, weren't you?" she said. She sounded surprised.

"Yeah," I said. "I…"

"You shouldn't have come," she said. Her voice sounded sad.

Suddenly I had a strong suspicion that all those announcements of missing teens and Regina's frequent absences from school might be connected.

"There is no serial killer, is there," I said.

Regina shook her head. There was dried blood on her lips.

"Did you drink her blood?" I asked.

She shrugged. "Some."

Regina began to move, and I jumped to my feet. Standing, I could see now that it wasn't just the dead girl's neck that had been opened. There were gory holes in her belly, and her breasts had been turned into hamburger.

"You ate her," I said.

Regina didn't answer me. It occurred to me in that moment that it

162

was probably in her best interest to make sure I didn't leave the house alive. And from the look of the body on the floor, she had no problem whatsoever with killing.

I turned and ran for the door.

I was across the carpet and back on the old wooden porch in five seconds, but it was the sixth second that fucked me up. My shoe caught on a raised plank just before the stairs to the gravel road. I grabbed for the wooden bannister, but missed, and then there was spark of white light as my forehead hit the flagstone path at the base of the stairs just a second before the rest of my body hit the ground.

***

"I promise, I'm not going to eat you," were the first words I heard when I woke up.

I was in a bed, tucked in beneath pink sheets and a fluffy sea-green comforter. My head was throbbing. I put my hand to my forehead, and felt a lump there; a thick gauzy bandage. Regina sat on the side of the bed. She'd washed her face, and was wearing a loose yellow cotton tank top. Part of me still managed to notice that she hadn't put on a bra.

"That was quite an escape," she said. Her voice was soft, with a hint of laughter rolled up inside it.

"Not very effective," I admitted.

She shook her head. "Do you want some aspirin?"

I nodded and groaned as I did. It hurt to move.

She got up and walked out of the room. She hadn't bothered to put on shorts. I wasn't sure whether to be excited or scared.

A minute later she was back with three pills and a glass of water. "Take an extra," she said. "I think you need it." I downed them and laid my head back. "Ow," I said.

Regina slipped her legs under the covers and slid in beside me. She propped her head up with one hand, while stroking mine with the other.

"I really appreciate it that you came out here to check on me," she said. "Though, of course, I also wish you hadn't."

"Because now I'm a problem," I said.

"Maybe," she said. "I guess that's up to you."

I couldn't help but close my eyes when she ran her fingers across my hair.

"No problem," I said.

"Good," she said, and pushed herself closer to me. I put my arm around her and drew her close. Her skin was cool, but her eyes were electric. My heart skipped when her lips touched mine, but she didn't bite.

***

163

Later, when the light began to wane, I sat up in her bed. "I have to go," I said. Part of me hated to call the question. Would she let me leave?

"I know," she said with a yawn. "But could you give me a hand first?"

"Sure," I said. "Whatever you need."

A minute later we were in the kitchen, and she pointed to the body. "I need to move that downstairs."

"Um..."

"Come on," she said. "I do it by myself usually, but you could make it easier."

"Usually?" I said. "How many times have you taken bodies downstairs?"

"Just grab the feet," she instructed.

And just like that, I was helping Regina carry a body down a flight of stairs through a concrete room to another set of stairs that led to a damp, horrible earth cellar. The stench almost made me lose my lunch.

We laid the body down at the end of a row of corpses. It was a small room, but she had nine bodies laid out there, most of them missing large amounts of flesh. I assumed that was from her hunger, not from decay, though the first bodies were just blackened husks. The buzz of flies filled the air.

"Thank God dad put a door on that room," she said as we stepped back outside, and she pulled the door closed with a snap.

"Where is your dad," I asked.

"Oh, he's in there. First row on the left," she said, and walked away from me towards the stairs.

"You promise you won't tell anybody," she said. "I mean... not anyone."

I nodded.

"And your head?" she asked.

"I hit a bad pothole and fell off my bike."

She smiled. "See you in school tomorrow?"

I shook my head. "Yeah."

The whole walk down the gravel drive to my bike, I wasn't sure whether to puke, or dance.

I'd just made out with the girl of my dreams. In her bed. Only problem was, afterwards, I'd carried a dead body down to a cellar. The body of a girl she'd eaten.

***

On Tuesday, Regina was back in class, and I caught her eye in English. She smiled, in that quiet, don't-notice-me way which guaranteed that nobody else in class even knew she was there. But I knew. I saw the

164

glint in her eye beneath that frost blond hair. And part of me… a growing part of me… yearned to be back in her bed, letting her stroke my hair… and anything else she wanted.

I caught her later at her locker and when nobody was in earshot, I thanked her.

"For what?" she said.

"For letting me go."

"Thank you, for helping me pick up my books… and other things," she said. "Can you come over today?"

"After school?"

She nodded.

"Sure."

***

It was dicey. Amy always wanted me around to do homework with. And, she managed to sneak in some other activities when her parents weren't around. I excused myself saying my mom needed me to help clean out the garage, and maybe I could come by after dinner. Instead, I made my way from the garage to Regina's house.

The next day, Amy had softball again after school, but on Thursday, I had to tell Regina 'no' so that Amy wouldn't get suspicious.

And so it went for the next few days. I was a ping pong ball between the girl I wanted to be with, and the girl who was my cover.

The hard part was the weekend. Regina wanted me to come over.

I wanted to be with her.

Amy wanted to go to the movies. There was an outdoor showing of *Star Wars* at the Park District on Sunday night and I agreed to take her… but I promised Regina that I'd come over afterwards. Tuck Amy back home, show my face to the parents, and duck back out to spend a couple hours with her. After all… she didn't have any parents to worry about a curfew. I just needed to convince mine that I was home and tucked in for the night.

It all went fine… except that I almost barfed when Amy put her tongue down my throat in the middle of the attack on the Death Star.

I realized at that moment that I couldn't keep the charade up any more. I had to let her go. I didn't know if Regina would want to be seen as a couple – that would only draw attention to her, and she definitely worked hard not to do that.

But I wasn't going to hide under the protection of Amy big boobs any more. I was done there. She had to go.

After the movie, I practically threw her at her front door, and hurried down the street to my house. A half hour later, I was on my bike and heading towards that by-now-familiar gravel road.

What I didn't notice, or count on, was Amy being at her bedroom

165

window and seeing me ride by.

Girls have a sixth sense when their guys are slipping away. Some of them are more possessive than others.

Amy... was pretty possessive.

The red LED on the alarm clock in Regina's bedroom said it was 1:24 a.m.

"I gotta go," I said. "It's Monday already." She stirred next to me. She'd been almost asleep.

"Mmm, no," she murmured.

"It's late," I said. I ran my hand across her cheek, and then down her neck and shoulder. She slipped her hand up my back and pulled herself closer, daring me to stay.

"No," I laughed. "Seriously... it's crazy late. If the cops catch me on the way home, I'm totally dead."

She shifted and brought her lips to mine. "Come back to me?"

"Always," I promised.

Five minutes later, I was pedaling hard past the Rollin Pesticide Plant, praying that I'd reach my house before anyone saw me on the road. The curfew was still in force.

What I didn't know, was that before I'd picked my bike out of the ditch, there had been a knock on Regina's front door.

***

Regina wasn't in school the next morning.

That wouldn't have phased me in the past, but now that I knew the score... I wondered what she'd done after I left.

The day seemed to drag forever, and I couldn't stop yawning. But then during the last period, we got that oh-so-familiar announcement once again.

"Students, this is a reminder that the Renfield Meadows curfew remains in effect. Police are investigating a new disappearance from the area. We do not want to alarm our students, but we want you to be safe. Please make sure if you are walking or bicycling to go straight home today. Be safe, not sorry. Thank you."

I was definitely not going to go straight home. Luckily, I'd ridden my bike to class this morning, and so I dodged Phil and Joe and hightailed it out of Renfield Meadows High towards the industrial park. The sky was overcast, but I didn't care if it rained. I wanted to know what trouble Regina had gotten into in the past 12 hours.

I dropped my bike and hustled up the steps of her deck. I pressed the doorbell a couple times, but when she didn't come, I tried the doorknob.

As usual, she hadn't locked it.

I let myself into Regina's house. This time, I didn't worry about

166

myself. I was worried about her. I crossed the thick carpet of the family room and saw her lying down on the kitchen tile. She was wearing her nightshirt... the same one she'd been wearing when I left her. Only now, it was soaked in blood.

On the floor next to her, was Amy.

There was no mistaking those kinky black curls.

"Oh Jesus fucking Christ," I whispered.

I knelt down at Regina's side and pulled her over until she lay on her back. Her lips and chin were still sticky with blood.

Amy's neck had been torn out, and I could see the yellow slabs of fat that Regina's teeth had exposed on her sides.

Those nicely cushioning boobs were no longer looking so inviting. Regina had chewed the hell out of them.

"What did you *do*?" I said.

Regina's eyes fluttered open.

"Huh?" she asked. She put her hand to her mouth to stifle a yawn.

"You *ate* Amy!" I screamed.

She scrunched her eyes together a moment, and then looked at the body beside her, then back at me. "Yeah," she said. "She was pretty good."

"Seriously?!" I said. I really didn't know what to say.

"She showed up after you left here," Regina said. "She was really angry."

"So you... ate her."

"It had been a week; I was hungry. You should be happy. She was a pain in the ass to you all the time anyway. Problem solved."

I face-palmed myself.

"I assume since you're here that I missed school again. What day is it?"

"Monday," I said.

Regina nodded. "She put me into a food coma. The good ones always do."

"Speaking of which," I began. I faked a grin and pointed at my teeth.

"Huh?" she asked and then understanding dawned and she poked a fingernail past her lips.

"A little more to the left," I said. "You've got a piece of Amy stuck right... there."

She swallowed and then showed me a clean grin.

"I suppose you're going to want me to help you move her downstairs."

"Yes," she said. "But not yet."

***

167

Digging Amy's grave was one of the most difficult things I've ever done. Aside from the putrid stench of the cellar, Regina wanted me to make it extra deep.

"It's time for me to start planning for the future," she explained. "This is the best place for them; close to the kitchen and totally private and contained. No suspicious outdoor graves. But this room is pretty small. So we need to go down far so we can stack them."

I dug down until my head was level with the ground. Then Regina helped me climb out. I was drenched in sweat and my arms were trembling from the effort.

"I don't know if I can do this," I said when we went back upstairs to the kitchen.

"She was a chunky one, wasn't she," Regina said, nodding as we stood over Amy's chewed up torso. "Not sure what you saw in her."

"That's not it," I said. "I was just thinking about... her parents. I know them and all, and they'll wonder what happened to her. They'll never know."

"You think it would be better if they saw that somebody *ate* her?" Regina asked. Then she shook her head. "Let them live with the hope that she's still alive somewhere."

Five minutes later, my bossy ex-girlfriend was at the bottom of a deep hole. And my bossy new girlfriend was handing me a pair of rubber gloves.

"Let's get my parents in first. They've been here the longest; we're going to need these."

Digging the hole may have been the hardest thing I've ever done. But grabbing onto the rotten flesh of Regina's mother's legs was definitely the most disgusting. A good chunk of her guts stayed stuck to the ground when we heaved her body up. They just kind of... ripped.

After I threw up, we picked the body up again and tossed what we could into the hole. Her dad followed, and I used the shovel to move the pieces that had grown a little too sticky with the ground.

"Why did you start doing this," I asked, after dropping what may have been her father's kidney onto his blackened chest at the bottom of the hole. Amy's white and gory flesh was still visible in spots beneath the grey and green and blackened flesh of Regina's parents.

"You mean, eating people?" Regina asked. She stifled a yawn and rubbed her belly. It stuck out of her otherwise thin frame. "I blame the pesticide plant."

I shot her a querulous look.

"Remember when they had that big explosion a few months ago, and they shut down the highway for hours while they cleaned up the mess?"

I nodded, and she pointed at another body. This one looked to be a teen, but the chest and guts were so gnawed on I wasn't sure if it was a boy or girl. That and the skin had taken on the dark colors of rot. I picked up the feet again, as Regina grabbed the arms.

"Well, after that, we all got really sick. Dad thought mom was going to die at one point."

"Did you go to the hospital?"

She shook her head, and then we heave-hoed the body into the hole. It was getting pretty full.

"Couldn't afford it. Neither of my parents had worked in months. So... we rode it out. They got better, but it wasn't long after that when I lost my appetite. Like... completely."

Regina pointed at the next body, and we picked it up together. This one wasn't quick so... mushy.

"My mom would call me to breakfast every morning, and I just sat there and couldn't eat it. Or if I did, I'd go to school and puke it right back up. One morning, she called me and when I came into the kitchen, I'll never forget it. She gave me a hug and asked if I was hungry. And that's when it hit me. Like... I can't explain it. I realized that, yeah, damn right I was hungry. I was *starving*. And she smelled like the most delicious thing I'd ever smelled in my entire life."

"And so you... ate her."

Regina nodded. "The next thing I remember, I woke up and mom was lying on the kitchen floor with blood everywhere. I didn't know what to do. But I knew my dad would be home soon. So, I dragged her body down the stairs and hid it here."

"What about your dad?"

"When he got home, I told him mom had gone out. When she didn't come back, he figured she'd finally just given up and run away. She never liked living out here in the middle of nowhere, and he blamed himself. He got all gloomy."

I started filling in the hole with the loose dirt as Regina finished her story.

"That was the worst week of my entire life. I wanted to kill myself, but I really didn't want to die."

"So what did you do?"

"I realized that I just couldn't eat normal food anymore, so I tried eating raw hamburger, and even a steak."

"No luck?"

"Barfed it right back up."

"So what did you do?"

"A week later, I ate my dad."

***

I couldn't believe that we got all those bodies into two really deep holes. I couldn't believe that I dug holes that deep, actually. And I really couldn't believe what Regina did to me in the shower when we went upstairs to clean up. She did have a way of taking a boy's mind off the stench of rotting bodies and burial of his ex-girlfriend. She said she always got horny after a good meal. I told her that the image of her eating Amy might not be the best foreplay.

Later, lounging in her bed after one of the most enjoyable hours I've ever spent, I told her that she really couldn't keep feeding so close to home.

"I know," she said. "I was thinking the other day and kind of hoping you could help me… um… find new sources. From out of town."

Great. First I'm her undertaker, and now I'm her cannibal delivery boy.

I couldn't go any further down that road, not right then. I'd had enough that day. But I did finally ask the question that had been plaguing me for days.

"You're not going to get hungry one night and eat *me*, are you?"

Regina's face fell. She looked positively hurt. Then she rolled over and lay on top of my chest. That beautiful white blonde hair hung like mist over my shoulders.

"Just don't make me mad," she said. Then she winked and added, "And don't let me get hungry."

***

People at school figured that Regina and I became an item because she showed me sympathy after Amy disappeared. Kind of a rebound romance. My parents were concerned at first, but they liked it that I actually had date nights every Saturday night, especially once the town lifted the curfew, after a few weeks passed without any further disappearances. I think my parents liked it that Regina was quieter than Amy, at least around other people. It wasn't so obvious that she had me under her thumb. But oh, she did. The difference was, I didn't mind being under her thumb as much as I had Amy's. If only my parents had seen what we did on our road trips to find what Regina called… new takeout food.

***

I'm with her every day now, except for Sunday mornings, when typically my ghoulfriend's in a coma, thanks to the food I helped her lure home the night before. It's like I said at the beginning. Whether they're dead, alive, or somewhere in between… all girls are really the same. They want your undivided attention. They want your love.

And they want you to pick up dinner.

And you know what… with Regina, I'm okay with that.

I just make sure she's never hungry.

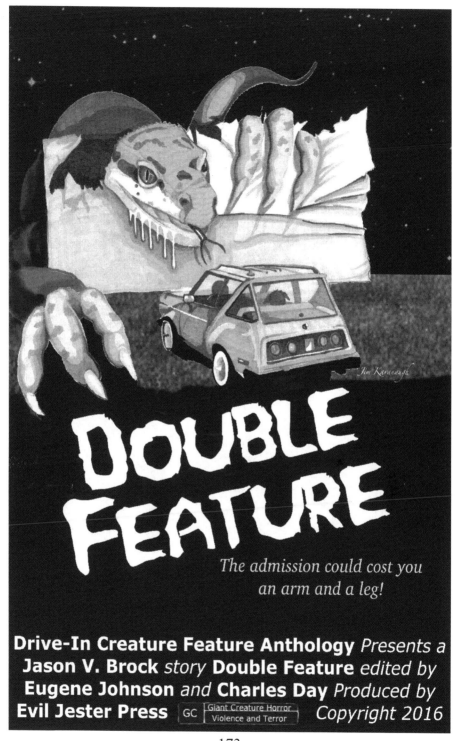

DOUBLE FEATURE

*The admission could cost you
an arm and a leg!*

Drive-In Creature Feature Anthology *Presents a*
Jason V. Brock *story* **Double Feature** *edited by*
Eugene Johnson *and* **Charles Day** *Produced by*
Evil Jester Press | GC | Giant Creature Horror / Violence and Terror | *Copyright 2016*

Jason V. Brock

Jason V Brock is an award-winning writer, editor, filmmaker, and artist whose work has been widely published in a variety of media (*Weird Fiction Review* print edition, S. T. Joshi's *Black Wings* series, *Fangoria*, and others). He describes his work as Dark Magical Realism. He is also the founder of a website and digest called *[NameL3ss]*; his books include *A Darke Phantastique, Disorders of Magnitude,* and *Simulacrum and Other Possible Realities.* His filmic efforts are *Charles Beaumont: The Life of Twilight Zone's Magic Man, The AckerMonster Chronicles!* and *Image, Reflection, Shadow: Artists of the Fantastic.* Popular as a speaker and panelist, he has been a special guest at numerous film fests, conventions, and educational events, and was the 2015 Editor Guest of Honor for *Orycon 37.* A health nut/gadget freak, he lives in the Vancouver, WA area, and loves his wife Sunni, their family of herptiles, running their technology consulting business, and practicing vegan/vegetarianism

DOUBLE FEATURE

Jason V. Brock

"Come on Val, don't do this." Jim glanced at his daughter as America's "Tin Man" swelled louder on the car radio:

Oz never did give…

Valerie was staring out into the darkness as the 1975 Gremlin raced along the interstate. She quickly wiped her face with a shirt sleeve, hiding behind a cascade of strawberry blonde tresses. As the song played, she fidgeted in her lap with the mood ring her boyfriend, Tommy, had given her.

"Mom said you'd keep me from going."

Jim huffed in irritation. "Did she now? What'd she say, exactly?" Adjusting the defrost to clear the windshield, he then grabbed the AM radio dial and twisted through the staticky swoops and squawks searching for something else to listen to:

…police report that alleged killer Ted Bundy has… daredevil Evel Knievel is still recuperating after a failed… while a new lead has emerged in the notorious Zodiac Killer case, New York City detectives are still stymied by the mysterious Son of Sam… Native American activist Leonard Peltier maintains his innocence from a jail cell in… a violent gang arising from the Irish Republican Army conflict called the "Shankill Butchers" has been plaguing… Woody Allen's Annie Hall *continues to delight both audiences and critics…*

Mirrors on the ceiling…

"Leave it there!" Justin yelped from the backseat. Jim threw his hand up as his son started singing along to himself.

"Mom said you think prom is just a big, stupid party. That it's become just an excuse for the spics, queers, spades, zipperheads and whores to screw around and get high—"

"Hey! Watch your mouth!" Jim exclaimed. He looked over at Valerie again, anger lining his face. He narrowed his eyes in annoyance. "Just *cool it*, especially around your brother. We never taught you to talk like that—"

175

"Like, *spare me*, dad! I know you think I can't handle myself. But I'll be a *senior* next year!" She whipped around to face him, tears streaking her features in the blue-green glow of the dash. "I mean, I'm *sixteen!* I can take care of myself. Besides, Tommy will be there—"

"Here we go with the Tommy shit again." Jim shook his head in bewilderment, smoothing his moustache. "For Christ's sake, Val! He's *too old* for you! He'll be a junior in *college* this fall—"

"*Yeah?* So what! I'm a grown woman, daddy! Deal with it! I'm liberated, and there's *nothing* you can do about that." Valerie slumped back into the car seat, sobbing quietly. "I mean, you voted for *Nixon!* You're part of the problem!"

Won't you sign in stranger?

"Turn it, dad. I hate this one," Justin said from the back.

"Okay, hold on, Doc." Jim dialed through the local and national bulletins as they were detailed on the quarter-hour newscasts:

...newly-elected president Jimmy Carter is hosting... FBI still voices concern over the rise of cults in the United... overseas, Queen Elizabeth II continues her Silver Jubilee... in the world of science, the recently discovered rings encircling Uranus have experts... anti-gay activist Anita Bryant was once again crusading... scientists have reported an increase in unusual solar flare activity for the past... rumors swirl that Tandy Corporation is preparing to release a new-fangled "computer" later this year...

"I want a computer!" Justin crowed from the back seat. "When are we getting to the *movie?*"

"Soon, Doc." Jim replied, winking at his son in the rearview mirror; the boy nodded his head, his blue eyes lively as his layered curls bounced in the dim light. "Another few miles."

"Right on! And I can stay up *all night*, right? I can see all the movies, daddy?"

Jim chuckled. "You sure can, Mr. Man." He looked back over at Valerie, his smile fading.

...in Antarctica, researchers have discovered previously unknown giant animals that... meanwhile, Elvis prepares for another... have been revived, even though they were believed long extinct; the Pentagon has issued a warning about... related, the notorious Sex Pistols are ready to... even as Disco continues to dominate the record charts, a new form of expression called "the rap" is making waves in...

"Elvis. What a joke," Valerie grumbled.

Jim's face tensed. "I suppose you want to see something like those horrible Sex Pistols, right?"

"Like, *yeah*. I mean, Elvis is a *chump.*" She smirked, twisting the ring on her finger. "I guess you know that, huh?"

Jim resisted the urge to say something cruel.

Distantly, thunder rumbled. On the horizon lightning flashed in

176

the evening sky. Fat drops of rain dotted the windshield as he turned on the wipers. As the shower grew heavier, he pulled a cigarette from the pack in his shirt pocket and placed it into his mouth before depressing the cigarette lighter on the control panel.

"Dream on, kiddo," he mumbled as he held the red hot lighter to the tip of his cigarette and took a long drag, the radiance of the igniting tobacco momentarily illuminating his olive complexion with a ruddy cast. "I mean, I *get it*, Val. I read *Jonathan Livingston Seagull* and took *est*, you know." He exhaled a lungful of stale bluish smoke.

Valerie looked over at him. "Can I have one?"

Jim glowered. "*No.* I told you I'm trying to quit. And I don't want you starting… But, sometimes, you and your mother…"

She crossed her arms, setting her mouth into a pout.

"Listen, Val. I *did* vote for Nixon. He said he was going to end the war. And he managed to do a few good things, like the create the Environmental Protection Agency, and continue funding for the National Endowment for the Arts. Granted, he turned out to be a *bad* man, a flawed man. *Corrupt.* I learned my lesson… But *every*one makes mistakes; I'm trying to help you avoid a few, that's all." Jim inhaled deeply. "'What is, is, and what ain't, ain't'; I get that you don't agree about the prom. But… but maybe, *maybe*, we can reach a compromise." The wipers slapped rhythmically as the buzzing radio crackled in the background.

Valerie's face brightened, her arms tightening as her leg kicked nervously. She peered up at her father from beneath her eyebrows, clearing her throat. "Oh, yeah?"

Jim sighed, letting the cigarette dangle from his lips, the smoke snaking into the dark beyond the reach of the dashboard lighting. Ahead he could see the animated neon sign for the theater—towering above the highway on an oversized, rusting spire—glowing through the haze of fog clinging to the ground as the cloudburst continued: **Viking Five Drive-In**. Beneath it was a large backlit marquee with red plastic letters that read:

JOIN US 4
ALL-NITƐ SHOCK-A-TH0N 2!
FRI - SAT: 7pm-???
5 F!LMS 4 $5/CAR
"JASON & ARGONAUTS"
"BuRNT 0FFƐRiNGS"
"GoDZILLA"
"DaRK S7AR"
"L!PS of BL00D"
In smaller letters below that:
PLU$ – "Pussycat" Screen!ngs NitƐly XXX
Hello my love, I heard a kiss…

177

"This one's *boring*, dad," Justin declared.

"Okay, okay. Let me keep going, Champ." He reached for the knob again.

Jim looked over at Valerie. "How about this... You can go—*until ten*—but no hanky-panky. I expect your grades to be *at least* a B average until then... And *no* drinking. I didn't survive Korea so you could give your virginity to the lowest bidder, for Christ's sake. Also, I want you to look after your brother after the prom—"

"No fair! He's a pain! How can Tommy... look, we need *alone time*. Mom said—"

"*What?* Said what?"

Defiant: "She *told* me about the swinging, dad! Come on! Stop being so uptight!"

Jim was shocked and felt nervous, unsure of how to reply. "I-I don't know *what* you're..." He paused, concentrating on his driving. He could feel beads of sweat forming on his forehead and rolling from under his arms. "Look: This has *nothing* to do with our behavior. We did what we did, and I *will not* discuss this with you. This is about *you*, and what's best for your future, nothing else." He stopped and held her gaze until she looked away. "So... what did your mother say with respect to *that?* That it was okay for you to risk getting knocked up? Oh, no! You're *still* my daughter, and we're still a family even if your mother and I are divorcing. That won't change even if the Equal Rights Amendment passes, so get used to it. You have school to consider, and then college. *Tommy Romeo* will just have to beat off if that's not acceptable." Jim's voice was booming in the confines of the car.

Valerie stared at him like he was an alien, shaking her head in disbelief, eyes huge. "Ha! My *God* are *you* a chump! *So square!* I mean, like, he's got *all* those girls at college. He chose *me*." Valerie sat back, massaging her forehead. "So, I *have* to keep him... *interested*, don't you get that?"

"Oh! I fucking *get* it, darlin'. Them's the terms," Jim said, pulling one last puff before flicking the butt out of the car window and rolling the glass back up. He ran a hand through his dark, curly hair. "Take it or leave it."

I watch the ripples...

Valerie slumped back in the seat, stunned as the song ended. Jim turned the dial again.

This is WSNI, your place for news, weather, music, and... embattled Black Panther Party leader Huey P. Newton... newspaper heiress Patty Hearst plans to appeal... the three major networks, CBS, NBC, and ABC, announced their schedules for next year today, renewing M*A*S*H, The Rockford Files, The Six Million Dollar Man, and others, as well as canceling Marcus Welby, M.D. and... Associated Press Breaking news: Explosions have been reported in Tokyo and Sydney.

178

Casualties have been confirmed; more as this story develops. San Francisco and Washington, D. C. are also reporting a military emergency; more information as… the Treasures of Tutankhamun *exhibition is making… as talk show host Phil Donahue continues to shock with his…*

Mountains come out of the sky…

"Good one!" Justin said and started singing along. His face was rapturous as he acted out the lyrics. After a time, the rain slackened off to a drizzle. Jim turned into the theater entry and slowed the car.

"Five dollars, sir," the attendant, an acne-scarred young man with feathered brown hair said.

Jim dug a ten out of his pocket and handed it to the teenager.

"Five is your change. Stay on the main strip here. It's past the other four screens and in the very back. Y'all have a good time."

"Thanks," Jim replied and rolled the window up. They drove in silence for a few moments while he fiddled with the radio again.

"Listen, honey," he said, softening. "I know you don't understand right now… but just humor your old man. Please? I mean, we're living in a world of terrorists murdering Olympic athletes and skyjacking planes… I-I worry about you, about Justin. Even though he's only seven years old, he admires you *so* much. So much. You're his big sister. Your mom and I… Well, we *tried*, but times are changing." Jim paused, took a breath, and rubbed the back of his neck. "Everything's going so damned *quickly* now. We've had the oil problems, the tensions in the Middle East, the Cold War. Hell, even Korea isn't *over,* not really. Plus Watergate… *Network* was so… *accurate.* And other things… Runaway teenage girls winding up in *Deep Throat* and *Behind the Green Door…* Vietnam… And prices just keep going up…" He trailed off.

Valerie turned to face him, her eyes shining. "Daddy, I understand. I-I… I just need you to trust me." She lowered her gaze, wiping her face. "I would *never* hurt you or mom. I promise you that."

Timothy, God what did we do?…

"Keep it right here, people!" the gravelly-voiced DJ interrupted. "Freeway Jack's got more tunes spinning up as we all try to figure out how much the Buoys left behind of poor Timothy. Next, Paul Simon's getting a little help from his friends as he remembers where he came from…"

In my little town…

Jim glanced over at Valerie as he cruised the pothole-lined side road leading to the main screen where the marathon was scheduled to show. He reached out and cradled her face in his hand. "I'll make it up to you, honey, I swear. I know you were upset we missed the big Bicentennial Celebration in New York City due to the budget being tight, but I was thinking we could do a summer trip to the World Trade Center and Manhattan. Just the two of us: A real father/daughter road trip like the old days. Justin wants to go to summer camp at Crystal Lake anyway. I'll take him to see that *Star Wars* thing when it comes out soon, keep him happy. He loved *Logan's Run*, so that's an easy one…"

Valerie nodded excitedly. "Yes! I love this idea."

"We just need a little more Johnny Carson and *The Waltons* and not as much Roger Corman and *The Exorcist* for now, y'know? That book scared the bejesus out of your mother, by the way. *Night Gallery,* too. And that Alice Cooper… Really: Your generation is growing up *so fast*… I mean, hot pants are fine on *women*, not girls your age. Gives the wrong message to young ladies, I feel. I'm with Archie Bunker on this kind of thing. Not *every*thing, but he's right about that one—"

"Oh boy! *Lesbians!*" Justin blurted from the back, pointing at one of the other screens as they passed: There was a close-up of two nude, buxom women engaged in *soixante-neuf.*

Valerie blushed, then burst out laughing. Her father grinned, raising an eyebrow as he peered into the rearview. "Where'd you learn *that*, Justin?"

"Are you *kidding?*" Valerie asked. "He's always looking at the magazines under the mattress at your place: *Playboy, National Lampoon, Penthouse.* When he was having those 'end of the world' nightmares and sleepwalking right after you guys split up, mom made him quit watching that horror host show, *Dead Ernest Presents.* Remember him?"

Jim laughed. "Good ol' Dead Ernest! Well, those nightmares have calmed down; it was probably just the stress of the move and stuff."

Valerie nodded in agreement. "I know. That was hard. For all of us… Anyway, I saw where mom threw out his old *Famous Monsters* and most of the *Vampirella, Creepy,* and *Vault of Horror* comics you gave him, too. So, I guess he's just left with naked chicks… Oh, he knows about lesbians, alright. Gets a little hard-on, I bet—"

"You stop that!" Justin protested.

"Probably why he was reading my copy of *Fanny Hill,* and mom's *Fear of Flying* and *My Secret Garden*—"

"Easy, now. Be nice to your brother, Val."

She leaned back into the seat, laughing softly. "Let's hurry, daddy; I don't want to miss *Jason and the Argonauts!*"

II.

Jim stroked his moustache as he pulled the car into a parking stall in front of the giant drive-in screen. The place was packed, and the rain had relented at last. Jim cut the engine and killed the headlights before cranking the window down to attach the speaker.

"Okay. We've got a few minutes," Jim said, adjusting the speaker volume; with the radio off, the silence was expansive. "I'm going to the concession stand. What do you guys want?"

"Baby Ruth!" Justin cried. "And an RC—no! A Cheerwine. And some popcorn, please."

180

Jim nodded. "And for the princess?"

After a moment's hesitation: "Pabst Blue Ribbon?"

Jim glared at her. "Be serious, would you? How 'bout a Fresca or Tab?"

"Oh, okay. Tab. Popcorn, please."

Jim left the car and lit up another cigarette as he walked to the stand. *Filthy habit...*

He looked up at the sky. Scattered clouds from the storm, but otherwise pleasant and breezy, if a little brisk without his coat. Out here away from the light pollution of the city, the stars were vivid; he could faintly make out the Milky Way, even a few shooting stars: *Beautiful. Wonder if one of those is Skylab?* He breathed the cool air in deeply, savoring the aroma of hot dogs, candy, and coffee drifting on the gentle wind.

Once at the stand, he smiled at the pale, bored-looking, mousy-haired girl in the striped outfit waiting on his decision for food.

"Hi... Can I get two popcorns, small—"

"It's only a quarter more to get mediums."

"I know, thanks, but that's too big."

"Your dime." She plugged the cost into the cash register and pulled the lever. The bell *dinged* loudly. A few others had gather behind Jim and were deciding what to get. He ordered the drinks and added the candy.

"$2.50, sir," the girl said. She favored him with a constipated smile as he reached into his pocket for the cash.

After paying, he wrangled the drink carrier and food back to the powder blue Gremlin. It was nearly time for the show to start.

III.

Jim woke up suddenly; he checked his watch: *12:03. Already asleep; damn job is killing me...*

"What... what happened to the intermission?" he asked.

"You missed it!" Valerie and Justin chorused. She added: "I forgot how good *Jason* was. And *Burnt Offerings* was *scary!*"

"Hush!" Justin yelled. "I'm watching *Godzilla!*" His sister nodded and rolled her eyes as she turned her attention to the screen, the reflected light illuming her features.

Jim rubbed his face, suddenly aware of the fullness in his bladder. "Anymore popcorn?" Valerie offered him the box.

"Thanks." After a few bites he felt more awake. "I have to pee. Back in a minute."

Exiting the car, Jim noted that the air was much colder. As he walked to the concession area, he tuned in to the sounds of *Godzilla* as the movie played, deep in thought. It occurred to him that there was comfort to be had in sharing this experience with his children. In some ways it made all the sad events of the last few years worthwhile, these little stolen

181

moments. *Only love matters in the end, doesn't it? It endures all travails, spanning dimension, time, place...* The overtly philosophical and melancholic nature of his ruminations amused him, and he chuckled to himself. "Come on, Jim. Lighten up a little."

After he left the restroom, he debated getting more popcorn but decided to wait until *Lips of Blood* started; he figured by then Valerie and Justin would be asleep, leaving him a bit of privacy to indulge in Jean Rollin's erotic horror vision. Overhead, he heard the rumble of what seemed to be very low-flying aircraft: deep and building in intensity, it eventually grew into a roar that rattled deep in his chest. *Christ!* He looked up into the night sky. *Shit, I know we're near the airport, but* fuck... He plugged his ears with his fingers. That was when he noticed the flashes on the horizon. *Damn, another storm coming.*

As he watched the screen while returning to the car, he vaguely noticed that something was not right: Godzilla was rampaging across Japan as he remembered, but above and behind the enormous movie screen, there was a strange... *void.* It was as though there was something vast blocking the light of the stars. And it was moving. Fast.

"What the *hell*," Jim murmured. "Is that a tornado or—"

His thought was interrupted by an incredible explosion from behind which knocked him to the ground as a shockwave of heat and pressure rocketed past him. Looking back, he realized that the concession area was engulfed in an inferno, a great fireball rolling heavenward. It was the last moment of true sanity that Jim would ever know.

As he watched the blaze, he realized that it involved not just the building, but several nearby cars; people were running away from the scene bathed in fire, screaming in pain and terror as the smell of cooking flesh wafted over to him. The horrors seemed to unfold in slow-motion: limbless victims lumbering around in shock; people with burning hair halo-ing scorched faces belched fire before collapsing into a heap on the molten tarmac. Jim shook his head, dazed by the scene, his ears ringing from the blast. The hairs on his arms were singed, and his shirt was smoking from the intense heat; the coppery taste of fresh blood filled his mouth where he had split his lip when he hit the rough pavement of the parking lot.

"*Oh my God.* I bet a natural gas line broke." As reasonable as this seemed in his moment of shock, Jim was soon to be confronted with the true cause of the chaos and fear unfolding at the drive-in. Pulling himself together, he was about to run over to assist the injured when he realized that the ground itself was shaking terribly, making it very difficult to stand or walk.

Then he saw it.

In the hellish glow of the building fire, a humongous, stout-limbed creature was moving toward him; though bipedal, it appeared to be some type of absolutely *colossal* reptile. For an instant Jim thought that he

182

must be dreaming; then the animal unleashed a thunderous roar and plodded forward. Jim understood at that point this was the cause of the violent tremors.

Jesus-fucking-Christ: This is actually happening.

The thing shifted forward again, and Jim could clearly see in the orange-red dancing of the flames that it was a chimerical blend of several species of lizard, only as large as a skyscraper—its scaly epidermis pulsing with multicolored bioluminescence, its rigid countenance an amalgam of alligator, skink, iguana. Even as he observed it, he remained mentally detached from the crazy scene while the leviathan stepped over the fiery remains of the concession area and moved toward him; then Jim noticed that there were at least *two other* creatures, slightly smaller, lurking behind it—all apparently the same alien species, whatever that species may have been.

Just as Jim was wrapping his mind around this scenario, a squadron of jets streaked past the monsters; one of the creatures reached out with staggering speed and grabbed at the planes. It clipped the tail of one and the wing of another, sending both aircraft into a downward spiral, trailing fire in a dual helix before slamming to the ground in a massive explosion on the other side of the theater complex, eliciting a terrific bellow of victory from the beasts which was so loud it caused the sinuses of his head to reverberate.

Bewildered, Jim finally had his bearings enough to run for the Gremlin as the remaining group of jets circled back around to fight the things again. As he watched, the dark mass he earlier thought was a tornado revealed itself to be yet *another* huge animal lurking behind the screen. It leaped forward in a crude emulation of the on-screen action of Godzilla destroying a train, demolishing a portion of the giant theater display. Landing on the asphalt, the impact it generated nearly brought Jim to the ground; in the light from the movie, it revealed itself to be a form of gigantic winged chameleon, its great eyes swiveling in their sockets, the huge zygodactyl-fused hands raised up in an absurdly defensive *kung fu* posture as it rose up on its hind limbs to an imposing height, towering over the damaged movie screen. The pointed, metallic-sheened face seemed to split open, and the thing released an earshattering rebuttal to the other creatures which reached a mind-numbing crescendo; the film continued to project Godzilla's black-and-white mayhem over its luminescent body in a macabre sort of parodic homage.

At last Jim reached the car: Flinging open the door, he was greeted with the music of his children screaming in terror. He jumped into the vehicle, grateful they were alive, and started the Gremlin. Before pulling off, he had the presence of mind to detach the speaker. As the chameleon-creature moved toward the other things—its watch spring, prehensile tail grasping for purchase and destroying the remnants of the screen—Jim peeled off. Other cars were trying to leave, but had collided,

183

or the owners had panicked and abandoned them, only to be crushed by the things as they converged, apparently to do combat.

Jim snapped on the radio in a bid to reassert control: "M-Maybe there's news about what's going on…"

…repeat: Civil authorities are requesting that people shelter in place; we are in the midst of an attack by an unknown force… This is a mass casualty event; the military has the situation well under control. Repeat…

"Bullshit!" Jim screamed in frustration. He gunned the car onto the easement to get back onto the interstate, speeding past the still-burning remains of the concession stand. He glanced over at Valerie, touching her leg: "Don't look."

In the rearview, Jim saw that Justin was simultaneously thrilled and afraid. "It's going to be okay, Champ." *God, please let it be okay…*

Ahead, he could see the exit to the theater: *"Come on,* baby." He patted the dash of the car. *"Come on…"*

Looking back in the mirror, Jim saw that the group of titans had at last engaged; the jets had been joined by a phalanx of helicopters that were shooting rockets and—he could tell by the tracers—withering machinegun fire. Moments later, he saw the entire group of them had been destroyed. Humans were no match for the reptilian overlords that they had been faced with. The creatures were now fighting each other, the flames of the concession explosion creating a mosaic of horror.

"Oh, *fuck!*"

Jim stood on the gas pedal, his world now reduced to the ever-expanding exit onto the interstate.

…scientists are at a loss to explain precisely what has… perhaps related to the recent asteroid…

"Daddy! *Look out!*" Valerie screamed, grabbing his arm. At the threshold, an immense leg—craggy, trunk-like—dropped in front of the Gremlin, causing him to take evasive action to avoid an accident. Justin was sobbing in the backseat; in the rearview he could see it was the forelimb of some variant of a supergiant tortoise with a feathered shell; the wise, beaked face regarded the car bemusedly before turning to stalk the action of the other combatants, its lumbering footfalls shaking the ground like the aftershocks of an earthquake.

…the entire planet is in a struggle for…

"Almost there! Hold on!"

The car fishtailed wildly, nearly flipping, as Jim took the interstate, headed back to the city.

…lter in place. Do not try to challenge the attackers. …orities will come to you…

"Daddy," Justin began, "can… can we help mommy?" The boy struggled to control his emotions.

Jim looked into the mirror at his son, his heart racing; he strained to smile, to be supportive, to calm himself. In the background, where the theater used to be, the creatures were fully embroiled, crushing everything in the area. There looked to be eight or nine different species now, all actively working to stop the initial aggressors. More planes and helicopters succumbed; Jim could see tanks moving in—and being destroyed as collateral damage by the giants as they fought one another.

About a thousand feet ahead, another curious animal was moving toward the scene in spastic leaps along the roadway: A glowing variation of *Uroplatus phantasticus*—the Satanic Leaf-Tailed Gecko, only the size of a stadium, its saturnine eyes shining in the headlights. Other cars tried to dodge the massive being, which simply picked them off the darkened highway like ants with its vast, sticky tongue and ate them. Jim dodged the creature, barely, speeding as fast as possible away from the bizarre scene.

"We're going back home… We're going to find your mother, and get her out of there. It… it isn't safe for her to be alone."

He twirled the knob on the radio, but it only crackled and popped with static, obscuring any further transmissions for the moment. They crested the hill taking them back home: a glimmering panorama of the city spread out before them. He brought the car to a stop, his jaw set in determination, keeping a wary eye in the rearview on the scene unfolding behind them. *This isn't good.* Past the yellowy headlights of the Gremlin, they could see that the glittering lights weren't from streetlamps and houses. Instead, what awaited them was like something out of a Bosch or Breughel the Elder painting, or perhaps Dante's *Inferno*: The entire city was ablaze; the town had been engulfed by the conflict from every angle—the land, the air, even the river and lake which surrounded it. The battle had laid waste to the entire cityscape; the military response was simply no match for the awesome power of these great beings, which were locked in a deadly combat beyond human understanding. Jim could make out the massive shapes of the animals—dozens of them—as the war raged on, humanity simply providing food and irritation to the combatants.

There's no winning this… it's between them, *not us and them. We don't even matter at all.*

Jim now understood, and accepted, that there were forces beyond comprehension, beyond petty human considerations. He pressed the radio preset button:

This is the end…

"Justin, Valerie…" As the car idled. he looked into the mirror at his son, who was calmer now, and then over at his daughter. "I love you both so much… Let's do this… Let's go get mom." He swallowed hard, his mouth dry, his hands damp as he pressed the preset button one last time, staring straight ahead, steeling himself for what was to come:

We were born to run…

Jim hammered the gas pedal; the tires squealed as he drove

toward the burnt-out city, into the breach of whatever fate lay ahead for him, his family. Night followed the car into the remnants of the town...
Then swallowed it completely.

—For my wife. To lost opportunities... and new beginnings.

THIS BRAIN WANTS TO LOVE, THIS BRAIN WANTS TO KILL!

The Dr. Hillstrom McGabble Show

HALF MAN... HALF HOMICIDAL MANIAC!

Drive-In Creature Feature Anthology *Presents a* Simon McCaffery *story* This Brain wants to Love, This Brain Wants to Kill! *edited by* Eugene Johnson *and* Charles Day *Produced by* Evil Jester Press TH Talk Show Horror / Mind Blowing Terror *Copyright 2016*

Simon McCaffery

Raised on a steady diet of drive-in creature features of the 1960s and '70s, Simon McCaffery writes science fiction and horror. His short stories have appeared in *Lightyear*, *Black Static*, *Alfred Hitchcock Mystery Magazine*, *Wily Writers Audible Fiction*, *Space & Time* and in anthologies including *Night Terrors III*, *Other Worlds Than These*, *Psychos: Serial Killers, Depraved Madmen, and the Criminally Insane*, *Appalachian Undead*, *Evil Jester Volume 2*, *Rocket Science*, *Book of the Dead 2: Still Dead*, *Mondo Zombie*, *The Haunted Hour*, and many others. He lives in Tulsa, Oklahoma.

THIS BRAIN WANTS TO LOVE, THIS BRAIN WANTS TO KILL!

Simon McCaffery

"This brain wants to love..."

Dr. Hill jabs a forefinger at Danny Tamblenson's youthful face, forever canted five degrees laterally outward on the right side of that massive torso.

"And this brain," Dr. Hill drawls, hooking a meaty thumb at Danny's swarthy brother, Vincent, "this brain wants to kill."

Vincent's smile reveals jagged teeth, his nostrils flare, and his tongue flicks out like a wolf's. The staff did their best with pancake makeup and hairspray, but he resembles a lycanthrope caught in the glare of a hunter's searchlight. Vincent's bristly, oblong face is slick with sweat from the hot studio lights. The audience is spellbound by this black-eyed brute, incredibly bonded to the mild choirboy.

"Kill," Dr. Hill repeats softy, nodding thoughtfully.

The simultaneous intake of breath from the audience is clearly audible inside the packed studio. Dr. Hillstrom McGabble's Emmy-winning daytime program is in its ninth season, facing stiff competition from a psychic pet therapist. His producers have begun roving farther afield from the typical format of exploring unhappy marriages, drug abuse, food addicts who can only be accurately measured at truck weigh stations, rebellious teenagers with more metal in their bodies than the Six Million Dollar Man, and grandmothers undergoing pelvic replacements to become the U.S. Pole Dancing Champion. Hence today's show, "He Ain't Heavy, He's My Transplanted Brother."

Try as you might, you cannot tear your gaze away from the bizarre conjoined brothers sitting on a cloth-covered bench, the oversized offspring of a settee and a sofa. The walnut stools with armrests that single-headed guests typically perch upon are simply not adequate. They are dressed in the homespun attire of their everyday lives – dungarees with suspenders, and a checked shirt altered to accommodate their double-wide chest and two necks corded with muscle from a never-ending workout.

Armed with a counseling degree from an open-admission online university, Dr. Hill has amassed a midlife fortune dispensing homespun soundbites and advice as cable television entertainment. He reclines in a leather high back chair with the button tufted backrest and elegant brass tack accents, strategically elevated a few inches above his guests, like shoe lifts.

"Boys, as a Dr. Hill exclusive this week, you've agreed to tell us how you came to be brothers; how you found true love, and your role in an averted massacre that some claim you orchestrated."

The cued audience applauds. Dr. Hill leans forward, rubs his butcher's hands together and directs his trademark basset hound gaze at both heads.

"We would be happy to share our story," Danny says, pausing smoothly so Vincent can bark, "We've waited a long time, you bet."

"Let's start at the beginning," says Dr. Hill.

***

This brain always wanted to love, and this brain always wanted to kill.

Danny and Vincent's lives intertwined on a lonely stretch of rural two-lane highway deep inside the swamplands near central Louisiana's Atchafalaya River, but their story begins decades earlier.

Daniel Tamblenson is the son of Dr. Richard "Nib" Tamblenson, an experimental neurosurgeon teaching at Bard College, an eccentric school tucked away above the Hudson River in the Catskill Mountains. Bard's apt Latin motto is *Dabo tibi coronam vitae* (I shall give thee the crown of life; Revelation 2:10). The translated verse reads like a prophetic summation of the heights of Tamblenson's ambitions, and his Dante-like fall and exile from the insular, prejudiced tower of science:

Fear none of those things which thou shalt suffer. Behold, the devil shall cast some of you into prison, that ye may be tried, and ye shall have tribulation ten days. Be thou faithful unto death, and I will give thee a crown of Life.

An intense man with chiseled Welsh features and no time for barbers, Tamblenson dared in 1971 to submit a paper to *The New England Journal of Medicine* outlining his unorthodox solution to sending men to the stars. Except for Trekkies, it was an accepted notion that visiting Proxima Centauri, Barnard's Star, and Sirius was the stuff of sedentary, underpaid pulp writers. Using nuclear propulsion systems would take centuries, and the science of cryonics was in its infancy. Dipping a man in liquid-nitrogen caused irreversible ice crystal damage to the brain's 100 trillion nerve connections. No!

The answer was…full head transplantation.

Young bodies could be grown during a long voyage, but a cloned brain is a blank slate! No atlas or technology existed to transfer its universe of chemically stored knowledge and memories. Only an advanced, computer-controlled medical procedure could transplant the astronaut's head from a senescent body to the spinal cord of a freshly decanted one. This process, Tamblenson's Process, could be established if properly funded. Launching astronauts packed like sardines inside a sealed aluminum can, pooping and urinating into bags during their jaunt to the Moon and back seemed…pedestrian and asinine. Navy frogmen who popped open Apollo 11 as it bobbed in the South Pacific reportedly vomited into their snorkels. Instead, send Buzz Aldrin to the stars.

The stars! A crown of Life!

The *NEJM* editors did more than reject Tamblenson's thesis; they declared him a vivisectionist; a raving lunatic. Bard expelled him, and after the two-headed hamster ensconced in his laboratory bit the department dean, Tamblenson's license to practice medicine was revoked. Prison seemed a real possibility, so he broke into his former laboratory to reclaim his research and as much of the brazenly redesigned surgical equipment as feasible. He rescued the cowering, near-starved hamster, Harry-Chinn, and fled the state.

Tamblenson ran for the next twenty years. A nomad, a heretic, a mad doctor straight out of a low-budget drive-in film, he shifted his meager possessions and equipment from town to town in U-Haul trucks emblazoned with slogans like, ADVENTURE IN MOVING and U CAN DO IT – FOR $19.95! Places like Pleasantview, Pennsylvania (rusted steelyards to the horizon), and Friendstown, Tennessee (they chased him out with torches and four-by-four pickups), and Monkey Run, Arkansas (the two-headed chimp escaped and terrorized the townspeople – oh, the irony). He used aliases and impersonated country veterinarians, sheltering the flickering embers of his dream to his breast like a Cro-Magnon carrying fire across a barren veldt. *One day*, he vowed, he would show all of those shortsighted fools!

Instead, Nib Tamblenson fell in love.

***

"Dad met Mom in Bugtussle, Oklahoma," Danny says.

Dr. Hills nods sagely, as if he is intimately familiar with the unincorporated community of 300 souls located on the southern shores of Eufaula Lake.

"Marta Deggendorf," Dr. Hill says. On the studio flat screens, a woman with corn silk hair holds a flax-haired toddler.

Dr. Hill pretends to consult the contents of a manila folder. "Your

191

father passed the house she was renting just as a neighbor's dog attacked her cat."

A disillusioned abnormal psychologist, Marta drifted like Tamblenson until she found herself living in the small lakeside town. Tamblenson, alias veterinarian "Dr. Mike Anderson," had neutered Sir Purrs A Lot, her adopted cat. The procedure blunted the tabby's gangster-like reflexes, and he was mortally wounded by the escaped dog.

Using the same process that might have sent space shuttle crews to Alpha Centauri B instead of hazardous, tile-cracking trips to and from low orbit, Tamblenson grafted the dying feline's head to the body of a smoke-colored, psychopathic stray dubbed Ratso. Ratso had been keeping the local rodent population under control.

Tamblenson led Marta to the recovery area, knowing his compassion had been a grievous error in judgment. When she saw the bandaged joining of Sir Purrs A Lot and the renegade, asocial Ratso, she would flee to inform the sleepy town that a monster resided nearby. In his mind, he began comparing his current checking balance with the cost of another U-Haul truck, extra padding blankets for his equipment, and the logistics of being on the road by nightfall.

"Mom didn't scream or faint like some creature-feature damsel," Danny says with pride. "It took her by surprise, but Dad had saved the life of her only companion."

Several audience members *do* scream at the sight of a yellowish, peel-apart snapshot of Marta with Sir Purrs A Lot / Ratso. The tabby nuzzles her, while Ratso tries to batten his needle teeth on her left ear. Marta's smile is radiant.

"They were still alive when I came on the scene," Vincent says. "Garfield gave kisses, but the other head bit like a mongoose."

"Vincent, isn't it true that you attempted to end the animal's life?" Dr. Hill dips back into the folder. "A trip to a nearby pond in a burlap sack?"

"Yes," Vincent says. His expression conveys the stupidity of the question.

"I stopped him," Danny says. "Mom understood the pain that society had inflicted on Ratso. He just needed a caring environment."

Dr. Hill mugs an expression for the cameras.

"Your father and Marta married. Did the two-headed kitty serve as ring-bearer?"

The audience laughs. Danny chuckles, but Vincent's black eyes narrow.

"She became your father's *lab assistant*," Dr. Hill continues, "and a year later she gave birth to you."

"It was a home delivery, yes," Danny says.

"Your parents changed identities and moved to Louisiana," Dr. Hill says. "They settled near Elba in St. Landry Parish, northwest of Baton

192

Rouge. Not long after, your mother succumbed to an aggressive, incurable brain cancer. You didn't attend school. Residents our staff interviewed said no one knew that Daniel Tamblenson existed. Later, university faculty and students were told you were biological brothers, rare conjoined twins sharing a single spinal cord who had been homeschooled. But that was a lie."

***

Danny had a rescued puppy named Bumper. One muggy July evening, he took Bumper outside to do his business, but it chased some scurrying animal down the dirt lane. Danny pursued it to the juncture of the two-lane highway and into the headlights of a 1974 Grand Prix driven by fifteen year old Vincent Delgrado, a veteran of the State of Louisiana juvenile system and a newly minted murderer. Vincent's face was flushed in afterglow and his rictus grin matched the Pontiac's front grill. Blood had dried on his hands, polyester shirt, and the green plastic steering wheel. There was more in the trunk, along with a gas station attendant bludgeoned with a tire iron. Vincent's eyes lost that frightening emptiness and he hauled on the wheel, overcorrecting. Danny was struck and thrown twenty feet into the weed-choked southbound culvert. The car left the road and rolled, coming to rest obscured by thick scrub.

"This was your father's first attempt using a human subject," Dr. Hill interjects. "Can you describe the experience?"

Here, the brothers must proceed with care.

"I thought I was paralyzed," says Danny. "It was numbness from the serum used to prevent Vincent's body from rejecting the transplant."

"My arms and legs were bound," Vincent says. "I had tubes down my throat, up my nose, and out my ass. Then Dad removed the breathing tube."

"Your *new* father," Dr. Hill clarifies.

Vincent ignores the bait.

"I never knew my real father or mother." He hawks and spits a blob of green that lands at the base of Dr. Hill's throne. Dr. Hill remains impassive. Many an angry guest have tried to push his buttons, and failed.

"What happened next?" Dr. Hill.

"I turned my head, and there he was. I thought he was lying next to me in an emergency room, then I realized the truth."

"How did that feel?"

"I wasn't happy about it," Vincent says.

"Do you think you over-reacted?"

"Am I sorry I bit off Danny's ear?" Vincent says. "I was after Dad pumped my stomach to sew it back on. That was worse than the breathing tube."

"You can hardly tell," Danny says, cheerfully.

193

"After the operation, you both stayed hidden. You learned to function together, even play the piano and ride a bicycle."

The brothers nod. Neither mentions how their father sank the wrecked Pontiac and its postmortem passenger into a bog, and swore them to silence. Danny shouldn't have to accompany his new brother to prison, and Tamblenson considered Vincent's involuntary sharing of his body a moral atonement, and preferable to the gas chamber.

Those first clumsy, crossed-circuited months were dreadful – the human body did not evolve to respond to the demands of two minds and two wills. Danny's abnormal psych mother wasn't there to help smooth their Janus-faced nature. The brothers learned to dress and complete chores. Vincent taught his new brother to shave when blond scrub finally appeared on his chin; using a disposable Gillette, never their father's seldom-used straight razor.

They learned to balance the extremes of their natures, and discovered a cognitive connection than transcended mere physical fusing. It wasn't a thalamic bridge, since their brains were not directly joined.

Nonetheless, an interface existed. How else could they occasionally share thoughts, emotion, and sensations?

"That's how you knew a sophomore named Corbett Malcolm Whitton planned to commit mass murder," Dr. Hill says.

"Yes," the brothers chorus.

"And this deeply troubled individual, still sought by law enforcement for questioning, intended to frame both of you?"

"Yes."

Dr. Hill's eyebrows rise and he spreads his hands. "Be--cause…"

"This brain wants to love, and this brain wants to kill," they say, pointing to one another.

***

After their joining, the brothers discovered song. Music led them to Amanda Benford, a collegiate choir champion, and true, unapologetic love.

Danny's lilting alto layered perfectly atop Vincent's baritone. Ignoring their father' disapproval of the performing arts, they dreamed of a life on stage, not freak-show specimens kept in perpetual hiding. They hunkered in front of the household's single, nineteen inch television to watch Ed McMahon put his contestants through their paces on "Star Search." They tried country, but discarded the bothersome cowboy hats in favor of Backstreet Boys goatees and mascara (for Danny) and moussed, blond-tipped hair (for Vincent). They contemplated the stage name In Sync.

"You obtained GEDs and applied to colleges using false information," Dr. Hill says. "Was your father surprised by the

194

acceptances?"

Vincent's expression telegraphs his desire to remake Dr. Hill's smug face into beef fagioli.

"We chose Oklahoma," Danny says. "They have a terrific college of fine arts program."

"And the door arches in the student union are really wide," Vincent chips in. The audience laughs, and he grins, glad to finally score some points.

***

Danny's brain always wanted to love; this attracted Amanda, whom they met auditioning for "Bye Bye Birdie."

Vincent's brain always wanted to kill; it was he who recognized Whitton, the psychopath masquerading as a student strolling the Collegiate Gothic-inspired campus. Whitton was perfectly camouflaged as just another smartly-dressed millennial who favored the packed coffee shop over the cavernous library lined with oil portraits of dead deans.

The school had fallen under an autumn spell of burning leaves and tailgate barbecues. Amanda was tall, with auburn hair and a fresh Midwestern beauty. She also loved to sing, but she knew that a law degree was in her future, not Broadway.

One day a young man passed them on the walkway to Amanda's dorm. Corbett wore slim-fitting slacks and a rolled-up slate shirt covered in a crew sweater vest with a "Boomer Sooner!" spirit pin. His eyeglass frames looked like smart, black Warby Parkers.

Whitton wore a smiley-button expression affixed to his face, but Vincent tracked his merry blue eyes as they hungrily scanned the comely Amanda. Whitton ignored the brothers; many of the students, obsessed with issues of race and LGBT discrimination, politely ignored their condition.

As Corbett stepped around them on the pathway, he brushed Vincent's bare arm.

Vincent's eyes widened. He sensed the pulsing bloodlust, barely kept in check. Always building, building, building, until a twist of the safety valve of butchery relieved pressure.

Vincent's prescient recognition of another apex predator was relayed to Danny, who involuntarily squeezed Amanda's slender hand. Danny relaxed his grip, but couldn't regenerate his carefree smile.

"What exactly did you see?" Dr. Hill says.

"He wanted to kill Amanda," Vincent says. "He wanted to kill everyone."

"His mind was a hurricane of limbs, gore, and faces," Danny says. "The dead faces of victims. Unimaginable intensity, and the storm was gathering momentum to make landfall."

195

"Did you tell anyone?" Dr. Hill says.

"Who would've believed us?" Vincent says to dumbest-question number two. "From the outside he looked like a Banana Republic ad."

He scores more laughs in this fixed match.

"We Googled him," Danny says. "We found missing persons articles where he grew up. We checked state websites for arrest records, but nothing."

"You filed a report with campus security about a break-in?" Dr. Hill says.

"It wasn't practical for us to live in one of the freshman dorms," Danny says. "The towers have keycard entry and cameras. But our apartment wasn't monitored, and it was easy for Whitton."

"Why Whitton?" Dr. Hill says.

"He ignored our laptop, TV, and wireless headphones," Danny says. "He only took personal items. He knew that we knew."

"Including a lock of Amanda's hair," Vincent growls.

"Police found a toy – a vintage 'Zeroids Zerak' robot that's apparently worth money on eBay – at the crime scene."

"Mom gave it to me as a boy," Danny says. "It was evidence to plant after his spree. He took Amanda's hair to enjoy before he killed her."

"It's true that psychopaths are methodical, as opposed to pure sociopaths, who are impulsive and disorganized." Dr. Hill stares at Vincent, who keeps his jaw clamped tight.

A missed jab.

"So, you concocted a plan to expose Whitton as the real monster," Dr. Hill says.

"We told Amanda," Danny says. "We knew she would believe us, and Dad…"

"Your father had pulled stakes again, right?" Dr. Hill says. "No doubt under another assumed identity."

"He had to move after we left for school, in case there was publicity," Danny says. "He promised to visit, but we haven't heard from him, and we're his only family."

"He'd hit the bottle hard since Marta's cancer," Vincent says. "We think Dad had some terminal illness. He just didn't want to upset us."

"He knew we would sacrifice our dream of an education and singing professionally to help him," Danny says. He swallows and composes himself.

"So you convinced your girlfriend to be the bait."

Amanda's fawnlike yearbook portrait appears, drawing agreeable murmurs from the audience.

"She's got more guts in her pinkie than most grown men," Vincent says. "She knew we'd protect her from Whitton."

***

196

Time is running out before Whitton's safety valve must be opened, so Vincent touches him again, while he stands in line at a popular campus eatery.

"Mosquito," Vincent says, brushing Whitton's neck from behind.

Whitton turns and regards the brothers.

"Oh, thanks," he says. "I guess it was that Indian summer."

"These tacos are really the best, aren't they?" Danny says.

"I prefer soft white corn tortillas," Whitton says tonelessly, turning back to the cashier.

It's happening, very soon.

Inside that crimson cyclone they glimpse a church spire; a foreboding forest; and Amanda's ashen face.

***

This brain wants to love Amanda, and this brain is quite willing to kill to save her.

The sky is a sobering gray blanket, and there is no moon. After three nights, the boys speculate whether Whitton is holed up inside the cozy coffeehouse, his finely attuned predator's radar alerted, sipping cappuccino and downloading folk music.

A figure emerges from behind Fassler Business Hall, across from McFarlin Chapel. Too far to positively ID Whitton, but the gait is right. He walks toward the entrance to the student mall, then swerves to the bench where Amanda sits, hugging herself against the chill.

The figure speaks to Amanda, then turns and waves, the gesture filling their stomach with ice.

The brothers rise from hiding, but the blood in their legs feels like sludge.

Whitton fells Amanda and deftly lifts her over a shoulder. He has the strength, size for size, of a worker ant. He flees toward the looming chapel.

The damp, grainy air muffles Amanda's scream. The brothers lumber faster, fogged breath streaming from their mouths like steam from a twin-stacked locomotive.

***

"You chased him up to the bell tower, and he tried to kill your brother?" Dr. Hill says.

"Yes," Vincent says. "He'd dumped Amanda in the center of the —"

"Belfry," Dr. Hill supplies.

"I saw a sleeping bag, bottled water, and food. And a big, mother-ass rifle on a tripod.

"Whitton popped out of this shallow curve in the wall. He pointed a nine-mill at me, grinning like a kid on his birthday. Then he shifted his aim to Danny."

"Why?"

To the amazed audience, Vincent's werewolf features soften, become human.

"He wanted to hurt me. I'd always been alone, thrown out like the trash, lashing out at the world – until I gained a brother who loved me unconditionally. A brother who was always there for me, and not just because I was the one packing the organs."

"Danny didn't really have a choice." Dr. Hill snorts, but many in the audience shake their heads, and several dare to audibly boo.

"Vincent twisted us and took the bullet," Danny says, his eyes bright with tears. "Just look what that lunatic did to him."

A close-up of Vincent's cheek, the runnel of scar-tissue, and the damaged left ear.

"Whitton didn't expect that," Vincent regains his werewolf grin. "I slammed the gun out of hand, and it discharged again. A piece of slug ricocheted."

"Hit our right butt cheek," Danny grins. "My cheek."

"I nearly got a hand around his throat, but I couldn't see clearly," Vincent says.

"Whitton fled," Danny says. "I, we, bandaged Vincent's face with a strip of my shirtsleeve. He needed attention, as did Amanda, so we didn't pursue. From the tower I saw Whitton slip into the woods."

"Police recovered a semiautomatic tactical rifle with enough ammunition to kill dozens," Dr. Hill says. "And the handgun, with two rounds spent. The fragment removed from your backside matched. But no fingerprints."

"Gloves," Vincent says. "He's a calculating monster, remember?"

"Amanda was unconscious in the bell tower, but claims she was attacked by Whitton," Dr. Hill says. "And speaking of Ms. Benford, our intrepid heroine is with us today."

Amanda appears from the wings, dressed in a robin's egg blouse, flattering black pencil skirt, and heels. A stagehand hustles out a bar stool, but she walks directly to the brothers and gives both a kiss on the cheek.

"We'll be back tomorrow to discuss the ongoing search for Corbett Whitton," Dr. Hill says, "but we have time for one more surprise."

The brothers stand and drop to one knee. Danny removes a jewelry box from his pocket and Vincent flips open the top to reveal a diamond engagement ring that dazzles under the studio lights.

Amanda accepts their joint proposal, the audience deliriously cheers, and Dr. Hill mentally tallies the ratings.

Corbett Whitton races through the woods on that fateful night, propelled by unquenched bloodlust, but he doesn't emerge under his own power. He peripherally sees a gaunt man appear from behind the bole of a tree. Whitton bucks as a Taser delivers nerve-sizzling volts. His last conscious sensation is the bee-sting of a needle. Fade to black.

A week later, somewhere in rural Kansas, Dr. Tamblenson wakes inside his computerized transplantation chamber that resembles an oversized MRI tunnel instead of a normal surgical theater. He's weak and muzzy from the anesthetic and the serum administered to quell the antigen uprising that results in tissue rejection. His new heart pumps and a pink, unmarred set of lungs draw air. His terminally ill birth-body has been cremated, along with Whitton's head.

His gray-haired head is now the sole transplanted occupant of this lean, youthful body.

Proof at last that the Tamblenson Process works.

A crown of Life.

-For John Skipp

199

STATIC

WHEN THE PHONE RINGS THE TERROR BEGINS...

Drive-In Creature Feature Anthology

Presents a **Taylor Grant** story **Static** edited by

Eugene Johnson and **Charles Day** Produced by

Evil Jester Press | R | ringtone / disturbing voicemail | *Copyright 2016*

Taylor Grant

Taylor Grant is a two-time Bram Stoker Award® nominated author, Hollywood screenwriter and award-winning filmmaker. His short films *The Vanished* and *Sticks and Stones* premiered at the prestigious Cannes Film Festival. His work has been seen on network television, the big screen, the stage, the Web, as well as in comic books, newspapers, national magazines, books, and heard on the radio.

Several of Grant's screenplays have sold or been optioned by major Hollywood film studios such as Imagine Entertainment, Universal Studios, and Lions Gate Films. His fiction and non-fiction has appeared in multiple anthologies and magazines, including Cemetery Dance Magazine, The Horror Zine, as well as four Bram Stoker Award® nominated books: *Horror for Good, Horror Library Vol.5, Horror 101: the Way Forward*, and *Horror 201: The Silver Scream*.

Taylor edited and co-wrote the bestselling horror comic book *Evil Jester Presents,* and his book *The Dark at the End of the Tunnel* was named Best Story Collection in the 2015 Solstice List which recognizes excellence in horror.

Taylor is currently working on his first novel, an illustrated novella, several commissioned stories—including a new release from Random House—a graphic novel, and is working with a video game company to bring one of his stories to life as an exciting RPG game.

Learn more about Taylor's dark imaginings at:
www.taylorgrant.com

STATIC

Taylor Grant

Midnight arrived with a phone call and a woman's scream.

Jack Bennett, who had been sleeping fitfully on the living room couch, awoke with a start. He yanked the snub-nosed .38 Special from his shoulder holster and scanned the cabin's shadowy interior.

In the adjoining kitchen, bathed in the light from the open refrigerator, was the lovely figure of Laura Cooper.

"Sorry," she said. "The phone...it scared me."

The continued ringing of the phone was amplified and shrill in the small cabin space. Jack so rarely used the landline that he had forgotten about it. He shoved his gun back in its holster and climbed off the creaky leather couch. The phone sat on a nearby wooden desk that was splintered and worn at the corners. He glanced at the caller ID box. It read: Anonymous.

Strange, he thought.

Laura watched him anxiously as he picked up the handset. He gave her a reassuring look.

"Hello?" Jack said into the receiver.

All he could hear on the other end of the line was the faint hiss of static.

"Hello," he said again.

The volume of the static increased.

This was highly unusual. His number was unlisted and he had a call blocker device that just allowed people with a special numeric code to ring through. Only his mother and his sister had that code.

The woman he'd been hired to protect was already tightly wound; there was no need to frighten her further. So he acted nonchalant as he hung up the phone.

"Bad connection," he said. "Probably a wrong number." He would check the call blocker after she went to sleep; the damned thing was probably faulty.

Laura didn't look convinced as she ran her long, perfectly

manicured fingers through her long, perfectly groomed tresses. The only clothing she wore was an oversized football jersey with the Denver Bronco's logo emblazoned on it.

Jack hated the Denver Broncos.

Her legs were long, tanned and shapely. Jack tried not to stare at them as she reached over the stovetop to turn on the kitchen light.

She caught his quick gaze anyway.

"Do me a favor," he said. "Put some pants on if you're going to wander around the place."

The tension in her face softened. A hint of a smile curved the edges of her lips. "Am I distracting you from your job?"

He shrugged. "I think we can both agree you have nice legs. No need to show them off to me. I'm just the hired help."

"Unless you're hiding some cabana boys in this dump, you're the only game in town."

Dump, he thought. *This little cabin cost me my life savings.* But he wasn't going to tell her that. "You know, you're always free to go and stay in a five-star hotel. Maybe one of their cabana boys will be your bodyguard."

He knew he should have been nicer to her. She was the client, after all. But interpersonal communications had never been his strength.

The tall blonde pouted her lips affectedly, giving the cabin a quick once-over. "No need to get sensitive. Your cabin has its... charms."

"Look, Ms. Cooper—"

"For the twentieth time, call me Laura. My mother is Ms. Cooper."

"OK, fine. Laura. It's late. We should call it a night."

Laura arched her back and stretched her arms over her head, revealing the shape of her ample breasts. "Oh, I'm too wound up to sleep now. Plus I'm so bored it hurts—those magazines in my room are ridiculous. *Soldier of Fortune,* seriously?"

Jack sighed. "There are some gossip rags in there, too."

She rolled her eyes. "Yeah, from like three years ago. Nobody on those covers is even married anymore." She reached inside the open refrigerator door. "You got anything stronger than beer?"

"Afraid not."

"It'll have to do," she said, and pulled out a cold one.

Jack tried not to gawk at her as she twisted off the bottle cap. Laura had the kind of body that attracted a man's eyeballs like moths ticking at light bulbs.

She caught him looking again and grinned.

Jack wasn't sure what annoyed him more: the fact that she knew she was attractive or that she knew he was attracted to her. God knows he didn't want to be. She was twenty-eight years old, which made her twenty-two years his junior. It was embarrassing. He was friends with her *father*, for fuck's sake.

Laura seemed to like the attention, though. She was undoubtedly used to it; model gorgeous, whip smart, and from an affluent, influential family. Well, by Yellow Creek, California standards, that is.

Jack had grown up in Yellow Creek, long before his life in Los Angeles. He'd gone to high school with Laura's father, Lou Cooper, who showed great ambition even then. He had campaigned hard to become class president, and-- as the legend went--had won by the biggest landslide in George Washington High School's history. So it was no surprise to Jack when he discovered that Lou had become an elected city council member and well-to-do dairy farm magnate.

Despite his own lack of success, Jack didn't hold Lou's against him. He figured the enterprising bastard had probably earned it. Plus, he'd been a loyal friend to Jack in high school, and loyalty was something rare in this life. He hadn't spoken to Lou in over fifteen years, until a week before, when he'd contacted Jack online seeking help. After a decade on permanent disability, it had felt good to be needed by anyone, especially Lou.

And it didn't hurt that he'd offered Jack a small fortune, either.

The phone rang again. Laura froze, staring at it like an animal transfixed by headlights.

Jack answered by the third ring. "Hello?"

He got an earful of static. Somewhere, there might have been a voice, but it was hopelessly lost in the roar of the receiver.

The line went dead.

Jack hung up and forced a smile. "Must be a problem with the phone line. I'll contact the phone company about it."

Laura's eyes shone with fear. She took a long swig from her bottle and went back to the refrigerator for another. He hoped she wasn't planning on getting drunk; their conversation was awkward enough as it was.

In fact, the whole situation was a bit.... peculiar. He'd been given three conditions for employment. Firstly, he was to provide protection for Laura outside Yellow Creek city limits. Secondly, Lou had asked for complete discretion, for his family's sake--it was a small town, after all. Thirdly, no questions asked.

The first two conditions weren't unusual requests, but the third would have been a deal breaker for any executive protection professional. They would have insisted on knowing everything about Laura and her stalker. It explained why Lou wanted him to babysit his daughter; it was much simpler to hire a disabled cop with joint injuries who had nothing better to do.

Jack didn't plan on looking a gift horse in the mouth, but there were some basic facts he needed in order to do his job with a modicum of efficiency. The most important question, of course, was who was he

205

protecting Laura from?

Not much was known at this point, other than an unknown stalker had been tormenting Laura for three months. And no matter how many times she changed her number, the son of a bitch managed to track her down. Lou was convinced that it was an angry ex-boyfriend, but didn't have anything substantive to prove his theory.

Laura had made several reports to the local police, but they didn't take it seriously because no threats of violence had been made. Yet the emotional toll on her had been severe. She was petrified to answer her phone or leave the house alone. In fact, she was convinced the caller meant her harm.

Now, as Jack stood in his kitchen with Laura, he suddenly realized that she had been waving a beer in front of his face.

"Join me for a drink," she said. It was a statement, not an invitation. It was pretty clear she was used to getting what she wanted.

Jack wanted to tell her 'no' on principle, but he supposed there were worse things than having a late night drink with a beautiful woman. Besides, beer always made him drowsy, and he was going to need all the help he could get to fall back asleep tonight.

He reached out his hand and accepted the cool bottle.

That seemed to change her mood considerably. A familiar grin crossed her lips, as if she had just won a small victory. She said, "I don't see a ring. No...Mrs. Bennett?

Jack didn't answer right away. He took a slow sip--savored it, he loved Mexican beer. It reminded him of his last trip to Acapulco. Now, the ladies there—they could be quite accommodating. He was also deciding whether or not he wanted to answer the question.

After an uncomfortable silence, he said, "Tried it once. Didn't stick."

She raised an eyebrow, and her head tilted ever so slightly. "Did you cheat on her?"

Now it was his turn to raise an eyebrow. "Even if I did, I wouldn't tell you."

"You're not very forthcoming."

He frowned and took another sip.

She seemed to be assessing him. "Different subject then. Dad said you were an ex-cop because of an injury." She looked him up and down. "All your parts seem to be working, as far as I can tell. Something I should know?

Jack nearly spit up his beer. "Wow. You have no filter, do you?"

"I'm just trying to get to know the person protecting me. We *are* living together, after all."

"We are not living together. I'm the hired help."

She chuckled. "Sure, keep telling yourself that. But technically we *are* living together. So...how are you injured?"

Jack had had enough. "Sorry, that subject isn't open for discussion." He skulked out of the kitchen and into the living room. "Excuse me, I'm all talked out."

He plopped down on the couch and the springs squeaked in protest. While he had tried to be civil, it was late, he was cranky, and the woman seemed to have a preternatural knack for asking the wrong questions. When he got into a mood like this, he knew it was better not to say anything at all, or he'd end up saying something he would regret.

Laura took a long, deliberate drink from her beer. Her eyes never left him. Somehow, she managed to make drinking a beer look sexy. "You know, most people on the payroll suck up to me and my family--but you don't. I like that."

Jack fluffed up a dingy-looking feather pillow and stretched out on the couch. "I don't think your dad hired me for my sunny disposition."

Laura was about to respond when the phone rang again. She nearly dropped her beer. Jack was amazed at how she could switch from complete confidence to anxiety in the span of a single ring.

"It's okay," Jack said, reassuringly. "Remember, *no one* knows you're here."

The phone calls were annoying him, though. It didn't make sense. All of his business and personal calls were via cell phone. And even if a telemarketer had somehow figured out a way to get through to his cabin, they wouldn't call at this ungodly hour.

He glanced at the caller ID again. As expected, it said: Anonymous. He gave Laura the universal sign for silence and then hit the speakerphone button. "Hello," he said, hoping he sounded as irritated as he felt.

It was quieton the other end for a few seconds--followed by static.

Laura's dark azure eyes widened with a look of horror and recognition.

"Is someone there?" Jack said, forcefully.

The static increased.

But Jack's annoyance was overshadowed by his curiosity.

And when the man on the other end of the line finally spoke, it was so abrupt and unnerving that Jack's whole body stiffened. The voice was cold, guttural, and seething with barely restrained rage. "Lauraaaaa...."

Laura threw her hands over her mouth, but a pathetic whimper managed to escape.

Jesus, Jack thought. *That voice. No wonder she's terrified. And how the fuck did he get my number?*

"Can I help you with something?" he said, not sounding nearly as calm as he wanted.

As if in answer, the static increased in intensity.

Jack gritted his teeth, "Who the hell is this?"

207

Laura's face had gone two shades whiter. She mouthed the words *it's him.*

The chilling voice repeated her name in the same manner, "Lauraaaaa."

She started to reply, but Jack held out his hand to stop her. He spoke instead, "There is no Laura here. How did you reach this number?"

There was a *click* on the other end--followed by a dial tone.

Laura's eyes welled with tears and her face shook with emotion. "I thought this was a fucking safe house! What the hell are we paying you for? We have to get out of here." She started to rush for her room, but Jack caught her by the arm. She gave a startled yelp and he pulled his hand away.

He held his hands out. "Sorry. I'm sorry," he said. "But I need you to stay calm. You're safe. I'm not going to let anything happen to you."

She wouldn't meet his eyes.

He spoke gently this time. "Listen, the fence is electrified. And I've got motion detectors and cameras installed. No one can get within 50 yards of this cabin without me knowing about it. Okay?"

Jack wished he was as confident as he sounded. He was stunned by this turn of events. He needed time to process how this could happen, time to figure out the best course of action.

Tears spilled from Laura's eyes as she began to pace. "I knew he'd find me again. I knew it."

Jack said, "I might be able to pull in a favor and get a trace if he calls again. But it's going to take a while to set up."

Laura looked beaten as she plopped onto a bar stool at the kitchen counter, her shoulders slumped in defeat. "I already tried that with the phone company. They couldn't trace it--said he probably used pay phones."

Jack grimaced. He'd had enough of this bullshit. He wanted answers.

"Look," he said, sitting at the stool next to her. "Your dad led me to believe that this wasn't a serious threat--told me you were overreacting. He thinks you just need a couple weeks of protection to feel safe again and this thing will blow over."

"Fucking armchair psychology from the dairy king," she said. "I'd laugh if it wasn't so pathetic."

Jack glanced at his watch. "Regardless, somehow this guy tracked you down in twenty-two hours. That means this isn't some run-of-the mill scorned ex-lover. The only thing that makes any sense is that he had some inside help, but the problem with that theory is that there is no one he could have gotten the information from--much less this quickly."

Laura continued to avert her eyes, which spoke volumes.

He placed his hand on her shoulder. "Laura, this is serious."

Reluctantly, she looked up at him.

Jack said, "If our security here has been compromised, I can't afford to be in the dark. For your protection, I need to know what I'm up against here."

Laura turned away again, buried her face in her hands and began to weep silently.

Jack continued to speak softly, "I know you've been through the wringer. And I'm sorry. But I need some answers."

It took several moments for her to regain her composure. He handed her a napkin from the counter and she dabbed her eyes. Finally, she said, "Everything I've told you is true, OK? He finds me no matter what I do. The police don't take me seriously and my dad thinks I'm nuts."

"That's not true," Jack said. "Although, I can tell he's worried about you."

Laura laughed, but there was no humor there. "He's not worried about *me*. He's worried about bad press. Don't you get it? He doesn't want any unsavory attention directed at his family right now because he planning to run for Mayor. He's just wants me out of his hair for a while and hopes I'll come to my senses."

Jack wasn't sure how to respond. So he didn't.

Laura's face hardened and her eyes narrowed. "You may have known my dad back in high school, but you don't know him like I do. He only hired you because he knew you wouldn't ask questions. He doesn't want me to tell anyone the truth."

"The truth?"

The kitchen light flickered twice...and went out. They were suddenly cloaked in darkness.

"Oh my God," she muttered.

Jack jumped up and tried a different light switch. Nothing. The electricity was out.

"It's okay. We're in the mountains. Happens all the time up here. Usually comes back on in a minute or two. Don't worry, the cameras and fence have backup batteries. Plus, I've got a generator in the garage, if we need it."

The phone rang. Laura gasped.

"Don't say anything," Jack said, moving toward the desk with the phone. He hit the speakerphone button.

The soft crackle of static never sounded so ominous.

Jack didn't speak. *Your move, asshole.*

Finally, the voice returned, like a whisper at the dark edge of his mind. "Do you... remember..."

Jack could see the whites of Laura's eyes, shining in the dark. She stared at the phone in horror.

"...your promise?"

She was trembling now, but Jack couldn't tell if it was terror, rage, or both.

Then, amidst an endless stream of eerie buzzing, the voice said, "Do you? Lauraaaaa?"

She lunged at the phone, "What fucking promise, Eddie? What the fuck do you want!?!"

Jack rushed to her but she was already smashing the phone against the corner of the desk with all of her might.

"Stop!" Jack said, and yanked it from her.

She collapsed to the floor, sobbing.

Jack checked the phone, but there wasn't even a dial tone. She had broken it. *Cheap Japanese piece of shit.*

He tossed the useless hunk back onto the desk and offered his hand to Laura. She smacked it away. "Leave me alone, goddamit."

"I can't do that. Your friend has my number. I'm officially involved. Now please…get off the floor." He offered her his hand again, and she took it.

He led her to the couch as he spoke. "No more bullshit, Laura. You called him Eddie. Who is this guy?"

She sighed as if a pressure valve had been released inside of her. "His name…is Eddie Verano. Haven't seen him since high school. He sat behind me in Social Studies--always smelled like ass. Had a thing for me; it was disgusting."

Jack sat next to her. "OK, we're getting somewhere. What happened?"

She looked apprehensive. "I need a cigarette."

Jack nodded and pulled out a pack of *Lucky Strikes* from the front pocket of his chambray work shirt--lit it with his lighter, watched as the tip began to glow in the darkness.

"Go on," he said.

She took a long drag before answering, as if the inhalation might somehow embolden her. When she spoke, it didn't seem directed at anyone in particular. "It was just a prank…"

"A prank?"

"Katie, Oliver and Candace. They were my buddies back then. They were behind it--told Eddie I had a crush on him. They convinced him I'd say 'yes' if he asked me out."

Jack's eyes had finally adjusted to the shadowy room; shafts of moonlight beamed through the living-room window and crawled across the floor. He studied Laura's face as she spoke; her gaze seemed to be focused far beyond the walls of the room.

"We all thought it was hysterical. And it was. Poor bastard actually thought I'd go out with him."

Jack sat forward. "Did you?"

Laura let smoke flow from her lips and curl back through her

210

nostrils. "Yeah. For a month, if you can believe that. By the fourth week, the whole school was in on the joke. Well...everybody but Eddie. He spent every dime he had trying to impress me. Stupid son of a bitch."

Jack reached for a cigarette of his own. "So this Eddie Verano returns ten years later for revenge--that it?"

She turned and met his eyes for the first time in several minutes. "Yes." There was barely concealed venom in her tone.

Jack lit his cigarette and pocketed the lighter. "Seems pretty straightforward to me. Why doesn't your father believe you?"

Laura slumped back on the couch and closed her eyes, shaking her head. "God help me..."

Jack's patience was at an end. "Why?" he said through gritted teeth.

Her eyes remained closed. "You'll think I'm insane, Jack."

"Damn it, why?"

Laura leapt up from the couch, startling him. "Because he's *dead,* OK! All because of the stupid fucking prank."

Jack stared at her hard. "What?"

She shook her head mournfully. "We set up a video camera at Barkley Park. I lured Eddie there by telling him I'd always wanted to make love under the stars.

"Candace, Oliver and Katie hid in the bushes, and watched us as I got the idiot naked. As soon as he had a boner, I gave a signal and they all jumped out, grabbed his clothes and we all ran away--laughing our asses off. He screamed something at us, but we couldn't stop laughing long enough to hear him.

"The next day Eddie showed up at the high school cafeteria, and found us at our usual spot. He just stood there. Staring at me. He had tears in his eyes. And for the first time, I felt really bad for what we'd done. The whole place went quiet and none of us knew what to do.

"But when he pulled out a handgun and pointed it at me, everyone started screaming and running in every direction. I didn't move and he didn't say a word, he just turned the gun around and shot himself in the face. I stood there with pieces of his brains in my hair...on my face...I watched him die. Staring at me from the floor with the one eye he had left. Don't you get it? I hurt him more than any gun could."

Jack's mind was racing; he remembered hearing about the suicide from his sister years ago. It was big news in a town like Yellow Creek. He had a thousand questions. "I remember hearing about this now. Jesus Christ."

Laura couldn't meet his gaze.

Jack said, "Your dad never mentioned any of this."

Laura shrugged. "Of course not. It's a stain on our esteemed family's reputation. He pretends it never happened."

Jack said, "OK, let's talk facts here. This person on the phone--

211

whoever it is--asked one thing specifically. He wanted to know if you remembered your promise. What does that mean, exactly?"

Laura waved her hands angrily. "I don't know! He keeps asking the same fucking question...over and over. And that's not even the worst part."

Jack wasn't sure he wanted to know the worst part. He reached for the ashtray on his coffee table--pulled it closer. "Let's hear it." ??

"Everyone who started the prank—Katie, Oliver and Candace--all disappeared under 'mysterious circumstances." And all over the past three months. Katie and I never left Yellow Creek, but Candace and Oliver lived in two different states."

Jack stared at her, uncomprehending. "This all happened in the past three months?"

She nodded. "I haven't spoken to any of them since graduation. When I finally figured out it was Eddie, I tried to reach them, but all of them seem to have disappeared. I got my first call on the tenth anniversary of Eddie's death."

Jack ran his fingers through his thick, graying hair. "And you haven't mentioned any of this to the police?"

"Absolutely not," she said, bending down to crush the butt of her cigarette into the ashtray. "Dad threatened to cut me out of his will if I did. Said there was no reason to dredge up the past. Besides, no one would believe me anyway--they'd cart me off to an asylum. I have to admit, he's probably right."

The woman's story was so perverse it was almost funny. "Yeah--they're not going to believe in the zombie killer angle, if that's what you mean. But this stalker of yours may have been close to Eddie--hell, it could be some vengeful family member for all we know."

"It's Eddie," she said. "He sounds...horrifying, but I still recognize his voice."

"You don't really believe a zombie is after you?"

"No," she said, glaring back at him. "A *revenant* is after me."

"A what?"

"A revenant. I've read all about them since this began. They're similar to zombies, except they retain their intelligence, and have supernatural powers. They're driven by vengeance or love, or a desire so strong it can overcome death."

A loud *crash* came from somewhere inside the cabin; it shook the entire structure. Laura screamed and spun toward the sound.

Jack snatched the .38 from his holster and turned to her. "That came from the garage."

"It's him...it's him."

Jack reached into his front pocket and pulled out his cell phone. "Here, take this. Call 911 and tell them there's a crime in progress—stay on the phone with the operator. Hide in the closet in your room. Don't

212

come out unless I call you."

"But--" she started to protest.

"Now!" he said, giving her a shove.

Her face was blanched, eyes wide and shining—not with tears, but with terror. She ran.

Jack heard a scraping sound from inside the garage. None of this made any sense. The motion detectors should have gone off. But there wasn't time to contemplate that. There was an intruder in the garage and he could already hear the door to enter the cabin being tested. It *rattled* wildly for a moment...then stopped.

Jack grabbed the wooden chair next to his desk and barricaded the door. He faced it squarely, taking a standard police shooting stance, his knees flexed at an angle and his arms extended. He hated the fact that the.38 shook in his hands.

What have I gotten myself into? He thought. This gig was supposed to be easy money. He was no goddamn hero. He'd never had the stomach for hazardous situations. It was why he'd faked his disability in the first place. Risk his life for a police officer's shit pay? A fool's game.

Outsmarting the system had been easy. He claimed his wrists, hands, left knee, back and neck were injured in an on-duty traffic accident. Sure, he'd been hurt, but it was only minor whiplash and he'd recovered in less than a month. He greatly exaggerated his physical problems so that he didn't have to go back to work.

Ultimately, he received a workers' compensation settlement for $92,000 and an annual disability pension of $47,000 from the Employees Retirement System.

Easy money. Easy life. Just the way he liked it.

One thing's for sure, he told himself. *If I survive this deal, my days as a bodyguard are over. I'm too old for this shit.*

There was a terrible crash as the large plate glass window in the living room shattered behind him. He spun around to see something that resembled a human being on the floor. It rose up in the darkness.

He thought he heard Laura cry out from the guest room, but then realized that the terrified sounds were his own.

The mutilated thing leapt toward him.

All of Jack's training and experience hadn't prepared him for this. At that moment, he realized that everything Laura had said was true. He fired at the creature until his .38 was empty. The gunfire in the confined space was deafening.

But the bullets had no effect.

The nightmarish thing cornered him. Jack tried to make a break for it, but in one swift motion its powerful arms were around him, lifting him off of the floor as if he were a child. He felt some of his ribs crack as the thing crushed him in its vice-like grip, and he cried out in a wave of unspeakable agony.

He glimpsed strange movement all over its body, and it took him a moment to process what he was seeing in the half light of the moon.

It was covered head to toe in wriggling maggots.

He gazed in horror and disbelief at the walking nightmare as it squeezed harder and harder. Finally, Jack's spine severed with a terrible *snap,* paralyzing him instantly. When it finally dropped him, he hit the floor like a slab of beef in a slaughterhouse.

He watched helplessly as the thing that was once Eddie Verano moved purposely toward the room where Laura was hiding.

#

Laura's hands were shaking so badly she could barely hold the cell phone. Not that it mattered. She couldn't get a signal in the back of the closet.

She'd have to leave the safety of her hiding place if she wanted reception. But then she would risk being heard talking or moving around. And even she got through to 911, no one would be able to reach them up in the mountains for an hour at best.

No, she thought. Better to stay hidden and hope to God that Jack was able to kill Eddie during all that gunfire. She would do exactly what Jack said; not move unless he came for her.

If I live through this, God, I swear I'll pray every day. I'll atone for what I've done somehow. And I'll move out of the fucking country. We'll see how well that fucker does trying to get across the Atlantic.

The phone in Laura's hand rang.

It startled her so much she dropped it to the floor. She scrambled to stop it from ringing and tapped the *decline* button several times.

But the call wouldn't be declined.

An unnatural hissing noise came from the other end. And there was something else, too. It was as if the energy of the static pulled together; and from it formed the sound of screams.

A familiar voice: "Lauraaaaa... do you remember your promise?"

She flung the phone away as if it had burned her. Then she hugged her knees and began to cry quietly. This was all about tormenting her, wasn't it? He could have killed her at any time--but he wanted to save her for last. He wanted her to know it was him, to remember what she'd done. And most importantly of all, he wanted her to know he was coming for her.

She jumped at the sound of a door being torn off of its hinges.

Oh my God. He's in the room.

She backed into the corner of the closet as strange, foreign noises born of fear emanated from her throat.

A large shadow appeared through the wooden slats of the closet door.

A ragged whisper through the slats: "Do you remember your promise?"

Laura screamed as the closet door was torn away as easily as rice paper. She wet herself upon seeing the grotesque thing looming above her. Half of its blackened, rotted head was missing, and the remaining half twitched and squirmed with an orgy of maggots. They fell to the ground in writhing clumps.

The revenant yanked her from the closet with the fury of a tempest and pinned her to the floor.

"Why did you come back?" she shouted. "What the hell do you want?"

Eddie's remaining eye looked deeply into hers as he tore open her jersey, exposing her heaving chest. She shrieked in unbearable pain as his rotted fingers dug into the flesh between her breasts to expose the bone beneath.

When he spoke, Laura saw dark things wriggling within the ruined shape of his mouth. "You promised me your heart...."

Buy a
Bucket..
Leave in
a Box!

Drive-In Creature Feature Anthology *Presents a*
Essel Pratt *story* **Popcorn** *edited by*
Eugene Johnson *and* **Charles Day** *Produced by*
Evil Jester Press Copyright 2016

Essel Pratt

Essel Pratt is from Mishawaka, Indiana, a North Central town near the Michigan Border. His prolific writings have graced the pages of over 60 publications. He is the Author *of Final Reverie, ABC's of Zombie Friendship*, the soon to be released *Sharkantula,* and many short stories.

As a husband, a father, and a pet owner, Essel's responsibilities never end. His means of relieving stress and relaxing equate to sitting in front of his dual screens and writing the tales within the recesses of his mind.

Inspired by C.S. Lewis, Clive Barker, Stephen King, Harper Lee, William Golding, and many more, Essel doesn't restrain his writings to straight horror. His first Novel, *Final Reverie* is more Fantasy/Adventure, but does include elements of Horror. His first zombie book, *The ABC's of Zombie Fri*endship, attacks the zombie genre from an alternate perspective. Future books, that are in progress and yet to be imagined, will explore the blurred boundaries of horror within its competing genres, mixing the elements into a literary stew.

You can visit Essel on Facebook at:
www.facebook.com/esselprattwriting,
On Twitter @EsselPratt,
Online at http://esselpratt.wix.com/darknessbreaks

POPCORN

Essel Pratt

As the closing credits faded to black, the drive in's dirt lot darkened under the moonless sky. The few cars that remained during the second half of the double feature rocked from side to side as the couples inside worked toward their own climax behind steamy windows. Silent screams muffled behind the glass until, one by one, the shaking stopped and engines roared. Dust and debris filled empty lot, signaling the end of the drive in's glory days of summer.

Old Man Danby peered out upon the empty lot, waiting for the dust to settle. He shook his head at the pot marked landscape that was scattered with mud-filled tire tracks and littered with paper wrappers and discarded popcorn. Each and every night, for twenty years, he was the last to stay behind and clean up after the uncaring patrons, gathering the paper refuse into large industrial bags and collecting the popcorn scatterings into a plastic barrel.

Sorrow filled his heart as he walked the lot one last time for the season, as it did at the end of every season. The drive in was his home away from home; his place to hide away from life's troubles and escape into the imagination of the movie producers' minds. He could recite the lines of every movie from memory, at least most of them, and appreciated the intricacies of even the worst B-rated flops that shined upon the big screen during discount weekends. His life was ending, at least in its manifested form, as the drive in closed for the season and his happiness prepared for a winter of hibernation.

He didn't have to clean the dirt packed parking lot after the last show, but he felt it was his duty to do so as the lights shut off for the last time and the other employees sped off toward home. He wandered the lot in a calculated path clearing each quadrant, leaving nothing left to mar the empty façade. The silence in the air was deafening, echoing his random sobs into the night, lost in nothingness with no one to hear.

After emptying the garbage into the rusted dumpster near the concession stand, Old Man Danby conducted his nightly ritual of sacrificing the barrel of discarded popcorn into a pile at the rear of the

219

towering screen. Under his breath he cursed the waste of food, muttering about third world countries that wished for scraps food to fill their bellies, while adding to the years' worth of popcorn that collected at his feet. Waste was his one pet peeve that infuriated him to no end.

"God damn kids," he muttered as he dumped the last bit of popcorn onto the pile. "A third of my life I've cleaned up after them and all I have to show is the pile of popcorn. I'd sell my soul to the Devil herself to avenge the spirits of the corn fields that so readily supplied their kernels."

A single burst of lightning shot from the sky, rocketing into the mound of popcorn, shooting fingers of electricity into Old Man Danby's wrinkled flesh; followed by a booming burst of thunder that shook the ground beneath his feet. His body stiffened and he collapsed into the burning pile of popcorn, his skin bubbling like the salted butter that covered each piece of popped corn, until his remains were cremated to nothing but dust, intermixing with the horrendous burning smell of the puffed corn. As if saying his final goodbye, a gust of wind lifted the ashes into the air, scattering them within the fields that surrounded the drive in's out lot.

***

As the sun gradually set upon the cloudless sky, a lazy breeze meandered upon wild corn stalks that flanked all sides of the revitalized drive in theater's exterior as the new season prepared to open. Near the back, towering over the plethora of cars lined up in rows, the large screen displayed a countdown to signal the start of the inaugural triple feature. On the agenda were two classic films, *Creature from the Dark Abyss* and *The Devil Never Knocks*, followed by the premier of 1985's summer blockbuster, *Nightmare in the Camp: Part 2.*

Children played upon the swings and slides at the base of the big screen as their parents lined up for buckets of popcorn and sugary drinks. Teenage boys flirted with the girls, the girls flirted with the boys, some of the boys flirted with boys as some of the girls flirted with other girls. Those that were lucky enough to have already found the crush of their lives spent time planning how they would make their best move toward the end of the night, hoping for a lock of their lips or a quick feel of forbidden flesh.

After one of the coldest winters in the small Indiana town's history, life was renewed within the heart of the drive in; Old Man Danby would have been proud at the turn out. The owners, partly in tribute to Old Man Danby's years of service and in tribute to his memory, outfitted the drive in with the latest technology. The oversized screen and state of the art projectors were calibrated to provide the clearest picture in the region, the best speakers money could buy gave clarity to the score that

220

accentuated the film with eerie detail, and the button call pad signaled waitresses to the cars, making trips to the concession stand a thing of the past. Luxury was the key focus; no need to leave the car unless nature called.

As the minutes counted down to show time, a baritone voice echoed over the loud speaker. *"Ladies and gentlemen, our first film will begin in only ten minutes. Please find your way back to your vehicle and enjoy the opening credits. As soon as the sun disappears behind the corn and darkness envelopes the sky, we will begin the show."*

"Hey Jennie," said Mike, a dark haired teen wearing a letter jacket.

"What's up, Mike?" asked Jen, his beautiful blonde girlfriend.

"The movie is starting; we'd better get back to the car before Steve and Lisa," said Mike. "Before they take the front seat."

"Won't the back seat be better?" she said grabbing his hand with a devious smile and guiding him back toward the car."

***

"Nice of you two to arrive," said Steve as he jumped into the back seat with Lisa; a crooked smile on his freckled face.

"We saved you guys the front so you can see better," said Lisa before placing a kiss onto Steve's lips.

"I hope your braces get stuck together," said Mike as he opened the door for Jennie.

Mike ran over to the driver's side and jumped in his seat, glancing a furrowed brow back to Steve and Lisa, their slurping kisses nearly causing him to gag. He tried to avert his attention to Jennie, grasping her hand within his while leaning over to plant a kiss upon her rosy cheek. However, his eyes met the rearview mirror just as Steve's hand reached into Lisa's shirt. Instead of kissing his girl, he pulled away and crossed his arms as he slumped in his seat. Frustrated, he turned up the volume of the movie and waited patiently as the movie began to start.

***

The night illuminated as the first preview exploded onto the screen; an action thriller with a horror twist starring Brice Gillis and Jane Lee Curts. Mike perked up as the trailer climaxed, revitalizing his anticipation for the first feature to begin. He reached his hand over to and rubbed Jennie's leg, while the next two trailers played above, and shuffled in his seat to get comfortable. He wanted to scoot closer to Jennie's side, but the center console made that a bit awkward, so he made do with intertwining his fingers with hers. Just her touch made the rest of the world fade from his mind.

221

Immediately after the previews, the screen glowed white as dancing hot dogs and soda cups welcomed everyone to the drive in. Their contagious song bellowed through the air as the soft breeze started to whip through the air, sending bits of corn stalk sailing through the air smashing into windshields. Steve laughed as Jennie jumped in the front seat, startled. Mike and Lisa joined in as Jennie playfully smacked Mike on the arm. The movie hadn't even started and the scared were already beginning.

The wind became fiercer as the animated food continued their song and dance. *"Soda, hot dogs, food for all your taste! If you love to snack at all, don't let it go to waste! If you want a salty treat, get right on the horn! Never fret, we won't forget to make some buttery popcorn!"*

The animated finale filled the screen with a creepy popcorn box with a sinister smile, spilling his kernels all over the other foods, drowning them in his buttery children. It was a strange and creepy finale to a typically jubilant concession commercial.

A couple kids in the car next to Mike and gang laughed, making jokes about the popcorn creature spilling his seed. Mike wanted to laugh as well, but held it in so he would appear more mature for Jennie. Hoping to take his mind off the joke, he reached back and smacked Steve in the arm.

"Hey, you guys want some popcorn?" he asked.

"Sure man, extra butter," replied Steve.

"Oh, do they have kettle corn?" asked Lisa.

"Yeah, that sounds good," said Steve, his expression rapidly changing as his eyes widened and his jaw dropping. "What the fuck is that?"

Jennie screamed as Mike turned back toward the screen. In the back seat Lisa also screamed, dropping her soda in her lap as she reached to lock the door, while grabbing onto Steve and pulling him close. Mike saw the young lover's fantasy fade in the rearview mirror and couldn't help but think it was more awkward than their sloppy kiss.

Mike tried to focus on the object everyone was screaming about, but couldn't quite see what it was. The screen went dark just before it collapsed to the ground, barely missing the cars in the front row. The moonless sky left little light to see the large object ahead. Car engines roared as their drivers turned the ignition and tried to speed off, kicking up clouds of dust in their wake, only to find themselves in a chaotic traffic jam where they wedged among each other, making it near impossible to leave unless the attempted to do so on foot. Car horns blasted and tempers flared as obscenities mingled with the screams of women and children. It was like a scene from one of the movies they were there to watch; only it was happening in real life.

"What the hell is going on out there?" said Mike as he opened his car door to get a better view.

222

Debris sailed through the air, nearly missing Mike as he walked toward the front of the car. He shielded his eyes with his left hand as he braced himself against the hood with his right hand. All he could see were the mass of cars and a mass of people zig-zagging in between where they could, each of their faces flushed with fear.

Mike grabbed a nearby guy by the shoulder. "Hey, what's going on?"

"Let go man, some sort of monster out there! Get out while can," the man said, pushing Mike away.

Steve exited the back seat and ran to Mike's side. "Dude, we need to get the hell out of here before that thing gets closer!"

"What thing...," Mike's words were cut off as a small SUV crashed atop a car two spots away.

"Holy shit," yelled Steve. "There was a family in there."

"We need to help them," said Mike running toward the smashed cars.

Steve ran after him, jumping over the car parked next to theirs. His feet slipped as he hit the ground, falling into a puddle of warm sticky liquid. "Damn, I think the transmission is leaking, got the stuff all over me. I hope it isn't flammable."

"That isn't transmission fluid, man," said Mike. "I think that's blood. No one in there survived. We need to get out of here, now."

Steve didn't respond as he hopped back over the sedan to get back to the girls. Mike was right on his heels, yelling at the Jennie and Lisa to get out of the car and run. More cars soared overhead, piling up near the entrance, blocking the only way out, trapping everyone inside.

"We can run through the corn," yelled Jennie.

"I've seen that movie," yelled Lisa. "I'm not going anywhere near the corn fields."

"Me neither," said Steve. "But, that fucking monster is destroying everything. We need to do something."

Mike looked around, searching for a way out, finally seeing the monster responsible for the chaos. The beast towered high above him, its entire body formed from popped corn kernels, sopped with butter and glistening with salt crystals. Buttery puss oozed from between the kernels, dripping to the ground in steamy puddles. The beast's powerful arms and legs were the size of tree trunks and its massive torso large than a luxury SUV. Mike's knees shook and the hairs on the back of his neck stood on end. He wanted to run, he wanted to scream, but his mind blanked as he stood motionless.

Steve grabbed Mike's shoulder, "Dude, we have to get out of here. Come on!"

"Do you see that?" said Mike, his words shaky.

"How can I not see it?" asked Steve. "It's a twenty foot tall popcorn monster. Now, let's not dwell on what that fucking thing is and

223

focus on getting the hell out of here."

"Get out?" said Jennie. "Where are we supposed to go? There is no way out."

"What about the concession stand?" asked Lisa. "There has to be a basement or some sort of shelter we can hide in until help arrives."

"She's right, it looks like our only chance at hiding from the buttery beast," said Mike. "Steve, I'll go first and you follow behind, the girls will be between us in single file. We need to stay low so it doesn't see us."

The four crouched down and weaved between the cars, taking the long route as far from the popcorn monster as possible, hoping they wouldn't draw attention to themselves. They didn't bother being too quiet, the air was ripe with noise as people screamed for help and salvation. However, they kept a watchful eye on the beast, ready to maneuver their way into another direction if it got to close.

As they neared the concession stand, it seemed salvation was near. Lisa ran ahead to get inside where it was safe. "We're safe, we're safe," she yelled. "Hurry, let's get inside."

Lisa was relieved to find the door unlocked as she hurried inside, not waiting for the others as they tried to catch up. Steve tried to run ahead but Mike pulled him back, shoving him down onto the ground between two older model cars.

"Slow down, the popcorn beast is right there," he said in a hushed tone, pointing to the north end of the lot. "We are safe here until he moves on, then we'll go in."

"But Lisa's alone in there," he said, anxious to get inside and hold her in his arms.

"You won't do her any good if you're dead," said Mike. "We'll wait it out here, she'll be okay in there."

Time seemed to stand still as the popcorn monster wreaked havoc on the drive in. He corralled a few people in between a Humvee and a pick-up truck, each huddling together hoping for a miracle to save them from their doom.

Towering above the group of five men and women, the popcorn beast opened his mouth and vomited gallons of steamy melted butter onto his prisoners. Their screams of agony faded as the boiling butter melted their flesh down to muscle and bone, cooking them in their own juices. The stench of scorched flesh filled the air. A group of younger teens that were hiding behind a small compact car nearby screamed and ran toward the concession stand, seeking refuge inside and out of sight of the beast. They found the same door that Lisa entered through, but the popcorn beast saw them as well. He lifted the Humvee above his head and hurled it toward the concrete building, smashing the side wall to dust. He followed his assault with the pickup truck, one of the poor victims melted to its side.

224

The bed of the truck, stocked with a couple large gasoline barrels, followed a similar trajectory of the Humvee, smashing into the roof, exploding into a fiery blaze, killing everyone inside, including Lisa.

"No!" yelled Steve, jumping to his feet.

Mike pulled him back to the ground as Jennie huddled in the fetal position, muttering to herself words that could not be recognized. Mike tried to calm both of them down, but neither was in the right mind to focus on anything but the confused thoughts in their heads.

"Come on guys," he said. "We have to move before that thing finds us. He's already taken out nearly everyone here. Look, there are bodies everywhere, scattered among the cars and garbage. Hell, the only thing not strewn about is bits of popcorn. Instead, we have their daddy here trying to consume all of us."

He held Steve and Jennie close to him, hoping to calm them enough to bring them back to their senses and get them coherent enough to get out of there. He knew they were out of time, but he couldn't rush it, not in their uneasy condition.

Jennie's sobs were amplified between the cars. Mike hoped they wouldn't draw attention to them, but he held her closer to his chest, hoping her cries would be muffled in the fabric of his letter jacket. Just to be safe, he pulled Steve in close as well. The air became suddenly silent around them; quite uncomforting.

The winds lessened as well, almost to the point that it was prior to the attack. Mike tried to look around, but his vision was limited and he could only see as far as his peripheral allowed. Once again, the hairs in the back of his neck stood on end and chills rushed down his spine; he wanted to run, but knew he had to be brave for his friends.

Not wanting to wait longer, Mike shook his friends, "Com on guys, we have to go. We need to be brave and get out of here before that thing gets us."

Both looked at Mike, nodding their heads in agreement, preparing to make their escape. Mike tried grasped each by the shoulder and looked them in the eye, making sure they were ready to make their next move. Each nodded to him, signaling they were okay, just as the car they leaned against flipped flung through the air, landing about ten feet away. All three fell to the dusty ground, finding themselves staring eye to eye with the popcorn beast.

Steve jumped to his feet, in a fighting stance with his fists out front, ready to take on the popcorn monster despite the odds. The monster, unconcerned at the threat Steve posed, raised his massive arm into the air and swooped it down, slapping Steve toward the concession stand where the flames still licked the sky. His body lost in the conflagrations.

Jennie screamed; her voice hoarse from all the cries that bellowed from her lungs. Mike grabbed her and tried to crawl away, but the popcorn beast was right atop them; escape was futile. Knowing the end was near, Jennie looked into Mike's eyes and whispered softly, "just hold me. As long as I'm with you, everything will be okay."

Mike held her tight, unwilling to let go, regardless of what hellish torture the popcorn beast was ready to dish out. With Jennie's face buried into his chest once again, Mike stared bravely into the popcorn beast's eyes, letting it know that he was not going to perish without facing his enemy down.

The popcorn beast's eyes were the color of buttery yellow kernels, shining against the remaining car headlights, its ominous glow foreboding and grim. The creature opened his mouth wide, a gurgling sound emanating from within its gut, as it readied itself to let loose a vomitus spray of salted butter bile.

Mike held Jennie closer, adjusting his body over hers, hoping to take the brunt of the attack and shield her from fatal harm. He knew the chances were slim, but had to try his best. He said goodbye, softly, and placed his lips upon hers, gently kissing her one last time before their demise. "We'll be together again soon, I swear to you."

A violent war cry roared from near distance. Mike, shocked, looked up just in time to see Steve running toward them, his body aflame. His pace was steady and swift, although his body weak from the heat, as he ran toward the popcorn beast. He took the popcorn beast by surprise as he jump onto its leg, grasping it as tightly as possible with his remaining strength, sending his flames upward, igniting the popcorn in an instant.

The popcorn beast roared, standing straight as the buttery bile dribbled down its chest. The flames consumed the beast as it stumbled backward, retreating into toward the surrounding cornfields, making its way to the area behind where the large movie screen once stood. The beast tripped over the many scattered cars, its body succumbing to the flames. As it neared the edge of the lot, the creature collapsed, spreading its flames to the stalks of corn. As the popcorn beast perished, the corn field came to life with dancing infernos pirouetting in the still air. The sky lit up with an eerie glow, leaving a single path left untouched at the entrance of the drive in.

Mike grabbed Jennie by the arm and lifter her to her feet. He made sure she was steady before ushering her toward the entrance, looking her in the eyes to let her know they would be okay.

"Let's go," he said. "This isn't the time to mourn our loss; it's a time to celebrate our lives. We'll come back later to grieve, when the time is right."

Hand in hand they walked toward the entrance, their shadows stretched into the center of the chaos as they approached the ticket booth, neither looking back as they continued down the path towards home.

THE BENEFACTOR

Feast
upon
the
creative
juices !

Jim Kavanaugh

Drive-In Creature Feature Anthology *presents a*
Mark Allan Gunnells *story* **The Benefactor**
edited by **Eugene Johnson** *and* **Charles Day**
produced by **Evil Jester Press** | L H | Literary Horror Disturbing Content

Mark Allan Gunnells

Mark Allan Gunnells loves to tell stories. He has since he was a kid, penning one-page tales that were *Twilight Zone* knockoffs. He likes to think he has gotten a little better since then. He loves reader feedback, and above all he loves telling stories. He lives in Greer, SC, with his fiancé Craig A. Metcalf.

THE BENEFACTOR

Mark Allan Gunnells

March 15

I moved into Monica's house today.

House? Mansion is more like it, the kind of home that has wings and servants' quarters, something out of a Merchant/Ivory film. I have my own suite of four rooms in the east wing, with a view of the tennis courts and swimming pool.

Hard to believe I only first met Monica less than a month ago. It was a Friday night, and I was where I always was on Friday nights, a coffee bar called Grounds. Every Friday they have an open-mike night for amateur writers who want to share their works with an audience.

That night I was reading a short story I had just written, "Milk and Honey," a dark little tale of a utopian society, which is maintained through the use of psychedelic drugs. It went over well with the gathered crowd, laughs coming at the appropriate moments, applause and a few cheers at the end. I felt pretty good as I stepped down off the stage.

Monica approached me, an elegant woman in her fifties, flaming red hair streaked with gray, wearing a stylish red dress that accentuated her small waist and ample bosom. I had seen her at Grounds before but we had never spoken. She told me my writing was what kept her coming back. She told me my stories were rich and textured, masterfully crafted tales that engrossed and enticed. She stroked my ego with an expert's hand.

I spent the rest of the evening at a corner table with Monica, enjoying her charming laugh and the way her eyes bore into me with candor and a certain hunger. She proved herself to be a woman of sophistication and intelligence, and her appreciation for my work was effusive. As a young man of twenty-two, I had never found myself particularly drawn to older women, preferring young and nubile flesh, but Monica made a convert out of me. Suddenly all the girls I had been involved with in my life seemed nothing but a gaggle of simpering fools, airheads and dumbbells, hollow shells that were all surface and no substance. Monica represented a new kind of woman, a woman whose physical beauty was infused and enhanced by an inner light. She had life experience that made her so much more vibrant and alive than anyone I had ever known.

I assumed that Monica's interest in me was primarily of a physical nature—not to brag, but my body is fit and my looks have charmed more than one young lady into my bed over the years—but the offer she made me at the end of the night was not sexual. She wanted to be my benefactor, my patron. She said she recognized the untapped potential inside me, and it was her hope that she could help hone that talent.

Her offer was this: that I move into her home for one year, allow her to cover all of my expenses for the duration, so that I could concentrate solely on writing the novel I had wanted to write for ages. I would not have to worry about finances or work schedules or anything of the sort. I could focus all of my time and energy on my writing, on creating a work of importance and grandeur.

I hesitated initially. It seemed a strange setup, like I would be her kept boy or something. In the end, however, the notion of finally excavating that novel from my brain and getting it down on paper proved too tempting. I was tired of working my ass off at two jobs and still barely making the rent, leaving me precious little time to write. Monica's offer was manna from Heaven, and I shelved my initial concerns and accepted.

And now here I am, in my own little apartment within her palatial estate. She has provided me with a new laptop, sleek and modern, quite a step up from the old Smith Corona typewriter that I was previously using. I brought my notes, the ones I've been jotting down for years, with bits of dialogue, possible scenes, character descriptions, a half-finished outline for the first several chapters of what I hope will become my masterpiece.

Tonight I settle in. Tomorrow I begin work on my novel. It is scary, but awfully exciting.

March 17

For such a large house, Monica has only 3 servants; a butler, a cook, and a maid. They all look to be in their early to mid-30s, but their faces are careworn, as if they've lived rough lives that have aged them beyond their years.

I mention them only because I would almost swear the maid is Amaretta Tyler, the stage actress that dropped out of the theater scene after a disastrous performance in a high-profile off-Broadway production last year. It seems unlikely she would now be working as a servant, but I once saw her as Blanche in *Streetcar Named Desire* and the resemblance is uncanny.

March 19

    Eat Your Heart Out Julia.
    That is the name of my novel. The plot in a nutshell involves a divorced man's new bride, Julia, trying to fit into the lives of her husband's two daughters when their mother, a deranged woman who feels Julia is usurping her life, reappears and begins a campaign of intimidation and violence in order to drive Julia away. The initial idea for the novel has been with me since my freshman year of high school. I was sitting in Algebra class, my mind on anything but Algebra, and began thinking how the stepmother in works of fiction is almost always wicked. I started to contemplate why that was, was it not possible that a stepmother could be good, could in fact be a better person in some cases than the biological mother? I had the seed of the story then, but it took eight years for that seed to blossom.
    When I first sat down at the laptop Monica provided for me, I had much trouble finding a way into the world of the story. Everything I wrote seemed derivative and trite. I had written nothing but short stories for so long, I began to wonder if I was capable of sustaining a longer piece of fiction. I was not able to immerse myself in the story, every word a struggle, every sentence a battle, every paragraph an all-out war. After two days of this, I was nearly ready to give up.
    And then it came to me, out of nowhere. It happens like that sometimes. You can spend days struggling over a story, practically pulling your hair out at the roots to work it out, and then it simply comes to you. The way in, the solution, just like that. Like a gift from the Muses.
    I needed to write the novel from the perspective of the youngest daughter. She initially sees Julia as the traditional wicked stepmother, agreeing to help her mother dislodge Julia from their lives. Only after a while does the daughter begin to understand just how sick her mother truly is. It was perfect, added a level of moral complication to the story that it had lacked before.
    I have so far only written the Prologue and the first chapter and a half, but I am pleased with the work I am doing and anxious to continue. This arrangement with Monica was just what I needed. I now have the time to devote to my craft that I never had before, the time needed to become a true artist.

March 21

    Monica and I had dinner together tonight. It was a delicious, extravagant meal. Not surprising, considering that she has a kitchen staff of five. We started with a salad of crisp spinach, fresh fruit, and some type of nut that lent the salad an intriguing smoky, peppery taste. Then we had crab shells stuffed with cheeses. This was followed by the main course of roasted duck marinated in a sumptuous wine sauce. Dessert was a mousse so rich and creamy that even now, hours later, I still taste it on my tongue. Only a week ago, I lived on take-out and delivery pizza; never have I had such a meal as this.

Monica seemed to take delight in my pleasure as I devoured the meal. She herself ate mechanically, seeming to derive no particular enjoyment from the food, eating only for the necessary nourishment. I suppose when one eats like this every day, it is easy to become immune to the lavishness of it all.

We talked throughout the meal. Monica asked me how the novel was coming, and I told her excitedly about the progress I was making. She did not ask to read the chapters I had thus far completed, but she did show much interest in the creative process. She asked about my childhood, past loves, my parents. She devoured my life story the way I devoured the food set before me.

She also told me of her life. She was an orphan, living on her own since she was fourteen. At nineteen, working as a chambermaid at a posh hotel, she had met a wealthy businessman and soon became his bride. Three years into the marriage, her husband had died from a massive coronary, leaving Monica his fortune. Smart investments and well-chosen business ventures had increased her wealth over the years. As a lover of art but with no true talent of her own, Monica had become a patron to the arts, giving of her time and money when she could. I was the first artist she had ever taken into her own home, but she believed in my talent.

I was more than a little tipsy from the wine by the end of the evening. She walked me back to my suite, and I thought that she would come into my rooms with me, spend the night in my bed, but instead she just kissed me; a deep kiss, a passionate kiss, the kind of kiss that stiffens a man. I was weak-kneed when she pulled away and took her leave. Even now her image is fresh in my mind, the swell of her cleavage, the scent of her perfume, the feel of her soft lips against mine. I will no doubt have to pleasure myself before sleep will take me tonight.

March 22

I slept until after noon today. And even then, I awoke reluctantly. My body was sore, my mind groggy, my tongue coated with fur by the feel. Normally I hold my alcohol better than this; the wine last night must have been particularly potent.

I attempted to work on the novel this afternoon, but I found it difficult to concentrate on the story. My mind kept wandering off, distracted by the slightest thing. At one point, I realized I had been merely sitting, staring at a single mote of dust floating in the sunlight, for at least a half an hour.

I took a walk around the grounds in an attempt to clear my head, regain my focus. When I returned to the house, I encountered the butler dusting the foyer. Looking for another distraction, I engaged him in a little conversation, talking to him about my writer's block. He told me he could relate; revealing that he had once been a poet of some renown in certain literary circles, publishing under the name Edward Malys (pronounced "malice"). The name was not familiar to me, but then poetry was never my forte. He confirmed that the maid is in fact Amaretta Tyler, and confided that the cook had once been a sculptor though not one of any great prominence. When I inquired how they all ended up in Monica's employ, the butler became evasive, probably due to embarrassment over his fall from notoriety.

I returned to my room more determined than ever to overcome this block. I would succeed; I would not end up like these servants who had lost their creative spark.

March 27

Today was a good day, in more ways than one.

After several days in which I had found writing more of a chore than a pleasure, I finally managed to get back in the zone. I was writing a confrontation scene between Julia and Teresa, the youngest stepdaughter, and it just *clicked*. I could hear their voices, I understood their motivations, and it flowed from me like water through a sieve. The characters came alive to me, like they weren't living only in my head but were in the room with me, and I was not creating their dialogue so much as simply recording their conversation as it happened. When it comes that easily, it is magical, as if I am merely a vessel through which the story is channeled. It is a feeling that is impossible to describe to those who have never experienced it, but its power is intoxicating.

I wrote for four hours straight, my fingers cramping but not enough to deter me, and only stopped when Monica came to my door. She wore a short summer dress, baby blue, riding high on her creamy thighs. She was barefoot and her hair was down and wild. There was a mischievous glint in her eyes that managed to pull me away from the computer.

She did not speak, merely came to me, straddled me where I sat and kissed me like she wanted to swallow my flesh. She unzipped me and freed my throbbing organ, pulling her dress up higher to reveal she wore no underwear. She mounted me and rode me like that, both of us still clothed, neither of us speaking. We made love with urgency and desperation, our bodies drenched in sweat, our cries of pleasure indistinguishable from cries of pain. When it was over, when we both had climaxed, she merely kissed me, thanked me, and left like a dream

233

dissipating in the light of morning.

I can smell her on me still, her musky female aroma all over my skin. Every time I breathe I am reminded of her beauty, her passion, her hunger. I think I am falling in love.

April 11

I am in hell.

For the past couple of weeks, I have been unable to write anything of substance or quality. My prose is flat, my characters lifeless, my dialogue stilted and inauthentic. Nothing I do seems to work. The novel has veered way off course, and I cannot seem to steer it back in the right direction. Sometimes as I sit in front of the computer, the cursor blinking at me in accusation and mockery, I get so frustrated that tears spring to my eyes.

Monica comes to me nightly, allowing me to take solace in her body. My time with her is the only joy I know these days, the pleasures of the flesh in which we indulge ourselves. We have done things I have never tried before, never even considered. The other day we made love in the garden amongst the lilies, knowing that Edward was tending the roses just on the other side of the hedge. She inspires me to acts of depravity that leave me breathless and exhilarated. I profess my love to her daily, though she has yet to return those three all-important words. But I am patient; I know I will hear them in time.

April 17

I deleted the last three chapters of *Eat Your Heart Out Julia*. I had introduced a subplot in which Julia discovers that she and her husband's first wife are actually fraternal twins separated at birth. However, recognizing the plot as the cheesy soap opera device it was, I abandoned it. I continue to slave over my novel, but I cannot seem to find my way back into the story, cannot find the key to unlock the door into that world.

Two days ago, I decided to take a break from the novel and write a short story or two. In the past, shorter pieces had always come easily to me. I could usually knock off a six-thousand word story in a matter of hours. Having had no new ideas since coming to live in Monica's house—I have been so focused on the novel that it has left me with little time to think on shorter works, I guess—I consulted my notes, where I keep scraps of ideas that have come to me over the years.

I took several ideas from my notes and tried to craft them into stories. Nothing too long, fifteen to twenty pages maybe, but even that was not working. I have suffered bouts of writer's block in the past, every writer has, but never anything this severe. It is as if I have developed the opposite of the Midas touch—everything I touch turns to shit.

I attempted to engage Edward in conversation again, thinking in him I may find a confidant who could understand an artist's pain, but he no longer seems open to this. Perhaps it is painful for him, salt in his metaphorical wounds, reminding him of his own artistic inadequacies.

So I continue to suffer alone.

May 2

Today was a beautiful spring day, warm and bright, full of promise and hope. In my darkened suite, sitting at my computer, fingers poised above the keys but not moving, all was bleak and dismal.

Monica rescued me from that misery. She insisted I leave the novel behind for the day, and we went on an excursion to the beach. I was hesitant at first, I did not want to feel I was running away from my problem, but she finally convinced me. Perhaps what I need is some distance. Perhaps my constant obsessing over the story is just making the block all the worse.

We found a private cove and had a picnic. Monica was wearing a stunning two- piece bikini that left me speechless. I could swear she seems to be getting younger right before my eyes. She no longer looks to be a widow in her fifties; if I were meeting her for the first time today, I would guess mid-to-late thirties. Maybe it is just that she has colored her hair. I noticed the other day that there were no longer streaks of gray, now her hair was just that startlingly vibrant shade of auburn. That could account for her younger look.

And yet I'd swear the wrinkles around the corners of her eyes and lips have melted away. Her body, seductively on display in the swimsuit, seemed more toned, firmer. Perhaps it is just part of the old cliché, that love makes a person grow more beautiful every day.

We made love in the sand like a scene from some melodramatic movie. Her body clinched around my flesh like a ravenous mouth, causing me to scream out my devotion to her. She merely smiled and thanked me, allowing me to climax inside her.

May 15

While attempting to write today, Amaretta came into my room to clean. I considered telling her how much I'd loved her in the Tennessee Williams' play but decided that would be cruel considering her current circumstances. She worked in silence, as always.

Except just before she left, she turned to me and said, "I was cleaning the other day when you were out with Monica and I read a few pages of your work."

Part of me was offended by this intrusion, but another part of me craved feedback. "What did you think?"

"Maybe you should add a succubus to the story."

"Excuse me?"

"A succubus. Look it up."

And then she left. What an odd comment for her to make about my novel. I didn't have to look up the word "succubus", as an educated man I know it is a mythical creature of great feminine beauty who seduces men to drain them of their youth and vitality.

But I fail to see what that has to do with me or my story.

June 17

I have not left my suite in days, perhaps weeks. I don't know, time seems to have lost all relevance. Day bleeds into night, night into day, on and on in a repetitive cycle that is as meaningless as it is predictable.

I merely sit at my desk, staring at the blank screen of my laptop, my face streaked with tears. The magic is gone, dried up, and I cannot find any means of reviving it. My imagination, which once seemed boundless, is a barren wasteland that can no longer sustain life. Tumbleweeds roll through the dusty expanse between my ears, but nothing else. There is no creative spark, no ideas, no living characters begging to be freed onto the page.

I have always been a writer; it is how I define myself. In some ways, it is *all* that I am. Without it, without my ability to craft fictional worlds and explore them, I do not know who I am. I do not know if I am anyone at all. I am lost.

Monica has not been to see me in weeks, possibly a month. The servants tell me that she is away on business and do not know when to expect her to return. She did not even tell me she was going, did not tell me goodbye.

I am lost.

I am no one.

June 30

I dreamt of Monica tonight. We were making love with her on top. She straddled and rode me like a stallion, her lithe body bathed in golden candle light. And yet the mix of this flickering illumination and the shifting shadows played tricks on the idea. Her beautiful face now seemed that of a crone, a dried crabapple with straw-like hair sprouting from it in sporadic patches. Her once pert breasts now sagged like socks full of pennies, and her nails were chipped and yellowed and clawed at my chest. Her sex seemed to clamp down on mine like a vise, and the pleasure which had only a moment before coursed through my body now

236

turned to tortuous pain.

I screamed…and woke, realizing I was still screaming.

Three hours have since passed, and sleep has not come again.

July 1

Monica returned home today, but she was not alone.

His name is Victor, and he is a painter. The house is now filled with his canvases. Victor favors surreal dreamscapes, Salvador Dali-esque portraits of a world gone mad. The paintings frighten me with the power of their conviction.

Victor himself is a contradiction. He has the physique of a bodybuilder and the meek disposition of a high school nerd. He speaks little, except of his art, and Monica seems completely enraptured of him.

July 15

I caught Monica and Victor making love today.

Caught is the wrong word; that implies they were trying to hide. They weren't. They were making love by the pool, right out in the open. I glanced out my window and there they were, coupling with animalistic intensity. Later, when I confronted Monica, she gave me a look so cold that I felt the marrow in my bones freeze. She said this was her house and she would do as she pleased.

She has asked me to move to a small room in the servant's quarters so that Victor can have the suite. He needs room to work, she says.

August 5

Monica came to me today and told me I needed to start earning my keep around the estate. She took the laptop, which I haven't used in months anyway, and informed me that I was to become her driver. My first assignment was to drive her and Victor to town so that she could buy him some new paints.

I cried, I admit it. I blubbered and pleaded with her, dropping to my knees and professing my eternal love to her. She merely looked disgusted. I asked her what had changed, why had she turned so cold to me? She smiled cruelly and said I was no longer of any use to her; I no longer had anything to offer. Once I had been brimming with creativity and artistry, and she had bathed in that brilliance, but now it was all used up, and she had found someone new and fresh, someone whose creativity was still strong and luminous.

She left me with this ultimatum: I could be her driver or I could leave the estate. Those were my options.

But as I sit here writing these words, the old straight razor sitting next to my left hand, I realize there is a third option.

Monica was right. My creativity is all used up, there is no artistry left in me. I am useless and have nothing to offer.

There have only ever been two things to give my life purpose, my writing and my love of Monica. Without those two things, I am nothing. I may as well not even exist.

So I won't.

THE FOLDING MAN

A TALE THAT WILL FRIGHTEN YOU TO DEATH!

Jim Kavanaugh

Drive-In Creature Feature Anthology *Presents a* **Joe R. Lansdale** *story* **The Folding Man** *edited by* **Eugene Johnson** *and* **Charles Day** *Produced by* **Evil Jester Press** | HH | halloween horror / scenes of brutality | *Copyright 2016*

Joe R. Lansdale

Joe R. Lansdale is the author of 48 novels and over 20 short story collections. He has written and sold a number of screenplays, has had his plays adapted for stage. His work has been adapted to film; *Bubba Hotep* and *Cold in July* among them. His best known novels, the Hap and Leonard series has been adapted for television with Lansdale as co-executive producer with Lowell Northrop under the title, *Hap And Leonard*. He has also edited or co- edited numerous anthologies.

THE FOLDING MAN

Joe R. Lansdale

They had come from a Halloween party, having long shed the masks they'd worn. No one but Harold had been drinking, and he wasn't driving, and he wasn't so drunk he was blind. Just drunk enough he couldn't sit up straight and was lying on the back seat, trying, for some unknown reason, to recite The Pledge of Allegiance, which he didn't accurately recall. He was mixing in verses from the Star Spangled Banner and the Boy Scout oath, which he vaguely remembered from his time in the organization before they drove him out for setting fires.

Even though William, who was driving, and Jim who was riding shotgun, were sober as Baptists claimed to be, they were fired up and happy and yelling and hooting, and Jim pulled down his pants and literally mooned a black bug of a car carrying a load of nuns.

The car wasn't something that looked as if it had come off the lot. Didn't have the look of any car maker Jim could identify. It had a cobbled look. It reminded him of something in old movies, the ones with gangsters who were always squealing their tires around corners. Only it seemed bigger, with broader windows through which he could see the nuns, or at least glimpse them in their habits; it was a regular penguin convention inside that car.

Way it happened, when they came up on the nuns, Jim said to William at the wheel, "Man, move over close, I'm gonna show them some butt."

"They're nuns, man."

"That's what makes it funny," Jim said.

William eased the wheel to the right, and Harold in the back said, "Grand Canyon. Grand Canyon. Show them the Grand Canyon...Oh, say can you see..."

Jim got his pants down, swiveled on his knees in the seat, twisted so that his ass was against the glass, and just as they passed the nuns, William hit the electric window switch and slid the glass down. Jim's ass jumped out at the night, like a vibrating moon.

"They lookin'?" Jim asked.

241

"Oh, yeah," William said, "and they are not amused."

Jim jerked his pants up, shifted in the seat, and turned for a look, and sure enough, they were not amused. Then a funny thing happened, one of the nuns shot him the finger, and then others followed. Jim said, "Man, those nuns are rowdy."

And now he got a good look at them, even though it was night, because there was enough light from the headlights as they passed for him to see faces hard as wardens and ugly as death warmed over. The driver was especially homely, face like that could stop a clock and run it backwards or make shit crawl up hill.

"Did you see that, they shot me the finger?" Jim said.

"I did see it," William said.

Harold had finally gotten the Star Spangled Banner straight, and he kept singing it over and over.

"For Christ sake," William said. "Shut up, Harold."

"You know what," Jim said, studying the rear view mirror, "I think they're speeding up. They're trying to catch us. Oh, hell. What if they get the license plate? Maybe they already have. They call the law, my dad will have my mooning ass."

"Well, if they haven't got the plate," William said, "they won't. This baby can get on up and get on out."

He put his foot on the gas. The car hummed as if it had just had an orgasm, and seemed to leap. Harold was flung off the backseat, onto the floorboard. "Hey, goddamnit," he said.

"Put on your seat belt, jackass," Jim said.

William's car was eating up the road. It jumped over a hill and dove down the other side like a porpoise negotiating a wave, and Jim thought: Goodbye, penguins, and then he looked back. At the top of the hill were the lights from the nun's car, and the car was gaining speed and it moved in a jerky manner, as if it were stealing space between blinks of the eye.

"Damn," William said. "They got some juice in that thing, and the driver has her foot down."

"What kind of car is that?" Jim said.

"Black," William said.

"Ha! Mr. Detroit."

"Then you name it."

Jim couldn't. He turned to look back. The nun's car had already caught up; the big automotive beast was cruising in tight as a coat of varnish, the head lights making the interior of William's machine bright as a Vegas act.

"What the hell they got under the hood?" William said. "Hyper-drive?"

"These nuns," Jim said, "they mean business."

"I can't believe it, they're riding my bumper."

"Slam on your brakes. That'll show them."

"Not this close," William said. "Do that, what it'll show them is the inside of our butts."

"Do nuns do this?"

"These do."

"Oh," Jim said. "I get it. Halloween. They aren't real nuns."

"Then we give them hell," Harold said, and just as the nuns were passing on the right, he crawled out of the floorboard and onto his seat and rolled the window down. The back window of the nun's car went down and Jim turned to get a look, and the nun, well, she was ugly all right, but uglier than he had first imagined. She looked like something dead, and the nun's outfit she wore was not actually black and white, but purple and white, or so it appeared in the light from head beams and moonlight. The nun's lips pulled back from her teeth and the teeth were long and brown, as if tobacco stained. One of her eyes looked like a spoiled meat ball, and her nostrils flared like a pigs.

Jim said, "That ain't no mask."

Harold leaned way out of the window and flailed his hands and said, "You are so goddamn ugly you have to creep up on your underwear."

Harold kept on with this kind of thing, some of it almost making sense, and then one of the nuns in the back, one closest to the window, bent over in the seat and came up and leaned out of the window, a two-by-four in her hands. Jim noted that her arms, where the nun outfit had fallen back to the elbows, were as thin as sticks and white as the underbelly of a fish and the elbows were knotty, and bent in the wrong direction.

"Get back in," Jim said to Harold.

Harold waved his arms and made another crack, and then the nun swung the two-by-four, the oddness of her elbows causing it to arrive at a weird angle, and the board made a crack of it's own, or rather Harold's skull did, and he fell forward, the lower half of his body hanging from the window, bouncing against the door, his knuckles losing meat on the highway, his ass hanging inside, one foot on the floor board the other waggling in the air.

"The nun hit him," Jim said. "With a board."

"What?" William said.

"You deaf, she hit him."

Jim snapped lose his seat belt and leaned over and grabbed Harold by the back of the shirt and yanked him inside. Harold's head looked like it had been in a vice. There was blood everywhere. Jim said, "Oh, man, I think he's dead."

BLAM!

The noise made Jim jump. He slid back in his seat and looked toward the nuns. They were riding close enough to slam the two-by-four into Williams' car; the driver was pressing that black monster toward them.

Another swing of the board and the side mirror shattered.

William tried to gun forward, but the nun's car was even with him, pushing him to the left. They went across the highway and into a ditch and the car did an acrobatic twist and tumbled down an embankment and rolled into the woods tossing up mud and leaves and pine straw.

***

Jim found himself outside the car, and when he moved, everything seemed to whirl for a moment, then gathered up slowly and became solid. He had been thrown free, and so had William, who was lying nearby. The car was a wreck, lying on its roof, spinning still, steam easing out from under the hood in little cotton-white clouds. Gradually, the car quit spinning, like an old time watch that had wound down. The windshield was gone and three of the four doors lay scattered about.

The nuns were parked up on the road, and the car doors opened and the nuns got out. Four of them. They were unusually tall. and when they walked, like their elbows, their knees bent in the wrong direction. It was impossible to tell this for sure, because of the robes they wore, but it certainly looked that way, and considering the elbows, it fit. There in the moonlight, they were as white and pasty as pot stickers, their jaws seeming to have grown longer than when Jim had last looked at them, their noses witch-like, except for those pig flair nostrils, their backs bent like long bows. One of them still held the two-by-four.

Jim slid over to William who was trying to sit up.

"You okay?" Jim asked.

"I think so," William said, patting his fingers at a blood spot on his forehead. "Just before they hit, I stupidly unsnapped my seat belt. I don't know why. I just wanted out I guess. Brain not working right."

"Look up there," Jim said.

They both looked up the hill.. One of the nuns was moving down from the highway, toward the wrecked car.

"If you can move," Jim said, "I think we oughta."

William worked himself to his feet. Jim grabbed his arm and half pulled him into the woods where they leaned against a tree. William said. "Everything's spinning."

"It stops soon enough," Jim said.

"I got to chill, I'm about to faint."

"A moment," Jim said.

The nun who had gone down by herself, bent down out of sight behind William's car, then they saw her going back up the hill, dragging Harold by his ankle, his body flopping all over as if all the bones in his body had been broken.

"My God, see that?" William said. "We got to help."

"He's dead," Jim said. "They crushed his head with a board."

244

"Oh, hell, man. That can't be. They're nuns."

"I don't think they are," Jim said. "Least not the kind of nuns you're thinking."

The nun dragged Harold up the hill and dropped his leg when she reached the big black car. Another of the nuns opened the trunk and reached in and got hold of something. It looked like some kind of folded up lawn chair, only more awkward in shape. The nun jerked it out and dropped it on the ground and gave it a swift kick. The folded up thing began to unfold with a clatter and a squeak. A perfectly round head rose up from it, and the head spun on what appeared to be a silver hinge. When it quit whirling, it was upright and in place, though cocked slightly to the left. The eyes and mouth and nostrils were merely holes. Moonlight could be seen through them. The head rose as coat-rack style shoulders pushed it up and a cage of a chest rose under that. The chest looked almost like an old frame on which dresses were placed to be sewn, or perhaps a cage designed to contain something you wouldn't want to get out. With more squeaks and clatters, skeletal hips appeared, and beneath that, long, bony, legs with bent back knees and big metal-framed feet. Stick-like arms swung below its knees, clattering against its legs like a tree limbs bumping against a window pane. It stood at least seven feet tall. Like the nuns, its knees and elbows fit backwards.

The nun by the car trunk reached inside and pulled out something fairly large that beat its wings against the night air. She held it in one hand by its clawed feet, and its beak snapped wildly, looking for something to peck. Using her free hand, she opened up the folding man's chest by use of a hinge, and when the cage flung open, she put the black, winged thing inside. It fluttered about like a heart shot full of adrenaline. The holes that were the folding man's eyes filled with a red glow and the mouth hole grew wormy lips, and a tongue, long as a garden snake, dark as dirt, licked out at the night, and there was a loud sniff as its nostrils sucked air. One of the nuns reached down and grabbed up a handful of clay, and pressed it against the folding man's arms; the clay spread fast as a lie, went all over, filling the thing with flesh of the earth until the entire folding man's body was covered. The nun, who had taken the folding man out of the car, picked Harold up by the ankle, and as if he were nothing more than a blow-up doll, swung him over her head and slammed him into the darkness of the trunk, shut the lid, and looked out where Jim and William stood recovering by the tree.

The nun said something, a noise between a word and a cough, and the folding man began to move down the hill at a stumble. As he moved his joints made an un-oiled hinge sound, and the rest of him made a clatter like lug bolts being knocked together, accompanied by a noise akin to wire hangers being twisted by strong hands.

"Run," Jim said.

Jim began to feel pain, knew he was more banged up than he

245

thought. His neck hurt. His back hurt. One of his legs really hurt. He must have jammed his knee against something. William, who ran alongside him, dodging trees, said, "My ribs. I think they're cracked."

Jim looked back. In the distance, just entering the trees, framed in the moonlight behind him, was the folding man. He moved in strange leaps, as if there were springs inside him, and he was making good time.

Jim said, "We can't stop. It's coming."

It was low down in the woods and water had gathered there and the leaves had mucked up with it, and as they ran, they sloshed and splashed, and behind them, they could hear it, the folding man, coming, cracking limbs, squeaking hinges, splashing his way after them. When they had the nerve to look back, they could see him darting between the trees like a bit of the forest itself, and he, or it, was coming quite briskly for a thing its size until it reached the lower down parts of the bottom land. There its big feet slowed it some as they buried deep in the mud and were pulled free again with a sound like the universe sucking wind. Within moments, however, the thing got its stride, its movements becoming more fluid and its pace faster.

Finally Jim and William came to a tree-thickened rise in the land, and were able to get out of the muck, scramble upwards and move more freely, even though there was something of a climb ahead, and they had to use trees growing out from the side of the rise to pull themselves upward. When they reached the top of the climb, they were surprised when they looked back to see they had actually gained some space on the thing. It was some distance away, speckled by the moonlight, negotiating its way through the ever thickening trees and undergrowth. But, still it came, ever onward, never tiring. Jim and William bent over and put their hands on their knees and took some deep breaths.

"There's an old graveyard on the far side of this stretch," Jim said. "Near the wrecking yard."

"Where you worked last summer."

"Yeah, that's the one. It gets clearer in the graveyard, and we can make good time. Get to the wrecking yard, Old Man Gordon lives there. He always has a gun and he has that dog, Chomps. It knows me. It will eat that thing up."

"What about me?"

"You'll be all right. You're with me. Come on. I kinda of know where we are now. Used to play in the graveyard, and in this end of the woods. Got to move."

They moved along more swiftly as Jim became more and more familiar with the terrain. It was close to where he had lived when he was a kid, and he had spent a lot of time out here. They came to a place where there was a clearing in the woods, a place where lightning had made a fire. The ground was black, and there were no trees, and in that spot silver moonlight was falling down into it, like mercury filling a cup.

In the center of the clearing they stopped and got their breath again, and William said. "My head feels like its going to explode....Hey, I don't hear it now."

"It's there. Whatever it is, I don't think it gives up."

"Oh, Jesus," William said, and gasped deep once. "I don't know now much I got left in me."

"You got plenty. We got to have plenty."

"What can it be, Jimbo? What in the hell can it be?"

Jim shook his head. "You know that old story about the black car?"

William shook his head.

"My grandmother used to tell me about a black car that roams the highways and the back roads of the South. It isn't in one area all the time, but it's out there somewhere all the time. Halloween is its peak night. It's always after somebody for whatever reason."

"Bullshit."

Jim, hands still on his knees, lifted his head. "You go down there and tell that clatter clap thing it's all bullshit. See where that gets you."

"It just doesn't make sense."

"Grandma said before it was a black car, it was a black buggy, and before that a figure dressed in black on a black horse, and that before that, it was just a shadow that clicked and clacked and squeaked. There's people go missing, she said, and it's the black car, the black buggy, the thing on the horse, or the walkin' shadow that gets them. But, it's all the same thing, just a different appearance."

"The nuns? What about them?"

Jim shook his head, stood up, tested his ability to breathe."Those weren't nuns. They were like...I don't know...Anti-nuns. This thing, if Grandma was right, can take a lot of different forms. Come on. We can't stay here anymore."

"Just another moment, I'm so tired. And I think we've lost it. I don't hear it anymore."

As if on cue, there came a clanking and a squeaking and cracking of limbs. William glanced at Jim, and without a word, they moved across the lightning made clearing and into the trees. Jim looked back, and there it was, crossing the clearing, silver-flooded in the moonlight, still coming, not tiring.

They ran. White stones rose up in front of them. Most of the stones were heaved to the side, or completely pushed out of the ground by growing trees and expanding roots. It was the old graveyard, and Jim knew that meant the wrecking yard was nearby, and so was Gordon's shotgun, and so was one mean dog.

Again the land sloped upwards, and this time William fell forward on his hands and knees, throwing up a mess of blackness. "Oh, God. Don't leave me, Jim... I'm tuckered...Can hardly...breathe."

Jim had moved slightly ahead of William. He turned back to help. As he grabbed William's arm to pull him up, the folding man squeaked and clattered forward and grabbed William's ankle, jerked him back, out of Jim's grasp.

The folding man swung William around easily, slammed his body against a tree, then the thing whirled, and as if William were a bullwhip, snapped him so hard his neck popped and an eyeball flew out of his skull. The folding man brought William whipping down across a standing gravestone. There was a cracking sound, like someone had dropped a glass coffee cup, then the folding man whirled and slung William from one tree to another, hitting the trees so hard bark flew off of them and clothes and meat flew off William.

Jim bolted. He ran faster than he had ever ran, finally he broke free of the woods and came to a stretch of ground that was rough with gravel. Behind him, breaking free of the woods, was The Folding Man, making good time with great strides, dragging William's much abused body behind it by the ankle.

Jim could dimly see the wrecking yard from where he was, and he thought he could make it. Still, there was the aluminum fence all the way around the yard, seven feet high. No little barrier. Then he remembered the sycamore tree on the edge of the fence, on the right side. Old Man Gordon was always taking about cutting it because he thought someone could use it to climb over and into the yard, steal one of his precious car parts, though if they did, they had Gordon's shotgun waiting along with the sizeable teeth of his dog. It had been six months since he had seen the old man, and he hoped he hadn't gotten ambitious, that the tree was still there.

Running closer, Jim could see the sycamore tree remained, tight against the long run of shiny wrecking yard fence. Looking over his shoulder, Jim saw the folding man was springing forward, like some kind of electronic rabbit, William's body being pulled along by the ankle, bouncing on the ground as the thing came ever onward. At this rate, it would be only a few seconds before the thing caught up with him.

Jim felt a pain like a knife in his side, and it seemed as if his heart was going to explode. He reached down deep for everything he had, hoping like hell he didn't stumble.

He made the fence and the tree, went up it like a squirrel, dropped over on the roof of an old car, sprang off of that and ran toward a dim light shining in the small window of a wood and aluminum shack nestled in the midst of old cars and piles of junk.

As he neared the shack, Chomps, part pit bull, part just plain big ole dog, came loping out toward him, growling. It was a hard thing to do, but Jim forced himself to stop, bent down, stuck out his hand, and called the dog's name.

"Chomps. Hey, buddy. It's me."

248

The dog slowed and lowered its head and wagged its tail.

"That's right. Your pal, Jim."

The dog came close and Jim gave it a pat. "Good, boy."

Jim looked over his shoulder. Nothing.

"Come on, Chomps."

Jim moved quickly toward the shack and hammered on the door. A moment later the door flew open, and standing there in overalls, one strap dangling from a naked arm, was Mr. Gordon. He was old and near toothless, squat and greasy as the insides of the cars in the yard.

"Jim? What the hell you doing in here? You look like hell."

"Something's after me."

"Something?"

"It's outside the fence. It killed two of my friends..."

"What?"

"It killed two of my friends."

"It? Some kind of animal?"

"No...It."

"We'll call some law."

Jim shook his head. "No use calling the law now, time they arrive it'll be too late."

Gordon leaned inside the shack and pulled a twelve gauge into view, pumped it once. He stepped outside and looked around.

"You sure?"

"Oh, yeah. Yes, sir. I'm sure."

"Then I guess you and me and Pump Twelve will check it out."

Gordon moved out into the yard, looking left and right. Jim stayed close to Gordon's left elbow. Chomps trotted nearby. They walked about a bit. They stopped between a row of wrecked cars, looked around. Other than the moon-shimmering fence at either end of the row where they stood, there was nothing to see.

"Maybe whatever, or whoever it is, is gone," Gordon said. "Otherwise, Chomps would be all over it."

"I don't think it smells like humans or animals."

"Are you joshin' an old man? Is this a Halloween prank?"

"No, sir. Two of my friends are dead. This thing killed them. It's real."

"What the hell is it then?"

As if in answer, there was the sound like a huge can opener going to work, and then the long, thin arm of the folding man poked through the fence and there was more ripping as the arm slid upwards, tearing at the metal. A big chunk of the fence was torn away, revealing the thing, bathed in moonlight, still holding what was left of William's ragged body by the ankle.

Jim and Gordon both stood locked in amazement.

"Sonofabitch," Gordon said.

Chomps growled, ran toward it.

"Chomps will fix him," Gordon said.

The folding man dropped William's ankle and bent forward, and just as the dog leaped, caught it and twisted it and ran its long arm down the snapping dog's throat, and began to pull its insides out. It flung dog's parts in all directions, like someone pulling confetti from a sack. Then it turned the dog inside out.

When the sack was empty, the folding man bent down and fastened the dead, deflated dog to a hook on the back of what passed for its ankle.

"My God," Gordon said.

The thing picked up William by the ankle, stepped forward a step, and paused.

Gordon lifted the shotgun. "Come and get you some, asshole."

The thing cocked its head as if to consider the suggestion, and then it began to lope toward them, bringing along its clanks and squeaks, the dead dog flopped at the folding man's heel. For the first time, its mouth, which had been nothing but a hole with wormy lips, twisted into the shape of a smile.

Gordon said, "You run, boy. I got this."

Jim didn't hesitate. He turned and darted between a row of cars and found a gap between a couple of Fords with grass grown up around their flattened tires, ducked down behind one, and hid. He lay down on his belly to see if he could see anything. There was a little bit of space down there, and he could look under the car, and under several others, and he could see Gordon's feet. They had shifted into a firm stance, and Jim could imagine the old man pulling the shotgun to his shoulder.

And even as he imagined, the gun boomed, and then it boomed again. Silence, followed by a noise like someone ripping a piece of thick cardboard in half, and then there were screams and more rips. Jim felt light headed, realized he hadn't been breathing. He gasped for air, feared that he had gasped too loudly.

Oh, my God, he thought. I ran and left it to Mr. Gordon, and now...He was uncertain. Maybe the screams had come from...It, the folding man? But so far it hadn't so much as made breathing sounds, let alone anything that might be thought of as a vocalization.

Crawling like a soldier under fire, Jim worked his way to the edge of the car, and took a look. Stalking down the row between the cars was the folding man, and he was dragging behind him by one ankle what was left of William's body. In his other hand, if you could call it a hand, he had Mr. Gordon, who looked thin now because so much had been pulled out of him. Chomps' body was still fastened to the wire hook at the back of the thing's foot. As the folding man came forward, Chomps dragged in the dirt.

Jim pushed back between the cars, and kept pushing, crawling

250

backwards. When he was far enough back, he raised to a squat and started between narrower rows that he thought would be harder for the folding man to navigate; they were just spaces really, not rows, and if he could go where it couldn't go, then—

There was a large creaking sound, and Jim, still at a squat, turned to discover its source. The folding man was looking at him. It had grabbed an old car and lifted it up by the front and was holding it so that the back end rested on the ground. Being as close as he was now, Jim realized the folding man was bigger than he had thought, and he saw too that just below where the monster's thick torso ended there were springs, huge springs, silver in the moonlight, vibrating. He had stretched to accommodate the lifting of the car, and where his knees bent backwards, springs could be seen as well; he was a garage sale collection of parts and pieces.

For a moment, Jim froze. The folding man opened his mouth wide, wider than Jim had seen before, and inside he could glimpse a turning of gears and a smattering of sparks. Jim broke suddenly, running between cars, leaping on hoods, scrambling across roofs, and behind him came the folding man, picking up cars and flipping them aside as easily as if they had been toys.

Jim could see the fence at the back, and he made for that, and when he got close to it, he thought he had it figured. He could see a Chevy parked next to the fence, and he felt certain he could climb onto the roof, spring off of it, grab the top of the fence, and scramble over. That wouldn't stop the thing behind him, but it would perhaps give him a few moments to gain ground.

The squeaking and clanking behind him was growing louder.

There was a row of cars ahead, he had to leap onto the hood of the first, then spring from hood to hood, drop off, turn slightly right, and go for the Chevy by the fence.

He was knocked forward, hard, and his breath leaped out of him.

He was hit again, painfully in the chest.

It took a moment to process, but he was lying between two cars, and there, standing above him, was the folding man, snapping at him with the two dead bodies like they were wet towels. That's what had hit him, the bodies, used like whips.

Jim found strength he didn't know he had, made it to his feet as Mr. Gordon's body slammed the ground near him. Then, as William's body snapped by his ear, just missing him, he was once more at a run.

The Chevy loomed before him. He made its hood by scrambling up on hands and knees, and then he jumped to the roof. He felt something tug at him, but he jerked loose, didn't stop moving. He sprang off the car top, grabbed at the fence, latching his arms over it. The fence cut into the undersides of his arms, but he couldn't let that stop him, so he kept pulling himself forward, and the next thing he knew, he was over the fence,

251

dropping to the ground.

It seemed as if a bullet had gone up through his right foot, which he now realized was bare, and that the tug he had felt was the folding man grabbing at his foot, only to come away with a shoe. But of more immediate concern was his foot, the pain. There hadn't been any bullet. He had landed crooked coming over the fence, and his foot had broken. It felt like hell, but he moved on it anyway, and within a few steps he had a limp, a bad limp.

He could see the highway ahead, and he could hear the fence coming down behind him, and he knew it was over, all over, because he was out of gas and had blown a tire and his engine was about to blow too. His breath came in chops and blood was pounding in his skull like a thug wanting out.

He saw lights. They were moving very quickly down the highway. A big truck, a Mac, was balling the jack in his direction. If he could get it to stop, maybe there would be help, maybe.

Jim stumbled to the middle of the highway, directly into the lights, waved his arms, glanced to his left—

--and there it was. The folding man. It was only six feet away.

The truck was only a little farther away, but moving faster, and then the folding man was reaching for him, and the truck was a sure hit, and Jim, pushing off his good foot, leaped sideways and there was a sound like a box of dishes falling downstairs.

Jim felt the wind from the truck, but he had moved just in time. The folding man had not. As Jim had leaped aside, his body turned, through no plan of his own, and he saw the folding man take the hit.

Wood and springs and hinges went everywhere.

The truck bumped right over the folding man and started sliding as the driver tried to put on brakes that weren't designed for fast stops. Tires smoked, brakes squealed, the truck fish tailed.

Jim fell to the side of the highway, got up and limped into the brush there, and tripped on something and went down. He rolled on his back. His butt was in a ditch and his back was against one side of it, and he could see above it on the other side, and through some little bushes that grew there. The highway had a few lights on either side of it, so it was lit up good, and Jim could see the folding man lying in the highway, or rather he could see parts of it everywhere. It looked like a dirty hardware store had come to pieces. William, Gordon, and Chomps, lay in the middle of the highway.

The folding man's big torso, which had somehow survived the impact of the truck, vibrated and burst open, and Jim saw the bird-like thing rise up with a squawk. It snatched up the body of Mr. Gordon and William, one in either claw, used its beak to nab the dog, and ignoring the fact that its size was not enough to lift all that weight, it did just that, took hold of them and went up into the night sky, abruptly became one with the dark.

Jim turned his head. He could see down the highway, could see the driver of the truck getting out, walking briskly toward the scene of the accident. He walked faster as he got closer, and when he arrived, he bent over the pieces of the folding man. He picked up a spring, examined it, tossed it aside. He looked out where Jim lay in the ditch, but Jim figured, lying as he was, brush in front of him, he couldn't be seen.

He was about to call out to the driver when, the truck driver yelled, "You nearly got me killed. You nearly got you killed. Maybe you are killed. I catch you, might as well be, you stupid shit. I'll beat the hell out of you."

Jim didn't move.

"Come on out so I can finish you off."

Great, Jim thought, first the folding man, and now a truck driver wants to kill me. To hell with him, to hell with everything, and he laid his head back against the ditch and closed his eyes and went to sleep.

The truck driver didn't come out and find him, and when he awoke the truck was gone and the sky was starting to lighten. His ankle hurt like hell. He bent over and looked at it. He couldn't tell much in the dark, but it looked as big as a sewer pipe. He thought when he got some strength back, he might be able to limp, or crawl out to the edge of the highway, flag down some help. Surely, someone would stop. But for the moment, he was too weak. He laid back again, and was about to close his eyes, when he heard a humming sound.

Looking out at the highway, he saw lights coming from the direction the trucker had come from. Fear crawled up his back like a spider. It was the black car.

The car pulled to the side of the road and stopped. The nuns got out. They sniffed and extended long tongues and licked at the fading night. With speed and agility that seemed impossible, they gathered up the parts of the folding man and put them in a sack they placed in the middle of the highway.

When the sack was full of parts, one nun stuck a long leg into the sack and stomped about, then jerked her leg out, pulled the sack together at the top and swung it over her head and slammed it on the road a few times, then she dropped the sack and moved back and one of the nuns kicked it. Another nun opened up and reached inside the sack and took out the folding man. Jim lost a breath. It appeared to be put back together. The nun didn't unfold the folding man. She opened the trunk of the car and flung it inside.

And then she turned and looked in his direction, held out one arm and waited. The bird-thing came flapping out of the last of the dark and landed on her arm. The bodies of William and Gordon were still in its talons, the dog in its beak, the three of them hanging as if they were nothing heavier than rags. The nun took hold of the bird's legs and tossed it and what it held into the trunk as well. She closed the lid of the trunk. She looked directly where Jim lay. She looked up at the sky, turned to face the rising sun. She turned quickly back in Jim's direction and stuck out her long arm, the robe folding back from it. She pointed a stick like finger right at him, leaned slightly forward. She held that pose until the others joined her and pointed in Jim's direction.

My God, Jim thought, they know I'm here. They see me. Or smell me. Or sense me. But they know I'm here.

The sky brightened and outlined them like that for a moment and they stopped pointing.

They got quickly in the car. The last of the darkness seemed to seep into the ground and give way to a rising pink; Halloween night had ended. The car gunned and went away fast. Jim watched it go a few feet, and then it wasn't there anymore. It faded like fog. All that was left now was the sunrise and the day turning bright.

Things

Some Things are meant to be left alone!

Jim Kavanaugh

Drive-In Creature Feature Anthology *Presents* *a* **Paul Moore** *story* **Things** *edited by* **Eugene Johnson** *and* **Charles Day** *Produced by* **Evil Jester Press** IH | Inhuman Horror / Disturbing images | *Copyright 2016*

255

Paul Moore

Paul Moore is a filmmaker who has written and directed four feature films, most recently *Keepsake* and *Requiem*. He is also the co-owner of the movie production studio *Blind Tiger Filmworks* and his first short story, *Spoiled,* was published in the well-received anthology *Appalachian Undead.* It was very rewarding experience and he is happy to follow that effort with *Things*; an homage to both the spirit of B-movie alien invasion films and several of the films that inspired him to pursue a career in filmmaking

THINGS

Paul Moore

The streets were deserted. Morning sunlight cascaded past aging brownstone buildings, dispelling the long shadows that stretched across the wet pavement. In the alleyways and beneath the awnings, the darkness shrank as the sun rose.

It was a picturesque sunrise that would have been the envy of any painter or photographer. Bright. Warm. Still. A morning filled with promise and hope for anyone who had weathered the previous night's storm. It was a perfect dawn.

It was also a lie.

A low rumble echoed along the empty streets, escalating into a tortured whine as a taxi cab screeched into the intersection. Its rear wheels skidded along the pavement as it careened into the turn and righted itself. The engine roared as the driver accelerated, the yellow sedan surging forward.

Inside the cab, Peter glanced at Maria, his hands squeezing the steering wheel. His wife's breathing had grown increasingly ragged over the past hour. With each of her labored breaths an insidious panic tightened its grip on his heart. She needed a hospital and that was now an impossibility.

He had tried Mercy General first, but the bridge out of the city had been transformed into a parking lot. He had debated carrying her over on foot, but decided against it when the sounds of gunfire had popped in the night air. The distant, staccato tattoo was unmistakable. Automatic weapons. Military weapons.

Peter had turned the cab around and nosed his way through the growing congestion. A few minutes later, his suspicions had been confirmed as warm, orange light cast a glowing reflection in the windows of the city's skyscrapers. He glanced at the rear view moments before the thunderous sounds of the explosions reached his ears.

His eyes had widened as he watched billowing flames engulf the bridge. On the rectangular surface of the mirror, the collapsing bridge was framed like one of the widescreen matinees he used to watch with his father. Peter watched as the bridge disappeared from sight; cinematic, surreal, dragging thousands of people into inky oblivion.

As a hack driver, Peter knew every shortcut, switchback and alley in the city. During the week he avoided them all, opting to take his fares on longer, leisurely rides. On the weekend, business was done in bulk and it behooved him to get his fares to their destinations as fast as possible. He could get from downtown to the airport and back in less than thirty minutes with the proper incentive.

Usually, that motivation came in the form of drunken revelers with overstuffed wallets and an overblown sense of gratitude. Sometimes it came from his own empathy when he saw apprehension in the faces of his fares as they feared a missed flight or meeting. Peter had seen none of those things that night.

He had only seen Maria's strained, sweat soaked face, frail hands clutching her swollen belly. At the possibility of losing their unborn child amid the chaos and bloodshed, his mind, paradoxically, had both focused and splintered.

His reflexes sharpened as he sped along side streets, chasing the unraveling fabric of his sanity. He had attempted to reach St. Mary's, but blocks from the institution he had abandoned hope.

A line of empty, blood streaked vehicles and shredded corpses informed him that St. Mary's was a lost cause. Either the hospital was overrun, or it had become a protected bastion that was beyond their reach. In desperation, he recalled Calgary Medical.

A veterans' hospital; Peter had transported more than his fair share of older, disabled soldiers to the obsolete facility. Because of its specialized nature and unassuming architecture, it was possible that most people had forgotten its existence. As far as Peter was concerned, a doctor was a doctor.

Peter was blocks away and hope was beginning to return. Maria's breathing was still unsteady, but she had stopped wailing. Her thin T-shirt was saturated with sweat, but her jeans were dry. Her water had not broken.

Peter counterfeited a smile, blurred by stubble, exhaustion and a few spatters of blood.

"How are we doing?"

Maria did not look at him as she responded between shallow breaths.

"It hurts."

"Hang in there, Baby," He spared a hand from the steering wheel and wiped a few stray locks of moist hair from her eyes. "Just breathe."

"I... can't," Maria moaned, "I need a hospital."

Peter peered into the rear view mirror. His own breathing faltered as he watched the spectacle unfolding behind them.

Things were flooding the street. Malformed bodies shuffled, scrambled, flopped and charged as the undulating throng spilled around the corner, a hideous mass of furious flesh. Wet teeth, talons, claws and tentacles gnashed and gnawed as each of the abominations sought to gain ground over the others.

Some of the *things* still bore a few traits that betrayed their human origins, but their humanity had been erased. Whatever they had been, they were now driven by blood lust, fueled by an insatiable appetite.

Peter focused on the intersection ahead. The street he was traveling dead ended at a cross street, and it would be a blind turn; a hard left into the unknown. So far, Peter had encountered barricades, vehicle collisions and, in one bizarre instance, a giraffe carcass. The *things* had dragged it from its enclosure at the zoo and had begun feasting on it in the streets.

He continued steady pressure on the accelerator. He had no idea what was around the corner, but he knew what he saw in the rear view mirror and he had decided they should take their chances on the unknown.

"I know, I know," Peter consoled as he prepared to take the turn, "but we can't do that now, Baby." His hands yanked the steering wheel as he shouted, "HANG ON!"

The cab's tires squealed as black smoke poured from the peeling tires. The sedan canted to one side and Maria bawled as it slid around the corner. Peter gunned the engine and snapped the steering wheel, the cab leveling with a chorus of squealing metal and rubber. The cab surged forward toward the next cross street. Another dead end, another blind turn.

Beside him, Maria unleashed a pathetic whine. Instinctively, his hand reached for hers.

"Please, Peter..." She moaned as she clenched her midsection, "I need a doctor."

"I've got this, Maria. Everything's going to be alright," Peter reassured as he squeezed her hand. It was a natural gesture, but it felt awkward. His fingers broke the plane between Maria's hand and her belly and immediately he felt like an interloper. Maria was fighting for the life of her unborn child and Peter knew that he was a distant second in that equation. And that was fine by him. They were united in a single purpose. Staying alive was just a means to an end.

"I promise," he added as he released her hand and looked into her eyes.

Maria smiled and, for a moment, Peter saw his wife as she had always been to him; strong, hopeful and kind. Beneath the agony and fear, he saw the woman he had married. The woman he loved.

Maria shifted as she looked through the window. Her eyes bulged and the illusion of tranquility was shattered as she screamed.

"*PETER!*"

Peter's eyes snapped forward as the horde of *things* poured around the corner and lurched into the street ahead. There were too many. A tumbling, stumbling mass of aberrations. He stomped on the brake pedal and the cab slid to a stop a half a block ahead of the oncoming throng.

Peter stared through the windshield at the advancing legion of malformed jaws and deformed claws. High pitched howls and grunts echoed along the street as phlegm and drool spilled over cracked, translucent lips onto rain slicked pavement.

It was a scene from a nightmare. The boogeymen had punched their way into the waking world and they had done it by inhabiting the bodies of the minds they used to haunt. They had transformed mankind. Perverted it for their own profane purposes.

"*Jesus...*" Peter uttered. It was the only prayer his baffled mind could muster. These *things* were as incomprehensible as they were real and Peter wished now, more than ever, that he had listened closer to Father Macy's sermons. And, more importantly, his warnings. Perhaps these demonic monstrosities were not the result of man's greatest sins, but the wages of his million minor ones.

Mountains did not crumble overnight. They crumbled over eons; one forgotten stone at a time.

But in this moment God, man and mountains were subjects best left to priests and philosophers. Peter was a son, a husband and a cab driver with a single ambition - to add *father* to that meager list. It was a simple goal for a simple man in extraordinary circumstances.

Hell had come for the human race, and maybe mankind was due to settle its debts. Peter did not know and did not care. His child was not in that ledger and if Peter was, he would pay his dues in time.

That time was not today.

Peter concentrated on the rear view mirror as he slammed the gears into *reverse*. He drove the accelerator into the floor as the tires spun and the cab swerved backwards down the street. The intersection grew larger in the rear view mirror as the mutated mob surged forward in pursuit.

Despite his best efforts, the cab had reached an unsteady velocity. Peter tore his eyes from the mirror as he looked over his shoulder. The cab was almost to the intersection, the widest point of exposed road. His free hand shot the handbrake and he squeezed the steering wheel. He would only have one shot.

He stole a glance at Maria. Her body contorted as another brutal spasm wracked her abdomen. Sweat mingled with tears as she cried out with a pathetic, simpering whine.

"*HOLD ON!*"

Peter yanked the handbrake, jerking the steering wheel as far as he could to the right. It was a near perfect bootlegger's reverse. The cab fanned across the intersection, the rear fender striking two of the *things* as the horde reached the cross street.

One of the creatures exploded like a sack of jelly. Inky fluids and

260

gelatinous organs splattered the side of the taxi as its body ruptured. The other bounced across the trunk leaving a trail of mucus and black blood in its wake as it toppled to the pavement.

To Peter, all of this was a blur in the cab mirrors as the two packs joined in the intersection behind him. He slipped the gear into *drive* and stamped' the accelerator as the taxi shot forward. It was the wrong direction, but it was also the only clear path. His plan was to double back through the alleys and lose the-

He saw it through the top corner of the windshield. A crudely crafted banner reading: *S.O.S HELP!* Three stories above the street and hanging over the roof of a brownstone. There was also a blur of something else. Something important.

"Peter, there are-"

"*NOT NOW!*"

Peter returned his attention to the road before him and his thoughts burst through the filter between his brain and mouth.

"*MOTHERFUCKER!*"

It was another legion of *things*. The creatures were pouring from the alleys and side streets ahead. A bizarre congregation of men, women and children who had been warped and transmogrified into a pack of primal, gluttonous devils.

Distended eyes set above labial fissures commingled with limp proboscises and pulsating veins as the legion grew and spread along the street. It was a tidal wave of soggy flesh and ruthless appetite and it was clawing and tearing its way toward the taxi cab.

Tires screeched as the cab rocked to a stop. Peter stared into the rear view mirror and a renewed river of sweat dripped from his brow. The combined mob of *things* was barreling toward them.

"Peter...?" Maria croaked through halted breaths.

Peter's eyes flicked between the mirror and the windshield as he tracked the converging hordes.

"Not now..." Peter exhaled as he felt his mind begin to slip. His mind was growing numb. "Not-"

"PETER?!"

His attention snapped toward Maria, proving that even the apocalypse could not overcome years of domestic conditioning. She raised her arm and extended a quivering finger toward the side window.

"*People.*"

Peter leaned backward as his eyes followed her finger.

Behind the brick parapet several people waved their arms wildly above the rudimentary sign. His angle of view was extreme and their gesticulations were wild, so it was difficult for Peter to ascertain what they were trying to communicate. *Beckoning? Warding? Warning?*

Peter glanced in the mirror, saw a sea of dripping maws and decided it did not matter. They were still human and there was strength in

261

numbers. The cab would not survive if he attempted to plow forward and the beasts would tear it pieces in matter of minutes if it stalled.

Reaching the veterans' hospital was an impossibility. His child's life hinged on Maria making it to that rooftop. He turned to her and unbuckled his seat belt.

"Can you run?"

Maria shook her head emphatically as another contraction seized her body. Peter placed his hand on her swollen belly and locked eyes with her.

"For our *son?*"

She choked back a sob and rasped.

"*Daughter.*"

He saw it in her eyes. The woman he married. The woman he *loved*. The only woman other than his mother who could ever cut through his charm to the truth. The only woman who could see his true self.

"Only one way to find out," he challenged. A tear slipped from the corner of his eye.

Despite the tears, he winked and Maria nodded. His hand moved from her belly to the glove compartment. He popped it open and rummaged beneath the papers. A moment later, he produced a revolver.

Peter held it in front of Maria.

"We can do this."

Her voice was hopeful as she responded through heavy breaths.

"We've got this?"

Peter looked from the revolver to the oncoming mob of *things*. He looked back at his wife. His expression was as steady as his hand.

"We've got this."

***

The driver's side door to the cab burst open as Peter leaped from the taxi. He held the revolver at the ready as Maria clambered through the door behind him. He hooked his arm around her waist as the guttural grunts rose into deafening howls. The *things* were moments away from the cab on both sides of the street. Their hunger was palpable.

Peter wasted no time as he dragged Maria toward the entrance to the brownstone. A small grid of window panes set into the front door revealed a small foyer containing a bank of mailboxes and an umbrella stand. Beyond the foyer was a glass door that opened into a small lobby. Two doors between the two of them and sanctuary and a chilling reality occurred to Peter.

At least one of those doors was locked.

It would be the outer door. Peter ushered Maria up a few cursory stone steps before he turned and looked back at the street. His heart simultaneously sank into his stomach and climbed into his throat.

262

The *things* swarmed the cab. The roof crumpled and the windows shattered as talons and fleshy pincers sought purchase. The creatures were dismantling the hurdle as they vaulted it. It was an awesome sight in the truest sense of the word; a symphony of destruction.

Maria yowled as another contraction seized her. Peter tore his eyes away from the advancing carnage as instinct commandeered his body. He swung the pistol and smashed the lowest pane of glass.

Small shards of glass raked across his arm as he reached inside the door and thumbed the latch. In one fluid motion, he threw open the door and shoved Maria inside. She stumbled into the foyer and moaned as she impacted the glass door to the lobby. She gripped the crossbar as her legs wobbled beneath her.

Peter slammed the door behind him as he ducked inside. He jammed the revolver into his belt as the *things* reached the door and he spun toward the umbrella stand. Behind him, the door shuddered in its frame as the first of the creatures threw its weight against it. Another pane shattered as enraged howls filled the foyer.

Peter ignored both Maria's pleading groans and the rising choir of carnivorous need. He was operating on a level that most men only discovered in times of war or tragedy. An adrenaline spiked cocktail of desperation and survival. Tiny, precise gears of knowledge and theory ticked inside him at impossible speeds.

He snatched an umbrella from the stand and slid it through the door's S-shaped handle. He grabbed another and wedged it between the first and the jamb. The *things* were intent and single-minded in their purpose, but Peter had seen no evidence that they retained any of their *human* intelligence. They were *pushers*, not *pullers*.

He turned and, once again, snaked his arm around Maria. He hefted her as he tried the crossbar on the glass door. It opened and Peter wasted no time as he thrust Maria through the opening. She yelped as she lurched across the hardwood floor and sagged against the ornate banister at the foot of a narrow staircase. Peter closed the door behind him and surveyed his surroundings.

Diffused sunlight cast a soft glow as it struggled to penetrate the frosted glass of the transoms and high windows. Two apartment doors flanked the left side of the lobby and a modest arch gave way to long and shadowy hallway. The right side of the lobby was dominated by heavy newel posts supporting a narrow staircase that led to a landing and, beyond that, the second floor landing.

Peter ignored all of this as his eyes settled on hall tree in the corner. Several rain slickers hung from curved pegs that extruded from the heavy wood.

"Peter..."

"Get upstairs."

It was an afterthought. He was intent on the hall tree. Peter began

263

peeling the coats from the hooks.

"*PETER!*"

He stopped cold as he pulled the last slicker from the rack and revealed a snow shovel leaning in the corner of the lobby. Maria was forgotten as a plan took shape in his mind's eye. Beyond the glass door, another pane popped and the umbrellas began to bend. They had a few minutes... at most.

"*GET UPSTAIRS, NOW!*"

It was the first time in their six years of marriage that Peter had raised his voice to the level of a shout. Even in the throes of their worst arguments, Peter knew that the louder his voice became the smaller Maria's ears became. He had learned that from his parents. Endless nights of pointless arguments that deteriorated into screaming matches. Volume over substance. Pain matched against greater pain.

On any other day he would have been ashamed, but today was not about the politics of living; it was about the laws of staying alive. The world had always been about predators and prey. Those rules predated civilization, but mankind had evolved and drawn a polite face on a world of primates. A world where station and influence had replaced sticks and stones.

Now the rules had changed and the humans had become the giraffes at the city zoo.

Beautiful in their simplicity, but out of their element. All it took was one wolf through the gate to expose the fraudulence of their existence. Now the world was the domain of wolves and the giraffes, for all of their passive elegance, were revealed for what they really were...

Meat.

Peter scooped the shovel from the corner and thrust it through the crossbar. It was just long enough by half a foot. He turned again and snapped the hooks from the hall tree, flipped it and slid it through the crossbar in the opposite direction. The engineering was crude, but it would hold until they reached the roof.

The outer door bowed inward as the *things* surged against it. Five minutes between the two doors. Ten at the most.

"*GODDAMNIT, PETER!*"

Peter backed away from the door and turned to face his wife. One of her hands clutched the stair railing and the other encircled her belly. Sweat dripped from her nose and her teeth pinched her cracked lips. A single droplet of blood traced the outline of her chin.

The adrenaline ebbed in his veins, but like alcohol, the effects lingered. His words sounded too harsh to his own ears when he spoke.

"*WHAT!*"

Maria released her belly and directed a crooked finger toward the arched entryway to the first floor hall. For the second time that morning, Peter's gaze followed his wife's finger. His hand curled around the butt of

264

the revolver.

A large pool of blood had spread across the floor at the far end of the lobby. As Peter approached, he saw a large swath of blood had streaked the hardwood floors and the trail disappeared into the dark recesses of the hallway. He thumbed back the hammer on the revolver as he reached the puddle and knelt.

He touched the coagulated blood with his fingertip. It was thick and tacky, at least a day old. Peter turned his attention the shadowy passage ahead of him. The blood in front of him belonged to a body and that body had been dragged into the darkness. Or dragged itself.

Neither possibility appealed to Peter. He looked back at the blood pool. It was possible that-

A heavy droplet of blood plopped into the center of the puddle and a syrupy ripple spread through the pool. Peter furrowed his brow as he looked upward.

The edge of the second floor landing was coated with blood. Viscous crimson strands hung from the molding. A Peter watched, one of the strands snapped and another dollop of blood splashed into the puddle. He rose and stepped backwards as he spoke.

"There are people on the roof. I saw them," he stated, more to himself than to Maria. "*You* saw them."

A renewed patina of sweat glistened on Maria's skin as she cradled her belly.

"I don't know what I saw, Peter. We should-"

"They were there!" Peter exclaimed in a sharp tone that he immediately regretted. Maria was frightened, possibly in labor and looking to him for protection and salvation. He was just frightened. A cab driver whose concerns, until yesterday, amounted to putting food on the table and making enough money to move his family into a two bedroom apartment. Now, he was tasked with safely delivering his child into a world that had been overrun by the denizens of Hell.

"I know what I saw. We need to get to the roof."

Maria slid upward along the newel post until she was standing. She wiped the sweat from her eyes and blinked. Even that simple act was the product of visible effort.

"These are apartments. They have phones, right?"

Peter returned his attention to the hallway as he squinted and peered into the darkness. Maria continued as though he was listening.

"We need to call someone," she stated as Peter took a step forward and tightened his hand around the revolver. "Call 911. Let someone know we're here. Maybe the police could-"

"We have to get to the roof." Peter said in a queer, disassociated tone.

Maria ignored the statement as she stepped behind him.

"We can lock ourselves inside until help arr-"

265

"We need to get to the roof..." Peter repeated as he took a step backwards and raised the revolver. "Now."

His words had a calm, dispassionate quality that was directly contrast to the quaking pistol he held in his sweaty hand. Maria looked past him and the revolver into the hallway beyond.

Twisted, lurching figures were emerging from the opaque shadows. Low hisses and guttural moans were accompanied by the sounds of heavy shuffling and moist stretching. Deep slurps and muffled cracks filled the air as the *things* shambled into the meager light.

The closest had been a woman in a previous life. Heavyset and in her late forties. Now, she was something that would have given Hieronymus Bosch nightmares. One arm had elongated past her knee and her fingers had been replaced with membranous claws. The other arm was vaguely human, but the skin had taken on the consistency of congealed snot.

Her countenance reminded Maria of a melted candle, if the candle in question had irregular sized, cataract filmed eyes and rows of needle-like teeth. Most of the *she-thing's* clothing had sloughed away to reveal sagging breasts and a foot that was transitioning into a malformed pincer. It was the breasts that disturbed Maria. One of them had *teeth*. Not fangs, but the small broken teeth of a child.

"Peter...?" It was a question laced with shrill desperation. Despite all that they had seen, Maria's mind was just now coming to grips with the insanity of their situation.

"Get up the stairs." Peter commanded. It was a directive devoid of emotion. It was a matter of fact. His eyes were locked on the second *thing* ambling from the shadows.

It had been a man and, judging from the pants that clung to its emaciated legs, most likely a delivery man or postman. Bubbling, black ooze seeped through the ripped seam of the pants and one of its orthopedic shoes had ruptured as jagged talons had burst through the leather.

It was an oddly dissociated observation, but Peter thought it would make sense that anyone who delivered packages or parcels would wear orthopedics. However, that was the only observation about the *man-thing* that made sense.

Wide lesions had split the *thing's* torso exposing its organs, pulsating sacs of bile and mucus that expanded and contracted with each step. Its arms were twisting into fibrous tentacles and its eyes had become conjoined. A slit of irregular fangs comprised its mouth and several of those were chewing through its gelatinous cheek as its jaw ground mechanically.

Behind Peter, Maria recoiled a few steps and looked up at the second floor landing.

"But there's blood up there, Peter..." she observed in a tone that mirrored Peter's mental state. It had an undercurrent of *this isn't really*

266

happening, is it?

Another creature stumbled into the hallway. Behind it, other *things* moved in the shadows. The jumble of growls had coalesced into a series of rising howls that echoed from the darkness.

"Get up the *fucking stairs*..." Peter snarled. "Right fucking now."

The howling in the hallway was reaching a crescendo as Peter stepped backwards and the things charged. He pivoted toward Maria as the sounds of damp flesh and sharpened claws smacked and clicked against the hardwood floors in the hallway behind him. It was an escalating, urgent composition of sounds that evoked two sensations. Speed and terror.

They had seconds at the most. Peter bolted forward and snagged Maria's wrist. He could feel her unsteadiness as he towed her toward the foot of the stairs. He could hear her distressed chirps as he bound up the first flight; dragging her in his wake. Her wrist had twisted queerly in his hand and, for a moment, the horrible image of him gripping a severed arm flashed through his mind.

The *things* had snared Maria. The creatures had ripped her into hunks of meat and were gnawing through her carcass in an effort to satiate their unholy appetites with flesh of his unborn child. He turned his head as hot tears welled in his eyes.

Maria was still there. She had simply lost her balance and caught herself on the rail. Rage flooded Peter. Rage at Maria for faltering. Rage at himself for misinterpreting the situation. Rage at the *situation*.

He looked past Maria and his rage dissolved into something else. Into fear.

The *things* had poured into the lobby. Their predatory eyes and obscene appendages searched and probed the space as veins ballooned beneath their gluttonous jaws. The raucous din outside the doors melded with the creatures' profane howls. The sound was maddening. A feral choir performing for a captive audience of two frightened mice.

Not two, Peter thought as he watched Maria support her distended midsection. *Three. Three blind mice... See how they run.*

Peter focused on Maria and repeated the sentiment.

"*RUN!*"

For emphasis, he tugged on her wrist and she started upward.

A few clumsy steps later, they had finished their ascent. Several apartment doors lined the second floor hallway and pools of deep shadows were collected along its length. Some of the doors were partially open. Too many.

A few shafts of weak sunlight spilled through the open doorways and, at the far end of the hallway, an *Exit* sign cast a red glow in the gloom. It was the shadows in the hall that concerned Peter.

The shadows that were *moving*.

He slid to a stop at the edge of the second floor hallway as Maria collided with him. Further down the hall, the shadows took form as they stepped into the light. Peter swiped the the back of his hand across his eyes as he peered into the gloom. Moist, translucent flesh gleamed in the slivers of light that penetrated the murky corridor.

The *things* shuffled forward as they filled the passage. Peter hefted the revolver and did the math. Six bullets. Four creatures standing between them and the door to the roof.

Several years ago, Peter had installed a police scanner in his cab. It had proven a wise investment as it had helped him avoid accidents, street closures and, on rare occasions, criminal pursuits that had crippled lanes on the highway. In the past twenty four hours, its value had exceeded its weight in gold.

As Peter had worked his way across town to retrieve Maria, he had listened to the fall of humanity as it was transmitted in bursts of short static. Garbled messages containing hints and observations that had become fact through repetition.

They're fucking everywhere!
Pull back! Let them burn!
They're too many! They're too Goddamn fast!
Use your sweepers! Blow their fucking heads off!
They keep coming!
Shred the fuckers!
Concentrate your fire on their heads, Sergeant!

Whatever these monsters were, Peter had gleaned from the panicked broadcasts that certain rules still applied. No eyes resulted in no sight. No joints meant no movement. And... no brain equaled no life. On some level, it made sense. These things were reanimated perversions of human corpses. Perhaps they were mutated with the genetic material of other animals, or they were something altogether different.

A new race built on the flesh of a dying one.

However, all of these thoughts were afterimages in Peter's brain. Strobes of memory and intuition. His attention was squarely centered on the passage ahead of him, and the threat rising behind him.

He cast a glance over his shoulder and immediately regretted it for multiple reasons. The first was the tears he saw on his wife's cheeks. Her face radiated terror and Peter could feel Maria's wrist trembling in his grasp.

His heart was both pounding and breaking as he looked past her to the stairs below. The *things* were lurching upward. Their misshapen feet navigated the steps with a waning uncertainty. Their new bodies were *learning* both their purpose and their environment. In a few minutes, the creatures would be moving with speed and assuredness.

Maria squawked as another contraction clenched her belly. She looked up at him as she doubled over and her eyes were like those of a newly born fawn. Wide, wet and confused.

268

"C'MON!" Peter barked.

Maria's gaze was pleading. Helpless. She was surrendering. Peter wrenched her wrist.

"MOVE!"

He yanked her arm and jerked her forward. Maria did not resist, but she did not respond. Her movements were limp and listless. One foot in front of the other in a pale imitation of running.

Ahead of them, the *things* were beginning to warble and yowl. The unsteady noises that were growing in intensity and tenor. The closest of the creatures burped thick bubbles of mucus that plopped over its swollen lips and onto its elongated chin before slipping down its leathery wattle. It was a repulsive sight, however it was the sound that followed that truly chilled Peter's blood.

It was a thin, reedy whistle that expanded into a bellowing howl. A sound imbued with rage and hunger. It was the anthem of nightmares. The hairs on Peter's neck stood at attention as he pressed forward into the inky passage.

Bony protuberances slashed upwards through the beast's sloughing skin as it tottered forward. Its howl continued to rise in pitch as it reached forward with bowed arms. Peter saw twitching suckers on the ends of its fingers. The same octopus-like suckers that were growing on its undulating jowls.

He dragged Maria forward as the *thing's* howl exploded into an ear piercing screech. Its greedy hands surged toward him from the shadows. Only a few feet remained between them.

Close enough.

Peter raised the revolver and fired. The flash of gunfire illuminated the hallway for a split second revealing the house of horrors ahead.

Once human bodies twisted and distorted into monstrous spectacles. Viscous sacs dropped from appendages both old and new. Extraneous limbs had melded with vital organs that hung precariously in hammocks of shredded clothing. Needles of bone and keratin had erupted from digits and joints.

The bullet hit its mark and the first *thing's* head exploded in a shower of black jelly and syrupy blood. Peter felt Maria's wrist tighten in his hand as she screamed. Bits of teeth and bone stuck against the walls as they charged past the collapsing creature.

The gunshot had snapped her back into the moment and Peter seized on the momentum. He rushed forward as he raised the pistol and fired again.

The bullet missed its mark as it chewed through the plaster wall. He squeezed the trigger once more and the revolver bucked in his hand.

The second shot caught the nearest *thing,* a shower of blood erupting from its chest as the creature was knocked against the wall. It wailed like a broken siren as it tumbled onto its back. Peter and Maria raced past the *thing* as it flailed and convulsed, splashing blood and bile across the hardwood floor.

Two down and two left and... three shots.

The noise in the hallway had grown from a few shrill voices to a demonic ensemble. Peter spared a glance over his shoulder and saw the silhouetted legion pouring into the hallway behind him. The distant sounds of breaking glass and splintering wood emanated from somewhere beyond the advancing mob of *things*.

The lobby had been breached. Turning back had never been a real option, but there was something about the *finality* of that realization, the knowledge that their only salvation lay in the dark recesses ahead, that began to throttle the last of Peter's *hope*.

There was no going back. There was no escape. Civilization would never be what it was before and his child would be born into a hostile world where survival was not measured in years, but days. His dreams of a family were his motivation for greeting each day. It was the reason he stuck with being a hack rather than spending his nights in a bar drinking away a government check.

Peter had wanted something better for Maria. He had wanted something better for his son or daughter. He had wanted to move them out of the city to a place where the grass grew in a backyard and his neighbors did not entertain junkies and whores at all hours of the night.

He wanted *better* and now all of his hard work; all of his *sacrifice* was undone by these *things*. Peter felt a fury building inside of him. Something more powerful than the simple reptilian need for survival. Something fundamentally human.

Righteousness.

This was his *family* and no man or monster was going to steal their lives from him. They deserved their lives. They deserved to see the sun. They deserved more.

Anger coursed through his blood as he raised the pistol and aimed at the next howling *thing*. Its distended skull bobbled in the revolver's sight. He squeezed the trigger and the flames bloomed from the barrel as the bullet drilled through a wooden door jamb.

Both of the creature's mouths opened and hissed. Its upper, once human jaw displayed rows of sharp, broken enamel, but it was the beast's lower jaw; seared onto Peter's eyeballs in the brief instant of muzzle flash, that drained his self-righteousness. A jagged row of needles that had carved its way through the soft skin of the *thing's* pubis to reveal a tendril-like tongue.

It was an orifice that could emit sounds. It could vocalize. It was the voice of Hell projected through the most obscene of Satan's designs.

Two Howlers... Two bullets.

Peter flipped the pistol and gripped the barrel. There was a door at

270

the end of the hallway that led to the rooftop. Maybe it was open, maybe it was locked. But one thing was certain...

There was no turning back. Even if they could make it to the street, there was nothing left for them beyond these walls. Perhaps everything that was happening was part of a greater design. What Father Macy called *God's Plan*, but God was not in this hallway. It was only Peter, Maria, their unborn child and the hosts of Hell and Peter was not ready to give their lives over to the grinding gears of the *Divine Machine*.

There was a door ahead and a chance it might be open. A chance that he might see his wife standing in the sunlight one more time. A chance that his child might see the world for even a moment.

The Howler was almost upon him when Peter struck. It was a savage blow that shattered the *thing's* teeth as its jaw collapsed. Spittle and broken shards of enamel spattered across Peter's face as the creature raised its bloated hands.

He released Maria's wrist and snared the beast's forearm as its claws swiped at his eyes. His fingers sunk into the *thing's* spongy flesh. It was a nauseating sensation and Peter felt his stomach sour as he struck again. The butt of his revolver cracked against the creature's forehead as he struggled to hold its ill-shaped talons away from his eyes.

The Howler was stronger than Peter anticipated. Stronger than the human body that was it progenitor. It was inhuman in every sense of the word. Peter swung the revolver again. It was a ferocious blow fueled by gut churning disgust and outrage. Ooze seeped over Peter's fingertips as his hand sunk into the *thing's* putrescent skin and the wooden grip of the pistol shattered its temple.

Black goo and ichor slopped across his hand as the grip of the gun lodged into the Howler's skull. Behind Peter, something skulked through the shadows. A dark figure moving with murderous intent. He strained to pull the revolver from the Howler's skull as the *thing* attempted to grapple him with its free arm.

Claws raked his exposed flesh as Peter shoved the *thing* against the wall and drove the Howler to the floor. The encounter lasted mere seconds, but they were seconds he could not afford. A tsunami of mutated and vengeful flesh was surging into the hallway and there were many steps ahead.

Perhaps too many. Perhaps not enough.

Maria screamed from the darkness behind him and Peter tore himself from the dying Howler. A shower of grue splashed across his face as he turned toward his wife. Maria's wide eyes were glossed with tears as the last *thing* descended on her. Its razor sharp teeth snapped at her upraised arms as it pressed its engorged body against hers and propelled her back against the wall.

Peter shrieked as he cracked the butt of the revolver against the back of the abomination's skull. The blow reverberated along Peter's arm as the Howler's maw gnashed at Maria's face and she slide down the wall. Steaming breath and hot saliva layered her face as she shrieked.

Despite the melee, Peter saw his wife's arm encircle her belly. Maria cringed as the monster's jaws unhinged to expose an impossible row of secondary teeth. Jaws within jaws. It was the mouth of a Hell-spawn. It was the ruthless abyss that all fathers saw in their nightmares.

It was the blackened depths of the unknown.

Every instinct Peter possessed shrieked at him to pull the trigger and obliterate the *thing's* skull. Only seconds remained before the monster descended on Maria and seconds after that, the hallway would overrun with torrent of Howlers. If the door was locked...

His only option would be the last two bullets.

Peter struck the Howler, again. And again. The sound of crunching bone mingled with Maria's screams and joined the swelling symphony of rage and appetite that echoed inside the crowded corridor. The *thing's* clawed hands darted toward Maria's pregnant belly. Her eyes were wide with abject horror as the serrated nails swiped at the forearms that barricaded her unborn child.

It was if the *thing* instinctively knew that she was protecting something precious. It was, as if, killing her was not enough. Consuming her was not enough. The monster wanted her to truly and completely suffer in the last moments of her life.

Or maybe it was just following some sort of predatory behavior encoded in the basement of its DNA. Kill the offspring. Eradicate the bloodline.

None of it mattered. Peter's wife was not giving her life for his child. Not to these *things*.

The wooden butt of the revolver split as Peter hammered it into the *things* face. The deflated proboscis that served as its nose disappeared as the monster's skull imploded and the Howler tumbled backwards onto the floor. Maria's eyes danced from the crumpling beast to her husband. In the chaotic dark, he was little more than a shade dripping blood and sweat.

The sight terrified her. He was the visage of a man on the verge of losing all of his humanity. The skin of civility boiled away in a crucible of madness.

The man standing in front of her was nearly an animal. His posture seethed with barbarism as black pus dripped from the revolver in his hand. It was a savage, gruesome picture. His every civilized edifice had been stripped cleanly down to his bones. Maria was frightened of that man, but she saw his *will* in his eyes. Glowing like iron plucked from a forge. Peter would not let her die here.

Peter would save their child.

Her hand reached toward him. Her skin had grown clammy and her forearms were greased with sweat. Peter closed his hand around her wrist as he pulled her up from the floor. Wild shadows danced and expanded along the walls as the howling horde surged toward them.

He locked eyes with her.

"We can do this," he stated through drawn lips. She nodded as they turned and he herded her down the hallway.

Slimy flesh smacked and thudded against the hardwood floor as the *things* lumbered and stumbled in pursuit. Angry howls competed with hungry slurps as teeth ground and wiped trembling lips. Somewhere within the pack of *things* a sac of fluid burst causing some of the beasts to slip and lose their footing. A few of the nightmare apparitions somersaulted and careened against the walls. Distressed wails ricocheted in the enclosed space.

Peter ignored it all. A misstep on the *things* behalf was a gain of precious seconds for himself and Maria and he was not going to squander that time with speculation or a backward glance. He watched as the *Exit* sign grew larger in his vision. A glowing red beacon of salvation or an ironic end, it did not matter. There was no stopping now. No turning back.

Maria's coordination was failing. Her legs were losing steadiness with each step she took. Her ankle turned twice as she struggled to match Peter's pace. Seconds later, they turned the corner and Peter was all but dragging her.

Two battery powered emergency lights burned at the top of a steel staircase. Behind them, a thin rectangle of sunlight outlined a door, the door to the roof. The door to that would allow them to see the sun once again.

The door that would open the world to his child.

Peter released Maria as he hit the stairs in a dead run. She crumpled onto the steps behind him as he hurled himself against the door. It did not budge. He frantically pushed the arm bar, but the result was the same. The door was locked.

Peter slammed his body against the door as he yelled.

"HELP US!"

He looked back down the stairs. Maria had crawled up the steps and was halfway up the staircase, but her breathing was sporadic. Deep, sucking breaths followed by shallow gasps.

Peter pounded on the door.

"OPEN THE GODDAMN DOOR!"

There was no response and the howling inside the hallway was reaching a fever pitch. It sounded as if they were inside and air raid siren. His ears ached.

"OPEN THE DOOR!" Peter screamed as he beat the door. "PLEASE!"

A shadow moved passed through the thin seams of sunlight that defined the door's edges. There **was** someone on the other side. A person. A human being.

Peter swung for the cheap seats.

"MY WIFE IS *PREGNANT!*"

The shadow disappeared and Peter's vision grew blurry. Tears flooded his eyes. Helpless rage cast a red tint across his vision as he kicked the door. His grasp on his own humanity was slipping. He was out of options.

And what came next was too horrible to fathom.

"OPEN THE *MOTHERFUCKING DOOR!*" He shrieked as he unleashed a savage kick into the door. It rattled in its frame as Peter turned away. Maria was helpless on the steps and the *things* were moments away.

If those were to be their last moments, Peter vowed to himself he would spend it with Maria in his arms.

He circled his left arm around Maria as he sat. His palm spread across her ample belly. The cacophony in the hallway was nearing bombastic levels. The *things* were moments from rounding the corner. He could feel her insides churning.

"It's okay, Baby," Peter whispered in her ear.

Tears spread across her cheeks as she emitted a thin, mewling whine. Peter did not know if it was the result of the contractions or if Maria realized what was about to happen. He laid his head against hers.

Fresh tears welled in his eyes.

"We've got this," he said, but his voice was distant, devoid of conviction.

Peter was not afraid for their souls. They had both lived good lives. He had spoken more truths than lies and he had done more good than bad. They had both attended Mass regularly and, to the best of his knowledge, they had both been consistent in their confessions and their contrition.

Father Macy would not approve of what he was about to do, but those were rules for a different world. The church served as a bridge between this world and the next and Peter had built his character on its fundamental principles. However, there was nothing in the Bible that had prepared them for earthly transmogrification.

In Peter's eyes, Maria was the most perfect of all God's creatures. She exemplified to him what all people should strive to become. She had her faults, as all men do, but she overcame them with a grace and intelligence that was only matched by her beauty. Other men would disagree, but as far as Peter was concerned, they were fools and that was their loss.

Maria was everything that made life worth living and the world worth saving and he would not let her become one of those *things*. What came next was not murder; it was salvation. Peter knew in his secret heart, the heart that he shared only with himself and the Lord God Almighty, that what followed was mercy and God would understand.

He said a silent prayer as her raised the revolver and placed the stubby barrel to Maria's temple. The shadows of Howlers fell across him as the *things* rounded the corner. It was a teeming mass of teeth and claws. Peter thumbed the revolver's hammer.

"I've got this," he whispered to himself as his finger tightened around the trigger.

A swath of sunlight blazed across the staircase and swept the hallway. It was blinding and the *things* hissed and yowled with confusion as they lost their bearings. They collided with one and other as spun and whirled in a display of furious disorientation.

Peter looked back up the staircase. Silhouetted against the morning sky, a hulking man stood in the doorway above them. His voice boomed as he raised his arm and aimed a pistol.

"MOVE IT!"

Maria followed Peter's gaze as the man descended a single step and fired. The resulting report was an ear shattering thunderclap. The nearest Howler turned its head toward the rooftop door as the bullet demolished its skull. The creature's head exploded like some sort of satanic piñata. Blood, mucus, teeth, and bone showered Peter and Maria as the other *things* shrieked their outrage.

"MOVE YOUR ASSES, NOW!"

The man fired again and the muzzle flash cast Peter and Maria in stark relief as Peter pulled his wife to her feet. Behind them, the bullet punctured a bloated sac dangling from one of the *thing's* necks. Ropy, white cords of sebum splatted across the steps as the beast snarled; exposing rows of bony, serrated teeth.

Peter forced Maria's head downward as they ascended and the man fired again. The bullet drilled through the milky orb that served as the Howler's right eye. The creature fell back against the wall as its legs slipped out from under it. It toppled to the floor as another; unable to slow itself, tumbled over its carcass.

The base of the staircase was a congested pile of sticky flesh, flailing limbs and snapping fangs. Peter ignored the pile-up as he hauled Maria up the steps and past their burly savior. The man fired one more shot and another Howler collapsed onto the blood soaked risers.

More *things* shredded its rubbery flesh as they clambered over the corpse and charged up the staircase. The man stepped backwards into the sunlight as the ravenous host of creatures flooded toward the door.

"CLOSE IT!" he commanded in a bellowing baritone.

The door swung shut; plunging the remaining *things* into a well of darkness.

***

Peter lay on the rooftop staring at the morning sun. Its warm light caressed his cheeks; drying his tears. He was alive. Maria was alive. His chest was heaving as he sucked fresh air into his starving lungs. Until that moment, it had not occurred to him how stale and fetid the air had been in the hallway.

The building may have started as an apartment complex, but it was now a mausoleum. It was a dwelling for the dead. And like all graves, it was beneath him.

A shadow fell across his face as a massive figure eclipsed the sun.

"Get up," the figure instructed. It was a soft directive delivered by a mellifluous voice, but the words were infused with gravitas.

Peter pushed himself to his feet and the effort was dizzying. He had been running on little more than adrenaline and hope for over twenty four hours and now that he was no longer in motion, the toll he had taken on his mind and body was evident. He was exhausted. Every fiber of his being pleaded for rest and his thoughts were jumble of raw emotions.

"I think she's in labor." The voice was feminine, but strong.

"Are you sure?" Another voice, also female, but imbued with less confidence.

Peter turned his head as attempted to isolate the women who were speaking. He blinked away the sunlight as he attempted to focus on the ill-defined shapes that hovered over Maria. Everything was blurry.

"Get her under the tarp and get her some water." It was the baritone voice from the hallway. Peter wiped sweat from his eyes as he sought the source. The man spoke again.

"You okay, son?'

Peter opened his mouth to respond as vertigo and nausea overwhelmed him. He doubled over. Almost immediately, large hands caught his shoulders and steadied him.

"Easy, chief," the soothing baritone cautioned. "Let's sit you down."

One of the meaty hands began to guide him forward as the other reached for the revolver.

"Let's just set that aside before someone gets hurt."

It was a sensible suggestion and Peter wanted more than anything to relinquish the responsibilities that came with the weapon. Power over life and death was a heavy burden and far too nuanced for a man in his condition.

The hulking man's fingertips touched the revolver and clarity crashed over Peter with tsunami force. The world roared into sharp relief as he broke free of the man's gentle grip and snapped the revolver to the ready.

The man took a step backwards and raised his hands. For the first time, Peter saw him clearly. The man was the definition of a *gentle giant*. He was easily six and half feet tall with broad shoulders and even though time had softened his midsection and expanded his waistline, it was evident he had been an athletic man in his youth. His ebony skin and shaved head accentuated his imposing presence, but his deep, wide eyes and soft wrinkles painted a different portrait.

The man standing before Peter projected neither malice nor menace. His expression was imploring and his posture was relaxed. Everything about his demeanor announced that he was not a threat to either Peter or Maria, but still Peter kept the pistol trained on him.

"My name is Bernard," the man stated in a plain, but subtly soothing tone. "And you are?"

"Peter." It was a mechanical response. "Peter Delgado."

"Good, Peter," Bernard encouraged. "Is that your wife?"

Peter glanced over at Maria. Two women, one older and another barely out of her teens, were positioning Maria beneath a makeshift lean-to. A tarp had been stretched from the brick edifice that housed the door and supported with a few pieces of scaffolding. Beyond the simple structure, several cans of paint and a stack of roofing materials sat exposed to the elements.

"Her name is Maria," Peter answered "She needs a doctor."

"I don't know if I can help you there, friend," Bernard said through a cautious smile, "But Jennifer over there is a nurse. How far along is Maria?"

"She was due days ago."

"Understood. We'll do what we can, but first I need you to do something for me," Bernard lowered his hands as he spoke. "I need you to put that gun away."

Peter's eyes looked from Bernard to the revolver in his hands. Until that moment, he had not realized he was aiming at Bernard. It had been an instinctual action born of fatigue and fear.

"I can see you're not a violent man, Peter," Bernard continued, "And you're just like the rest of us. Confused and scared. But the best way for all us to get through this is to make sure none of us get shot. Your wife is over there and she needs you."

Peter looked from Maria and Bernard. The barrel of the revolver dipped, slightly.

"That's right," Bernard soothed, "I'm armed, you're armed, but I let you on this roof because it was the *decent* thing to do. The right thing. Please, don't make me regret that."

As rapidly as it had dissipated, the fatigue returned. Peter had no fight left in him and he could see that Bernard recognized that he was at the end of his wits.

Peter lowered the revolver.

"Can I keep this?"

"As long as you don't point it at me or them," Bernard said with a reassuring smile, "It's all yours."

"Thank you. And..." Peter extended his hand, "I'm sorry. We owe you our lives and I'm grateful."

Bernard shook his hand.

"Let's go see about your little lady."

The two men began walking toward the shelter.

"How are things out there?"

"It's..." Peter's weary brain searched for an answer, "It's Hell on Earth."

It was a simplistic and overly melodramatic answer, but Peter, normally articulate and composed, could not find the reserves to offer anything more than a simple cliché.

"I suppose that sums it up." Bernard said as he rubbed his chin. "Did you see any police? Military?"

"You're talking about the cavalry?"

"I'm talking about *hope*," Bernard responded. "It's in short supply up here."

Peter placed his hand on Bernard's shoulder as they neared the women. Bernard stopped and turned to face him.

"The city is on fire. I watched those *things* overrun the police, the National Guard, everything in their path. Somebody blew the bridges hours ago."

"Yeah, we saw the flashes before dawn," Bernard said as he nodded toward the horizon. "You can still see the smoke."

Peter looked in the indicated direction and saw the faint pillars of smoke as they climbed into the morning sky. He locked eyes with Bernard.

"I think we're on our own."

"We were always on our own, Peter." Bernard mused. "Now we're alone. And I'm not going to lie... The situation is not good up here. You may have been better off locking yourself in one of the units downstairs."

"Units?"

"Sorry," Bernard chuckled, "Force of habit. I'm the building superintendent. Correction... was the super. If your toilet is clogged or your AC is out, I'm your man, but... when your neighbors turn into flesh eating monsters, I guess I was the first guy on the roof."

"I don't believe that."

"I don't believe any of this. Two days ago, I went to check on Mrs. Goldberg in two-oh-nine. She had her groceries delivered and she wasn't answering. I knocked a few times, let myself in and found her on the bathroom floor. Shower was running, but she was on the floor. Soaking wet and clutching her chest." Bernard paused as his eyes lost some of their focus.

"What happened?"

"I called 911, but when I got back to the bathroom she was dead. Heart attack. So, I covered her with a sheet and waited."

Bernard ushered a Peter a few steps further away from the lean-to.

"No one came. I waited for an hour and the next time I called I got the *All circuits are busy* message. So I had this kid, Rodrigo, a good kid who lived downstairs, stay in the room in case they showed up and I went out to find help."

"Did you?"

"No. I went down to the corner store. Open and empty. Went down the block to the Chinese joint and it was locked tighter than the Queen's drawers. That's when I heard the first shots. And this ain't that kind of neighborhood."

"What did you do?"

"Hightailed it back to the building, but..." Bernard's eyes had completely lost focus and Peter did not have to ask why. He knew Bernard was replaying that initial moment. The same moment they had all experienced.

The first moment they saw a Howler. Peter decided it was best for them both, to skip the details. Instead he opted for the facts.

"Rodrigo?"

Bernard shook his head.

"Some of the tenants got out, but we had a lot of older people in the building and I couldn't leave them." Bernard sighed, "Not if I ever wanted to sleep again."

"What about them?" Peter asked as he nodded to the two women hovering over Maria.

"The older one, Ms. Patterson, had nowhere to go. I tried to get her to leave, but she's got salt and vinegar for blood. I think her exact words to me were..." A small smile crept over Bernard's face as his eyes returned to the here and now, "They were... *I'll be God damned if I'm going to run from a fight in my own home.*"

"Tough customer." Peter nodded toward the younger woman, "What about her?"

"Jennifer?" Bernard rubbed his chin absently, "She's a nurse at Mercy, but she refused to leave after we realized that no ambulances were on their way. Last night there were six people on this roof... Two of them wounded."

"What happened?"

Bernard squared his shoulders as he looked up at the sky.

"It rained."

"What do you mean, *it rained?*"

Bernard looked back at Peter. His eyes were narrow and dark cloud passed behind them.

"You've been watching the news? All that stuff about the weather and those meteors?"

The realization hit him with the force of a runaway train.

It was *the rain*.

The meteor impacts. The resulting atmospheric disturbances. The dust, the changes in weather patterns, the nightly rainstorms...

For days, the twenty-four hour news networks had been talking about the meteors that had impacted half of the globe. Few were large enough to cause significant damage, but most were sizable enough to survive that trip through the atmosphere. It was a scientific anomaly that had fueled a large amount of sensational speculation. Armageddon scenarios, tales of alien invasion and announcements of the Rapture had all found their way into prime time broadcasts. None of it had seemed important. It was simply wild conjecture allowed over the air waves due to a slow news cycle.

The only thing everyone could agree with, but no one could explain, was the rain. The second night after the meteor shower, heavy rainfall had been reported across the world on every continent. That in and of itself was not unusual, but it was the *when* and *where* that had piqued the interest of the scientific community. Areas that usually received no rain at that time of year were flooded with downpours. And all of them began in the late evening and ended before sunrise.

The next night, it was the same event, but in different areas. Opposite areas. For five nights, the storms continued in an alternating pattern until most of the world had been affected by the night storms. It was a meteorological anomaly.

"Mr. Parsons was critically wounded. He was gutted and there was no way he was going to make it. And we didn't have enough room under the tarp anyway," Bernard continued as the clouds behind his eyes gathered, "So we put it to a vote and left him out here for nature to take its course. His neighbor, Juliet, she was a good woman and good friend of his, decided to weather the night with him."

Bernard rubbed his chin, again. It was a practiced, exhausted motion, as though he was attempting to wipe away an invisible stain. Or more accurately, a stain that *was not visible*. Some sort of blemish that had spread beneath the skin that he was unconsciously worrying.

"What happened?" Peter prompted.

"It rained and in the morning, they were dead. Parsons was a foregone conclusion, but Juliet..." Bernard stopped rubbing his chin and sighed. "She just... *died*. We found her huddled next to him, but..."

"*But?*"

"It wasn't natural. Her eyes had gone jet black and her skin had become..." Bernard eyes were searching his memories as he spoke, "Have you ever used those sole inserts for your shoes? The ones made out of gel?"

Peter nodded.

"It was like that. Soft but thick. Also, it was..." Again, Bernard was searching, but this time it was for a word. "Not see through, but you could see what's underneath."

"Translucent?" Peter offered.

"That's it." Bernard now locked eyes with Peter. "It was translucent. And... Both of their bodies were moving. Not like they were alive, but like things were shifting inside of them."

"So, you threw them over?"

"What would you have done, son?" Bernard's eyes were as sharp as his tone.

"I wasn't an accusation, Bernard," Peter found himself rubbing his own chin, "I was just filling in the gaps. I'm sorry."

"No, no. That one's on me. It's been a rough couple of nights. We've all been through a lot."

"It was a sensible precaution," Peter acknowledged. "Considering. But you said there were three people."

"Right," The clouds returned to Bernard's eyes. "Barry Garrett. He was a drunk and a card carrying asshole. Racist, sexist... Basically if it ended in *ist* or *ism* he was your man. The only person up here I would have thrown off the roof just because it's my job to take out the trash around here."

"Is that what happened?" Peter said in a carefully measured tone. He knew that, at this point, he was navigating tricky waters and he did not want to upset Bernard again. However if the group had murdered a man for any reason, justified or not, it was information he needed.

"No. These are good people." Bernard stated. "I am a good person."

Peter was not sure if that last statement was for his benefit or Bernard's, but he acknowledged it with another nod, nonetheless.

"Garrett was also wounded," Bernard continued, "But it wasn't fatal. Or at least that's what we thought. The guy had been bitten during the rush to the roof. One of those *things* took a nasty chunk out of his arm, but Jenny patched him up."

Bernard turned to look at Jennifer as she tended Maria and Peter followed his gaze. For the first time since he and Maria had escaped the building, he was now actually seeing things.

Jennifer was an attractive young woman. Her long, thick hair was tied back in a ponytail and she was actually wearing her scrubs, although Peter was sure the grimy garments had seen better days. Next to her, Ms. Patterson held Maria's hand as Jennifer encouraged the pregnant woman to sip from a bottle of water. Ms. Patterson's gray hair was cut short in a no nonsense style and her narrow face was lined with deep wrinkles. The slogan *ADK: Teachers Do It With Class!* was stenciled across the front of her T-shirt and her jeans were almost as filthy as Jennifer's.

Both women had heavy, purple bags beneath their eyes. However, Peter suspected that if he had a mirror, his would look every bit as weary and war torn. He sighed inwardly at the thought because, until now, he had not made the connection. This was the first stage of a war.

It was an invasion. Whether it was an intentional incursion or a

281

cosmic accident, the meteors had contained something alien. Perhaps it was simply a virus or perhaps it was something more sentient, but either way, it was the end of humanity. An inexhaustible army that grew exponentially with each attack. The math was irrefutable.

None of this had any bearing on Peter and Maria's current situation with a single exception, that it was still not too late to spare his wife and child from the inevitable. Their chances for survival were slim to nonexistent. Even if his child was born without complications, they would still be trapped on the rooftop with no hope of rescue.

"Are you okay, son?"

Peter looked at Bernard and saw the older man studying him. It must have been obvious that the wheels were turning in his head and perhaps Bernard was beginning to rethink allowing Peter and Maria onto the roof.

Should he be worried?

It was a dark thought with darker implications, so Peter dismissed it with a shrug.

"Sorry," Peter returned his attention to Bernard. "So what did happen to Garrett?"

"He died," Bernard exhaled, "Just after sunup. And then he began to... to change."

"Like Juliet?"

"Not exactly. His..." again Bernard searched for the words, "His transformation began before he died."

"The transformation... what was it like?"

"Near dawn, he started screaming." Bernard explained as the storm clouds dispersed behind his eyes. However, they were replaced with a waxy focus. It was obvious that he had no desire to review the images that his mind was projecting. "His bones were tearing through his skin. They were sharp like... horns. One of his eye sockets was growing... right in front of us. His teeth started falling out. It was..."

Peter felt his mouth go dry as he stared dumbly at the older man. To Bernard, Peter was sure it looked like he was respectfully allowing him time to tell the story, but in reality, it was something different altogether.

The sleeves of Peter's overshirt had unrolled during his struggles in the apartment building. His forearms were now covered. His wounds were covered. The Howler had clawed him and the wounds had been deep. But...

No blood had seeped through the fabric. The blood had coagulated. He had not given the injury a second thought until that moment.

"Awful." Bernard said, finishing his thought. "Whatever was happening to him, killed him. But the changes didn't stop. His insides were still cracking and popping when we dumped him over the edge of the roof."

"You did what you had to do." Peter stated. It was an automatic response. Beneath his dull expression, his mind was racing.

It will happen to you.

It is already happening. Humans bleed.

Monsters do not.

"I appreciate your saying that," Bernard said as his eyes returned to the present, "But too many men have said that to help them sleep easier. Like I said, the man was garbage and nobody will miss him, but..."

Bernard turned and looked toward the city. The plumes of smoke had increased in size and number.

"He was a human being. And I've seen enough people die to last several lifetimes." Bernard said as Peter stepped next to him. "Not to mention, that one less of *us* is one more of them."

"You were in a war?"

"One war, one *military action.*" Now it was Bernard who sounded automatic. "I got a medal, a handshake and a lifetime of government checks for my efforts."

Peter turned toward him.

"So as a soldier, what is your assessment of our situation?"

"We're outnumbered, outgunned and there are no reinforcements coming." Bernard's words were clipped as he spoke. "We have five bottles of water, two snack bars and a bag of chips left behind by the roofers. The same roofers that left us the tarps, scaffolding, three coils of rope and a box of tools. Phones don't work and, with the exception of you and your wife, everyone we've seen on the streets has been overrun and killed long before they reached us. So..."

Bernard turned and met Peter's gaze. His eyes were as clear as crystal for the first time.

"In my opinion, we are well and truly fucked." Bernard's eyes softened. "I'm sorry. I know that wasn't what you wanted to hear."

"It's the truth. And I'd-"

An agonized wail interrupted Peter and both men turned toward the shelter.

"It's time." Jennifer announced. Her voice was low and her tone cool. Despite her youth, Peter was immediately relieved. The woman was a professional.

Peter and Bernard rushed to the lean-to. Peter knelt beside Maria and took her hand as Bernard stood behind Jennifer.

"How do you feel?" Peter asked his wife. Their eyes were mutual pools of anxiety and hope.

"*Madre Dios!* It hurts." Maria exclaimed through a crooked smile. "Why couldn't you have been a drug dealer?"

"Because..." Peter started as he squeezed her hand and smiled, "I have a hard enough time with your parents as it is."

"I have to get her pants off." Jennifer stated as her hands began to

283

work the buckle of Maria's belt. Peter glanced at his wife's waist. Her crotch was soaked with water. "Evelyn, I need some towels."

Evelyn Patterson met Jennifer's eyes and shook her head. Without thinking, Peter stripped his over shirt from his body. He handed the wadded garment to Jennifer.

"Use this."

Jennifer accepted the shirt, but her eyes lost their intense focus as she spied the dark furrows on his forearm.

"Thanks." she muttered as her attention returned to the task at hand. "Evelyn, stay here. You two..."

Jennifer peeled the jeans from Maria's legs, folded the shirt and continued speaking as she situated it beneath Maria's buttocks.

"Give us room."

"No." Peter stated, flatly.

Jennifer stopped in mid-action as she nailed Peter with a hard stare.

"This baby is coming." Jennifer plainly stated. "The best chance it has for life is to let me do my job. But if you'd rather stay and complicate that, it's no skin off of my teeth if your stubborn ass wants to watch it die from a ringside seat."

It was a cold statement that had its intended effect. Peter released his wife's hand and kissed her sweat slicked forehead.

"I'm a few steps away." he said as his hand tightened around hers. "And I love you."

"I love you, too." Maria said as her eyes watered.

"You've got this." Peter said as he kissed her cracked lips and whispered in her ear. "We've got this."

Maria smiled and opened her mouth to speak as another contraction rocked her body. She cried out as Jennifer once again pinned Peter with her eyes. No words were exchanged. Peter released his wife and stepped away from the shelter. Jennifer maintained her hard stare as she turned her head.

"You too."

Bernard nodded as he joined Peter away from the shelter and the women focused on Maria.

***

Alien incursions, mutated abominations and the collapse of civilization were all violent, apocalyptic events, however...

They had nothing on the spectacle of childbirth.

Maria's cries, wails, shrieks and pleadings continued for hours as the sun crossed the sky. For Peter, it felt like an eternity. As with any expectant father, he worried about the health of his wife and their child. What if there were complications? Would Maria survive? Would their child?

Peter knew these were typical concerns for any man who had been banished to the waiting room. But he had not been dismissed to a waiting room. He had been sent to stand at the corner of a rooftop that stood above hundreds of bloodthirsty monsters.

In truth, there were very few Howlers in the streets. Bernard, perhaps sensing that Peter needed space, chose to spend the time fiddling with items in the toolbox and periodically consulting his phone. It was simple busy work as no one had been able to make a call or send any messages for two days. The infrastructure of the modern world had collapsed with alarming speed.

Peter considered the ramifications of that collapse as he watched the few creatures that had not retreated indoors or skulked into the shadows listlessly wander the streets. Even if Maria gave birth without complications, where did they go from here? Women had been giving birth since the dawn of time without medical aid, but still had access to food and shelter. In a few days, their resources would be depleted and they would be forced to leave the roof. How far would they get with no car and two bullets?

But as critical as these concerns were, they paled in comparison to the shadow that shrouded Peter's mind. He had been wounded by one of those *things* and his body was not reacting normally. His finger traced the gouges in his forearm. It should have been an uncomfortable sensation at best and a painful experience at its worst.

It was neither. The truth was that there was no sensation at all. It was as though he was running his fingers over a prop created from foam latex and rubber in a special effects workshop. It looked like a wounded arm, but it was devoid of sensation. It was dying or dead and Peter knew it was just the beginning. He could feel his body changing.

His skin had grown clammy and although he was hungry whenever he considered eating his stomach would do a lazy roll. In addition, he had found himself absently picking at his own flesh for no obvious reason. Sounds were becoming sharper; the afternoon light had become overly saturated. The dull headache that had begun when they had reached the roof had grown into a sliver of heated pain that lanced his brain.

Peter knew he was sick and on a level he refused to acknowledge, he knew the outcome of this disease was as undeniable as it was inevitable. Soon he would have a family to protect and he was unable to dismiss the one inescapable thought bounced around his feverish brain.

How can you protect them from yourself?

***

In the fourth grade, Bernard had been tapped as the lead in his

285

school play. He had been tall for his age and lanky, so he had been the natural choice to play Paul Bunyan. He had prepared dutifully for the role and had proven very good at taking direction. He was proficient at his marks on stage and looked as striking as a fourth grader could in his rudimentary costume. There had been only one problem.

Bernard could not act.

No one in the audience had noticed, but when the next play rolled around, Bernard had been asked to play a tree. Apparently, being regulated to standing stock still and muttering lines like *Soon my cherries will be ripe for the picking!* and *Please George, don't chop me down!* or *Timber!* were still beyond his talents as a thespian. Finally, his teacher had accepted that Bernard was better suited for a career backstage and had regulated him to stage management, a position he had found much more to his liking.

Now almost sixty years later, Bernard found himself again trying to give a convincing performance on an entirely different stage. And once again, the audience was paying him no mind.

He had been watching Peter for the last two hours as he pretended to busy himself with mundane chores. The young man was bright, resilient and Bernard believed he was sincere. He had managed to transport his pregnant wife through a crumbling city infested with demons and delivered her, miraculously, to the one place where there was both a nurse and a safe haven for her to give birth.

Much of it had been luck and coincidence, but the fact still remained the man was a fighter and was not afraid to make hard choices. When Bernard finally made the call to open the door, he saw just how committed Peter had been to protecting his family. He had seen the revolver and where it was aimed. Peter had been a heartbeat away from pulling the trigger and ending Maria's life.

And the life of their child.

It took a man to make that call. Bernard had known those men and respected them. They were not soldiers, they were leaders. He himself had made a few of those choices in distant jungles during battles that failed to qualify as footnotes in history. They were moments that few men knew about and had transpired in a time most people wanted to forget. It was a lonely place for a man to find himself and in Bernard's experience, a man who was capable of doing that...

That man was capable of just about anything.

He had seen the wounds on Peter's arm and had not deluded himself. Peter was dying and he would not stay dead. He would return as one of those *things*. Bernard knew it and he was certain that Peter had drawn the same conclusions. The real question remained,: had Peter *accepted* it?

The clip in Bernard's pistol still contained four rounds. It had been his service weapon during the war and, like many soldiers, he had

286

managed to hold onto it after the Army had decided he had spilled enough blood. Most of that blood had belonged to the enemy, but some of it had belonged to Bernard. After he had been discharged, the pistol had been tucked into a bedside table, largely forgotten.

Now as Bernard feigned interest in a collection of drywall screws and wire clippers, he was considering if he was once again going to have to spill the blood of another human being. It was not something that a man did easily and it was not something easily forgotten.

He needed to address the situation with Peter, but he knew that until the child was born his words would fall on deaf ears. Bernard could not blame Peter for that. The man was in an impossible situation and he deserved to hold his child as long as the sun was in the sky. After that, the night would descend and the storms would begin. Bernard glanced upwards.

It was a few hours from sunset.

***

Maria was delirious. Her body was soaked with sweat and her muscles felt like taffy. She had no idea how long she had been in labor, but she felt as though someone had lodged a burning freight train in her pelvis and jammed a few railroad spikes in her abdomen and neck for good measure.

To make matters worse, some hateful bitch kept yelling *PUSH!* from the end of a wind tunnel built at the bottom of a well. Every sound was drawn out as though it was coming from the far side of time and space.

Poooooooosssshhhh!

Her spine felt like a wet towel being snapped back and forth and her vision ebbed with each contraction. It was as if Maria had contracted malaria, scarlet fever and food poisoning simultaneously. Her fingers threatened to crush the hand of the elderly woman looming above her.

Is that Evelyn?

Who the fuck is Evelyn?

Where the fuck am I?

Where is Peter?

Am I going to die?!

Without warning, hands were inside her. Maria screamed and the blurred harpy hiding behind her bloated belly barked again.

"This is it!" The woman who might be named Jennifer or Jenny announced. "Push!"

Maria shook her head madly as drool flung from her mouth.

"*NOW!*" Jen-something commanded.

Out of nothing more than pure spite, Maria crushed the muscles of her abdomen inward. Inside her, something gave and she was rewarded

287

with a tide of mucus spilling across her buttocks and an anticlimactic plopping sound. Her entire body went limp as the pressure inside her unwound.

She heard it with a clarity only a mother possessed. A smack and a strangled cry. Tears erupted from her eyes and her body began to shake. Maria was laughing. For the first time in two days she was devoid of fear, anxiety and depression.

She was flooded with joy, suddenly overwhelmed with the need to see her child. From the corner of her eye, she could see Peter racing toward the shelter as she propped herself on her elbows. Her breath caught in her throat as she looked over at the baby and felt her heart stop.

It was beautiful.

In actuality, its face was pinched and its sausage-like limbs seemed too stubby for its plump body. However, it was healthy and screeching. An understandable fuss when yanked from a warm, comfortable sleep and dragged naked into the afternoon sun. All thoughts of ravenous beasts, burning buildings and defiled carcasses were banished from Maria's mind. The ugliness and terror that had occupied her thoughts found themselves eclipsed by the immeasurable promise of the future.

Whatever was to come, her baby was alive and she and Peter were now a complete family. They were safe for the moment and their son...? Daughter...? An unexplained panic flashed across Maria's face.

As if Jennifer could read her her mind, she smiled an leaned forward.

"It's a girl."

A renewed tide of tears spilled over Maria's cheeks as Peter knelt beside her. Maria looked up at her husband's watery eyes. His face was beaming, but there was something irregular about his smile. Maria's own smile faltered as she looked deeper into his eyes. Something was not right.

Peter closed his arms around her and the distraction was instantaneous. Whatever she sensed evaporated as he whispered in her ear.

"You did it." he croaked. "I'm so proud of you."

When he pulled away from her, Peter was crying freely.

"I love you so much." he said in little more than a hoarse whisper.

"Yo también te amo."

Evelyn finished wrapping the infant as she lifted it from Jennifer's arms. She stepped forward and offered it to Maria.

"Would you like to hold her?"

Despite the warm afternoon sun, Maria's naked thighs were quivering with exhaustion and Jennifer was doing her best to clean them. However, Maria was unaware of those efforts as she scooted backwards and extended her arms. Evelyn gently handed her the swaddled baby and Maria looked from the child to Peter. He beamed back at her.

***

288

Bernard stood as he watched Peter and the women congregate around the infant. He had never had children, although it was not for a lack of trying. His wife, Sarah, had been a strong woman. She had suffered neither fools nor nonsense and had a temper like a matchstick. It flared hot and bright, but burned out quickly. Most people found her to be like a storm, an event you had no choice but to weather if you wanted to survive.

But Bernard was not most people. He understood that storms carried great power and a majesty unparalleled in the natural world. They were fascinating spectacles that washed away anything that was not strong enough to survive on its own. They rid the world of the dead and dying. They were the great purifiers and if you did survive them, you were rewarded with sunrises of heartbreaking beauty.

That was Sarah, and she would have had untapped wells of love and strength to offer a child. However, God had not seen fit to give her the gift of childbirth. Instead, he had given her the gift of cancer. The kind of cancer only a woman could have. An insidious decay that had stolen her life and dignity one day at a time until there was nothing left for it to take.

On some level, Bernard resented the Lord for that, a grudge he had carried with him for decades after Sarah's death. However, he had never hated God for what happened to his wife. He truly believed that God had a plan. A plan so painful in its execution that he had given his only son, but so glorious in its realization that all men and women would find themselves basking in an eternal sunrise of unfathomable love.

He pondered those feelings as he watched Peter hold his child for the first time and gently kiss its forehead. He knew that this was a defining moment in any man's life and wondered how Peter felt about such a divine mechanization. It was the question that had consumed him for hours, but in the end he was afraid it came down to mathematics, not providence.

Four bullets against two.

***

Five years ago Peter had given the eulogy at his father's funeral. It was a small service and only a handful of his father's surviving friends and family had attended. Peter had given considerable thought to what he was going to say. He had mulled over each word in an effort to sum up the entirety of the man and all he meant and had accomplished in a handful of paragraphs. It was an impossible task and like all sons who had stood at their fathers' graves before him, he had failed miserably.

That was the most difficult moment of Peter's life, until he had to hand his child to Evelyn. When the older woman opened her arms to receive the baby, Peter found himself unable to relinquish it.

A queer expression crossed Evelyn's face as Peter struggled with his indecision. It was an expression he had seen before in the faces of police officers, teachers and landlords. It said, *Is this going to be a problem?* It was the same expression Bernard was wearing as he watched from the far side of the roof.

Though he had pretended to be occupied, Peter knew Bernard had been watching throughout the delivery. Both men were anticipating the moment that was coming.

Peter could not stay on the roof, but Peter could not leave his weakened wife and his newborn child. Peter would become a monster, but Peter *was not* a monster. Peter had two choices: surrender his life to Bernard or take it himself.

Neither of those options appealed to him. Nothing was certain; all of their theories were based on circumstantial and specious reasoning.

Meteors were responsible for a supposed plague. The rain infected people. A human bitten or scratched was destined to become a Howler. The government had failed and no help was forthcoming.

It was all conjecture. Nothing more than fear based rationale from the minds of people who had been reduced to quaking rabbits in the face of the unknown. There was no science behind the reasoning. It was all speculation.

Peter smiled as he released the infant. Like Bernard, acting was not his forte and Evelyn's expression reflected his performance. Her retreat from Peter was a step too hasty. He was unconcerned.

Peter turned away and set his mind to his argument. His business was with Bernard. The rest would understand once their guardian came around to Peter's way of thinking.

* * *

Bernard watched as Peter walked toward him. Inwardly, he sighed as his stomach sank. The man had held his child, and the rest of the world had shrunk beyond his vision. The last of the afternoon sunlight struck the young man's face where the sheen of sweat glistened. Peter's eyes were wide, but his pupils were pinpoints.

There was never a chance of the situation ending well, but now Bernard knew it would not end peaceably. Still, he chose to believe that humanity and reason would prevail. He held out his hands, palms exposed.

"I know what you're thinking," Bernard said in the calmest tone he could muster.

"Do you have children?" Peter said as the distance between them closed to ten feet. Just enough to talk at a civilized volume, but not enough for either of them to reach the other. Physically or otherwise.

Gunfighter distance.

"I don't," Bernard confessed, but added "And neither did you an hour ago."

290

"But I do now." Peter swallowed. Bernard was not the only person he was trying to convince. "Now, I have a family."

"We all have families," Bernard hands drifted downwards as his eyes darted to Peter's clenching fists. "And if someone was on this roof, someone who had been clawed by one of those things, what would you do to him to protect your family?"

"I..." Peter hesitated as he felt the edges of his argument begin to crumble, "I'd watch him. Closely."

"That's the first time you lied to me."

"It's not a lie. We don't know what will happen."

"That's true, but I didn't ask you what you know," Bernard countered, "I asked you what you would do. I asked you what kind of chance you would take with the lives of your family."

Bernard leveled his gaze at Peter.

"Would you let your baby girl sleep next to a man who had been bitten?"

"I would-"

"BULLSHIT!" Bernard snapped. Behind Peter, Jennifer looked up from a sleeping Maria and Evelyn looked up from the baby. "You would kill him. You would murder him in his sleep."

Peter looked down at his feet as he searched for an answer that would satisfy both himself and Bernard. For the first time, he noticed just how bloody his clothes had become. Some of the stains were fresher than others, but all of them had soaked through the cloth. He was suddenly aware of the crusting fluids against his skin and the congealed muck clinging to the edges of his soles.

That was it. The human race was drowning in an ocean of its own blood. And the only people who would survive were those that sought the higher ground. Those that found themselves on the rooftops.

"Is that what you're going to do, Bernard?" Peter asked as he looked up from his shoes. "Murder me?"

"You're not getting it, son." Bernard felt a flutter of sorrow behind his eyes as he spoke. "You're already dead. Those *things* killed you. That's as much a fact as rain is wet."

Bernard's hands were at his waist.

"It's just up to us how you go out."

"I can't let you do this, Bernard." Peter said. His eyes had taken on a fevered cast. "I have a family now."

Bernard offered a sympathetic nod.

"Then do right by them." Bernard looked over toward the door. "I can open the door. Let you back inside and you can take your chances in there, but..."

"*But* what?"

"But," Bernard said as he looked back toward Peter, "We both know what's going to happen to you and I don't think you want to be

291

walking around as one of those *things*."

Something was not right. Peter felt as though he was suddenly being watched. He furrowed his brow as he puzzled through the sensation and realization clicked. It was the fact that he *was not* being watched.

Bernard was looking toward him, not at hi*m*. Bernard was looking past him.

Peter spun as Evelyn rushed him. She clutched a short length of steel pipe and she yelled as she charged. There was fifteen feet between the two of them, but the retired teacher was spry. The sight of the old woman's lips curled back over her teeth as she raised the pipe and sped toward Peter like some octogenarian Valkyrie was as frightening as it was absurd.

A gunshot bellowed behind Peter as he ripped the revolver from his waistband. The bullet tore through his back and chunks of flesh exploded across Evelyn's face as it exited Peter's shoulder. Unfortunately for Evelyn, it was his left shoulder.

Peter's right hand thrust the revolver forward and he squeezed the trigger. Flames flashed from the barrel as the bullet drilled through Evelyn's throat. A spray of blood showered Peter's face as the pipe tumbled from Evelyn's lifeless hand and her corpse collided with Peter.

Another report from Bernard's pistol cracked the afternoon air, but Evelyn's death charge had knocked Peter off balance. He dropped to one knee as he deflected the old woman's body and Bernard's shot missed its mark. Peter splayed his free hand against the rooftop to steady himself as he sought Bernard.

Sunlight seared Peter's eyes as a colossal shadow fell over him. Bernard had stepped into the path of the sun and now towered over Peter like a mythological giant. A silhouetted Titan gripping a handful of thunder and death.

Both men fired. Peter's bullet punched a hole in Bernard's chest, just above his heart. A near perfect shot, but half a second too late.

Bernard's bullet shattered Peter's teeth, tunneled through his tongue and chin and buried itself in his sternum. A hiss of air escaped as blood filled Peter's lungs. His rattling breath came in fits and starts as he watched Bernard crumple to his knees.

The larger man teetered on his knees as he looked from the fountain of blood pumping from his wounded chest to Peter. He opened his mouth to speak. Peter's vision was dimming, but he could plainly see the river of blood that sloshed over Bernard's chin.

The man who had saved his and Maria's life, the man who had refused to abandon the people in his charge, the man who risked the lives of everyone on the rooftop because he refused to give the world over to monsters, refused to abandon his humanity, collapsed face first into a pool of his own blood.

Peter dropped the revolver and began to drag himself toward

Bernard. The magnitude of what had transpired echoed hollowly inside of him. His mind was not his own. Thoughts, emotions and *something* else, something *vile*, clacked and ricocheted inside his dying mind.

He knew what he had done was awful. He knew it was wrong. He knew that Maria would never have wanted any of this. Not for herself, not for their child. The part of him that was still human knew all of these things. But a gross union of monster and man was occurring inside him and the protective instincts of newfound fatherhood had merged with vulgar appetites he did not fully understand. He was becoming something else.

Something that did not care about right and wrong. Something that only cared about need.

Peter's blood drenched hand closed around Bernard's pistol. His body was sizzling with pain and his mind was churning like a volcano. His memory was a fractured slideshow of disconnected thoughts.

How many shots?

You have to end this.

How many bullets?

You did not name your daughter.

Where are they?

You are not you.

You can not-

"Peter?"

A hand clamped around his good shoulder and a razor of confusion sliced through his brain. Peter lurched forward and twisted as he swung the pistol in front of him and fired. A flash of brilliant gunfire illuminated a woman's face as the sound of the shot split Peter's ears.

The bullet punched through Jennifer's stomach and splintered her spine before exiting her back in a meaty explosion. Her face was frozen in shock and bewilderment and, for a moment, she swayed in the waning afternoon light. Like Bernard, her mouth attempted to work, but it was a futile attempt.

Peter watched the last of the light leave her eyes as she toppled onto her side. He looked at the gun in his hand and tried to reconstruct the last few seconds. There was little reason left in his dying mind. Just nervous twitches that disappeared before he could mold them into thoughts.

Despite the murky whirlpool of his mind, Peter knew that there was one last task he needed to complete. One final action that would help ensure Maria's survival and the survival of his daughter. The survival of his family.

He placed the barrel of the pistol against his temple and closed his eyes as he pulled the trigger.

There was a metallic *click* as the hammer fell.

The magazine was empty.

Peter took one final look at his wife and child before the last of his blood drained from his body. There was something wrong with the blood. It was too dark, too thick. None of this was right. He had... He needed to...

Peter fell face first onto the rooftop as the last of the afternoon sun disappeared from the sky.

***

Maria held the child as she watched the sun's halo disappear behind the edge of the building and darkness fell across the rooftop. She had not seen what had transpired, but she could see the aftermath. Her dreams had been chaotic. Filled with loud flashes and booming noises. But she had also dreamed of her wedding and the night that followed.

She had dreamed of fields populated by tulips and roses. A wonderful, colorful place where she, Peter and her daughter could run and laugh. She could even remember watching Peter, smiling and chuckling, as he taught their daughter, giggling in her white dress, to catch butterflies. He was explaining to her why they were beautiful; why it was important to release them.

Maria pulled her daughter closer. The howling sounds in the street had grown louder and the air smelled like a slaughterhouse. On the other side of the rooftop door, something banged rhythmically. Something hungry. She had never felt more frightened or alone in her life.

She wondered what would become of her and her child. She wondered what would become of the bodies. Mostly, she wondered what the night would bring. Moments later, she had her answer.

It began to rain.

ABOUT THE EDITORS

Eugene Johnson

Eugene Johnson is a filmmaker author, editor, and columnist of science fiction, fantasy, horror, and supernatural thrillers.

He has written and edited in various genres. His anthology *Appalachian Undead*, co-edited with Jason Sizemore, was picked by FearNet, as one of the best books of 2012. His story *"Bitten"* appeared in the *Zombiefeed Volume One*, edited by Bram Stoker Award® nominated Jason Sizemore. His articles and stories have been published by award winning Apex publishing, The Zombiefeed, Evil Jester Press, Warrior Sparrow Press and more. He has worked on various movies including the upcoming *Requiem* staring Tony Todd and directed by Paul Moore. His short film *Leftovers*, a collaboration with director Paul Moore, was featured at the Screamfest film festival in Los Angeles, CA as well as Dragoncon.

He is currently working on several projects including *Brave an anthology honoring people with disabilities, Where Nightmares Come From*, a non-fiction book on the art of storytelling in the horror genre, and his children's book series *Life Lessons With Lil Monsters*.

He resides in West Virginia with his wife, daughter, and two sons.

Charles Day

Charles Day is an active member of the Thriller Writers Association and a Bram Stoker Award® nominated author of the YA novel, *The Legend of the Pumpkin Thief*. His other published works include *Deep Within*, his first co-authored novel with Mark Taylor, *Redemption*, and the *The Hunt For The Ghoulish Bartender, Book 1*, a YA weird western trilogy.

His forthcoming publications and/or projects in development for 2016-2017 will see the return of his *Legend of The pumpkin Thief* characters which are being made into a middle grade series, with Month 9 Books, and he's also slowly illustrating a comic book series based on his *Adventures Of Kyle McGerrt* trilogy. He also has another middle-grade series, *The Underdwellers*, and his third YA novel, *My Father, Assassin*, an action-packed thriller set in NYC, which he's trying hard to bring to fruition.

Charles is also an artist and illustrator, who's totally passionate about creating with all types of media on paper and digitally, which include some of his fictitious characters in published or soon to be published novels and comics.

You can find out more about his upcoming writing projects, check out his illustrations and art, or find out what he's cooking up next by visiting his Facebook page:

https://www.facebook.com/charles.day.92

ABOUT THE ARTISTS

William Neal McPheeters
Cover Artist

Award winning artist William Neal McPheeters has designed and illustrated hundreds of book covers over the years including volumes produced by just about every major publisher in America. Discovering that one or more titles sporting one of his covers is listed among The New York Times' best sellers is not uncommon. He also writes and illustrates graphic novels and exhibits his easel paintings in galleries and museums across America.

James Kavanaugh
Interior Artist

A Lifelong art fan, Jim Kavavnaugh has been illustrating professionally for the past 5 years. His influences include Basil Gogos, Frank Frazetta, and Daniel Horne. Jim's artwork has been featured in gallery openings, the covers of paperback novels, and various magazines. From assorted mediums Jim tries to breathe life into the characters he creates.

SPECIAL THANKS TO OUR
INDIGOGO SUPPORTERS

Elizabeth S Massie
Taylor Grant
Cecilia Dockins
John M MacLeod
Vasilia Staley
B Luke Styer
Simon P McCaffery
Elena DeGarmo
Paul Legerski

John M MacLeod
Heather Remaly
Dana Fredsti
Angela Bradley
Lynda Lampert
Dwayne Russell
Brenda Ricketts
Gary taylor